"Amid this detailed, often hectic sci-fi narrative, the plot threads of Pack's high schoolers remain the most compelling. The Terrorians' fear of cats is hilarious, but the drama wrought by Logan's obsession with becoming a successful news intern—and reporting the Library to the world—is exceptional. Longtime readers may miss the intimacy of earlier volumes but should brace themselves for the darkest, most rewarding installment yet.

The complexity deepens in this kaleidoscopic adventure series."

—Kirkus Reviews

"Wars and battles, alliances and prejudices, this book has everything you would find in the real world, but on a monumental scale." ... "If you like science fiction which has some great depth, then you'll find Fourth Chronicles of Illumination has a lot to offer."

—Reader's Favorite

FOURTH CHRONICLES OF
ILLUMINATION

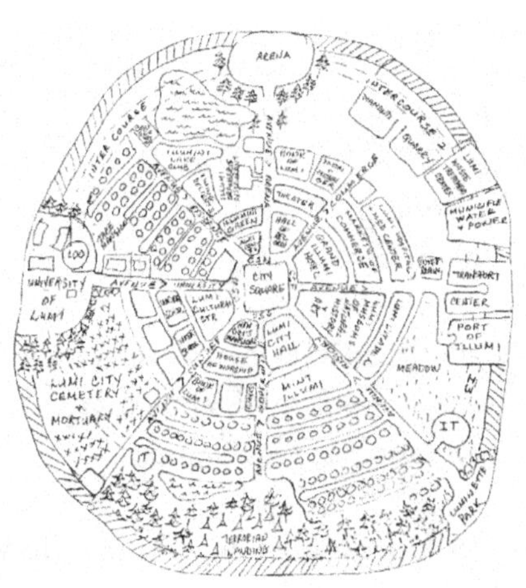

BOOKS IN THE
LIBRARY OF ILLUMINATION SERIES

Becoming Johanna
A Library of Illumination Prequel

Chronicles: The Library of Illumination
Book One: The Library of Illumination
Book Two: Doubloons
Book Three: The Orb
Book Four: Casanova
Book Five: Portals

Second Chronicles of Illumination
First Book of the Knowledge is Power Trilogy
Book Five: Portals
Book Six: The Overseers
Book Seven: Myrddin's Memoir

Third Chronicles of Illumination
Second Book of the Knowledge is Power Trilogy
Book Eight: Games

Fourth Chronicles of Illumination
Third Book of the Knowledge is Power Trilogy
Book Nine: Endgame

A Library of Illumination Christmas
Book Ten

FOURTH CHRONICLES OF
ILLUMINATION

Endgame

Third Book of the Knowledge is Power Trilogy
Library of Illumination: Book Nine

by

C. A. PACK

Artiqua Press
www.artiquapress.com

Artiqua Press

www.artiquapress.com

ARTIQUA PRESS
info@artiquapress.com
Westbury, NY 11590

TRADE PAPERBACK

April 3, 2018

FOURTH CHRONICLES OF ILLUMINATION
Endgame
Library of Illumination—Book Nine

ISBN-13: 978-0-9979084-7-3

Library of Congress Control Number: 2017919745

When we last left the Library of Illumination…

Nero 51 had broken free of the layers between time and space, while his dream to dominate all the realms in the Illumini System continued to fester. Traveling in the time machine, he made an unexpected appearance in the Fantasian (aka Earth) library cupola, into which Emily, Jackson's new girlfriend, had practically forced her way to pose for prom pictures. Johanna happened to be in that area as well, leading heartthrob Cameron Thorne—a new library member and potential date material—on a special tour of the facilities.

In a mad attempt to score a coup, Nero 51 grabbed Emily. But Johanna couldn't allow that to happen and offered herself as a hostage in Emily's place. The Terrorian grabbed Johanna and—POOF—they disappeared.

Unfortunately, or fortunately—depending on how you look at it—Johanna wasn't the only Fantasian who ended up on Terroria.

Read on!

Illumini System

The Illumini System is a constellation made up of thirteen worlds including the prime realm, Lumina, where the College of Overseers and the Library of Origination are located. All other realms have Libraries of Illumination and each realm is represented by a dean from the College of Overseers who benevolently governs and acts as a liaison. Each library also has a curator, or in the case of Fantasia, co-curators, who take care of its day-to-day operation. The deans live on Lumina. The curators live in the libraries on their designated realms. Ryden Simmdry is the Master of all the deans, and he oversees the main Library of Origination on Lumina, which is the center of the Illumini system. Overseers go by both their first and last names—you would never say a first name without the surname. They are each identified by a symbol and can speak telepathically.

Prime Realm: Lumina, Master Ryden Simmdry

⌘Master: Ryden Simmdry (a.k.a Myrddin Emrys; Merlin the Magician)
✠Dean: Horatio Blastoe
∑Dean: Artemus Rexana
⇌Dean: Grappho Pluck
✳Dean: Galio Abbingdon
§ Dean: Zenith Fullova
★ Dean: Pru Tellerence
☿ Dean: Reichel Bean
■ Dean: Marsh Kierand
Ψ Dean: Proteus Bligh
π Dean: Rubicon Zenicon
▥ Dean: Selium Sorium
Ω Dean: Plato Indelicat
Odyon/Robert Birk/Peter Dakion—shapeshifter
Milver Dunstable—Lumi domicile dealer; realtor

Realm One: Romantica, Dean Horatio Blastoe

Natalia Dalura—curator of Romantican Library of Illumination
Dame Erato—former curator on Romantica
Ingur Aguri—white witch
Selestra (a.k.a. Bel)—Pru Tellerence's child
Arraba, Felicia, and Milencia Jolen—three sisters who helped establish the militairres on Romantica
Annabeth—militairre recruit
Stasia—militairre recruit
Bethany—militairre recruit

Marin—militairre recruit
Nicoletta—militairre recruit
Lei—militairre recruit

Realm Two: Adventura, Dean Artemus Rexana

Prophet IAN c.—hu*bot curator of Adventuran Library of
   Illumination
Prophet CARL a.—gold-armed medi*bot
Prophet CHRIS h.—gold-armed leader*bot
Prophet DANIEL p.—gold-armed strategi*bot
Prophet DAVID l.—gold-armed leader*bot
Prophet ANDREW r.—gold-armed leader*bot
Prophet PATRICK c.—gold-armed leader*bot

Realm Three: Educon, Dean Grappho Pluck

Dr. Infinitis—curator of the Educonian Library of
   Illumination

Realm Four: Scientico, Dean Galio Abbingdon

Galon Senter—curator of the Scientic Library of
   Illumination

Realm Five: Juvenilia, Dean Zenith Fullova

The residents of Juvenilia only live to age fifteen and are
then re-incarnated as three-year-olds. Their lives are not
short, however, because each year on Juvenilia is equivalent
to five Fantasian years. Peer Meap, the curator of their
library, is a transplanted teacher from Educon and is the

only adult who lives in the realm.

Peer Meap—curator of Juvenile Library of Illumination
Duddu—teen leader
Pollo—Duddu's right hand man
Marbol—the oldest teen and the inventor of the sonic
    scrambler
Guffle and Flugle—teen twins
Waxmo & Pokkie—teen twins
Selly & Cici—teen twins
Dee-Dee—youngest Juvenile
Boxer, Bungie—Juvenile teens

Realm Six: Dramatica, Dean Pru Tellerence

Furst—curator of Dramatican Library of Illumination
Pondor—Dramatican Judge
Dungen—Pondor's son
Mudge—Dramatican strategist
Ozzro—Dramatican soldier
Emorie—Official in charge of Dramatican Court/Jail
Lenc—young Dramatican soldier
Benger—Dramatican who lost a loved one in battle
Lylle—Dramatican who lost a loved one in battle

Realm Seven: Comedia, Dean Reichel Bean

Abbello Abbato—curator of Comedian Library of
    Illumination
Milbo Fatufo—Mayor of Comi, the capital city of Comedia
Neli Flo—Young Comedian woman
Tropo—Neli Flo's pig

Realm Eight: Inspiracon, Dean Marsh Kierand

Issiopia—curator of the Inspiric Library of
Illumination

Realm Nine: Mysteriose, Dean Proteus Bligh

Hue the Elder—curator of the Mysterian Library of
Illumination
Dron the Elder—Mysterian Elder
Sean of Oster—Mysterian Elder
Harva—Mysterian politician
Drefol, Tensia and Garon—Mysterian family

Realm Ten: Numericon, Dean: Rubicon Zenicon

Pi—curator of the Numeric Library of Illumination

Realm Eleven: Fantasia, Dean Selium Sorium

Johanna Charette—18-year-old prime curator of the
Fantasian Library of Illumination
Jackson Roth—17-year-old co-curator of the Library of
Illumination
Malcolm Trees—the former curator of the Library of
Illumination who brought in Johanna as his replacement
(Mrs.) Niamh Fitzpatrick-Roth—Jackson's mother
Chris Roth—Jackson's 16-year-old brother
Ava Roth—Jackson's 14-year-old sister
Cameron Thorne—Dean of English, Cranford University
Ophelia—Johanna's kitten
Logan Elliott—Jackson's best friend

Michael Elliott—Logan's father
Cassie Turner—Logan's girlfriend
Emily Brent—Cassie's best friend
Zach Maybrecht—Emily's ex-boyfriend
Trey Onderdonck—Exeter High School senior
Jennifer O'Loughlin—GRUNT assignment manager
Channing Daniels—GRUNT reporter
Luke Harris—GRUNT program manager
Reeve Rinaldi—GRUNT cameraperson
Andrew Sigurdsson—Exeter High School student
Kara Biels—Exeter High School student
Mr. Chander—Exeter High School physics teacher
William "Buffalo Bill" Cody—famous 19th/20th century
    cowboy/soldier/showman
Myrddin Emrys/Merlin the Magician/Ryden Simmdry—
    see Master Ryden Simmdry under the listing of overseers
Thor—God of Thunder
Eahta Frean fram Drycræft—The Eight Masters of
    Wizardry who live in various countries on Fantasia
    and protect Myrddin's Memoir, a collection of Merlin
    the Magician's spells.
Robert Birk (Odyon)—representative from Switzerland
Brychan Rhydderch (Beck)—representative from Wales

Realm Twelve: Terroria, Dean Plato Indelicat

Nero 51—curator of the Terrorian Library of Illumination
Garpa—Nero 51's long-dead grandfather
Welt 87—Terrorian surgeon
Bener 411—Terrorian soldier
Barzic 922—Terrorian General
Senet 83—Terrorian soldier
Kelsis 384—Military strategist

This is a basic index of characters. Not everyone who appears in this book is noted above. For a more inclusive list of characters, please consult the Illumini Compendium or search the files at:

www.libraryofillumination.com

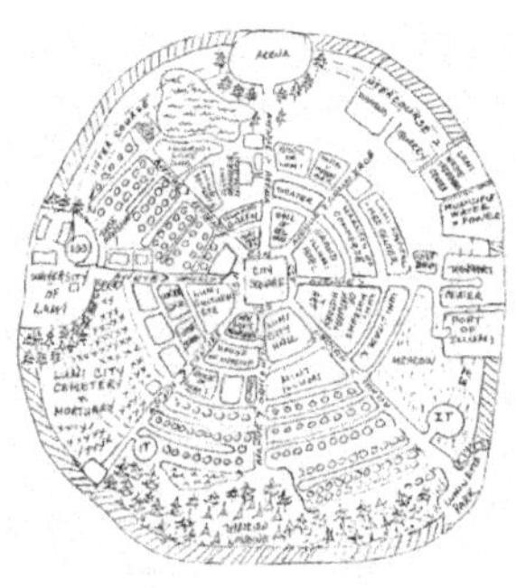

CHAPTER ONE

Cameron Thorne, the dean of English at Cranford University, grimaced and twisted his face to one side with his eyes tightly closed. "What is that smell?"

"Terrorians."

He squinted just enough to see Johanna Charette, curator of the Fantasian Library of Illumination. "Am I dreaming?" he asked. "I just had one hell of a nightmare."

"It's a nightmare all right, but it's very, very real."

"How can this be real?" He struggled up to his feet to try to put some distance between himself and the Terrorian vapor that swirled across the floor. "Wait. Don't tell me. We're inside one of your books. It's the Library of Illumination, right? Books come to life here."

"I wish it were that simple." She sighed. "We're on Terroria, a dark, toxic world filled with oversized beings with multiple tentacles for arms. Nero 51, the Terrorian who brought us here, is the curator of their library. He wants to take over the entire Illumini System, a constellation of thirteen worlds, by destroying all the Libraries of Illumination, so his library alone holds all knowledge. And as Francis Bacon said, 'Knowledge is power.'

"Anyway," she summarized, "we're a long way from Fantasia."

"Fantasia?"

"That's what the College of Overseers, who are in charge of all the libraries, call Earth. 'Fantasia.'"

"I have absolutely no idea what you're talking about, but I can say for certain, it's not because I doubt you. Should I be scared?"

"You've got nothing to fear from me. But I can't say as much for our tentacled abductors. They absolutely hate me and would love to see me die a slow, painful death."

"That doesn't sound promising."

"I hope Jackson managed to secure the library after we were taken."

"Is that difficult to do?"

"It is with the Terrorians. They have our time machine, but I thought they were stuck between the layers of time and space. I guess they figured out how to break free."

"Did you just say *time machine?*"

"It's a long story."

"*Meow.*"

"No!" Johanna swatted away the vapor in the area of the mewling. "I don't believe it." She lifted a bundle of fur and hugged it to her chest. Ophelia purred at her. "Now, I have to worry about you too?" she said as she bent to kiss the small, white kitten. She pulled away sharply. "You smell like Terrorian poop."

Cameron scratched the top of Ophelia's head. "You know," he said to Johanna, "everything you've told me so far sounds totally off the wall—like you're just grabbing bits and pieces of your favorite sci-fi stories and mashing them together. Yet, my insides are tied up in knots, because I believe every word of it."

Johanna managed a small smile. "I'm sorry I got you mixed up in this. It really was just supposed to be a pleasant lunch and a library tour for my future college professor—just a way for you to see one of our enchanted books spring to life."

"What do you think our chances are of getting out of here?" Cameron walked around the enclosed space that imprisoned them, looking for a way out.

"Normally, I'd say slim to none. But I've got a few tricks up my sleeve, thanks to the *Eahta Frean fram Drycræft*."

"Welsh?"

"Yes. It's a secret society formed to protect the works of Myrddin Emrys, who is more popularly known as Merlin the Magician."

"Merlin the Magician is fictional."

"Nope. He's as real as you and I."

"I'm the dean of the English Department. I did my doctoral dissertation on medieval Arthurian literature. Myrddin Emrys may have been real, but Merlin is a complete fabrication."

"When we get back to the library, I'll prove it to you."

"Well, at least you're optimistic about us getting back to the library."

Johanna sighed. "I'm so sorry, Cameron. I really wish the Terrorians would have left you and Ophelia behind."

"But then you'd be all alone. At least you have me to protect you and your furry little friend."

His comment took her breath away, if only for a moment. "Thank you," she whispered.

FURST USED HIS diary to contact overseer Pru Tellerence. He wanted to tell her about the Terrorians' sneak attack and how the invaders captured his kinsmen outside the Dramatican library. He walked back to the window on the halo level and looked out onto the field behind the library. The inhabitants of Dramatica, a normally peaceful realm where people lived simple lives, had risen up to fight the Terrorians and were now being taken prisoner.

Furst could see a half-dozen soldiers and a dozen immobilized Dramaticans. At least, the fighting had stopped, although four troopers faced out from the field with their decimators ready.

Pick them off, I could, Furst thought. But the sealed library window would pose a problem. *The cupola?* The curator looked at the railings above him before staring at the base of the cupola staircase below. *Too much time, that would take.* He slid the decimator behind his back and flexed his knees before jumping from the halo level to the cupola.

Furst took a deep breath after his feet connected with the floor. Dramaticans were known for their jumping abilities, but he took a leap that would be considered well beyond normal. He rushed into one of the alcoves and found an octagonal window that opened for roof maintenance. He opened his diary to ask Pru Tellerence if the window was sealed. He did not expect to see the words, *Furst, we are under attack*, as her reply.

THE TERRORIANS WHO invaded the predominantly female realm, Romantica, were so intent on removing the arrows that had pierced their tentacles, they didn't notice Milencia Jolen's late arrival on the field.

She fell to the ground after crashing into Natalia Dalura and found herself staring into the curator's eyes. "Are you all right?" Milencia whispered.

"I can't move," Natalia answered, keeping her voice low. "Apparently, we've all been incarcerated in our own personal force fields."

"But you can speak."

"Yes. But I can't turn my head or use my limbs."

Milencia tried to touch Natalia, but the force field repelled her hand. "Did I hurt you when I crashed into you?"

"No. I think it is also protecting me."

"What do you think I should do?"

"Unless you believe you can overtake six large invaders with eight stretchy tentacles each before they see you, I'd say not much. At least, not here. It would be better for you to sneak away and warn everyone to lock themselves inside their homes."

Milencia peeked beyond Natalia's inert body. She stiffened. "Dame Erato doesn't look good. Is she dead?"

Natalia might not have been able to move, but that didn't stop a tear from pooling on the bridge of her nose. "I don't know. It wasn't supposed to happen. One of the militairres shot an arrow at the Terrorians, but the arrow went wild. If Dame Erato dies, it's *our* fault."

"*U zego a inca-gi.*"

Milencia froze when she heard the Terrorians speak. She looked around for a means of escape. A massive willow tree was just a few arm-lengths away. She turned her head and watched the Terrorians cluster together to discuss something. Milencia crawled behind the tree and held her breath. Even though she didn't exert a lot of energy, her heart thumped heavily, and she tried as hard as she could to quiet her heartbeat and control her breathing. What felt like several minutes passed without incident. Milencia slowly crept around the trunk of the tree to see what the Terrorians were doing. Her jaw dropped when a large glass bubble appeared and two militairres were loaded inside. She gasped, ducking back behind the tree when they disappeared.

The invaders lined up the other frozen militairres two-by-two. At this rate, it could be hours before the Terrorians completed their task and departed. *Or maybe not.* The bubble suddenly reappeared, empty, and two more militairres were carried onboard.

A MELANCHOLY SPIRIT pervaded the overseers' meeting room in the Library of Origination on the prime realm. The outward appearance of calm and perfection in the capital city of Lumi belied the internal turmoil created by the Terrorian betrayal. The overseers had their work cut out for them.

⌘*The Terrorians have invaded Romantica and managed to capture overseers Pru Tellerence and Horatio Blastoe, as well as the militairres. Fortunately, they ensnared their captives in force fields rather than killing them.*

Σ*We must go free our brethren.*

⌘*We do not need to free them. The deans are still wearing their miters and can remove themselves at will. Right now, they are acting as our eyes and ears.*

■*How interesting. They say the prisoners are apparently being removed in the stolen time machine.*

❋*This calls for an entrapment snare.*

⌘*Pru Tellerence and Horatio Blastoe do not have that capability. Only you, Galio Abbingdon, and I, can engage an entrapment snare.*

■*Will you be traveling there, then?*

⌘*It is wiser to allow them to be taken to Terroria. They can give us information on what is transpiring on that realm.*

Ω*If I'm not mistaken, although I have no memory of the actual event, I did not fare well on Terroria, even though I'm an overseer.*

⌘*Ah, Plato Indelicat, that is only because you became separated from your miter. Pru Tellerence and Horatio Blastoe will transport themselves away if they fear that is about to happen to them. You have provided them with that important lesson.*

Σ*Can we also discuss Adventura, which is under attack by its sun?*

⌘*By all means.*

Σ*The power grids have failed across the entire realm.*

Previously, only their tissue-cloning operation appeared threatened. Now, their very existence is at risk. They have no way to refrigerate the plasma they use to keep their brains and hearts functioning, nor any way to recharge their non-organic sensors. In less than six weeks, their civilization will cease to function if a solution is not found.

Scorching winds blew debris across the deserted landscape of Adventura's main cities. The massive explosions caused by their raging sun had destroyed the realm's interconnected power systems, plunging everything into darkness.

In the capital city of Venit, *gold-armed* hu*bots gathered in cohorts to discuss strategies that might sustain the majority of their citizens in stasis. Physicians discussed ways to maintain heart and brain health. Scientists studied the phenomena that caused the massive blackout. Mathematicians calculated how long the solar storm would last and how much further damage it might do. Engineers concerned themselves with developing new mechanisms for generating power. And, violet-eyed gold arms—the most elite echelon of all—weighed the various approaches and considered how they might mesh together.

Few would admit it, but never had the Adventurans felt so helpless, at least, not since the nuclear aftermath of the Two Millennia War nearly annihilated their civilization. Each of them still carried the cloned remnants of those same ancestors, and their forbears' ancient emotions stirred back to life.

The young people on Juvenilia were amazed to see an

overseer. Juveniles didn't survive past the age of fifteen, so most of them had never seen anyone old. They circled around Zenith Fullova, touching his robe and marveling over his beard and hat. The overseer had visited Juvenilia regularly but mostly confined his stays inside the Library of Illumination. He was as concerned as the children over the disappearance of their curator.

§ *When was the last time you saw Peer Meap?*

One of the younger boys stared at the overseer, his eyes wide. "Did you see that?" he asked, without taking his eyes off Zenith Fullova. "His lips don't move. He can talk with his mouth closed."

All the Juveniles took a step closer to Zenith Fullova, hemming him in. "Say something," one of them called out.

§*Allow me to restate the question. When was the last time any one of you saw your curator?*

"Wow. Could you teach us how to do that?"

Zenith Fullova smiled. §*First, you must tell me about Peer Meap.*

"He's been gone an awful long time," Duddu answered. "I haven't seen him since before the monsters came."

§*Are there monsters here, now?*

"They're mostly dead. One drowned in the pond. We fried one in the storm drain. The others are making a big stink in the library. We don't want them here."

§ *They don't belong here. It is the reason why we sealed the libraries. However,* Zenith Fullova looked at Duddu and Marbol, §*you boys still managed to get inside.*

Marbol held up his homemade weapon. "I used my

sonic scrambler. The first time, it broke the glass in the window and the monsters escaped. But then, something happened, and we couldn't get inside, even though there was no glass left. I modified my scrambler and tried it again on a different window. It doesn't look like I broke the glass, but now we can get inside like there's nothing there."

Zenith Fullova carefully studied the device. §*May I borrow it?*

Marbol hunched his shoulders and hugged the scrambler against his chest. "It's the only one I have."

§*I can get it back to you, unchanged, within moments.*

Marbol repeatedly sucked in air and rapidly blew it out through pursed lips, making them quiver.

Duddu placed a hand on Marbol's shoulder. "It'll be okay. He's Peer Meap's friend. He'll give it back to you." But Marbol continued to clutch the sonic scrambler to his chest, breathing heavily.

§*I have an idea. Let's take a trip.*

"All of us?" someone asked.

§*No.* Zenith Fullova put his hands on Marbol's and Duddu's shoulders. §*Just these two lads and I.* In the blink of an eye, they disappeared.

Malcolm Trees, the Chancellor of the Exchequer, hid on the floor behind a stone bench at the far end of a Mysterian discussion circle. He and curator, Hue the Elder, hoped the bench would shield them from invading Terrorians. Mal's biggest concern was his inability to commune with the overseers. He had left his robe and chaperon—a special hat designed by the overseers—at Hue the Elder's home after lunch. Without the special properties built into the chaperon, he could not inform anyone of the attack upon the priests and priestesses of Mysteriose, a realm where half the inhabitants dabbled in witchcraft and sorcery.

"This is quite undignified," Hue whispered, "and uncomfortable. But we must remain here until we can get away to the caves without being detected."

Mal nodded but doubted the curator could see his sign of agreement. He wriggled his way to the edge of the bench to try to peek around it. He caught a glimpse of a Terrorian trooper walking out of the building with each of his tentacles wrapped around an immobilized Mysterian.

Jackson Roth frantically searched the Library of Illumination's circulation desk for Johanna's diary. "She used to keep it in here. I'm sure of it."

Emily Brent, his prom date, wrapped her arms around her body. "I don't want to stay here. This place gives me the creeps. Those ugly beasts tried to kill me!"

Jackson stared at her. "They're called Terrorians. You're okay now, which is more than I can say for Johanna."

"They dangled me from five stories up. I could have been killed."

"You weren't," Jackson answered as he continued to search.

Emily glared at her best friend, Cassie Turner, who in turn nudged Jackson's best friend, Logan Elliott.

"Are you calling the cops?" Logan asked.

"No. I need to get in touch with the overseers."

"If you're not calling the cops, I'm not hanging around here for a repeat performance." Emily turned to Cassie. "Do I look okay? Have I been slimed?"

"No," Cassie answered. "You look beautiful."

"Can we get out of here? I want to go to the prom."

"The prom?" Jackson couldn't believe his ears. "I can't go to the prom. I'm the co-curator here. I have to save Johanna."

"I'll probably be voted prom queen. You have to escort me." Emily stamped her foot. "You're supposed to be my king."

Jackson looked at Logan. "Can you help me out here?"

Logan shook his head. "Leave it to this place to turn prom night into a weirdo missing persons case."

Cassie gripped Logan's arm like she'd never let go. "What about that other guy?"

That got Emily's attention. "The cute college guy?"

Jackson sighed. "Who did she say he was?"

"The dean of English at Cranford University," Logan answered.

"I've got to get them back." Jackson continued to root around the desk.

Cassie tugged on Logan's arm. "Do something," she said between clenched teeth.

Logan kissed the side of her head before saying to Jackson, "Dude. How about I take the girls to the prom, while you take care of business here? There's not much reason for us to hang around. You know where to find us when you're done."

"Yeah. Sure. You go ahead," Jackson said, without stopping his hunting expedition.

Logan placed his free hand on Emily's back and led her and Cassie out the door.

"Wait," Jackson called out. He grabbed the corsage he had purchased for Emily and ran over to her. "This is for you."

She took the corsage without looking at him. "Thanks."

Once they were outside, Emily leaned toward Logan. "What was that all about? What is this place?"

"It's the Library of Illumination, and if you don't want to be considered an airhead, don't repeat anything that happened tonight to anyone. Jackson didn't want us coming here to begin with, and now I can see why."

Cassie pulled away from him. "Somebody needs to know what happened here. It's… unnatural."

Logan helped the girls slide into the back of the limousine they had hired to take them to the senior prom. "You're right. But if you say something without any proof to back it up, no one is going to believe you. And they'll start calling you a *whack job*. Just leave it to me. This gives me an idea about how to put my summer internship to good use."

"Where are you interning?" Emily asked.

"Graydon Ransom University News Tonight. I'm going to be one of their new reporters. And, boy, do I have a story for them. I think tonight just turned into my springboard to stardom."

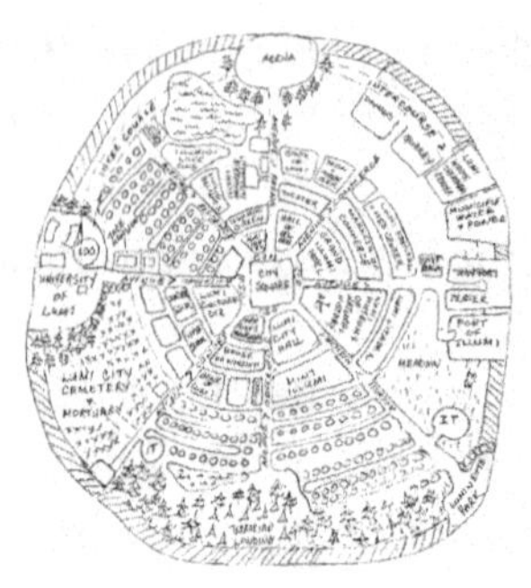

CHAPTER TWO

The Overseers focused on crisis abatement.

⌘*We have not heard from Malcolm Trees. He should be back from Mysteriose by now with his report.*

■*Unusual, but not unheard of. Perhaps he is strengthening relationships.*

⌘*Perhaps. However, I require his counsel.*

The deans suddenly sat back in their chairs, startled by the sudden appearance of Zenith Fullova and two teenagers. All but Galio Abbingdon, who leaned forward and stared at a small weapon one of the boys held in his hand. ❀*What an interesting-looking device.*

Zenith Fullova nodded. §*These lads are from Juvenilia, where they have found a way to breach the library seal we enacted. Young Marbol is reluctant to hand over his 'sonic scrambler' to a stranger. I thought it best if I brought him and his friend Duddu along, so you could see it.*

Ryden Simmdry's brows shot up. ⌘*It allowed them to breach the library?*

§*Oddly enough, it changes the composition of the glass in the windows. It looks like the glass is intact; however, you can pass through it quite freely.*

❋*Like a hologram.*

§*Exactly.*

⌘*What of the Terrorians on Juvenilia?*

§*None remain.*

■*They've escaped?*

"They're all dead. Bam!" Duddu smacked the palm of his hand with his fist.

❋*Is the climate inhospitable to Terrorians?*

§*Not as much as the inhabitants are.*

Galio Abbingdon walked over to the boys and placed his hand on the sonic scrambler. ❋*How does it work?*

Marbol, eyes wide, let go of it. "You just aim it at the window and hold the trigger in for 15 seconds."

The overseer did as the Juvenile said, and then lowered the arm holding the weapon, confused. ❋*Nothing happened.*

Marbol walked over to the window and put his hand through it. It passed freely through where the glass should have stopped it.

❋*Remarkable. What principles did you based this on?*

"Sound waves. I scrambled them. The other scrambler I made just confuses people, but this one confuses windows."

Galio Abbingdon beamed. It had been a long time since the overseer for Scientico had smiled. His thin lips pulled back until they were nearly invisible, revealing a remarkable set of teeth for someone so old.

❋I would like to take these lads back to my lab. It intrigues me that someone so young invented something so industrious.

Duddu made a face. "Do you have any chocolate there? It's snack time, and we need something *feasty.*

❋I'm sure that can be arranged.

CAMERON'S STOMACH GROWLED. He lifted his lids just enough to know he still sat trapped in a Terrorian cell. He had leaned against the wall and closed his eyes for a moment, and he must have fallen asleep. He now sat on the floor with Terrorian vapor swirling around him.

Johanna reached out her hand to help pull him up. "I don't know how you can sit in that muck and sleep. It's really vile."

"It smells awful." Cameron tried to brush himself off. "Do you think it's dangerous?"

"All this vapor is Terrorian waste. Their floors are their sewers."

"Just when I thought it couldn't get any worse."

MEOW. Ophelia jumped from Johanna's arms and disappeared into the mist.

Johanna and Cameron both turned at the squeal of door hinges.

Nero 51 and another Terrorian entered the room, taking up most of the space and crowding the fugitives into a corner. "*Zig a otos sika aug-ig?*"

Johanna mumbled a translation charm. "Could you repeat the question?"

"When we are finished with you, you will wish you

had never been born, Johanna Charette." One of Nero 51's tentacles snaked toward the Fantasian curator.

Johanna pressed back into Cameron and felt his arms protectively encircling her. "That isn't the question you originally asked me," she stated without breaking eye contact with her Terrorian counterpart.

"It seems you are the overseers' pawn. I demand to know what they are doing with the portals."

Johanna crossed her arms over her chest. "They closed the portals to keep you from entering and destroying libraries. You're a curator. Why would you even do that?"

"You are a weak and ignorant creature. Most of the other curators are just like you. You all lack vision. The Libraries of Illumination are suffering from nonconformity. Irregularity. Inconsistency. I want to save them. Unite them. Make them better."

"The differences in the libraries and the realms they're on is what makes them unique and wonderful. That isn't nonconformity. It's individualism and originality."

Nero 51 stood up straighter. "It weakens them. I will make them strong, again."

Johanna could feel her blood coursing through her veins. "By invading the other libraries and killing everyone who gets in your way?"

"You are a stupid girl. We will not kill anyone, as long as they choose to embrace our leadership."

"No one wants your leadership," she said through clenched teeth. "Each realm is autonomous—as it should be."

"There is no autonomy among realms. You are all under the overseers' control. They are old and decaying.

Their time to rule is long past. Their ideas are stale. They show no initiative.

"I had planned to torture you in the slowest, most painful way possible," Nero 51 continued. "However, if you proclaim to the other realms that you have heard my plan to unite the libraries and believe in it, I will consider allowing you to live."

"Really?" Johanna said. "You would use me as *your* pawn?" Her voice dropped an octave, dripping with ice. "I would rather die."

Cameron leaned into her and whispered, "Don't be too hasty. Maybe agreeing with him will buy us enough time to figure out how to get out of here."

Johanna raised her voice. "I would never support you, Nero 51. And, I won't ask anyone else to do what I wouldn't do."

The Terrorian stretched his tentacles toward Johanna's neck.

A guttural growl erupted from beneath the vapor and in an instant, a white mass of hair jumped out of the mist and sunk its claws and teeth into Nero 51's tentacles.

"No. No. No," Nero 51 screamed as he shook his tentacle ferociously, trying to dislodge Ophelia.

"White cat," the other Terrorian screamed. "The sign of doom."

Nero 51 whipped his tentacle with all his might, dislodging Ophelia who flew through the air into Johanna's arms. The Terrorians fled the room, slamming the door behind them.

Cameron twisted Johanna around till she faced him. "What is going on here?"

The corners of her mouth curved upward. "The Terrorians are apparently afraid of cats."

"More than afraid of them. They looked terrified," Cameron said. "Too bad. I was hoping you would play along with them to buy us a little time."

"They had no intention of working with us. They just want to use me to improve their chances before they torture me."

"Us," Cameron said. "Before they torture *us*. Like I might know something."

"We're not going to let it get that far." She pulled out the miniature diary she had worn around her neck since the last time she was forced to spend time on Terroria. "Mal," she asked, "why are Terrorians afraid of cats?"

MAL HEARD JOHANNA'S voice in his head. "I can't talk now," he whispered, hoping she could get along without his advice for a while.

Hue the Elder poked him. "Shhhh…." The distance quickly closed between them and the Terrorians, and the Mysterian curator did not want to be discovered. Mal wriggled back out of sight as the Terrorians' work brought them closer.

Most of the noise came from the center of the discussion pit. Mal couldn't help but notice a new sound coming from behind him. Before he could turn his head, someone placed a hat on his head and took his arm. Ψ*It is time for us to leave.* Moments later, Dean Proteus Bligh crouched over the prone figures of Mal and Hue the Elder in the center of the conference room on Lumina.

Ryden Simmdry cut into Mal's thoughts. ⌘*Is there*

a problem, Malcolm? I'm sensing a great deal of angst from you.

Mal stood up. "Mysteriose is under attack. The Terrorians have captured many of the residents in force fields and are taking them somewhere." He reached up and removed the hat from his head. "My chaperon."

Proteus Bligh handed him his robe. Ψ*You very nearly got captured yourself. I would advise not leaving these articles behind in the future.*

⌘*Did you overhear the Terrorians say anything of interest, Malcolm?*

"No. Although Johanna asked me a question. She wants to know why Terrorians are afraid of cats?"

Ryden Simmdry raised his eyebrows but said nothing for several seconds. ⌘*I had almost forgotten.* He paused as he nodded to himself. ⌘*You will not find cats on Terroria, at least, not any more. Even when they did exist, felines were kept in captivity because they are believed to be evil omens. All cats are despised, but white cats, which are not native to the realm, are especially hated. Terrorians believe only deities harbor cats and use them to mete out justice to subjects who don't follow the laws of the gods. Even before the Two Millennia War, a widespread belief said a white cat had killed Terrorian ruler, Hanro the First. He was responsible for enacting a draconian law demanding the delivery of all first-born offspring of non-ruling class citizens into slavery to be used for the pleasure of the rich and powerful. Not long afterward, he was found dead with a pure white cat sitting on his body. It is believed the cat trod through erabatum, a highly toxic plant that is poisonous to Terrorians, although apparently not to cats. According to legend, the cat jumped on Hanro the First, and its claws pierced the ruler's skin, depositing the poison. Try as they might, Terrorians were unable to trap the cat and prove it responsible for their leader's demise. There are many similar stories, but that is the most famous one. Why is she interested?*

"I don't actually know. I was trying to avoid the Terrorians, and," he winked at the master of the overseers, "I was *shushed* by Hue the Elder."

Hue immediately became flustered. "Oh, no Malcolm, I did not mean to get in the way of library business. I was just trying to keep you safe."

Mal smiled and placed his hand on Hue's shoulder. "I'm only teasing you. I'm sure Johanna is fine. But just to make sure, I'll go there now and relay what Ryden Simmdry just said."

FURST COULD FEEL his curls tighten into tiny ringlets. *By all means, the Terrorians must be stopped. Take them out, find a way to, I must.* He switched his decimator to force field and aimed at the Terrorian who stood farthest away. He eased the trigger back and waited for something to happen. *Miss, did I?* he questioned himself. He took aim at another Terrorian and fired. Once again, nothing appeared to happen.

The faint sound of angry voices slowly increased in volume. Furst ran to another window in the cupola and saw a crowd of Dramaticans rushing toward the fighting. *Annihilated, they will be.*

He ran back to the open window to see if the Terrorians had heard them. He watched as several troopers started running toward the noise, but not the two he had shot at. *Works, the force field.* He located another open window with a view of the impending clash and aimed at a Terrorian in the rear flank. The trooper froze in mid-step. *Three, that makes.* Furst managed to freeze one more trooper before the two sides began firing on each other. He saw his cousin disappear. *Using the decimator, they are!* He switched his weapon to decimate and managed to obliterate another enemy soldier, but not before the Terrorians turned several more of his kinsmen into dust.

Furst trained his weapon on the only Terrorian left.

"I BELIEVE WE'LL find what we need in here," Prophet IAN c. said to gold-armed Prophet CHRIS h. They rummaged through the defunct machinery of civilizations past, looking for old technology.

"What are we searching for, exactly?" CHRIS h. asked.

"They are called generators and are powered by the vats of oily substance we found in the previous room."

"What does a 'generator' look like?"

"Like this," IAN c. answered, pointing to a bulky mass. "We have found one." He pulled away a massive tarp that covered the machine. They soon discovered a half-dozen more.

"Do you think they still work?"

"We will soon find out."

The two men walked into the next room, which reeked of petroleum. IAN c. tipped a sealed, barrel-shaped vat on its side and rolled it into the room with the generators. They poured a small amount of fuel into the closest one, and after tightening the cap, IAN c. pushed a throttle to the right before he pulled a large lever. The generator thumped as it tried to power up, but it would not operate.

"Why doesn't it work?" CHRIS h. asked.

"Help me move it into the light. We may have to check its system of hoses and valves," IAN c. said, pointing to them, "to make sure they are not clogged. This is not a very efficient or clean way of generating power, but it's our only hope."

ON THE WAY to his lab, Galio Abbingdon stopped by the Library of Origination's duplication chamber and created a basket of sweets that would make any chocolate-lover drool. Marbol and Duddu each tried to claim ownership of the candy, nudging the other away, but a stern look by Galio Abbingdon stopped the tussle, and the boys settled on carrying the basket between them.

Inside the lab, Marbol took apart the gun and explained how he had created it. He discussed his reasoning with the overseer for Scientico, who was enthralled by Marbol's genius.

The boy put the scrambler back together. "Are you going to try to make one like it? I can help you if you need me to."

Galio Abbingdon smiled. ❋*I have a better idea.* He led them back to the duplication chamber and made a copy of the scrambler. Then he made a copy of the basket of sweets so each boy would have their own.

Finally, they returned to the overseers' conference room where Zenith Fullova took charge of returning the teens to Juvenilia.

*

Milencia slowly backed herself away from the Terrorian soldiers and into the shadows of trees in the forest abutting Militairre Meadow. She doubled around the library toward a residential area and began pounding on doors. "Lock yourselves in!"

She explained to each family what had happened and asked them to alert everyone else in their neighborhood to lock their doors. She ran to the next section of homes to spread the message. Some Romanticans volunteered to travel to the other side of Roma, the capital city, to start informing people there to barricade themselves inside. Others ran into the heart of the city's business district where they told proprietors to return home quickly and protect themselves. All were forewarned to run in the opposite direction if they saw a Terrorian approaching.

"What is a Terrorian?" many people asked. "How will I recognize one when I see it?"

"You'll know immediately," Milencia answered. "They are huge and have tentacles. They do not resemble us at all, although they do walk on two legs and wear clothing. They are armed and will shoot to kill."

The description of Terrorians traveled like wildfire. Romantica's use of technology was very limited, but they had developed a strong grapevine for gossip, and in no time at all, the Terrorians became the talk of the city.

Jackson found the diary Johanna had given him shoved in the bottom of his backpack. He opened it and wrote, *Johanna, can you see this?*

He heard her voice in his head. "Jackson. Are you

all okay?"

He sat on the floor behind the circulation desk and continued writing, *Everyone here is fine. Where are you?*

"Cameron and I are in a small room with a heavy door. It could be one of the Terrorian library storerooms, but there are no windows. It might be located on one of the sub-levels. They were here a little while ago but abruptly left after Ophelia attacked Nero 51. She's with us, too."

Jackson's pencil scribbled noiselessly across the page. *Ophelia is with you? I didn't notice her missing. I was too busy looking for a way to contact you.*

"Have you heard from Mal?" Johanna continued. "I asked him why Terrorians are afraid of cats, but I haven't heard back yet."

Nope, Jackson wrote back. *What can I do to help?*

"Sit tight," she answered. "I don't have enough information yet to formulate a plan."

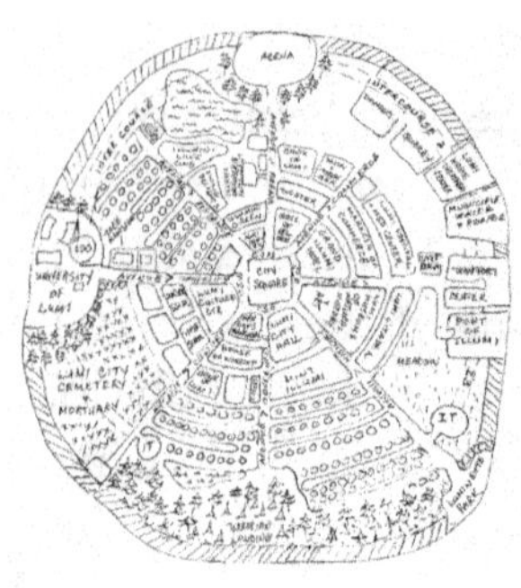

CHAPTER THREE

A chunk of the library structure next to Furst's head disappeared. A Terrorian trooper had spotted him and seemed intent on eliminating him as a threat.

Take down one Terrorian, I can.

But he spoke too soon. Outside, Terrorian reinforcements had arrived, and when Furst sneaked a peek, they were releasing the soldiers he had placed in force fields.

Killed them, I should have.

He suddenly felt his blood run cold. His hands started to shake. Dramaticans were, for the most part, peaceful. Killing anything was anathema to them. Yet here he stood, wishing he had killed the enemy. The thought nearly paralyzed him.

The sound of Terrorian feet stamping up the cupola stairs snapped him out of it. He ran back to the maintenance window and looked outside. No one. From the sound of it, all the soldiers were inside the library pursuing him. Furst squeezed out the maintenance window. It was a long way down, but he had to jump to freedom or die trying. He took a leap of faith and safely landed on the back lawn, freeing as many of his kinsmen as possible and telling them to flee the library grounds. One of the people standing close to him suddenly disappeared. Furst leapt out of the way, using his powerful legs to propel himself to the front of the library. He grabbed a Dramatican military recruit and pulled him to the front of the library where he aimed the decimator at the roots of a small tree. The roots disappeared, and the tree fell. Furst pointed at the library entrance, and he and the recruit soon jammed the sapling through the door handles to keep the Terrorians inside.

"Hold, will it?" the recruit asked.

Furst stared at the tree for a second, then grabbed the recruit's decimator and jammed it through the door handles, as well. It was a tight fit but made a much stronger barrier. "Everyone, you must get. Surround the library, we must. Break the windows, they might. Now, go."

Furst stepped back so he could see as much of the library as possible. Many of the windows were narrow, and he thought the Terrorians would be least likely to escape through those because they probably would not fit. He circled to the side of the library near the board room. Those windows were larger and Terrorians would definitely be able to escape through them. Around the corner, another large expanse of windows could be breached. Furst tried to position himself in a way that he could fire at either side.

Soon, others came to aid Furst's defense. He

positioned them in bunches around the building where Terrorians were most likely to emerge. He cautioned them that he had initially incapacitated Terrorians by shooting at them from the maintenance windows in the cupola. He pointed them out, warning the Dramaticans that the Terrorians might try to pick them off in the same way.

Furst's diary was still inside the cupola where he had dropped it after reading that Pru Tellerence was under attack. There was no way to contact her, or the overseers, to tell them about what was happening on his realm.

MAL LOOKED AROUND the unusually quiet Fantasian library. "Is anyone here?" he called out.

Jackson's head popped up from behind the circulation desk. "Mal. Johanna said she was trying to reach you."

"I know. Where is she? I couldn't answer her because I was nearly caught and detained by a Terrorian invasion team on Mysteriose."

"They have her. Nero 51 and one of his ilk were here, and he took her. She gave herself up so he wouldn't hurt my prom date. It's all my fault. If Emily wasn't here, maybe Johanna would have been able to fight the Terrorians off."

"Your prom date?"

"Yeah. Johanna and I kind of split up. It's stupid, and that's all my fault, too. I love her more than she'll ever know, and now the Terrorians have her." Jackson swallowed as he tried to maintain his composure.

"The Terrorians have a lot of people," Mal said. "A couple dozen at least from Romantica and Dramatica, and as I said before, Mysteriose."

"I thought the time machine was trapped between the portals."

⌘*Apparently Nero 51 found a way out.* Ryden Simmdry had arrived so quietly, no one realized he was there.

They turned to greet the master of the overseers. "What else can you tell us? Mal asked.

⌘*I'm quite sure Odyon orchestrated their sudden liberation. Nero 51 could never have pulled that off by himself. Odyon is powerful, nearly as powerful as I am, and his vast knowledge of sorcery makes this invasion totally unpredictable. He will not allow himself to be impeded by the laws of man and nature. Odyon will bend circumstances to suit his needs.*

⌘*Where is Johanna?*

"The Terrorians have her," Mal and Jackson said in unison.

⌘*I guess she no longer cares about the history of cats on Terroria, then.*

"But she does," Jackson said. "Apparently, the Terrorians didn't just take Johanna and Dr. Thorne. They took her cat Ophelia as well. But something must have happened because she told me to ask Mal why Terrorians are afraid of cats."

⌘*You're able to converse telepathically?*

"She gave me a diary. I write, and she answers in my head."

⌘*Ask her where she's being held.*

"I already did that. She says she thinks she's in a sub-level chamber because there are no windows, and the door is reinforced."

⌘*Did she say anything more?*

"Just that there's nothing I can do for her right now because she hasn't 'formulated a plan' yet."

The overseer nodded, and turned away, but then blinked and jerked back toward Jackson. ⌘*Who is Dr. Thorne?*

Milencia recruited two new Romantican militairres, Annabeth and Stasia, to travel back to Militairre Field with her. They crept through the woods trying to avoid being spotted. It took twice as long as normal, and when they got there, the Terrorians and captured militairres were all gone. Only Dame Erato's limp body lay crumpled in the open meadow.

The militairres approached Dame Erato tentatively. Milencia explained how a member of the militia had shot an arrow at a Terrorian invader but had hit Dame Erato instead. When they arrived at her resting place, they knelt down to pay their respects to her spirit. "May you forever be at peace, Dame Erato," Milencia said aloud.

"Mmm…" Dame Erato moaned.

"She's alive," Annabeth said.

Stasia jumped up in a flash. "I'll get help."

Dame Erato moaned again. Milencia took her hand and squeezed it. "We're here for you, Dame Erato. Stasia has gone to get help. Just lie still a little while longer."

It seemed like an eternity before Stasia returned with a white witch from the Maroqi District and a small child who bore the mark of a Maroqi priestess.

The woman pushed Milencia out of the way. "I am Ingur Aguri. Was the arrow tipped in poison?"

"I don't know," Milencia said. "I don't think so. It is one of our own."

"Is the arrowhead carved into the wood or was it an added embellishment?"

"Our arrows are carved to a point. We do not add embellishments. They only weigh the arrows down," Milencia replied.

Ingur opened a satchel and withdrew a small bottle containing a thick yellow substance. She poured some around the wound where the arrow pierced the skin. Then she took out a vivid blue powder and sprinkled it on the shaft of the arrow. "We must roll her on her side. I will get behind her, and you must pull her toward you without allowing her to turn completely over."

Milencia took hold of Dame Erato's shoulder and waited for Ingur's command.

"Now," the witch said, working quickly to pour the same yellow substance on the exit wound where the point of the arrow stuck out. She quickly sprinkled the blue powder on the tip, chanted for a moment and clapped her hands twice. The arrow burst into flames, and Dame Erato screamed in pain.

Milencia stiffened, her face contorted. "What are you doing?"

"Saving her life," the witch replied.

Once the flames died out, Dame Erato's body sagged in Milencia's arms. "You killed her," the young woman cried.

"No. I destroyed the arrow that pierced her chest by causing it to burn hot enough to seal the wound in her flesh." Ingur placed her ear to Dame Erato's chest. "Her heart still beats. Her breathing is weak. I suspect the arrow pierced her lung. The wound is sealed, but she may have lost some ability to breathe easily. It is the difference between breathing shallowly and not breathing at all. Which would you prefer?"

Milencia stared at the witch, then put her own ear to Dame Erato's chest. Her eyes opened wider. She looked at Annabeth and Stasia. "What she said is true. Dame Erato's heart continues to beat."

The little girl who had arrived with the witch walked over to Dame Erato and kissed her pale cheek but said nothing. Ingur smiled at the child. "This is my granddaughter Selestra. She is destined to be a powerful Maroqi priestess. She has given this woman her blessing."

Stasia reached into the pockets of her skirt. "What can we give you to pay for your services?"

"Harrumph." The witch grabbed her satchel and took Selestra's hand. "I require nothing from you. I know Dame Erato. Tell her Ingur Aguri healed her. The rest will be up to her."

A LARGE GROUP OF Mysterians fled the Terrorian invaders and hid in one of the caves that safeguarded their resources. They could not breach the gates to reach the assets stashed within; however, the cave had several other chambers where they could wait out the invaders.

"Where is the curator, the overseer, and the chancellor of the exchequer when we need them?" one of the men asked.

"I saw them for a moment inside the town hall," a woman answered.

"Did they escape?" the questioner pressed on.

"I don't know," she answered. "My attention was diverted by a bright light inside a glass bubble that our people were disappearing into. When I looked back at where the curator and the others had been, no one was there."

"Maybe they went to get help," a young boy said.

"More than likely, they took to ground just like us," his mother answered, "and are waiting for the invaders to leave."

"Or they traveled to somewhere safe and have abandoned us completely," the first man continued.

"I doubt it," someone else replied. "They would never leave without collecting their precious taxes."

"They already have them," the woman countered.

"No. They don't," Sean of Oster said. "They prepared the notes they gave us and catalogued all our resources and put them behind impenetrable gates, but they have taken nothing. We were supposed to hear more about their plan today, but the Terrorians put an end to that."

"Well then," the first man said. "Maybe they will come back, if only to take a share of what is ours."

MARBOL AND DUDDU reappeared in the Juvenilia Town Hall, each carrying a huge basket of treats. They soon discovered they had a lot of "best" friends. The large number of treats gave the boys instant power and popularity, and they found themselves bartering chocolate and taffy for goods and labor. Zenith Fullova watched as the pop-up marketplace thrived. He knew it was not what Galio Abbingdon wanted to achieve by giving the Juveniles so much candy, but he also didn't want to interfere with their free trade. The overseer quietly disappeared without notice.

"So where did you go?"

"What did you do?"

"Did that old guy teach you how to speak without moving your lips?"

"Can you go back and get more candy?"

The questions were quick and random. At that moment, the Juveniles didn't really care where the candy came from, as long as they could get their hands on some.

"She's the belle of the ball," Cassie whispered to Logan, "but she's not smiling. And she hasn't said two words to me all night. I saw Kara Biels in the ladies' room, and she says Emily hates Jackson for not escorting her to the prom and blames me for setting them up. I think what happened at the library really messed with her mind."

"It is your fault. If you hadn't pushed me into convincing Jackson to date her, this would have never happened."

"You could have said no, you know. You didn't have to convinced him."

"And face your wrath? You would have made my life a living hell."

Cassie scowled, unlinking her arm from Logan's.

Overhead, hundreds of balloons nestled against the ceiling with different colors and lengths of curled ribbon hanging from each one. A stage stood off to one side with an overhead banner proclaiming *Exeter High School Senior Prom.*

"Anyway, it wasn't my idea to come here," Logan

answered. "She said she wanted to go to the prom. So, we took her to the prom."

The dancing ended, and everyone stood around expectantly as the principal made his way to a microphone at the front of the stage. "Are we all having fun?" he asked.

A few students said, "Yeah," but most remained silent. It was time to announce this year's prom queen, and while Emily had been favored to win, her breakup with Zach Maybrecht meant some late voters might have switched to a different candidate. A member of the student council walked over to the principal and handed him a sealed envelope.

"What is this," Logan asked, "the Academy Awards?"

"Shush," Cassie whispered, elbowing him in the ribs.

He took a step away from her. "That hurt, you know."

Cassie made a face, then turned away and ignored him.

"First, we will announce the members of the royal court." He named four girls and four boys. None of them were Emily, but her two closest competitors had been selected, as were their boyfriends. The girls were guided stage right, while the boys were positioned stage left.

"And now for your prom king and queen." He received a new envelope, pulled out a white card, and smiled. "The queen of this year's Exeter High School prom is…Emily Brent."

Emily lifted her chin and walked up onto the stage, smiling along the way at students who congratulated her. When she reached the microphone, the principal motioned her to wait. "And this year's prom king is…Zach Maybrecht."

There was a smattering of applause before someone shouted out, "He's not here."

The principal's eyes narrowed. "He has to be here. He's prom king."

"He decided not to come after Emily broke his heart," a girl shouted. Several people said "Aww," while others laughed.

Emily nearly shoved the principal off the stage as she pushed in front of the mic. "Whatever Zach told you is a lie. It's just as well he's not here, because he shouldn't be my prom king. He only won because he was dating me. Since I'm prom queen, I'm going to choose the king who will stand by my side."

"Yeah who?" another student shouted.

"My prom king—" Emily paused for effect, "is Logan Elliott."

Cassie's mouth opened and stayed open. Logan smirked at her before making his way on stage. Once he arrived at Emily's side, the president and vice president of the student body walked over to them. The president placed a silver tiara embedded with rhinestones on Emily's head, while the vice president placed a manlier version on Logan's.

The band began to play a slow dance. Logan led Emily down to the dance floor. He took her in his arms, and the rest of their entourage filed suit. As the chosen couples danced, the rest of the students applauded, except for Cassie who stood alone looking miserable. Once the dance ended, Emily took Logan by the arm and led him around like a prized possession, completely avoiding Cassie, who stood quietly by herself, fighting back tears.

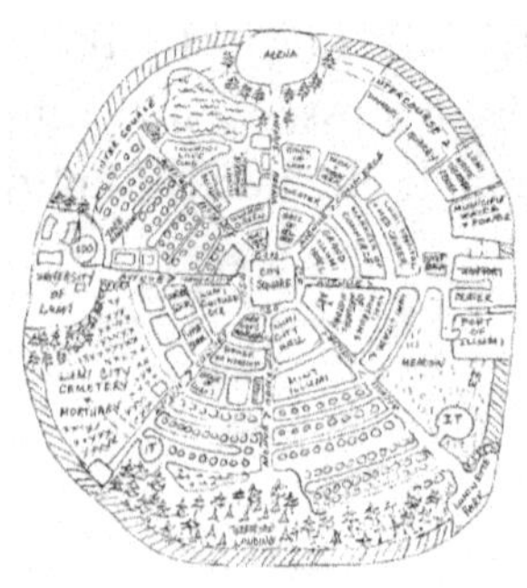

CHAPTER FOUR

SUDDENLY, BOOKS CAME crashing through several of the Dramatican library windows as the Terrorians trapped inside began hurling them like missiles. The Dramaticans held their fire. A tentacle slithered out one of the windows. When nothing happened, a second tentacle clutched the edge of the window, and soon a head appeared behind it. Furst set his weapon to decimate and fired. The Terrorian disappeared.

Furst soon heard the yelps of some of his kinsmen as the Terrorians picked off his neighbors. "Fire!" Furst yelled. All the Dramaticans with decimators took aim at the windows and fired. Some Terrorians were turned to dust. Others were caught in force fields. After several moments, the silence grew thick.

"All of them, is that?" One of the soldiers asked Furst.

"Know, I do not," Furst answered. "Enter the

library, I must."

"A trap, it may be," Mudge warned.

"Maybe," Furst replied, "but to know, go in, I must." He took a step and turned back. "Careful, be."

Furst asked the soldiers in front of the library to cover him, and he told them to shoot at anything that moved, besides him. He removed the decimator from the handles of the front door of the library. He knew once he dislodged the sapling that secured the door, one or more Terrorians could come rushing out and grab him.

He stepped back. With his weapon still set to decimate, he aimed at the door handles and fired. The tree disappeared along with the door. There was nothing to stop the remaining Terrorians from running out, and three of them did, firing at the line of Dramatican soldiers. It was a quiet battle. The decimators barely whispered as they picked off five Dramaticans and two Terrorians. The third invader retreated back into the library after being shot with several arrows.

The Dramaticans didn't have time to wonder what to do because they suddenly heard screams from behind the library. Furst told the men to his right to stay put and guard the front, while he motioned for those on his left to follow him as he ran toward the back. The Dramaticans suffered more casualties after being surprised by three new soldiers arriving in the time machine. Furst ran toward the vehicle, only stopping when it disappeared from sight. Mere seconds later, it loomed back in view and without hesitation, Furst aimed his decimator and fired. There was a loud boom and a flash of bright light before the time machine disappeared with the Terrorians still inside.

*

RYDEN SIMMDRY PACED in circles around the information desk while Jackson explained who Dr. Thorne was and Johanna's connection to him.

⌘*So, it's not bad enough that the Terrorians are invading several realms at once and taking prisoners. Now, there's a civilian from Fantasia on Terroria as well.*

"I'm afraid so," Jackson answered contritely.

"Don't sound so defeated, Jackson," Mal said. "It's not your fault Nero 51 invaded."

"But it is," Jackson lamented. "If my prom date didn't come here, Nero 51 couldn't have dangled her over the balcony railing, and Johanna might not have been forced to bargain with him to take her instead of Emily."

⌘*Emily? There's another civilian involved?*

"Yeah. But it's okay. Nero 51 gave Emily back and she went to the prom with my friends Logan and Cassie."

⌘*Were all these people present when the Terrorians showed up?*

"Kind of."

Ryden Simmdry turned toward Mal. ⌘*We must return to Lumina at once. We need to formulate a containment plan for this situation before word gets out and there's a panic. The major cities on other realms are less populated and more separated from the rest of their worlds, and the problems on those worlds are not as acute. But given the density of Fantasian cities, their naiveté about the Illumini constellation, and the way technology controls the inhabitant's lives, we'll have our work cut out for us.*

Mal held up his hand. "One moment, Johanna has another question."

*

A REALM AWAY, JOHANNA and Cameron were politely excusing their growling stomachs.

Johanna had given up on avoiding the Terrorian mist and, like her companion, she sat on the floor with her back against the wall. She played with the miniaturized diary that hung around her neck as she asked it a question. "Mal, could you ask Ryden Simmdry if there's any way I can conjure up food out of thin air?"

A moment later on Fantasia, Mal turned to the overseer. "Johanna is asking if there's a way to conjure food."

⌘ *You're in contact right now?*

"Yes."

⌘ *Tell her to concentrate on my name and try to contact me telepathically.*

"What are you going to do?" Jackson asked.

⌘ *I'm going to find her.*

Mal answered Johanna by stating Ryden Simmdry's request.

The overseer closed his eyes, suddenly opened them, and transported from the Fantasian library to Johanna's location on Terroria.

"Oh!" Johanna exclaimed.

⌘ *Johanna.* He looked at her companion. ⌘ *And Dr. Thorne, I presume.*

"Yes." Cameron stood up, trying not to stare at the overseer. He had never seen anyone dressed so oddly, especially someone who magically appeared out of thin air and knew his name. His stomach growled. "Excuse me."

Ryden Simmdry waved his hand and turned his palm up. A platter appeared containing fruits and vegetables.

Cameron reached for an apple. Johanna just stood there staring at the food, then into Ryden Simmdry's eyes. She moved her hands in unison, mimicking the overseer's movement, and for a second, a bottle of water seemed to appear in each of her hands and then disappear.

⌘*Your growing abilities continue to astound me.*

"What ability?" she asked. "The bottles disappeared."

⌘*Practice, Johanna. Anything that comes too easily may not be worth having. Through practice, you will earn the right to be able to summon what is necessary. However, be careful what you wish for, for there is no filter on magical apparitions, and what appears may not be what you thought you requested.*

As the Exeter High School Prom wound down, couples with plans to continue their celebration by the lake moved outside. Emily slid into the limo and smiled at Logan, who remained standing by the open door. "Come on. We're going to be late, and if I'm not mistaken, you're the person with the key to the cabin at the Dunes."

"Cassie's not here," Logan said. "I don't see her anywhere. I'd better go take a look inside."

"You're going to leave me sitting here alone?" Emily asked, her voice devoid of sweetness.

"Cassie was my date. I can't just leave her here. I'm responsible for her."

Emily leaned out of the car. "Trey," she called out, waving at one of the players from the school softball team. "Have you got plans for after the prom."

The shy, redheaded player walked over and smiled.

"No."

"Well, you do now," Emily purred. "Cassie Turner is somewhere in the gym. Go find her and tell her you're taking her to the Dunes for the after-prom party."

"Uh…" Trey didn't know what else to say.

"That's settled, then." Emily turned to Logan. "Get in the limo."

Logan hesitated.

Emily slipped her hand up the front of his vest, grabbed his waistband, and tugged. She smiled sweetly. "I'll make it worth your while."

Logan shrugged and slid onto the seat next to her.

Trey walked back into the school looking for Cassie. Few students remained. He walked into the gym where a couple of custodians were clearing out the detritus from the prom. He looked all over but couldn't find her. He returned to the hall and asked a couple of students if they'd seen her.

"I think she's crying in the ladies' room," a girl said.

"I'm supposed to take her to a party. Could you go get her for me?"

"What did you do to her?" the girl asked.

"I didn't do anything…"

"She's Logan's girlfriend," her friend said. "Or she was, until tonight when Emily Brent got her claws into him."

Trey sighed. "Could you get her for me, please?"

"Sure," she answered.

A minute after she walked in, she walked out, without Cassie. "She said she's calling someone to pick her up and take her home."

"I can give her a ride home if she wants."

"What do I look like, your personal assistant?"

Trey's face turned red. "Is there anyone else in there?"

"No, she's the only one."

He turned and strode into the ladies' room. He didn't see anyone, but he could hear someone crying inside one of the stalls.

"Cassie?"

"Go away."

"It's Trey Onderdonck. Emily told me to take you to a party at the Dunes."

"And everyone does everything Emily says because she's…Emily."

"I know you walked in with Logan, and he just left with Emily. If you don't want to go to the party, that's fine. I can take you home."

"I can find my own ride home."

He could hear her sob. "Look, I can leave. But I only live a few blocks away from you. I'm here, now, and you're on my way home. Why bother someone else?"

Emily remained silent.

"Look. I'll wait right outside the door for a while," Trey continued. "If you want to take me up on the offer, take a moment to splash some water on your face and take a deep breath. When I came in, there were only a few people standing around and they're probably all gone by now, so you won't have to face anyone. I already know you've been crying, so it's not like I'll be shocked and start spreading rumors about you."

"Why are you being so nice to me? Because Emily

asked you to?"

"No. I have five sisters. If one of them was left in the lurch like you are, I would hope someone would give her a break and take her home. I'll be outside."

Five minutes later, Cassie slowly opened the door and poked her head out to see if anyone was still there.

"Cassie." Trey smiled at her.

Her lip quivered, like she was going to cry again, but she took a deep breath and nodded at him.

"Where would you like to go?"

"Home. Just…home."

He took her arm in his. "Your wish is my command."

Cassie managed a small smile. "Thank you."

The Adventurans worked through the night, cleaning or replacing the hoses and hardware on old generators. They could not quit until they had restored each piece of equipment to its proper working order. With that in mind, they carefully studied their handiwork, in an effort to make it reliable.

"Shall we start one up?" Prophet CHRIS h. asked.

"My brain requires sustenance," Prophet IAN c. answered. "Perhaps we should shut down and hook up for a couple of hours, so we are working at our very best capacity."

The gold-armed hu*bot's head moved from side to side. "We may lose what little living tissue remains of our forefathers. I do not think it is advisable to delay."

Prophet IAN c. nodded. "We will continue then." He filled one of the generators with fuel. If the curator could have closed his eyes as he pulled the switch, he would have, but he couldn't block out possible failure, nor could he pray. Adventurans did not believe in a greater power than the whole of their civilization. All IAN c. could do was pull the switch and witness the results.

Terrorian troopers laid in wait outside the Romantican Library of Illumination. The foliage from the plants, which had just been replaced in the library garden, barely concealed them. They didn't want to invade buildings they weren't familiar with, and which might contain unimaginable horrors. They preferred to pick off their victims one by one, until they received further instructions from Nero 51. The soldiers had no way of knowing Milencia informed local citizens to stay off the streets.

The Terrorians did not see Milencia return Dame Erato to her home near the city center, nor did they see the group of Romanticans she had recruited at their back doors sneak through the woods to the site of the Militairres' encampment.

Milencia had a decimator, but the single weapon—no matter how deadly—would not be enough to sustain them. Several people had their own bows and arrows, while others were willing to use shovels and garden rakes to rattle their enemies' brains. Milencia hoped several of the original militairres had run into their enemy's line of fire before stopping to grab their weapons.

In fact, many weapons remained at the camp, and Milencia made quick work of distributing them, showing the new recruits how the decimators worked.

After they were fully briefed, the new militairres made their way through the woods to the far side of the library, using the last of the early morning shadows to hide their approach.

SEVERAL HOURS AFTER first hiding in Mysterian caves, elders and priests who had escaped Terrorian capture, ventured outside. They were several measures away from the capital city. Everything close by, appeared to be normal.

"Is it safe to go back to our homes?" someone asked.

"We cannot tell from this distance," Dron the Elder replied. "Who will volunteer to return to the town hall to see if invaders remain?"

There was a moment of silence as each Mysterian looked at his neighbor to volunteer. No one spoke up.

"It seems I must appoint someone—"

"Why don't you go? You're a high priest. You must have some spell you can use on them to prevent them from attacking you," one of the citizens said.

"You're absolutely right. I will go. And, you will accompany me."

"I was not volunteering," the startled citizen replied.

"I'm appointing you. Let's go." Dron grabbed the man's arm and pulled him away from the others. "We shall return," he told them. "Please do not do anything to call attention to yourselves in case the invaders remain in our midst."

MARBOL AND DUDDU lay on their backs on the grassy slope leading to the pond.

"My teeth hurt," Duddu groaned.

"My stomach aches," Marbol moaned.

"Do you think that old guy will ever come back

and give us more chocolate?"

"I don't want any more chocolate."

Duddu rolled over and stared at his friend. "How could you say something like that?"

"Today," Marbol said. "I don't want any more chocolate—today."

Duddu flopped onto his back again and stared at the clouds scudding overhead. "Oh. For a while, there, I thought you were losing your mind. I'm glad you corrected yourself."

Marbol groaned again. "My stomach hurts real bad."

"Maybe it wasn't the chocolate," Duddu reasoned. "I saw you eating an apple before the old guy took us to that new place. I bet the apple made you sick."

"Yeah. You have to be right. Chocolate is too good to make me feel this bad."

A distant sound, like a child shrieking, grew louder as the moments ticked by.

"Do you hear something?" Duddu asked, still staring at the sky.

"Mmm…" Marbol moaned.

"Someone is definitely screaming," Duddu said. Neither of them moved as the screaming became more intense.

A few moments later, Marbol felt a shadow cross his face followed by an ear-piercing screech right next to his ear. He opened his eyes to see a little girl's face just inches from his own. "What's the matter Dee-Dee?"

"Aiaiaiaiai—" she screamed and suddenly she was lifted five feet in the air.

"Monsters!" Duddu shouted.

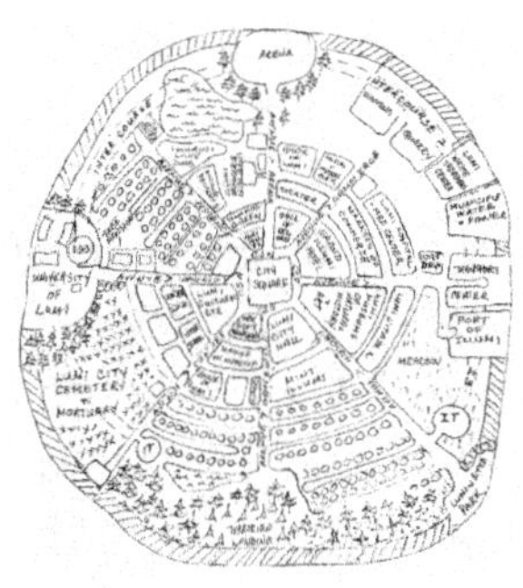

CHAPTER FIVE

"Destroyed the time machine, you have, Furst."

"Maybe," the curator answered. "But far from over, this is. Into the library, I still must get. Terrorians inside, there still may be." He took a deep breath. "Luck, wish me."

"Come with you, I will," someone called out.

Furst turned to see who volunteered and found Ozzro. "Accompany me, I am glad to have you. That you want to come, are you sure?"

"Yes," Ozzro replied. "Stand by you, I will."

Furst nodded at the soldier and the two of them headed for the front of the library. He approached the soldiers guarding the front door. "Seen any movement, have you?"

"No," one soldier answered, as others shook their heads.

"Decimator ready?" Furst asked.

"Arrows, I prefer," Ozzro said. "But more efficient, decimators are."

"In front of the door, stand directly, do not. From the right, approach. At an angle, try to look in. From the other side, do the same, I will. Before entering, for my signal, wait. Right behind me, enter low. Ready?"

They split up and snuck up to the front door from either side of the library. Furst stole a look though each window he passed looking for movement. Once they reached the door, they nodded to each other that they were ready. Furst leapt high into the air, aiming to land on the circulation desk. Ozzro rolled in right behind him, alert for signs of enemy fire. He saw a pillar to his right disappear as he rolled for cover behind the circulation desk, and heard Furst say, "Down is one," as Furst dropped down beside him.

"Are there, how many?" Ozzro whispered.

Furst shook his head and shrugged. "Be the bait, I must. Any attacker, you must shoot." He took a deep breath and leapt up to the railing outside the curator's residence, before rebounding to the halo level. A shelf full of books next to the residence disappeared, and Ozzro rolled out from behind the desk and took a shot, as did Furst.

Ozzro quickly rolled back behind the cover of the desk. He looked up but could not see Furst. He waited quietly for several minutes, his fear growing with each new breath.

"Clear, all is," Furst called down from the cupola. "Terrorians in the library, there are no more."

Furst picked up his diary before returning to the

main level and signaled out the front door for several soldiers to come inside. He positioned several of them by the portals, explaining they couldn't depend on the portals to be sealed. He also positioned soldiers near the broken window and front door.

Furst turned to Ozzro. "Rilli and Roxo Rodo, please get. Boards and fasteners, tell them to bring. Secure the library, they must." The curator used his diary to contact Pru Tellerence. *Attacked again, we were. Destroyed the time machine, I may have. With a decimator, I shot at it. A bright light and a big noise, there was. Safe for now, we seem to be. Safe, are you?*

MARBOL GRABBED HIS scrambler and tried to get up but suddenly found he couldn't move. He could still hear screaming all around him. "Duddu, you still there?"

"Yeah, but I can't move."

"What happened to Dee-Dee? I saw her for a second, and then she flew up in the air, and I lost sight of her."

"I bet the monsters got her," Duddu said. He tried to twist around. "What is stopping me? I can't see anything but I feel like I've been tied down."

Marbol tried to throw himself from side to side. He felt himself roll a little. "Are the monsters nearby? I think if we rock enough, we can roll away. But it will only work if the monsters aren't here to stop us."

"What if we roll into the pond and can't swim? Will we drown?"

"Good point," Marbol muttered. He tried rocking again. He felt his finger press against the scrambler trigger.

Too bad this isn't the scrambler that makes bullies scared. He started daydreaming about how cool it would be if he could disorient the monsters. He smiled, thinking about them walking around, dazed, bumping into each other. Maybe they'd wander into the pond and drown. And then he and Duddu, and who knew how many of their friends, would remain stuck like this forever until they died. *That's not good.*

Marbol heard more screaming in the distance. "That sounds like Selly and CiCi." He tried to move again and felt himself roll. His finger pressed the trigger and stayed in that position. After several more seconds, he found himself free and rolled onto his stomach. He looked up, hoping the monsters hadn't seen him move. He could see Duddu, still lying beside him, but Dee-Dee was gone. He looked in the direction of Selly and CiCi's screams and saw a monster carrying each of them away.

Marbol aimed his scrambler at Duddu, and several moments later, Duddu scrambled to his feet. "I'm free."

Marble got up. "Storm drain." The two of them hurried down the hill leading toward the oversized conduit that would take them back to the town hall.

⌘*SHALL WE GO?*

The Terrorian store room was not a place Ryden Simmdry wanted to stay longer than necessary.

"You should go," Johanna said. "But I think I should stay."

"Stay?" Cameron said a little louder than he might normally.

"Yes," she answered. "You can go if you want, but I think I should stay and see what the Terrorians are planning."

⌘*Are you trying to get yourself killed?*

"No."

⌘*If the Terrorians return and find Dr. Thorne missing, they'll know something is up. Why would he suddenly be missing while you're still here?*

"There is that…"

"So, we all leave," Cameron stated, "or we all stay."

Johanna searched his face before speaking. "I can't ask you to do that."

"You can. And I'd stay, but I get the impression you already know what's going on, and I can't see how being cooped up here in a locked cell is going to help you."

"It's easier to see what the Terrorians are doing if I'm already here."

"In a locked cell?" Cameron shook his head.

"I think I may be able to get myself out."

⌘*Yes. But you may inadvertently land yourself in harm's way before realizing it. I think it might be better for you all to come back to Fantasia now, and if you want to do a little covert exploring on Terroria, I'm sure I can arrange to transport you back here.*

Johanna closed her eyes and covered her ears with her palms to block her senses while she thought. Several moments passed before she dropped her hands and nodded. "You're right. Although I wish I could see Nero 51's face when he returns here and finds out I'm gone. That we're *all* gone." She smiled. "It will drive him crazy."

A SHADOW MOVED IN the Library garden, and Milencia signaled her new recruits to crouch down and be quiet. She concentrated intently, as she stared at the garden, looking for anything out of the ordinary. Suddenly, a Terrorian stood and Milencia watched as a tentacle shot out from behind another bush and pushed the impatient soldier back under cover. Milencia slowly removed her decimator from its holster and aimed at the soldier she had seen. She waited before taking her shot. Afterward, she tried not to move a muscle. Nothing changed. A breeze ruffled the leaves on the trees in the garden. Milencia watched as nearby foliage swayed as well, but not on the bush she had targeted. The bush, and hopefully the Terrorian behind it, were now caught in a force field.

She motioned for the recruits to stay where they were, and she changed position. Her peripheral vision caught a small movement in a corner of the garden. It looked like a tentacle rubbing a sore muscle or scratching an itch. It didn't matter. She surreptitiously took aim and shot the invader, wondering if he could still feel the discomfort of his pain or itch while stuck in a force field that left him unable to relieve it. She moved further away from the recruits. She surveyed the area for several minutes but did not see anyone else. That didn't mean they weren't there; they were just better at hiding.

What would Natalia do? she asked herself. *Or Arraba?* She barely moved, while hosting an inner dialogue. When she had reasoned out the answer, she did what she thought was necessary. She lowered her weapon and stepped out of the shadows making herself a target. She heard the new recruits gasp. *So much for staying hidden.* Any nearby Terrorians would immediately be alerted to their presence. Suddenly, a giant Terrorian burst from the newly-filled fountain in the center of the garden and aimed his decimator at her.

*

JACKSON STARED INTO space as he balanced a plastic fork in his hand. He still wore the dress shirt and pants from his tuxedo but had long ago shed his jacket and tie. On the counter in front of him, the butter on his pancakes had melted away and strips of bacon lay sodden under a layer of syrup in the disposable take-away container.

His brother, Chris, walked into the main reading room, eyeing Jackson's outfit. "Did you ever get to the prom?"

"What?" Jackson asked, as if Chris had spoken to him in another language.

"The senior prom? Last night? You're still wearing your tux. Did you ever meet up with Logan and Cassie? And your date?"

Jackson sighed and shook his head. "That was a mistake. A HUGE mistake. I can't believe I let things go that far."

"Are you talking about the Terrorians? Or your date? Although, the way things turned out, she probably won't be dating *you* again."

"No. By now, she hates me. It doesn't matter, as long as she's okay. Anyway, Johanna should have been my date."

"That wouldn't have stopped the Terrorians from causing trouble," Chris reasoned. "They probably would have taken Ava instead. Or maybe even Mom."

Jackson looked up suddenly. "Where *are* Ava and Mom?"

"Relax. They went to church."

"Well, at least someone has their priorities in order,"

a voice behind them said.

Jackson turned around so fast he knocked over the gong on the circulation desk. "Johanna!" Ophelia jumped out of Johanna's arms and skittered away.

Jackson ran to Johanna and grabbed her in a bear hug, closed his eyes, and let out a deep sigh. When he opened them—looking over Johanna's shoulder—he saw Cameron studying him, with his head cocked to one side. Jackson's eyes widened with recognition, and he straightened up. "You're Dr. Thorne."

"Yes."

Jackson let go of Johanna, and she took a step back. He looked at her and then at Cameron. Then he took a step forward holding out his hand. "Hi. I'm Jackson Roth." After he let go of Cameron's hand, he turned back toward Johanna. "I guess you formulated a plan."

"No. Ryden Simmdry pointed out that it wasn't fair to Cameron to make him stay, and if I stayed by myself, the Terrorians would know something was up."

"Well. I'm glad you're home. All safe and stuff."

She smiled. "How was the prom?"

"The prom? I couldn't go to the prom. Not with you missing. I went crazy trying to find the diary you gave me so I could contact you."

"What did your date have to say about that?"

"She wasn't very happy. She left here with Logan and Cassie."

"Sorry," Johanna said.

"Why? It's not your fault. It's Nero 51's fault." Jackson stared off into space for a moment before shaking his head. "Why can't he just mind his own business and stay in his own realm?"

"Johanna!" Ava squealed as she and her mother entered the library. The young girl's voice was pitched so high, it could have shattered glass. She ran to the curator and flung her arms around her. "We were so worried about you."

"I'm fine." Johanna looked at Cameron and then back at Ava. "We're fine."

Ava took a step back. "You don't smell so good," she whispered.

"Terrorian waste product," Johanna mumbled.

The younger girl made a face. "Ewwww."

"It's better to smell like waste," Cameron said, "than decomposing flesh, which is what I believe our abductors had in mind for us."

"Good point," Chris said, taking a bite out of the muffin in his hand.

"I need a hot shower," Johanna said, "to wash this stench away."

"I guess I should go home and do the same," Cameron said.

"You can shower here," Johanna offered.

"And put the same dirty clothes back on?" he said with a smile. "That would certainly defy logic."

"Jackson," Mrs. Roth said. "There's a clean sweat suit in the bottom drawer of your dresser. Get if for Dr. Thorne and show him where the shower is."

"The hotel shower?" Jackson asked tentatively.

"What other shower would I mean?"

"You could have meant Johanna's shower. But… uh…the hotel shower." He turned to Cameron and pointed toward the corner of the library. "I hope you're ready for this."

Jackson led Cameron into the George V suite. Cameron stopped in the middle of the sumptuous living room and turned full circle. He walked toward the glass doors to a balcony, opened them and walked out. The Eiffel Tower stood off in the distance. Cameron gaped, not moving for several seconds. He looked from the landmark tower to the rooftops below and then back at Jackson, who had followed him out. "How is this possible?"

"You're in the Library of Illumination. A lot of stuff is possible here."

"Yeah," Cameron replied, staring at the Eiffel Tower again.

"You want to see where the shower is?" Jackson asked.

"Yes. Of course. I'm just a little dumbstruck by all this."

"Yeah. We all are."

While Cameron looked at the toiletries provided by the hotel and played with the shower faucet to regulate the pressure and temperature, Jackson went to get him a change of clothes.

Minutes later, he walked in carrying a sweat suit and a plastic trash bag. "I never wore this," he said, handing Cameron the sweat suit. You can keep it. But you're going to have to go commando. I'm not sharing my underwear."

Cameron grinned. "Understood."

"And you may want this," Jackson gave him the plastic bag, "to carry your clothes in, or dispose of them. Whatever."

"Yeah."

"I'll leave you to it, then."

THE ANCIENT GENERATOR in the Adventuran storeroom sputtered and backfired.

"That's promising," Prophet IAN c. said.

"This generator is still not working. Why would you call that promising?" Prophet CHRIS h. asked.

"Because it is trying harder to start than it did before," IAN c. answered.

"Then we must try harder as well. Start it up again."

It took three more tries before the generator roared into action.

"Let's start the rest of them," IAN c. said, "to make sure they all work." The two hu*bots spent another hour fine tuning the generators, before having them delivered to facilities, where rapidly-warming refrigeration units stood waiting.

EMILY HAD CONSIDERABLE animal magnetism, and Logan was much more attentive to her than he had ever been to Cassie. The Exeter High School Prom king and queen took advantage of every indulgence their after party offered, as they drank, ate and danced the night away. Word of their post-prom beach party had spread, and half the senior class ended up there. There was no shortage of cell phones, and instant snaps of Logan and Emily's public displays of affection popped up all over the Internet.

Many of the revelers drifted away or headed home by the time the horizon lightened. Emily took Logan's hand and led him back to the cabin. While Logan played around with the tap on the now-empty keg in an attempt to extract the last dregs of beer, Emily did a quick check of the cabin. Everyone had taken their belongings and gone. She locked the door and sidled up to Logan, pressing herself up against his back and slipping her hands around his waist. "Forget about that. I have something much better in mind," she said, before lowering her hands a few inches, making Logan groan. He turned around to face her and slid his hands behind her back. Emily felt him untie her bikini top and then work his hands down her back and slide them inside her bikini bottom.

"Not here," she whispered, "in the bedroom."

"We'll get there…eventually, but right now, this is as good a place as any." He yanked down her bikini bottoms. "Time waits for no man," he paraphrased.

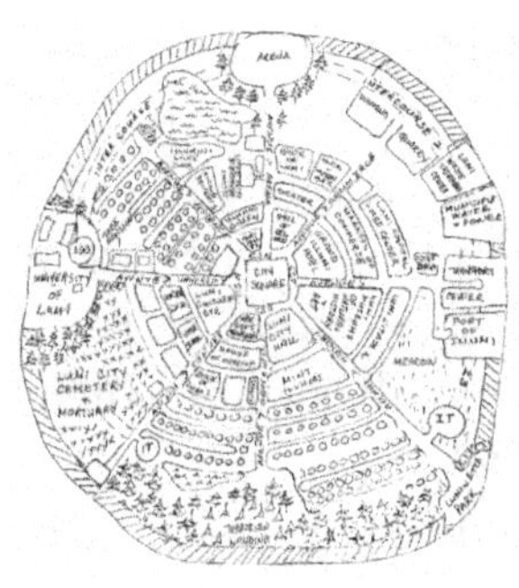

CHAPTER SIX

WHEN CAMERON EMERGED, he found Johanna, Ryden Simmdry, Mal, and all the Roths sitting around the dining table eating brunch.

"Cameron," Johanna called out. "I saved you a seat. Come have something to eat."

He walked over to the table and stared at a giant frittata, trays of pastries, bowls of fruit, and cups of steaming coffee and tea. "This looks great," he said, sitting down. "Thank you."

"I don't know if you've met everyone." Johanna introduced him.

"This is quite the place," he said as he filled his plate. "I've never seen a room like this in a library."

Johanna gave him a brief explanation of how they could have brunch in Paris, even though they were inside a library in Exeter.

"It sounds like you can travel anywhere from here," he said.

"And we have. Jackson and I have used the library to get to a meeting in Prague when we didn't have enough time to travel by air." She turned to Jackson. "Right?"

"Yeah," he mumbled, immediately picking up his coffee and taking a long sip.

"Johanna said you're a college dean. Do I have that right, Dr. Thorne?" Mrs. Roth asked.

"Yes. Johanna says she and Jackson will be attending Cranford University this fall, so I expect to be seeing a lot of them."

"The former dean recommended Cameron for library membership, so he'll have privileges to use the books here in the future."

"Yeah," Chris pointed out, "but did you make him take the oath to keep its secrets?"

"She wanted me to sign it in blood," Cameron said, and Johanna laughed.

⌘ *That brings up a very grave matter. Aside from Dr. Thorne, it has been brought to my attention that there were several other young people here in the library, when Nero 51 showed up.*

"Logan, Cassie, and that other girl," Ava said, loath to mention Emily's name.

⌘ *Would you please invite them here? I must speak to them.*

"Are you going to use one of those memory erasers, like they had in *Men in Black?*" Jackson asked.

Chris suddenly took notice. "Can you do that? Can you make them forget?"

"Do you think they'll even come here, again?" Ava asked. "I wouldn't."

⌘*Jackson, I will leave this up to you. If you cannot get them to come to the library, at least get them to meet you someplace private, so I can speak to them.*

"You could always invite them to our house," Mrs. Roth said. "We haven't been there in a few days. It would be good if you checked on it and opened the window while you're there to air it out. And pick up the mail, too?"

"I'll call Logan later," Jackson said. "We'll get them there."

"ONCE WE ARE through these woods, we will enter the city," Dron the Elder told Harva, the Mysterian politician he had forced to accompany him.

"We'll pass right by my home, where I will take my leave of you," Harva said.

Dron shook his head. "We must stay together. If one of us falls to our enemy, the other must inform everyone that it is not safe to return yet."

"I do not wish to fall, as you put it. Why don't I follow you from a safe distance?"

Dron grabbed the other man's shoulder with an iron grip. "You will stay by my side or be branded a coward. Do I make myself clear?"

The politician wrenched away from the Elder and rubbed his shoulder. "I did not volunteer for this."

"You are a politician. You receive certain rewards for the position you hold. In return, you must serve the people of Mysteriose. I will not only discredit your character, I will have your special privileges revoked if you defy me."

Harva grumbled but remained at Dron's side. Considering how close they were to the city, the area was eerily quiet. They heard neither the patter nor chirp made by the small creatures who lived naturally in the surrounding environment.

The men passed several quiet residences that appeared dark and lifeless. Before long, the domed top of the Library of Illumination came into view. The two men slowed, seeking the cover of nearby trees and the webs that shrouded them to shield themselves from aliens.

MILENCIA SCRAMBLED TO lift her weapon, but she knew she wouldn't be able to save herself. The Terrorian seemed frozen in mid-air for a moment, and she prepared to take her shot. He immediately moved and as his mouth dropped open, he froze again. She turned around. Bethany, one of the new recruits, was not too far behind her with a decimator swung over her shoulder.

"Nice shot," Milencia said.

"Thank you," Bethany answered. "Do you think there are any more of them around?"

"I don't know." Milencia walked tentatively toward the library garden. "When I saw them arrive in Militairre Meadow, only three of them fit into the vehicle they used. Maybe this is all of them, at least for now."

"What are we going to do with them?"

"Nothing. They're too large to move, and we have no place to keep them, even if we could move them."

"If we leave them there, and there are more of them," Bethany said, "the others will set them free."

Milencia stared at her for a while without speaking,

while she considered the problem. "We could kill them, but they did not kill the militairres they captured. They merely put them in a force field. If we kill these creatures, it may be seen as an act of aggression, and they may start killing our friends and neighbors. Do you want to be responsible for that?"

Bethany shook her head. "I wish we could hide them. They kind of stick out."

"We can knock them over and try to cover them with branches and leaves."

"How are we going to knock them over?"

"Like this," Milencia said, and began running at full speed toward one of the Terrorians.

WELT 87 SHARPENED THE blades in his surgery. He took pride in his work and considered himself precise and effective. He barely looked up when a soldier burst into the room.

"Nero 51 needs you, now."

Welt 87 hated to be interrupted. He would just as soon fling one of his scalpels at the soldier than jump at the call of Nero 51. But he had finished the task at hand and wanted to speak to the curator about getting assigned a larger facility. He started toward the door empty-tentacled when the trooper stopped him. "Take your blades with you."

"Has someone been hurt?"

"Not yet. That's your job."

They found Nero 51 in a foul temper.

"It's about time, Welt 87. I have business to conduct and was forced to postpone it until your arrival."

"Why not start without me?"

"I need your expert throwing arm. I see you brought your blades."

"As requested. They're newly sharpened."

"I hope your wits are as well. We have a spy to question and a hostage who may need some physical adjustment as an inducement to get the spy to talk. Then there's a white cat to get rid of."

The surgeon appeared to shrink, pulling in his tentacles. "No one mentioned a white cat."

"This spy is in league with the devil. I'm sure of it. The white cat is her doing."

"I will give you my blades."

"No! You will exterminate the cat."

"Why not use your weapon to make it disappear?"

"Like I said, this spy is in league with the devil. I have seen our weapons' force turned against us by others of her ilk. I believe the blades with get the point across much more efficiently. Your precision at throwing one is renowned. If it makes you feel any better, I will be right behind you."

Welt 87 didn't trust Nero 51's assessment, but he had little choice in the matter. He followed the curator down to a labyrinthine level of the library, where he stood poised to strike.

Nero 51 unlocked the door and pushed Welt 87 inside. There was no movement. The Terrorians waited.

"Where is this spy and her creature?" Welt 87 asked.

Nero 51 forced himself to stick his head into the room. He used his tentacles to sweep through the mist. His ensuing, anguished screams echoed through the halls of the library.

*

ADVENTURANS SPENT THE afternoon installing one or more generators at each of the sites they set up for clone refrigeration. Some of the living tissue had already started deteriorating, but the specimens packed deep in the middle of the freezing units remained viable.

"We have averted a serious disaster," Prophet IAN c. said.

"And we did it ourselves without outside interference," a leader*bot added.

"That's not entirely true," IAN c. said, shaking his head. "The overseers gave us extra refrigeration units. Without their help, we would have suffered a great loss."

"If they are so wonderful," the leader*bot reasoned, "why didn't they give us generators for the refrigeration units at the same time?"

IAN c. took a moment to consider the idea before answering. "We had just rejected their offer of tissue from some of their most noted scholars to keep our diversity from diminishing. I mentioned that our civilization had always taken care of itself in the past without outside interference and would continue to do so. Perhaps, they thought an offer of generators would be construed as meddling."

"Not that it matters, now," the leader*bot replied. We have taken care of keeping our legacy alive. Now we must find a way to recharge the millions of hu*bots who will soon run out of power.

DUDDU AND MARBOL bumped elbows together in victory, once they were back inside Juvini Town Hall. "You get the flamethrowers," Duddu told Marbol, "while I see who's here." Duddu took off up the stairs, while Marbol searched the basement for weapons and fuel.

Fifteen minutes later, he met up with Duddu and several other boys. "We've got three roasters. I don't know what happened to the other one. But these are all fueled up and ready to go."

Duddu took one and handed another to Pollo. "They've got Selly and Cici. Their screams were coming from the direction of the library. Pollo, you circle to the back. I'll take the front door. And Marbol, you go check the window that we used to enter the library. They may have taken the girls inside."

"Just one change." Marbol handed Guffle his flamethrower. "I'm going in with my scramblers. I know this one disorients them," he waved the original scrambler in the air, "and this one dissolves glass and force fields." He stuffed the second homemade weapon in his belt. "Let's go."

They hurried out of the building, each group approaching the library from a different side.

Logan banged on the front door of the library for several minutes before Jackson finally opened it. "Took you long enough," Logan said, sauntering inside.

"Yeah. Well, Johanna is taking a nap. Mom decided I wouldn't know how to clean our house, so she went home to clean. And Chris and Ava went to a movie. I'm downloading music on my phone and didn't hear you. Until now."

Logan grabbed Jackson's shoulder. "Did you just say Johanna is taking a nap?"

"Yeah."

"How'd you get her back from those…things?"

"It's a long story that I'd rather not get into right now."

"Yeah. But I want to get into it. And you owe me."

Jackson's brow furrowed. "I owe you?"

"Yeah. I'm the one who talked the girls out of saying what happened here to their friends last night."

"You did?"

"Yeah. And in return, I need you to keep your promise to give me a summer job here, especially now that Johanna is back."

"I told you I have to ask Johanna first, and I think I should wait until after she recovers from last night."

"You don't sound like much of a best friend."

"Johanna and I are a team. We make decisions together."

"And I thought you were a man. Sounds more like you're her little toady."

Jackson pointed to the door. "You can leave now.

Logan's lips tightened. *I've outgrown Jackson.* Too bad he needed information from his "former" best friend if he wanted GRUNT to run his story about the library. If he left now, he might never get it. He changed the topic. "So why is your family always hanging out here?"

"Johanna and I sometimes get called away, unexpectedly, and my mother takes care of the library until we return."

"Called away, or kidnapped by beasts like the one who was here last night?"

Jackson stiffened. "Does it matter?"

"Yeah." Logan played with his cell phone, turning on an app that recorded audio. He slipped it into his shirt pocket without telling Jackson he was recording him. "I want the whole story."

"Let me talk to Johanna first."

"Yeah. And let me post what happened here on prom night on social media."

"That's blackmail."

"I only said that because you're being unreasonable. Friends usually confide in friends."

Jackson sighed. "Whatever I tell you is just between you and me. Not a word goes beyond these walls."

Gotcha. Logan smiled as he crossed his fingers out of Jackson's sight. "Why don't you start by telling me about that thing that dangled Emily over the balcony."

"Nero 51."

"It has a name?"

"Yeah. He runs a library sort of like this one. Except they have glass statues instead of books."

"Like a museum?"

"No. It's a library. But the information is etched onto glass statues that look like miniature Washington Monuments instead of printed in books."

"That sounds dumb. Or are you just making this up as you go along?"

"It's real. Trust me."

"And how did he just appear like he did?"

"He came through a portal."

"Like a computer portal?"

"Like a portal to different realms."

"What exactly do you mean by 'different realms'?"

"Jackson?"

Jackson swirled around, turning red when he saw Johanna. "Hey—"

"What exactly are you telling Logan?"

"He's…uh…interested in working here at the library for the summer. I…uh…told him that would be up to you. Considering what he saw when he was here, maybe it's for the best, and you can make him take the same oath my brother and sister took."

"I thought we were going to invite them to your house to explain everything." She emphasized the word "explain" by raising and lowering her eyebrows.

"Right." He turned to Logan. "Here's the thing. We know what everyone experienced last night was kind of upsetting, so I thought maybe we could talk to all of you at my house, tomorrow. It's a neutral place, so the girls shouldn't be scared of meeting there—as opposed to coming here."

"That way we can clear up any and all problems," Johanna finished the invitation. "After school, say 3:30?"

"I'll have to ask the girls and get back to you."

Johanna nodded. "I can see Emily balking, but Cassie will come, won't she?"

"Um, like I said, I'll have to get back to you. In the meantime, what do *you* know about that thing that grabbed you last night?"

Johanna gave Logan a half smile. "Tomorrow. At 3:30." She took him by the arm and led him to the front door. "I'm sorry to rush you like this, but Jackson and I have work to do."

Logan broke free. "It's Sunday."

"No. She's right," Jackson said quickly. "We have a lot of…reports to write to…the Library Council." He pushed Logan out the door. "Paperwork and red tape," he added.

More like smoke and mirrors, Logan thought.

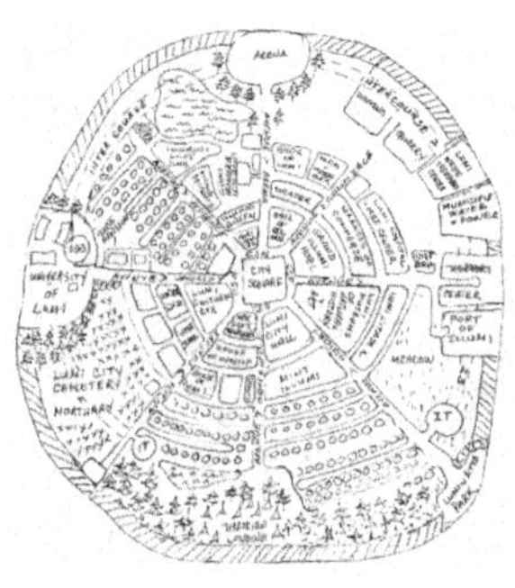

CHAPTER SEVEN

As the Mysterian trees thinned closer to the center of town, Harva and Dron found it more difficult to hide.

"There is no one here. I'm going home," Harva said.

Dron the Elder grabbed the man's arm. "If you're so sure there's no one here, why are you afraid to continue this journey with me? We need to ensure the area is safe before telling the others they can return to their homes."

"I'm sure you can do that on your own," Harva replied, no longer bothering to keep his voice down. "I'm going home." He stood up slowly. When nothing happened, he emerged from the cover of the trees. All was quiet. Harva continued walking in the direction of his home, his figure diminishing in size as he traveled further away from Dron. He suddenly stopped, frozen in mid-step.

Dron held his breath waiting for something to happen. Moments later, two Terrorians walked over and picked up Harva as if he were a bale of cuttings for the fire. He could hear Harva's screams, but there was nothing more he could do. His skin prickled when he heard a twig crunch behind him and he held his breath, waiting for something else to happen.

NERO 51 SPENT THE night stomping around his personal residence, complaining aloud to Garpa—his long-dead grandfather.

"I do not know if the Fantasians still remain on Terroria with their infernal cat, or if they've returned to their own realm after the little beast sunk her claws into me." He looked down at the puncture marks the cat had left behind. "It's likely the overseers had a hand in this, although it may just be that the Fantasians found a way to escape the room I locked them in. I have no idea how that is possible, but they may simply be hiding." A vision of Odeon flashed into his mind. "Unless they are shapeshifters." He swirled around to face the portrait of Garpa. "What if all the Fantasians are shapeshifters? But then, why wouldn't she have disappeared during her previous incarceration here?" His tentacles went limp. "Garpa, if only you were here to guide me. You would know what to do."

IN NO TIME at all, the three Terrorians captured in force fields lay on their sides, hidden behind the foliage in the garden of the Romantican library. The new recruits had to move a small pile of paving blocks to hide one of the Terrorian's large feet, but they felt sure a casual observer would no longer be able to see the hidden troopers.

"Now what?" one of the new recruits asked.

"I think we will visit Dame Erato. I left Stasia and Annabeth there, to take care of her. Normally, Natalia would figure out how to handle what's going on; however, she's been taken prisoner, so Dame Erato is our best bet." *If she's still alive*, Milencia added to herself.

They took a circuitous route to Dame Erato's cottage, just in case Terrorians still lurked in the area. Milencia knocked on the door in a previously agreed upon pattern, so the women inside would know it was her.

"What's happening?" Annabeth asked.

"We've captured some invaders in force fields and have hidden them near the library. We're hoping Dame Erato might have some insight on what we can do next."

Annabeth led them into a small sitting room. Dame Erato was sitting in a chair with a pillow on either side holding her in place. Stasia was feeding her a thick soup with a heady aroma.

"Milencia," Dame Erato said in a weak voice. "Please tell your friends I can feed myself and would do so if I were hungry enough to warrant it."

"You need to build up your strength," Stasia said.

"Maybe, but I can do that on my own. I don't need to be force fed. Perhaps a white witch's potion will help."

"Is Ingur Aguri a white witch?" Milencia asked.

"Yes." Dame Erato nodded. "Maybe you could ask her to visit me?"

"She visited you on the battle field," Milencia said quietly. "She saved your life. We tried to pay her, but she went off in a huff saying she knows you, and the rest would be up to you."

"Ingur," Dame Erato murmured, and shook her

head, appearing lost in thought.

Milencia squatted down next to Dame Erato's chair and took her hand. "Is everything all right? Is it okay that we asked her to heal you?"

Dame Erato studied the concern in Milencia's eyes. "My sister and I have not spoken since we were both young women. She stole something from me. Now I owe her my life. Not something I would have knowingly sought but serendipitous in its own way. We are not getting any younger and maybe it's time to grow closer, rather than further apart. It might be too much to ask that she visit me again. Milencia, would you visit the Maroqi District and ask her if she could recommend a potion that would build my strength? Tell her I would be very appreciative."

"I'll go now," Milencia said.

"But first," Dame Erato added, "please open the middle drawer of the cupboard and bring me the box you'll find inside."

Milencia returned a few moments later carrying a highly polished box made of animal horn, embedded with mother-of-pearl accents. Dame Erato lifted the lid and took out a small sac stuffed in the bottom corner. She removed an intricately carved locket from the sac and opened it. Inside, the image of a beautiful young girl faced the image of a dashing young man. "Tell her I know both these people loved her very much."

"Who are they?" Milencia asked.

"She may tell you," Dame Erato answered. "Or not. It is her story to tell."

JACKSON WALKED OUT of the bedroom, not quite ready to face another Monday at school.

"Boy, are you in for a hell of a day today, Bro."

"Go away," Jackson answered.

"You don't want me to go away. You want to see all the pictures posted on the Exeter High School page. A lot of people took pictures at the senior prom."

"I didn't go to the prom, and I don't care about the pictures."

"I guess you never heard the phrase, 'forewarned is forearmed.'"

Jackson sighed. "What?"

Ava came bursting into the room and stopped short when she saw Jackson. "Have you seen the pictures posted on the school's social media page?"

"I wasn't even there. Why would I care about the pictures?"

Ava nudged Chris out of the way, shoving her phone in Jackson's face. "This is your best friend and your date." One picture showed Emily and Logan hand-in-hand as prom king and queen. Another image showed a full-length snap of Logan and Emily kissing with his hands conspicuously placed on her derrière. A third picture showed the couple laying on a blanket on the beach in bathing suits, passionately kissing.

"I wonder what Cassie had to say about that?" Jackson said, more to himself than anyone else.

"She wasn't happy. Someone snapped this in the girls' room." Ava scrolled through pictures until she found the ones of Cassie. There was an image of her standing alone in the corner of the gym with tears streaming down her face. Another picture taken over the top of a bathroom stall showed Cassie in her gown scrunched up on the toilet, crying her eyes out.

Jackson closed his eyes and shook his head. "I hope she still shows up this afternoon."

"I don't know, Bro," Chris said. "Brittanie and I were talking about the pictures last night, and she said if she were Cassie, she wouldn't show up at school today. It would be too hard to face all the people who knew her and Logan as a couple."

"She has to show up." Jackson didn't exactly whine, but it was close.

Chris grabbed a backpack and headed for the door. "If you're smart, you'll get to Cassie's homeroom early. If she doesn't show up, you can go to her house and tell her that it's important she meet with you later, so you can explain what happened."

Ava snorted. "Ain't gonna happen. She probably hates Jackson. If he had taken Emily to the prom, Logan would still be with Cassie. But Jackson didn't go, so Cassie probably thinks losing Logan is all Jackson's fault."

"Why do women have to think that way?" Jackson wailed.

"Because we can," Ava said, following Chris out the front door.

She didn't bother closing it because Johanna stood just outside the entrance to the suite. "Can I come in?" she asked Jackson.

"Sure." He pulled out a chair for her at the table. "Do you want me to order you breakfast?"

She smiled. "No. I realize you don't have a lot of time because you have to get to school. But Ava showed me some of the prom pictures before, and I'm wondering if I shouldn't go see Cassie."

"I was going to go talk to her until Ava told me Cassie probably hates me."

"I don't know if she'll even talk to *me*," Johanna said, "but I've got to get her to agree to go to your house this afternoon."

"Better you than me," he replied. "Thanks." He kissed her on the cheek. "I really appreciate it."

Johanna studied Jackson's face.

He blushed under her stare. "What?" he asked in a defensive tone of voice.

"Nothing," Johanna replied. "You'd better get going. I'll see you at 3:30."

LOGAN DECIDED TO start his internship early. On Monday morning, dressed in khakis and a long sleeve, button-down shirt, he walked through the doors of Graydon Ransom University News Tonight, ready to take on the world. The news program aired year-round, so he knew people would be there.

Several students, not too much older than him, sat around drinking coffee and reading newspapers. He tried to make eye contact with someone before speaking, but everyone pretty much ignored him. The noise of a closing filing cabinet drawer attracted his attention, and he watched a woman walk over to a desk and take a seat.

He got there just a second later. "Hi. My name is Logan Elliott. I'm a new reporter here."

"You're either very late starting the spring semester, or very early for the summer."

"I'm registered for the summer, but I've got a lead

on a hot story. I thought, why not start my internship now, so I can cover the story?"

She gave him a tight smile. "That's not how it works."

"How's it work?" he asked.

"New interns receive instruction in writing, camera operation, and editing before they go out in the field. That class started two months ago and ends in a couple of weeks. The summer class doesn't start until the beginning of June."

"But I have a hot story."

"If there's a hot story, it should be mine," someone else said.

Logan turned to see a guy a few years older than himself, dressed in a blazer and tie. "It's my story."

"I just heard Jennifer say you're starting between terms. You've got no experience. What's the story?"

"You don't understand. It's *my* story. I witnessed something in a place most people aren't allowed into. No one will talk to you about what happened there. But they'll talk to me."

"What are the police saying?" Jennifer asked.

Logan looked at her. "The police don't know."

The other guy raised his eyebrows and asked, "Have you even graduated from high school, yet?"

"Yes," Logan replied.

"What did you say your name is?" Jennifer asked.

"Logan Elliott."

She punched up a screen on her computer. "This says your graduation from Exeter High School is pending. I'm pretty sure they're still in session and graduation isn't for several more weeks."

"So, you're a liar," the older boy said.

"No. I'm a graduating senior."

"That's not what you just told me. You said 'yes' when I asked you if you'd graduated yet."

"That's just a technicality. I already have all the credits I need. I took AP credits."

"And you're ready to start today?" Jennifer asked.

"Yes," Logan said, smiling at her.

"Okay. Why don't you tag along with Channing today so you can see what goes on out in the field?"

A look of horror crossed the other guy's face. "Aw, come on Jen. Why do I have to babysit him?"

"Because that's the way this internship works. The experienced students help break in the inexperienced students. You accompanied another reporter when you first got here. Now, it's Logan's turn to observe you."

THE DRAMATICANS TRIED to resume normal life with an uneasy calm. They performed their routine daily activities, but always with a quick look over their shoulder. Sudden or unexpected noises startled them, and many of them appeared jittery, which contradicted their usually placid stoicism. Soldiers helped Furst attach boards over broken windows, and a local craftsman and smithy built a new front door. The entryway to the Dramatican Library of Illumination did not have the same properties as its counterpart on Fantasia. In the past, citizens would never have vandalized or stormed the library like they might on other realms.

Dungen, Furst thought. *Dungen or Terrorians, worse, who is?*

Maybe the time had come to ask Pru Tellerence or Ryden Simmdry if a reinforced door might be in order.

THE SOLAR STORMS on Adventura raged on, and attempts to restore parts of the power grid proved to be futile. However, leader*bots took solace in knowing they had stemmed the tide on losing their entire civilization. They had managed to find enough archaic generators to keep the first sixteen orders of gold and silver-armed leader*bots activated. The remaining hu*bots were placed in stasis, receiving just enough nutritional drip to keep their human tissue alive. The lowest four levels of silver-arms were tasked with rotating the hu*bot nutrition drips, a job they considered unrewarding and mundane. However, the chance to contribute to society and accumulate prestige points kept them from complaining too loudly. They would have complained even less, if they knew how lucky they were.

THE TERRORIANS KNEW the Adventurans' library was defunct. They also believed the servers that contained the information previously housed in that library would be very well protected. The Terrorians were privy to that information because they had joined forces with Adventura for the Two Millennia War. The nuclear aftermath of that war served as a warning to anyone who might ever consider a subsequent takeover attempt.

For that reason, Nero 51 refused to consider launching an attack against Adventura this early in his invasion plans. If he knew how limited Adventuran resources were at the moment, and how few hu*bots struggled to maintain the status quo, he could have mounted a tactical mission that would have overwhelmed that particular realm and struck an early victory for Terroria.

Instead, the Terrorians and Adventurans were both so focused on their immediate needs, neither gave any thought to what might be happening on the others' world.

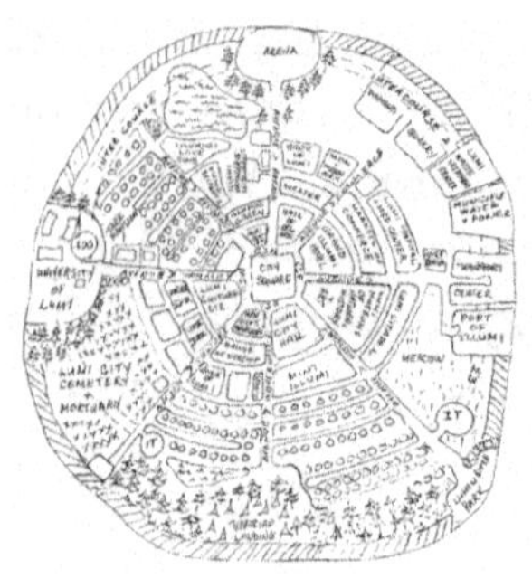

CHAPTER EIGHT

Jackson texted Logan saying he wanted to explain the assault and kidnapping at the library on prom night. MEETUP @ CASA ROTH 3pm. BRING EMILY AND CASSIE.

Logan texted him back: GRUNTING—U CALL CASSIE.

Okay. He didn't mention Emily, so I guess she's coming. Johanna will take care of Cassie. Hoping he had everything under control, he left for school.

Inside Exeter High School, everyone gossiped about the prom.

"Hey," Darrius thumped Jackson on the back. "What happened to you Saturday night?"

"I couldn't make it," Jackson said softly.

"Yeah. Well, your date found solace in your best friend's arms. And his girlfriend had a meltdown."

"I heard."

"Today should be pretty interesting," Darrius said as they walked together toward homeroom. Everyone around them went silent after Jackson turned the corner near Emily's locker, where she stood fixing her hair. She had made sure the previous week that everyone knew Jackson was her date for the prom, so when he didn't show up, and she switched her affections to Logan, the gossip mongers worked overtime.

Emily looked around to see why everyone had gone silent and made eye contact with Jackson. She scowled, slammed her locker, and walked away, with her friends trailing behind her.

"I guess there's not going to be a friendly reconciliation," Darrius surmised.

Jackson's lip quirked to one side forming a dimple. "I don't think so."

"Is there an underlying reason why you hate each other?"

"I don't hate Emily. I liked her. But considering what happened, I can see we're not right for each other. Obviously, she feels the same way." *That's an understatement,* Jackson thought, *but there's no way I can tell anyone what happened.*

"Covering stories at federal facilities is tricky," Channing said aloud from the front seat of the car. "Even though we report for Graydon Ransom University News Tonight, we don't have press passes because we're not full-time journalists. So, there's the chance we may not be able to get in."

"Which is the norm," Reeve added. Reeve Rinaldi,

another GRUNT student, was Channing's cameraman and their driver.

"Where are we going?" Logan asked.

"AccuGyroBotics. It makes all kinds of hardware for the government, and it's announcing something new today."

"Like a weapon," Reeve said.

"Or a big government contract," Channing added.

Logan hid his smirk by looking out the window. *This should be interesting.*

An electrified fence topped by coils of barbed wire, and a gate manned by armed guards, protected the facility. Reeve pulled up to the gate and rolled down the window. Channing leaned over and showed the guard his school ID. "I'm Channing Daniels from Graydon Ransom University News Tonight. We're here to cover the press conference."

"Do you have press passes?"

Channing fumbled with his wallet and pulled out a card. "I have my driver's license."

"That's not going to cut it. There's no one behind you. Back up and turn around."

"Wait," Logan said. He grabbed his own license and his father's business card and handed them to the guard. "There shouldn't be any problem."

The guard looked over Logan's credentials and handed them back. He stepped inside the guard booth and picked up the phone. A moment later, he raised the gate.

"What did you give him?" Channing asked.

"My ID, along with the business card of the regional vice president of this facility. Most people here call him Mr. Elliott, but I prefer to call him 'Dad.' You may have worked at GRUNT longer, but I have connections you'll never have."

Milencia handed Ingur Aguri the locket. The witch slowly opened it and stared at the contents but shook her head and refused to answer when the young woman asked about the people pictured inside.

Ingur stuffed the locket in her pocket, threw on a shawl, and took Selestra's hand. "Let's take a walk, child. You would like that, wouldn't you?" The three-year-old nodded as if she could read the mind of her pretend grandmother.

Rather than follow her, Milencia continued with her duty to gather new recruits.

Stasia pulled open the door to Dame Erato's cottage when Ingur knocked. "I would like to speak to my patient," Ingur said crisply.

Stasia admitted the woman and child inside. However, Ingur froze when she saw Annabeth sitting at Dame Erato's side. She looked from Annabeth to Stasia. "Alone. I would like to speak to her, alone."

"Where would you like us to go?" Annabeth asked.

"Go home," Ingur said. "If you're needed here, I will send someone for you."

"That may not be easy. We're under attack by Terrorians. Travel isn't safe."

Ingur Aguri walked to the front door and opened it. She looked at each of the young women who had taken care of Dame Erato and swept her arm in an arc until she pointed out the door. Annabeth and Stasia felt something pushing them forward, until the door slammed at their backs.

Outside, Annabeth found it difficult to keep her voice down. "Do you believe that woman?"

"She is the most respected white witch in the realm," Stasia answered. "I doubt it's for her manners."

Inside, Ingur settled Selestra by the fire. She opened her bag and fished out an apple for the child to keep her content. When she felt confident Selestra was fully-occupied eating, she sat on the chair across from Dame Erato.

"I guess I'm supposed to be nice to you now," Dame Erato said, "because you saved my life. At least that's what they tell me. I have no way of knowing for myself."

"Really?" Ingur said in a flat voice. "You believe you recovered from an arrow through your chest on your own?"

Dame Erato stared into Ingur's dark eyes. "Saving my life does not make up for stealing the love of my life."

Ingur huffed. "If you were the love of his life, he would not have left you."

"But he did. He couldn't fight your spell any more than those two young women could stop you from ushering them out the door. I hope you and Ren enjoyed your two years together. I know I enjoyed the past half-century of not having to listen to you lie to me."

"Then why did you send me this," Ingur fished the locket out and held it in front of Dame Erato's face, "and have that girl tell me you *both* loved me."

"So, for the next half-century, it would remind you of what you'd stolen. This locket was an engagement present to me. He had given it to me only a few days earlier. Then you set your sights on him." Dame Erato's focus faltered as her thoughts drifted to memories from decades past. "Mother always said men are not to be trusted. Our ancestors learned that the hard way when the men of this realm wanted to suddenly shift sides halfway through the Two Millennia War. Romantican women were always more intelligent than the males of our species, and oppressing them until they accepted our dominance was a necessary evil. I should have known better than to give my heart to a man. You should have, as well."

"I'm almost sorry I saved your life."

"And I'm sorry I wasn't saved by someone, anyone, other than you. For the past forty years, I've been content to believe my *sister* was dead."

"Too bad the women who asked me to heal you weren't content to believe *my* sister was dead."

"You didn't have to heal me." Dame Erato leaned forward, placing the flat of her hand over the wound in her chest. "You chose to. Now you must live with your decision."

DRON KEPT TO the bushes, traveling as quietly as he could behind the webs stretching across the branches of Mysterian trees. He covertly picked out a path to Hue the Elder's temporary home. Once there, he trembled, afraid to knock on the door; he didn't want to attract undue attention. Hue heard Dron's fingers scratching at the door, and after peering out a corner of the window to confirm the identity of his visitor, he let his inside, quickly bolting the door behind him.

"Have you news?" Hue asked.

"It is not good. All seemed quiet here, until Harva became overconfident and strode off on his own, only to be captured by the Terrorians. I was afraid they might trace his path back to me, but the Terrorians don't seem to be critical thinkers. They apparently caught him inside one of their force fields and hauled him away."

"How long ago was that?"

"Late last night," Dron replied. "I proceeded home carefully and waited. The Terrorians would have been too difficult to see in the dark. I did not want any surprises.

"I believe you should confer with the overseers," Dron continued. "They always seem to step in and lend a hand when someone from another realm decides to become dictatorial, arrogant, and aggressive."

"The overseers do not seem to be taking any direct action. Apparently, the Terrorians have launched incursions on several realms, and the overseers want to gather information and sort things out before proceeding."

"I know little of other realms. It's the people here I would like to calm and protect. Is there nothing we can do to help prevent them from being carted off like Harva?"

"Harva's sense of self-importance and lack of good judgement is what got him into trouble," Hue said.

"A description that applies to a great many Mysterians," Dron pointed out, "so any kind of outside assistance would help. We obviously can't depend on the full cooperation of our citizens."

THE JUVENILES APPEARED fearless as they marched toward the library with their weapons held high. They split up into three groups as planned. Duddu led his group to the front door and gave the handle a firm tug. The door was bolted tightly.

"Change of plans," he said as he led his group around to where he and Marbol had previously entered. Marbol was already climbing through what appeared to be solid glass.

"How can he do that?" one of the boys asked.

"He scrambled it," Duddu answered lightly, as if he actually understood how the scrambler worked. He followed Marbol inside with two other Juveniles trailing after him.

"Where is everything? Where are the shelves? Where are the books?" Waxmo asked.

"Shhh," Duddu whispered, "the monsters destroyed everything." They poked around the main level, keeping their distance behind Marbol and his scramblers, and when he went up the curator's staircase, they followed him up to the residence level.

"There's nothing up here, either," Waxmo said.

"There's stuff in Peer Meap's residence," Duddu answered. "Go look."

Waxmo tentatively stepped inside the apartment, waiting for something to happen. When nothing did, he walked in further.

"You see anything in there?" Duddu asked.

"No. Wait—yes." Waxmo saw something shiny under the couch and approached it carefully.

Duddu followed him and when Waxmo got down on his hands and knees, Duddu could see over his shoulder. Waxmo pulled out a metal bookmark. "There's a book under here, too." He retrieved that as well.

"That's Peer Meap's favorite bookmark," Duddu said.

"How do you know?"

"Because he always uses it. He probably used it in that book," he said pointing to the book Waxmo had picked up.

"Okay," Waxmo said, opening to a random page and sticking the bookmark inside. All at once, Peer Meap sprang from the book. He appeared so suddenly, the boys ran screaming from the room.

"Wait," Peer Meap called after them. He followed them out into the library and his eyes widened at the destruction. "What have you done?"

"It wasn't us," Marbol said calmly, while the others searched frantically for the window they came in through. "It was the monsters."

Peer Meap put both hands on his hips. "The monsters? Really. Is that the best you can do?"

"They *were* monsters. The old guy who spoke without moving his mouth called them Terrorians."

Peer Meap turned white. "There are Terrorians here?"

"They got Selly and Cici. Pollo is out behind the library searching for them."

"I've got to inform the overseers," Peer Meap muttered as he patted his pockets, looking for his diary.

"If you're looking for your book that answers questions, I've got it." Marbol pulled the curator's diary out of his pocket. "We used it to find you, but it didn't work. Just the old guy came. Then he took us to see a bunch of other old guys and they gave us heaps of candy just for letting them see my scrambler. I hope those are the guys you're calling now, because I'm all out of chocolate."

*

Johanna did not look forward to calling Cassie but knew she had to. When Cassie failed to answer her phone after several tries, Johanna called Jackson. "Is Cassie at school today? She isn't picking up. Maybe she has her phone muted because she's in class."

"Nope," Jackson answered. "Haven't seen her. I'm here. Emily is here but is apparently not speaking to me. Logan went to his internship. At least that's where he said he was going, but I don't know why. He still has classes here, and internships usually don't start until after finals. I'm guessing he wanted to avoid all the slings and arrows flying around the school."

"I'll take a ride over to Cassie's house," Johanna said. "If I'm lucky, she'll talk to me."

"Yeah." Johanna heard Jackson huff before he continued. "Good luck with that."

A short while later, Johanna knocked on Cassie's front door. When no one answered, she knocked harder. She saw a window curtain twitch. Someone was inside. *Why aren't you answering?* She took a deep breath and knocked even harder. The door opened a crack and Cassie's puffy, tear-stained face peeked out. "Hey."

"Cassie, how are you? I tried to call, and I got worried when you didn't pick up. I know you had a rough weekend, and I wanted to make sure you're all right."

"It's worse than you know."

Johanna took a deep breath and decided to be truthful. "I know all about the prom. About Logan and Emily…"

Cassie sniffed and her shoulders shook as she

lost control of her emotions. Johanna stepped inside and put her arms around the sobbing girl, as she pushed the door closed with her foot. "I know exactly how you feel," Johanna told Cassie. "I felt the same way when Jackson told me he was going to date other girls."

"At least you weren't humiliated in public. They did it at the senior prom. My boyfriend and my best friend. I've never felt so worthless in my life. I don't think I could ever feel any worse."

"It couldn't have been worse than what happened inside the library."

Cassie stopped sobbing as quickly as if someone had doused her with cold water. She suddenly turned lucid, acting and speaking clearly. "I'd almost forgotten about that. It's almost like it wasn't real. Like it was a virtual reality game or something. That thing should have dropped Emily over the balcony railing. I'd feel bad, but I'd still have my boyfriend." She suddenly broke into sobs again.

"Cassie, I need your help."

"No. I'm not going to Jackson's house this afternoon to talk about what happened. I listened to the messages Jackson left on my phone. But I'm not going to sit in disgrace in front of the two of them."

Johanna thought about the overseers reversing Cassie's memory—reversing everyone's memories. *If Logan forgets he dumped Cassie and that he and Emily were together at the prom, and if Cassie suddenly doesn't remember she was dumped, everything will return to normal. Well, almost normal, except everyone else in the school would know what happened and the images from the prom would continue to live on the Internet—forever.*

"Unless we get pizza," Cassie said, "and we poison it. You can warn Jackson, so only Logan and Emily will eat it, and then…and then…oh my God—"

"Right." Johanna shook her head. "We'd be tried for murder and that wouldn't make anything any better."

"It's not that," Cassie croaked.

"What is it?" Johanna asked, pulling the girl into another hug and rubbing her back.

"I'm…I'm…pregnant," Cassie blurted out, before she completely melted down, her composure dissolving into heartfelt wails and shuddering sobs.

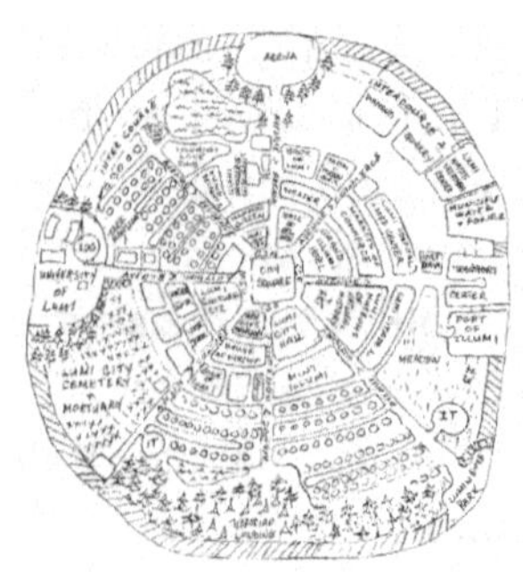

CHAPTER NINE

NERO 51 SEARCHED FOR his grandfather's journals, hoping something Garpa had written down for posterity would help him face his current problems. He had them stored just one level below his residence, so they would be nearby if he needed them, but not so close as to always rely on them and never exercise his own judgement. He retrieved them all and spent hours poring over Garpa's philosophies on the political landscape of modern-day Terroria, and his beliefs about why his realm lost the Two Millennia War.

THE BOND LINKING TERRORIA WITH MYSTERIOSE AND ADVENTURA WAS STRONG, AND MANY OF OUR AGREED UPON PRECEPTS WORKED WELL. SEVERAL OF THE OTHER REALMS THAT MADE UP THE COUNCIL OF TWELVE HAD RELINQUISHED THEIR HOLD ON POWER, AFTER LEARNING VOLUNTARY COMPLIANCE WOULD BE REWARDED IN A MORE POSITIVE MANNER THAN RESISTANCE. THE TERRORIAN ALLIANCE HAD ALL

BUT WON THE WAR. HOWEVER, THE OVERSEERS AND FANTASIANS APPEARED TO HAVE FORMED A UNION THAT DEFIED BREAKING. THE OVERSEERS, WHO HAD ALWAYS CLAIMED THEY NEVER INTERFERED WITH THE GOVERNANCE OF INDIVIDUAL REALMS, MEDDLED BY SEALING THE PORTALS. TERRORIA, MYSTERIOSE AND ADVENTURA AGREED TO TAKE PART IN THE FIRST INTER-REALM PEACE COUNCIL, TO GET THE OVERSEERS TO LOOSEN THEIR HOLD ON THE PORTALS AND RE-OPEN THEM. WE WERE READY TO SEIZE THE OPPORTUNITY FOR OUR FINAL DRIVE TO VICTORY; HOWEVER, THE CAPTURE OF OVERSEERS NARA SIERRA, MYRDDIN EMRYS, AND LEYLLAND ERITHEON DID NOT TURN OUT AS EXPECTED. WE HELD THEM IN CUSTODY ON TERRORIA AND CLAFF 8 ORDERED THEM EXECUTED, BUT THE FANTASIAN—MYRDDIN EMRYS—MANAGED TO ESCAPE AND BORE WITNESS TO TERRORIA'S PLANS BEFORE A MEETING OF OVERSEERS. THAT ALL BUT SIGNALED THE BEGINNING OF THE END TO EVERYONE BUT US. WE REJOICED WHEN WE RECEIVED WORD THAT THE PORTALS WOULD BE OPEN SO A SECRET EMISSARY COULD TRAVEL BETWEEN WORLDS, BUT IT WAS A LIE. ALL THE PORTALS WERE RECONFIGURED TO LEAD TO A LUMINAN CELL, AND OUR BRAVE REBEL WARRIORS, AS WELL AS CLAFF 8, WERE CAPTURED—ENDING THE WAR.

It is the Fantasians' fault, Nero 51 thought. *They attempt to thwart me at every turn. But this time I will not be outsmarted. I will find Johanna Charette, and the little white beast she brought with her, and I will smash the superstition that white cats are the devil's advocates by turning its cruelty on itself, thus making an example out of it.*

Nero 51 felt so overwhelmed, first by the appearance of a white cat on Terroria, and second by the sudden disappearance of Johanna Charette, that the fact he still held overseers Pru Tellerence and Horatio Blastoe as prisoners completely escaped him.

The overseers, on the other hand, were glad of the oversight. Each imprisoned overseer had taken an opportunity to transport outside their shared cell on Terroria, and telepathically commune their findings. The overseers had yet to find the time machine, but they were able to assess the buildup of forces and eavesdrop on some of the Terrorians' discussions.

They knew from their brethren that Johanna and Dr. Thorne had returned to Fantasia, but it was a fact Nero 51 kept hidden from the Terrorian population at large.

They wondered how he would feel if he discovered that they, too, were gone? They had certainly gathered as much intel as they could, however, Ryden Simmdry asked them to stay on Terroria a while longer and continue searching for the time machine. Without the time machine, he reasoned, the Terrorians would be left powerless to wage war, except amongst themselves.

Peer Meap grabbed his diary and within seconds, Ryden Simmdry and Zenith Fullova were standing by his side.

⌘*Peer Meap, you've returned.*

§ *We've been wondering what happened to you.*

"I was reading a book about celestial holidays and thought I'd immerse myself in it for a short while. It was marvelous, traveling through space, and witnessing novas from afar. I even gazed upon the breathtaking beauty of the Illumini Constellation as it drifted through space. I soon felt homesick and hungry; however, I found when I tried to return home, I was quite trapped. I'm not sure what happened to delay me. All I could theorize was that the pages of the book had closed. I'm glad the Juveniles managed to find it and bring me back.

"Now that I'm home, though, I can't tell you how alarmed I am to learn the Terrorians were here and destroyed the library. How long have I been gone, exactly?"

§*By my calculations, several weeks. Possibly as long as two months.*

"I can't believe I've been away so long, although in retrospect, you managed to end the Terrorian invasion quite quickly."

⌘*The invasion continues. The boys are looking for some Terrorians right now, who they believe have kidnapped Selly and Cici.*

"That's terrible."

⌘*A lot has happened while you've been gone. It's good to see you back, but now we must ask you to help us find the young people who are tracking the Terrorian abductors before they become victims, as well. I believe they were heading out behind the library.*

The odd entourage exited the building and followed the sounds of overexcited screams.

"ARE YOU SURE you're pregnant?" Johanna asked Cassie. "Did you see a doctor?"

"No," Cassie cried. "He would call my parents, and I would be grounded for life."

"This goes way past the 'grounded' stage. How can you be sure you're pregnant?"

"I bought one of those tests at the drugstore."

Johanna took a step back. "You know, sometimes those tests are wrong."

Cassie's eyes widened. "Do you really think so?"

"It's possible. I think you should see a doctor."

"I can't. I told you why."

"Look. I'll make an appointment for you out of town with a doctor I know. I'll go with you and you can use my name and information, so nothing gets back to your parents. It's better to know for sure than to rely on a drugstore test."

"You'd do that for me?"

"Yes. But I need a favor from you in return."

Cassie scrunched up her face and then covered it with her hands. She stood like that for several minutes without saying a word.

"Cassie?"

"Okay. But this may turn into the new worst day of my life."

"Get dressed. We're going to a spa."

"What?"

"If you're going to face Logan and Emily, you may as well look fabulous. My treat."

"I can't let you do that."

"Of course, you can. Go change into something nice for later, and let's get going."

They both had facials and had their hair styled. A makeup artist then gave them a new look. No one would ever know Cassie spent half the day crying.

"Are you sure I look okay?" Cassie asked on their way to Jackson's house.

"Is that a new outfit?"

"I bought it for the post-prom party. I wanted something nice to change into after spending the night on the beach." Cassie's smile drooped.

"You look more beautiful than I've ever seen you. And you want Logan to think so, too, so you have to look like you don't care what they think. Pretend you're acting in a play."

"I can do that," Cassie said. "I was in the Drama Club." She smiled. "I've got this."

Johanna did her best to conceal her sigh of relief. "Good."

JACKSON BOLTED OUT of his last class before the bell rang, so he could arrive at his house before the others. He had phoned Logan, who said he would get there as soon as he was able to leave his internship. Logan assured Jackson he would pick up Emily along the way.

LOGAN NOT ONLY got GRUNT into the press conference, he also got Channing an interview with his father. As far as Logan was concerned, Channing now owed him, and he would be sure to take advantage of his IOU when the time was right. He made sure Jennifer knew he was the one who pulled strings to get them the story.

He stuck around and answered some questions for Channing while the older boy wrote his news package, but Logan left early—telling Jennifer he had signed up for a community service project through his school he couldn't miss. "People are depending on me."

"Will we see you again next Monday?" she asked.

"You may see me even sooner than that," he answered, knowing she would not turn him away.

He drove to Exeter High School and picked up Emily at a previously agreed-upon spot.

"Let's go to the mall," she said. "I need some serious retail therapy. School was horrible. Everyone was horrible, snickering and pointing. At least Cassie wasn't there. But neither were you."

"I told you about my internship. I needed to start it today."

"Will you be reporting tonight on the news?" she asked, ready to make sure all her friends tuned in to see her new boyfriend.

"Not tonight. I had to get the feel of the place first and set some groundwork for the future."

"How did that go?"

"Like clockwork," he said pulling his car up to the curb in front of Jackson's house.

Emily's brows drew together. "What are we doing here? This isn't the mall."

"I promised a friend we would meet him here. We'll be in and out." He walked around to the passenger door and opened it for her. She allowed him to help her out of the car, even as she looked at the house with distaste.

"Just in and out," she said.

Logan offered her his arm without speaking.

Emily visibly stiffened when Jackson opened the front door. "What are you doing here?" Her tone was less than pleasant.

"I live here. Come in. I just want to apologize for what happened at the library."

Logan slapped him on the back. "You got pizza."

"Yeah, Jackson said. "To paraphrase a friend, 'a man's gotta eat.'"

Logan literally pulled Emily into the room and

dragged her onto the couch with him. After scarfing down a pepperoni slice, he stared at Jackson. "Start talking."

The doorbell rang saving Jackson from having to speak before everyone was in place. He admitted Johanna and Cassie. He looked from one to the other. "You look different, both of you."

"Spa day," they replied in unison and laughed.

Emily jumped off the couch when she saw Cassie. "What's she doing here?"

"She deserves an explanation, too," Jackson explained.

"Don't worry," Cassie said doing her best to smile. "I'm happy to ignore the two of you."

She sat in an overstuffed arm chair, and Johanna sat on the arm of the same chair, perched at Cassie's side.

Jackson looked at his co-curator. "Do you want to handle this, or should I?"

"I will," Johanna answered before standing up and moving to a place where she could see everyone equally. "As some of you may know, Jackson and I are the co-curators of the Library of Illumination."

"You're a librarian?" Emily said with a sneer. "That sounds about right." She looked at Cassie. "Are you a little librarian, too?" She slipped her arm into Logan's and curled sideways, snaking one of her legs around his.

Johanna shook her head imperceptibly at Cassie, then plowed on with her speech. "As co-curators, we are tasked with taking care of an extremely important facility that has very special properties." Johanna made eye contact with each one of them before going on. "Sometimes, it appears that people, places, and things that exist inside of books, have escaped the pages and appear real. Call it a 'special effect.'"

"That was no special effect," Emily said her voice rising. "It was horrible. It dangled me over the balcony. It smelled bad. It tried to kill me."

"But of course, it didn't, because I, knowing it was just a special effect, knew it could never hurt you. However, I wanted to show Dr. Thorne one of the special properties of the library. And when the Terrorian came to life, he played along."

Logan disagreed. "That's not possible. I know what I saw, and that was no special effect."

Jackson looked at Logan and said evenly, "If you want to work part-time at the library, you're going to have to learn about the special effects. I thought you, of all people, would understand."

"I'm not buying it." Logan jumped up, but with Emily's leg wrapped around him, he went down hard.

At the same time, a bedroom door opened and Ryden Simmdry stepped out signaling Johanna and Jackson telepathically to close their eyes. An acid green light strobed throughout the room for a few seconds, and then the overseer and the light disappeared.

"What happened?" Emily screamed, stepping away from Logan. She looked around the living room, her eyes stopping on Jackson. "Where are we?"

"My house."

"What are we doing here?"

"We picked up a pizza after school and stopped here to chill."

"I don't remember doing that."

"Logan," Cassie cried as she rushed to his side.

"What are you doing on the floor?"

"I may have tripped him by accident," Jackson said, waiting for Johanna to back up his story. When she didn't answer, he looked for her, but she'd slipped away before anyone noticed.

Logan moaned before opening his eyes. He woke to find Cassie stroking his face. "Cassie?"

"I'm so glad you're okay. Jackson tripped you by accident. You were out for a minute. I hope you don't have a concussion."

"I'm fine," he said, sitting up.

"Jackson," Emily said, "I have a splitting headache. Will you walk me home?"

"Sure," he answered.

"We'd better go, too," Cassie said. "Give me your keys. If you have a concussion, I'd better drive."

Logan wrenched his head from side to side as if stretching his neck. "I'm a little confused."

Cassie placed two fingers on the nasty red lump forming on his head. "I'm not surprised."

"Ow."

Cassie pulled him up to a standing position. "Come on, let's go."

When he didn't hand her his keys, she snatched them out of his jacket pocket and pushed him out the door. "Do you guys want a ride?" she asked Emily and Jackson.

"No, we'll walk," Jackson answered as Emily slipped her hand inside his and leaned against his shoulder.

PROPHET IAN C. PLAYED an important part in the complicated scheme to keep Adventura functioning during the solar storm. Besides having access to the overseers, he was one of the few of his kind who still read books for pleasure. Other hu*bots believed it frivolous to waste time reading, except to research specific information for a given task.

Because of his love of reading, IAN c. was highly knowledgeable in a number of fields, including engineering, natural science, and history. It integrated well with his position as curator of the Library of Illumination, and he was revered by his fellow citizens. It stood to reason that any weakness or failure on his part would assuredly hurt the realm as it struggled to remain viable.

Unfortunately, IAN c. worked too many long hours without a break in his quest to conquer the problems laid before him by the solar storm. He had given up his period of nourishment and maintenance to another hu*bot, with ill effect. IAN c.'s very human heart gave out on him quite suddenly.

He was alone in the lab when it happened, and no one was there to help him when his heart seized. As he blacked out, he wondered if he would ever see the light of the sun again.

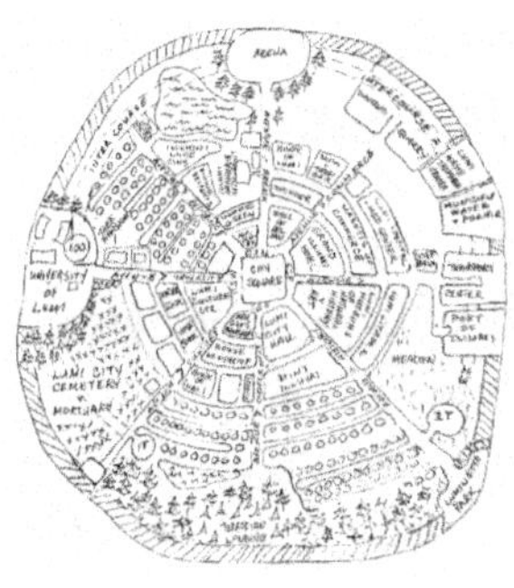

CHAPTER TEN

PRU TELLERENCE AND Horatio Blastoe had two ways to surveil Terroria: either they could miniaturize to roughly the size of a fist, or they could appear and disappear full sized. In miniature form, they were less likely to be seen, as long as they had some objects to hide behind, but they risked becoming a predatory animal's next meal. And if they landed on the floor in the foul Terrorian mist, they not only would have a limited view, they could also be stepped on. Full size gave them more control over their surroundings, but it would not allow them to spy on the Terrorians without being seen. And so, they chose to miniaturize.

Unfortunately, being tiny had more limitations than expected, because smaller eyes and ears also affect the distance they could see and the conversations they could listen in on. But they were intrepid and continued to explore as much of the Terrorian landscape as possible.

That morning, they transported themselves in miniature form behind the library, to see if the Terrorians were keeping the time machine outdoors. The two of them stood on a brick half-wall, and they were pleased to note an absence of Terrorian mist in the mostly open field.

✠*I can state unequivocally that a time machine is not hidden here, nor has one landed here in the recent past.*

★*How can you be so sure?*

✠*The grass is not crushed. A machine of that size may appear to be as light as a bubble, but it has significant mass. This grass shows no signs of having been encumbered.*

★*How can you tell? It looks dead.*

✠*It may not appear as vibrant and green as it might on some other realms; however, if flattened by weight, the individual blades would show some markings. These are not creased.*

A sudden movement forced them both to hit the deck. They were less obvious lying flat and hoped that small action didn't call attention to themselves.

They watched as Nero 51 quickly strode through the library yard and across the meadow behind it.

★*We should follow him.*

✠*It won't be easy. We can't keep up with him and will probably lose him.*

★*Not if we ride on the tail of his cloak.*

✠*He is not wearing a cloak.*

★*That—we can take care of next time.*

✠*Manipulating the weather is something we, as overseers, have always frowned upon.*

★*Tweaking the weather, during times of war, is*

probably something we could take a chance doing.

Horatio Blastoe shared the idea with the other overseers, and while there were some initial concerns, the consensus agreed that desperate measures could be taken.

SEVERAL HOURS HAD passed since Dame Erato's confrontation with her sister, Ingur Aguri. Neither Annabeth nor Stasia had been summoned back to the cottage, but Annabeth was worried and stopped by Stasia's home to tell her she was going back.

Daylight had waned, and they found Dame Erato sitting alone in the dark.

"Why didn't Ingur Aguri call for us when she left?" Annabeth complained. "She threw us out. The least she could have done was make sure we returned here, after she left. She knows how serious your injury is."

"I do not wish to talk about Ingur Aguri."

"As you wish," Stasia said as she removed a cloak and laid it over a chair. "Oh!"

Dame Erato watched as Stasia stooped down and picked up a bit of knitting. "What have you found?" the older woman asked.

"Your knitting. I didn't notice it earlier, or I would have picked it up from the floor."

"I do not knit," Dame Erato answered. "It probably belongs to the child. Who is that child? Do you know?"

"That's her granddaughter, Selestra."

Dame Erato raised her eyebrows. "Ingur Aguri never had any children. After Ren died, she swore off men. I've kept track of her over the years. She does not have a grandchild."

*

IMPATIENCE GREW AMONG the groups of Mysterians hiding in caves while waiting to hear if the Terrorians had retreated. Unfortunately, impatience makes some people act irrationally. Mysterians are no exception, and many of them struck out for home, either en masse or one-by-one, and the impatient fools were picked off by the Terrorians and carted away.

Hiding in widely scattered caves left the survivors incommunicado, so no one knew many of their friends and neighbors had been taken.

Meanwhile, Mysterian priestesses, locked in their homes, brewed potions meant to stop the Terrorians in their tracks, or make them disappear completely. During that time, many priests and politicians remained in the caves where they could talk to each other, at least, if not to the masses of people who routinely gathered in the discussion pits to argue their grievances.

"What has become of the chancellor of the exchequer?" one of the priests asked. "Has he given up trying to collect taxes from us?" Some of the men laughed, but others paused for thought. *Why aren't the overseers and the chancellor of the exchequer helping us?*

JACKSON FOUND JOHANNA behind the circulation desk, preparing to ship a bundle of books. "Do you really think Ryden Simmdry's memory flash will work? What happens when someone questions why Logan and Cassie are back together again?"

"Have you looked at the Internet lately?"

"It's full of pictures of the prom, especially them."

"Look again."

Jackson pulled out his cell phone and called up pictures of the prom. There were plenty of them, but the only ones he saw of Logan, Cassie, and Emily were the ones his mother took outside the library. There were no images of any of them beyond that. "This thing isn't working right. I'm borrowing your computer." He searched the computer for nearly an hour but couldn't find any pictures of Logan and Emily's illicit bang up. It was as if it never existed. He did find one girl's blog about a dream she had that accurately described the prom and post-prom party, but she only referred to it as her ridiculous imagination and never insinuated that it actually happened. "Do you think students are likely to ditch reality in favor of someone's blog about a dream they had?"

"Yes."

What Jackson didn't know was that students who ate one of the free Illuminate candy bars—practically spilling from large, open cartons around Exeter High School as a treat for graduating seniors—would most likely forget what really happened at the prom. There might be a few who escaped the overseers' virtual sugar-fueled net, but they would be in the minority and be chastised into forgetting what actually happened.

"I guess I'm going to have to date Emily again."

"Isn't that what you wanted?" Johanna asked as she picked up a piece of junk mail.

"I only wanted you to get jealous and miss me and commit to a relationship."

Johanna stared down at the paper she held in her hand. She barely breathed. He had hurt her so much. *It was all a stunt*, she thought. Without saying a word, she crumpled the envelope in her hand and flung it at him. Then she fled up the curator's stairs to the privacy of her residence.

LOGAN SAT ON his bed, considering everything that had taken place that afternoon. *Strange.* He remembered falling and hitting his head. *Something happened, but what?* When he had opened his eyes, Cassie—whom he thought would never speak to him again—was cradling him gently, and Emily seemed like she couldn't care less that he had fallen. And then Cassie drove him home, and Emily left with Jackson. *Like the prom never happened.*

He grabbed his iPad and scanned the web, looking for references to the Exeter High School Prom. There were pictures, but none of the ones of him and Emily making out on the beach. *What happened to them?* The harder he looked, the more confused he became. Finally, he stumbled upon a blog that accurately described what had happened. He recognized the blogger as a girl in his English class, but she claimed it was all a dream. *Nope. Not a dream. It really happened.*

His phone rang. He looked at the caller ID. *Cassie.* "Hey."

"Hi. I'm calling to see how you feel?"

"I'm fine. You know me."

"Yeah," she agreed.

"I'm glad to see you're not holding the prom against me."

"The prom?"

"You do remember the prom, Cass, don't you?"

"I barely remember it. Were we drinking beforehand?"

"We had a drink. Yes."

"That explains it. I don't even remember going to the beach afterward." She laughed. "Did we have a good time?"

"I had a *very* good time."

"At least there's that. I'd better go. I've got to study for my French test. I just wanted to make sure you're all right."

"I'm raring to go." He heard her giggle as he hung up.

DUNGEN EARNED THE distinction of being the first Dramatican in modern history to hurt a member of his own species. His jailbreak only emphasized his break with sanity. He pretended to choke on a bone during his evening meal. A guard noticed him thrashing and opened the cell door to help him. Dungen grabbed the guard around the neck. They struggled for several minutes, but the guard's movements eventually subsided. Dungen dragged his fresh kill into the corner of the cell and left, locking it. He raced out of the jail, but was confronted by Emorie, the official in charge of running the courthouse and detention facility. Emorie kept a desk by the front entrance so he could keep track of everyone who entered and exited. Dungen lunged at the official before he could arm himself and banged Emorie's head against the floor until he knew he was dead. Dungen jumped up like a rabid animal. The decimator that had been taken away from him at the time of his arrest, lay on a table behind the desk with a tag identifying it as evidence. He grabbed it. *Hah. This will right all the wrongs mounting against me, starting with my dear father.*

He looked out the door to make sure the path was clear. It was late and most Dramaticans were already at home taking their evening meal. He disappeared into the darkness. He would need time to think about the most effective ways to eliminate his enemies. *I'll save Furst for last. Once he's gone, I'll be the curator of the Library of Illumination.*

PROPHET CARL A. KNEW he had seen specific research regarding a process to slow down the degradation of tissue, and he rushed into the Adventuran lab where he had last seen it. He forgot all about the research, however, after he nearly tripped over Prophet IAN c. who lay inert on the floor. A gold-armed medi*bot, CARL a. did a quick assessment of the curator and physically dragged him out of the lab and carried him down two floors to the nearest charging station. He propped IAN c. against a wall and worked quickly to hook up an intracranial drip that would nourish the curator's organs. He also set up a medical monitor to assess and correct the beating of IAN c.'s heart. The medi*bot worked to regulate the curator's heart rhythm, and only when he was assured of continuing function, did he take the time to hook his patient up to a unit that would recharge his robotic parts and lubricate its inner workings simultaneously.

IAN c. suddenly twitched. CARL a. reached over and pressed what most humans refer to as a "belly button" to activate IAN c.'s sleep mode.

CARL a. returned to the lab and found the research

he needed. He had been delayed at a time when every moment counted for the continued existence of the entire civilization. Because of the collapse of the power grid, he could not start the cloning process to grow a new heart for IAN c. and hoped he hadn't wasted the time he spent trying to preserve the curator.

THE JUVENILES STOOD in a half circle with their flame throwers aimed at absolutely nothing.

⌘ *They have gotten away.*

"It was there," one little boy said, pointing, "and then it was gone. Poof. Like a bubble."

"It was," Duddu agreed. "It looked like a giant bubble. I ain't never seen nothing like it."

§ *Well, now that we've confirmed that the time machine remains operational, perhaps Pru Tellerence and Horatio Blastoe will be able to locate it.*

⌘ *Our visits to Terroria are becoming all too common.*

§ *When you wish to find fruit, you go to an orchard.*

⌘ *I don't know if that metaphor holds true when it comes to Terrorians.*

§ *Perhaps not. It seems that we are so busy handling small emergencies, we may be losing sight of the bigger picture.*

⌘ *Of course you are right. We need to consider all aspects of a new war and its consequences to create a course of action that mitigates damage and preserves life. You may return to Lumina. I must go to Fantasia to see someone about the distant past.*

§ *Who on Fantasia has the ability to remember the distant past?*

⌘ *An old wizard who was put down by his enemies long*

ago and supposedly laid to rest. But resting is not something he allowed them to foist upon him.

§*Who is this wizard? Have I ever met him?*

⌘*Let me speak to him first, and then I will tell you all about him.*

RYDEN SIMMDRY TRAVELED back to Lumina with Zenith Fullova only long enough to answer questions about the time machine the Juveniles had seen.

⌘*There is so much more we need to know before we decide what to do. And as I've told Dean Zenith Fullova, I know someone who may be able to help.*

RYDEN SIMMDRY'S SUDDEN appearance on Fantasia should have startled Jackson, but the teen barely moved.

⌘*Is there a problem?*

Jackson sat at the information desk with his chin in his hands. He looked at the overseer, but didn't move as much as a hair. "Yeah."

⌘*What new catastrophe has developed?*

"Nothing new. I'm still mired in the same old catastrophes, and no amount of innovation on my part seems to help. It's like drowning. Every time I come up for air, another wave hits."

⌘*Does this have anything to do with your friends and the actions we took at your school today?*

"Not really. It plays a part, but an infinitesimal one. I screwed up when I told Johanna we should date other people. I thought it would be a wake-up signal that would bring us closer. Instead, it turned into a wedge that drove us apart. And now she knows I only did it as a ploy, and she's really upset."

Ryden Simmdry sighed and his face softened as he got lost among his thoughts. ⌘*Women have a habit of making the best of the male species do crazy things. They give us life and help us establish our place in the universe, but they can also turn vicious and vituperative and rip out our hearts in the blink of an eye. They are extremely difficult to figure out.*

Jackson lifted his head and stared at the overseer. "It happened to you?"

The overseer snapped to his senses. ⌘*A very long time ago.*

"Can you tell me about it? What did you do?"

⌘*Maybe one day we can talk about it. But right now, I need to speak with Merlin.*

"The real Merlin who's locked in the vault among a zillion books?"

⌘*I can speak to his counterpart who is accessible through another book. Do you have that book, here?*

"I don't know where it is." Jackson's shoulders slumped. "I'll have to ask Johanna."

⌘*Let me. It may be easier.*

"You've got that right," Jackson said as he returned his head to his hands and resumed the position Ryden Simmdry first found him in.

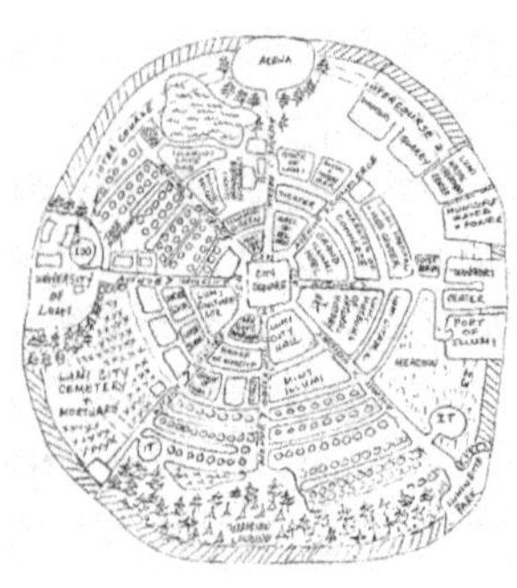

CHAPTER ELEVEN

Johanna handed Ryden Simmdry the book that would allow him to speak to Merlin.

⌘*I'll take this into the conference room if you don't mind. I'd like to compare notes with my younger self.*

"Of course," Johanna answered. "Take as long as you need."

When he was alone, Ryden Simmdry opened the cover and Merlin appeared. The magician raised his eyebrows in inquiry when he saw Ryden Simmdry. "To what do I owe the pleasure?"

⌘*If you don't mind, I'd like to pick your brain about the Two Millennia War.*

"Why would you have to pick my brain? Whether called Ryden Simmdry, Myrddin Emrys, or Merlin, we are different renderings of the same man. You were there, just as assuredly as I was."

⌘ *That may be true, but you do not have the events of the subsequent fifteen centuries muddling your memory.*

"You want to know what I remember of Odyon."

⌘ *Yes, but I'm more interested in discussing the Terrorians. They seem incredibly determined and tenacious, if not innovative and bright.*

"Everyone always believed the Terrorians created the triumvirate, but I seem to recall your friend Odyon playing a major part in initiating that particular dynamic."

⌘ *He always had a knack for suggesting something audacious and making others believe it was their idea.*

"You're quite right. His strength was influencing people. I've always believed we were the stronger sorcerer, but while we excelled at altering aspects of the physical world, he mastered the art of psychological manipulation. That makes him very dangerous."

⌘ *I knew speaking with you would bring the past into more precise focus.*

"I had more than a millennium locked in my own private prison to put my thoughts in order and dwell upon what I wish I had done differently."

⌘ *What would you have changed?*

"First of all, I would have cherished Pru Tellerence more ardently. I remember quite clearly when she first visited Lumina for the Longevicus Blessing. I thought of myself as a very dynamic individual with a lusty passion for life and little need for commitment, except with regard to the Illumini System. As an overseer, I wasn't allowed to have a family or romantic attachments. But something about the rare beauty and guileless goodness of *Pruelle* changed me forever.

⌘ *The young Pru Tellerence. I remember.*

"It wasn't easy keeping our relationship under wraps." Myrddin grinned. "We met secretly for so many years, telling ourselves our love was special and precious, and we didn't want it spoiled by outsiders. In retrospect, you could say we were hiding.

⌘*I agree. Our relationship became so second-nature to us both, we never considered the consequences when Pru Tellerence became an overseer.*

"It brings up an unusual possibility. As overseers, both you and Pruelle received the Majorious Longevicus Blessing, meaning each of you would only age one year for every thousand years going forward from the day of your blessings. If your union had ever produced a child, I wonder if your offspring would age in a similar way, or perhaps multiply other aspects of the blessing in a much different way?

⌘*She did, you know.*

"Pruelle gave birth to a child, fathered by you?"

⌘*By us. We are, as you just reminded me, the same man.*

"How intriguing. I have a child! How old is the child now? What special abilities manifest within the offspring of two overseers, especially when one is a noted sorcerer?" He drew himself up proudly.

⌘*She is a girl, now approximately three years of age, and as far as I can tell, she has no special abilities.*

"Are we assuming, then, the birth took place approximately three thousand years ago, long before history recorded either of our current personas?

⌘*As far as I can tell.*

"Perhaps the next time you visit, you will bring Pruelle with you. I would like to talk with her directly."

⌘*She is on Terroria, right now, pretending to be a prisoner.*

"Will she be gone long?"

⌘*All things considered, she'll be back before we know it.*

"Is there anything else you wish to discuss?"

⌘*When I asked what you would have changed, you used the qualifier 'first' before talking about Pruelle. What else would you have done differently?*

"I would have thought twice before agreeing to educate Viviane in the uses of spells and charms. She hid her treachery well. I can only surmise that Odyon played a hand in her betrayal."

⌘*I gather you're right. That most certainly did not turn out the way we expected. At least I found a way out of there.*

"Is there any news of Odyon?"

⌘*As far as I know, he was last seen with the Terrorians, but now that they are back to invading, he could be anywhere.*

The Grand Illumi Hotel had its perks, but Odyon found it to be a veritable vacuum when it came to news of Nero 51 and his multi-realm invasions. *That oaf probably hasn't even realized I'm gone.* Rather than waiting around to teach the Terrorian curator how to become a shapeshifter, Odyon took advantage of being one. He used his last trip to Juvenilia to escape—unseen—as a beam of light. From there he managed to attach himself to Zenith Fullova's robe as a piece of lint and travel back to Lumina with the overseer.

Once in Lumi, Nero 51 merely had to make himself over as a prosperous offlander and use a little shapeshifting thievery to find adequate funds to get started on his new life.

He only wished he could get inside the Library of Origination. Even traveling with Zenith Fullova, he found himself suddenly outside the walls when the Juvenilian overseer arrived back in Lumi. Unfortunately, a long-ago transgression during his tenure as an overseer had gotten him the boot, and his DNA was banned within the well-protected facility.

Still, it gave him time to set up his new identity. He had spent so many centuries on Fantasia, he decided to adopt it as his "birth realm." He would present himself as Peter Dakion, a Hollywood movie investor with deep pockets and a penchant for privacy. He would also need a way to alter his DNA, so he could gain access to the Library of Origination.

Pru Tellerence was not responding to diary inquiries. Furst's attempts to contact the overseer failed, and he worried that the Terrorian invasion was even more serious than he originally thought. The new front door slammed open as Ozzro rushed in.

"Happened, what has?" Furst asked.

Ozzro put his hands on his knees as he bent over to catch his breath. "Dungen," he said between gasps for air.

"About him, what?"

"Escaped, he has. Told me himself, Pondor did."

"Escaped!" Furst took as deep a breath as Ozzro. "Say to do, what did Pondor?"

"To find you, he said. To him, take you."

Furst picked his diary off the information desk and slipped it into his pocket. "Go, let's."

Johanna did not emerge from her apartment all evening, so Jackson asked Chris to guard the cupola until midnight, and then wake him for night duty.

For the rest of the night, Jackson fought to stay awake. He hoped—prayed—that Johanna would make an appearance, but she kept to herself. It was time to get ready for school, but he knew he couldn't leave the portals unprotected. *This sucks.* He wanted to see what was going on at school after the memory flash. But, he refused to leave the library until Johanna took over.

He felt himself suddenly jarred out of nodding-off by a heavy tread on the stairs. A man with a mustache, goatee, and unruly hair topped by a broad-brimmed Stetson hat came into view. His holster and revolvers left Jackson speechless, but the teen didn't need to say a word.

"You Jackson?"

The teen nodded.

The cowboy put out his hand. "William Cody, but you can call me Buffalo Bill."

Jackson's mouth opened, but no words came out.

"A pretty little lady told me you may be expecting some trouble up here. I've got my own firearms, but she says you have a special rifle I should use."

Jackson looked down at the decimator.

Buffalo Bill eyed the weapon. "Well, ain't that the ugliest thing you ever did see. Just like a big pipe. There ain't no finesse to it." He squatted down and stared at it. "No fancy engraving. You can't even tell the front from the back. What kind of weapon is this?"

"A very deadly one," Johanna said, her voice coming from behind him. "Just so you know what you're dealing with—" She placed an apple on an empty book cart, took the decimator, aimed, and a moment later, the apple disappeared.

"Well ain't that something. Where did it go?" Buffalo Bill asked.

"It's gone. Forever. It dissolved."

"That's a waste of a perfectly good apple."

"Maybe, but I want you to understand why you shouldn't shoot at anything except an intruder who enters through one of these portals. Do not shoot at anyone coming up the staircase. They probably belong here. You'll be the only one up here." She pointed to one of the portals. "However, you can shoot at anyone or anything who appears in one of the alcoves."

"Don't you worry your pretty little head. Buffalo Bill Cody is here to protect you."

"Thank you," Johanna said before turning to Jackson. "I believe you have school?"

"Mmm-hmm," he muttered as he slipped past her and made his way down the stairs.

A GUST OF WIND took the door nearly off its hinges when Nero 51 attempted to leave his library the next morning. A fierce storm had materialized overnight, and icy rain pelted down on anyone who ventured outside. The curator grabbed a cloak out of a library closet and attempted to leave again.

✠*Now*, Horatio Blastoe advised Pru Tellerence.

The two miniaturized overseers caught onto the hem of Nero 51's cloak and held on tightly. The folds of the cloak flapped wildly in the wind, forcing the overseers to send a telepathic communication requesting a break in the storm. Almost immediately, the wind died down and the rain lightened.

★ *Thank goodness. I don't think I could have held on if the wind and rain continued at full force.*

Nero 51 circumnavigated the library and crossed the meadow behind it. He cut through a thinly wooded area to a weed-infested field obscured by the trees. What looked like a desolate, abandoned building loomed over them, darkened by precipitation.

✠ *I wonder what we're doing here?*

★ *I'm sure we'll find out.*

Horatio Blastoe let go of the cloak and slid down to the surface, gingerly making his way to the front of the curator to see what he would do next. He watched as Nero 51 pushed a branch against a rock and the ground began to rumble. Horatio Blastoe scurried back to Pru Tellerence and grabbed the curator's cloak.

★ *What's going on?*

✠ *We're about to find out.*

Prophet CARL a. and several other medi*bots worked all night immersing batches of living tissues into vats of enzyme-rich broth to help prolong the tissue for a few more days, until a more long-term solution to the Adventuran grid crash could be put into place.

When they completed the task, he advised them all to re-charge, before they too followed in the footsteps of Prophet IAN c. Only then, did he check on the curator to see if IAN c. had pulled through his own personal crisis.

The monitor showed IAN c.'s heart beating at a normal rhythm. CARL a. removed the empty drip bag and re-animated the curator.

The violet lenses on IAN c.'s eyes shielded the optical mechanization of them switching into focus. He jerked when he saw CARL a. standing so close, staring at him. "What happened?"

"You collapsed, IAN c. I found your inert body on the laboratory floor. You are recharged now and should be functioning."

"The grid—"

"Is still off-line. However, we did manage to give an extensive store of tissue a protein bath. We must move ahead, but you will have to do it without me for a period, while I recharge. We cannot allow ourselves to become as rundown as you did. It looked like we might lose you, IAN c. That would be a severe loss to the realm."

A high-pitched buzz caught them off-guard, and the overhead lights blinked on, only to go out again.

JACKSON MET UP with Logan outside the school. "Hey. How's your cracked skull?"

Logan involuntarily reached up to feel the bump where he hit his head. "Seems okay." He paused. "Except for the revisionist history."

"What are you talking about?"

Logan grabbed Jackson by the shoulder. "What do you remember about the senior prom?"

Jackson narrowed his eyes. "Why are you asking?"

"Because *I* remember the senior prom, but Cassie doesn't. Does Emily?"

As if on cue, Emily turned the corner and walked over. She kissed Jackson on the cheek. "Hey baby." She looked at Logan. "Where's Cassie today?" She linked her arm in Jackson's and pulled him toward her homeroom.

Logan seized the opportunity. "Emily, wait. Let me ask you a question."

Jackson glared at Logan. "Leave Emily alone. She doesn't want to answer your dumb question."

"Dumb? That's what you think of me trying to uncover the truth?"

"You just sound paranoid. Let it go."

No way, Logan thought. He turned to Emily. "Do you remember what you said to me at the prom?"

Emily paused, "What I said to you when…"

"What you said to me when you took my arm after becoming prom queen?"

Emily's face got serious as she thought about the prom.

Why would I take Logan's arm? Emily thought. *Wasn't Jackson my king? I heard Zach wasn't going to show up, and I said I'd announce Jackson was my king.*

"I don't remember taking your arm."

"Who was your prom king?'

Jackson literally pushed Logan away. "Leave it alone."

"No," Logan answered. "I want to see what Emily has to say."

The bell rang, signaling the start of homeroom.

"What do you remember, Emily?" Logan pushed.

Mr. Chander, Logan's physics teacher, walked up to the trio. "People, into your homerooms. Now."

The three teens separated, each heading to a different room.

"This isn't over," Logan called out.

What is he talking about? Emily wondered, as she pushed open her homeroom door and walked to her seat.

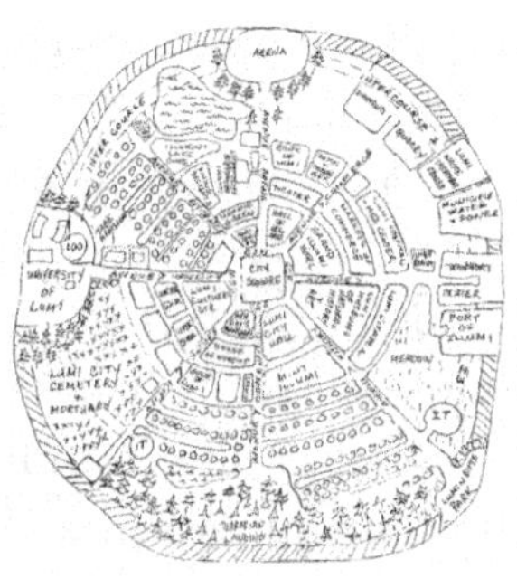

CHAPTER TWELVE

ODYON CHANGED INTO an insect and entered an open window in the Hall of Records in Lumi. When he was sure he was quite alone, he morphed into a tall, lanky, blond Luminan and searched the records for an identity he could steal. He copied most of the information for a reclusive offlander onto a new registration form under the name Peter Dakion and added his signature and image. Finally, he added his fingerprint. He placed both in the file and left the way he entered.

Odyon's new persona was in the guise of a swarthy Fantasian from America. He had thick, dark hair pulled back in a low ponytail and wore tinted glasses with heavy frames. That afternoon, he chose to wear all black clothing, simply cut with no remarkable details. The only thing anyone might remember about his general appearance was the bandage obscuring the Illumini Constellation embedded in his left palm. He entered the Hall of Records and waited patiently for someone to help him.

"My name is Peter Dakion. I have lost my credit and identity cards—my entire wallet, actually. I need an identity card replacement."

"Please step up to the scanner and rest your forehead against the upper indentation. Don't blink."

He did as he was told. A muted light scanned his eye.

"You are not in the system," the Hall of Records clerk said.

"That's impossible." He allowed his voice to go up a notch. "You should have all my information and prints on file."

"Just a moment." The clerk reached under the counter and brought out a small box. "Place your right hand inside." The clerk pressed a button. After an audible click, a transparent screen automatically raised up on the counter showing a registration form for Peter Dakion. "I don't know why we're missing your retinal scan, but I can remedy that right now. Please rest your forehead against the indentation again."

Odyon did so, and the clerk made sure his scan appeared on his file.

"Just one moment." The clerk walked out of the room and returned a moment later with a new identity card.

"Thank you so much," he said, smiling at her. "I'll make sure I'm much more careful about holding onto this one."

*

DAME ERATO WAS standing over a cup of tea when Annabeth entered the older woman's cottage.

"Dame Erato, what are you doing up?" Annabeth cried. "I should be doing that for you."

"I'm not helpless," the injured woman answered. "It hurts, and I'll take it easy until the wound heals. If Ingur used any of her potions or powders on it, it will probably speed up the healing. She's very good at what she does, even if she exasperates me to no end."

"Take your teacup and sit down." Annabeth laid a small bouquet on the counter. "I saw these flowers blooming in Sasha Kaye's front yard and she said I could pick some to make you fresh brichi."

"That would be nice," Dame Erato said, sitting down at the table. "Fresh brichi always makes me feel better, regardless of what ails me."

Annabeth gently rinsed the flowers and tore the blooms into tiny pieces. She blotted most of the moisture and laid them on a linen cloth to air dry. After placing a large bowl on the table, she looked in the cold storage room for the other ingredients she would need. She returned to the table, laden with flour, honey, butter, and yeast and assembled all the other pinches and sprinkles that would go into the brichi.

Dame Erato sipped her tea, then lowered her teacup. "Perhaps, this afternoon, we'll take a walk."

"It may be too soon for that, Dame Erato. Isn't it enough that you're up and about and have made your own tea?"

"I am not to be coddled," the older woman said with some force. "Life is going on, and may be going haywire.

We need to stay on top of everything that is happening if we want to protect ourselves and our realm."

Annabeth's frown turned into a smile. "So, you want to go out for a good gossip?"

"No. I want to visit the Maroqi District and get some answers out of my sister."

THE TIME MACHINE did not reappear on Juvenilia.

"What should we do now?" Duddu asked.

"Wait here with the scorchers and see if they come back," Marbol answered.

"We should hide," Waxmo added.

"We should build a fort," Pollo said.

The others shouted in agreement.

Pollo puffed out his chest. "We can grab those boxes from behind the library to get started."

"We're gonna need rocks, too," Marbol said. "Big ones."

The teens all scrambled looking for bits and pieces to build their fort. One person searched for broken branches from the edge of the woods and stripped down the ones he found with a knife. Another ran home and grabbed a shovel, so they could dig holes for the supports for their barricade. Others found the largest rocks they could move and rolled them over to where Duddu and Marbol stood.

"The front wall should be here," Marbol said, dragging a stick through the dirt to mark off an area less than a stone's throw from where they had last seen the time machine.

Pollo and Waxmo dragged over a fallen tree. "Anyone got an axe?" Pollo asked. "We need to cut this in half. We can sink a log into each corner and attach our fence to it."

"Fence?" Marbol shook his head. "That's too flimsy. We need a rock wall."

"Sure, we do," Duddu agreed, "but we need something to rest the rocks against to keep them from falling over.

"Whatever," Marbol said. "I'm getting hungry."

"Yeah," one of the younger boys said. "You told us the old guys gave you chocolate. So, how come they didn't give us any?"

"Maybe they're out of chocolate?" another boy guessed.

"Do you still have Peer Meap's book?" Waxmo asked. "We could always ask them to bring some when they come back."

"What makes you think they're coming back?" Duddu countered.

"There may still be monsters here, and if there are, that will make them come back," Marbol said.

"With chocolate?" a boy asked.

"That's a tough call," Marbol answered. "Maybe we better ask Peer Meap to ask the old guys to bring chocolate."

"Yeah," Duddu agreed wholeheartedly. "That's a plan!"

LOGAN HAD PLANNED to attend only his first period English class, but his physics teacher had already seen him, so he had to attend his physics class as well, delaying his planned departure. As soon as he successfully used static electricity to bend water, he left the building and drove straight to

Graydon Ransom University.

Inside the GRUNT newsroom, Jennifer O'Laughlin worked alone at her desk.

"Is everyone out on a story already?" Logan asked.

Jennifer looked up. "The newsroom opens at 8:00 a.m. and interns are expected to be here no later than 8:30."

"Sorry. I had a couple of classes I needed to attend this morning if I want to graduate in good standing. Is there anything I can do around here to help?"

Jennifer set Logan up in front of a computer terminal and showed him how to log into the newsfeed. "Rewrite this story for tonight's show." He read a brief account of a brawl that broke out behind a local school, involving a gang of students.

Logan rewrote it quickly and gave it to Jennifer. She read it, then gave Logan a phone number and told him to call the police and ask for a statement.

Once he worked the police statement into the story, he handed it back to her and said, "Do you want me to take a camera and get some video of the school?"

"Do you know how to operate the camera?"

"How hard can it be? I'm good at stuff like that. Give me a quick lesson, and I'll be on my way."

A half-hour later, Logan walked out of the newsroom and drove to the school where the brawl had taken place. He took a variety of shots of the school and looked for signs of the fight: a broken fence, some torn up grass, and then—*do my eyes deceive me?*—he saw what looked like blood on the pavement. *I should interview some kids.* He looked around but didn't see anyone. *In class. I'll come back later.*

He got in his car and drove to Exeter High School. He shot the exterior of the school, then walked around to the back of the building where the door to the gym was usually left unlocked. It was the middle of the period, and all the students were out on the field. He ducked inside and took pictures of the gym and the stage where the prom queen and her court had been announced.

As he walked back to his car, he ran into Kara, a girl from his homeroom. He had hoped to leave without being seen but decided to take the chance meeting and use it to his advantage. "Hey, Kara."

"Hi, Logan."

"I'm making a video of my time here to remember my senior year, and well, can I interview you on camera? Just ask you a few questions about the school?"

Kara shrugged. "Sure. I guess."

Logan switched on the camera and focused as he framed his first question. "The senior prom was the best. I know you were there, and you looked great by the way. So, let me ask you, what did you think about everyone's choice for prom queen and king?"

"I knew Emily Brent would win. I voted for her and so did all my friends. She's the prettiest." Kara paused.

After a few seconds, Logan filled in the silence. "What about the prom king?"

"Zach won, of course."

"But he wasn't there," Logan said.

"Right…but I can't remember who was crowned king. Does it matter?"

"I guess not. Thanks."

A bell signaling the end of the period rang in the

distance. Kara hurried off, and Logan headed back to his car.

Just as he reached it, he saw Andrew Sigurdsson approaching the vehicle next to his. "Hey, Andy. I'm putting together a video. Can I ask you a quick question on camera?"

"It's got to be quick. I'm working the lunch shift at The Meister Burgerie."

Logan flipped on the camera. "What did you think of the guy who was named prom king?"

Andrew's brow furrowed. "Who was the prom king?"

"That's what I'm asking you."

"Who can remember, and what does it matter? It's not like it's going to impact the fate of the world. I've got to go." Andrew got in his car and drove away, as Logan stood by, wondering why he was the only person around who remembered the outcome of the prom.

THE FOLLOWING MORNING, Mal and Proteus Bligh transported inside the Mysteriose Library of Illumination. The Terrorians had managed to destroy all the printed matter on the upper floors, leaving an empty shell.

Mal tested the front door. "Illuminate." It remained tightly shut.

Ψ*I do not believe the Terrorians will return to the interior of the library. We should be safe here.*

"Let's find Hue the Elder. He'll know what's happening and be able to help us formulate a plan to limit the Terrorians actions on this realm."

Proteus Bligh nodded and a moment later, the two

men appeared in front of Hue the Elder.

The curator gasped at their sudden appearance and covered his chest with one hand. "Gentlemen, you quite alarmed me for a moment."

Ψ*Our apologies. We think it's time to forge a plan to stop the invaders, or at least stall their efforts.*

"We were hoping you and Dron could help us out."

Hue rushed to a cabinet and poured three servings of essential water. "Just a little something to settle my heart after your surprise visit, and to welcome you back to Mysteriose." He handed them each a glass and raised his in salute.

"Has anyone reported seeing more Terrorians?"

"I spoke with Dron last night. He and Harva managed to walk as far as the library under cover, without incident. He said that as soon as Harva became brazen and walked out in plain sight, the Terrorians immobilized him, picked him up, and carried him away. Where exactly, I cannot tell you. Dron did not follow them.

"He asked me to contact you," Hue continued. "I had planned to do that today. Apparently, you are one step ahead of me."

"Where is Dron now?"

"I believe he returned to the cave where he and Harva originally hid, to tell the others it is still not safe to venture out."

"Can I talk to you?" Jackson had just returned from school and found Johanna doing paperwork behind the circulation desk. "I need to sort things out. Talking it over with someone usually helps, but I can't rely on Logan for this.

"I know you and I have been kind of distant lately," Jackson continued, "so I'll understand if you want to blow me off."

She laid down her pen. "What's the matter?"

"I don't think Ryden Simmdry's memory flash worked on Logan. It definitely worked on Emily. She's forgotten everything that happened between them. But this morning, he was pushing her to remember the prom. He kept asking her about her prom king. The only thing that saved us from his pushing the question was the homeroom bell. One of the teachers told us to go to our classrooms, so Logan had to stop badgering her. But I'm pretty sure he remembers."

"Then, besides us, he's the only one."

"I guess. Some girl blogged about what happened, but said it was a dream."

"There's your answer. If Logan says something, tell people he discussed reading the blog with you, before he fell and bumped his head. You can say that's why he thinks the blog is real."

Jackson nodded. "Fake news."

Johanna smiled. "I guess. Just remember, we have to protect the library at all costs."

"Is it safe to assume you're no longer mad at me?"

"Mad…at…you…?" She stretched out her words.

"For saying I wanted to date other girls to make you jealous."

Johanna stiffened.

Jackson watched as she took in a deep breath, held it and released it. He winced. "You're counting to ten, aren't you."

She took another deep breath before speaking. "I like you Jackson. I really do. And just before you pulled your little trick, I was ready to admit I loved you, but then you hurt me. Badly. And then I met Cameron. I like him. It's not that I don't have feelings for you. It's that I want to know—need to know—how I feel about him." She picked up a book and headed down to the duplicloner room inside the chamber of doors.

Jackson followed her down. "I screwed up."

She placed the book in the duplicloner. "Royally."

"What should I do now?"

She removed the book and turned toward him, studying him intently. "I don't know."

The duplicloner turned on unexpectedly, startling her. A moment later, Ophelia walked out and another cat mewled from the box where the duplicloner spit out cloned products.

Jackson's eyes widened. "We can clone cats?"

"Apparently," Johanna answered.

"They're already good at reproducing without our help."

"I didn't plan it. I didn't even know Ophelia was down here."

"Do you want to keep it?"

Ophelia hissed at her counterpart and swatted at her.

Johanna shook her head. "We need to find it a new home."

"Mrs. Caruthers's cat died a few weeks ago, and Mom said she misses it."

They headed upstairs and Johanna slipped the new cat into the pet crate she used for Ophelia when she didn't want the cat underfoot. "Great. Your sister and Chris can take it over later."

"What about me?"

She reached for Buffalo Bill's book and closed it. The sound of a decimator clattering to the floor echoed through the library. "Go upstairs and guard the portals."

CHAPTER THIRTEEN

Odyon entered the Prime Bank of Lumi as silent as a whisper and searched for a place where cash might be left unattended. Apparently, the Luminans paid a lot of attention to their money. He eventually found a guard sitting at a desk outside the bank's main vault. Odyon settled against the wall as a shadow. At some point, someone was either going to move money into or out of the vault, and he would be there when that happened.

Late in the afternoon, a Luminan bank teller wheeled down a cart containing a tray of long, flat, polycarbonate cards coded with information about the bank clients who had done business that day. The teller slipped the tray of cards through a special opening in the bars, and the guard placed them on a counter outside the vault, before returning to his desk.

Odyon changed into a scanning ray and studied

the information on the cards. He found one belonging to a well-to-do-citizen and changed the coding to show his name and identity.

A moment later, a woman used a special key to gain access to the vault and inserted the cards into a terminal. When she was done, she used her thumbprint to sign a tablet the guard handed her and left.

Odyon changed back into a whisper and floated out of the bank, morphing into Peter Dakion in a dark passageway. He then re-entered the bank, inserted his identity card into a terminal, and extracted enough currency to pay for his living expenses for the foreseeable future.

BACK IN THE GRUNT newsroom, Logan put together the video for the school brawl, then slipped the camera's memory card in his pocket. He'd buy one just like it on his way home and put that one in its place. He wanted to use the card he took for his breakout story on the Library of Illumination. Better yet, maybe he'd buy his own camera. He'd tell his father he needed it for his internship, and his father would pay for it. Then he could work on his *exposé* whenever he wanted.

He spoke with the show's engineer about the best type of camera to buy and went home with a brochure and plenty of information. On his way, he stopped to buy a new memory card. He didn't want GRUNT to know what he was doing. He couldn't prove most of the story yet because of some type of massive cover-up. He didn't know how Jackson and Johanna pulled it off, but he was sure it wasn't a figment of his imagination.

His father's car was parked in the driveway when he

got home. He went directly to his father's office and found him sitting at his desk going over plans. "Hey, Dad."

"Logan. What can I do for you?"

"You know my news internship?"

Michael Elliott laid the plans on his desk. "Yes. I was surprised to see how professional they acted at the press conference. I knew they were from the university because you were with them, but other than that, they were as professional as all the other news outfits."

"I'm learning a little more every day. And I was talking to the people there about getting my own camera. Their stuff is good, but different people use it every day, and sometimes it doesn't work the way it should. I guess it gets knocked around a lot. I've given it considerable thought, and being a broadcast journalist is what I really want to do with my life. A new camera wouldn't cost too much," he handed his father the brochure the show engineer had given him, "maybe the cost of a single college credit, but it would insure that my stories never get trashed because some jerk messed up the school's equipment."

Mr. Elliott looked over the brochure and then stared at his son for a moment. "Do any other students have their own cameras?"

"One or two of them. The really serious ones. And if they see something happening outside of normal newsroom hours, which are only 8:00 to 6:00, they have a leg-up on getting the story. Please, Dad."

"It would be your graduation gift."

Logan nodded. He was hoping for more than that, but he had set this ball rolling and he had to stick with it. "I know it's a little early for my graduation present, but could

I get it now?"

"I don't see why not. We'll go this week. Will you need anything else to go with it? Most of the news people had tripods, but not all of them. Will you need that? Or a camera case? What about lights?"

"I'll find that all out and get recommendations so everything works together." Logan broke into a big smile. "Thanks, Dad. This means a lot to me."

"You're welcome, son. I'm glad to see you're thinking seriously about your future."

DUNGEN'S GRANDPARENTS—his mother's parents—had lived outside the capital city of Adventura, in the small village of Ulster. They had never strayed far from home during their lives, and were buried nearby, next to Dungen's mother. He inherited the dwelling after his grandparents died but had never visited it, or thought about it, until now. He needed a place to stay and hoped it was long forgotten by everyone who knew him. He knew his father had never felt comfortable there and prayed the location had long disappeared from Pondor's radar.

Dungen arrived without fanfare, only stopping at the UB—that's what his mother called the Ulster Barter—for some staples. He hated giving up some of the jewels from his caftan but told himself he had no need for them anymore.

He found the cabin boarded up, but it didn't take much brute force to open the front door. He didn't care about removing the rest of the boards from the windows. The more derelict the place looked, the less chance any nosy neighbors would be likely to stop by. It had a remote location, well off the main road, on the edge of Cirra Lake. There was a burgeoning community on the opposite side of the lake, which had a sandy beach. But this small dwelling on the north side had no sand to speak of. The cabin sat on a bluff with a nearly-sheer drop to the water some 50 feet below. He doubted anyone from the opposite side would notice him, and even if they did, they were too far away to care.

He spotted a couple of old, oil lanterns, *just like I remembered*, and pulled a can of oil he had just bartered for out of a box of supplies. He lit both lamps, which helped illuminate the interior, but he knew he would have to remove the boards from one or two of the windows in order to see adequately if he didn't want to tote an oil lantern every time he moved.

He opened the door his grandparents' bedroom. The lamp gave off enough light for him to see rodents scurrying into the shadows. He would have to snare them and stuff up the holes they entered through. He shuddered. *I am above this.* His father was a judge. He came from a superior family. *I shouldn't have to clean this myself.*

He explored the area surrounding the structure, looking for signs of nearby neighbors or encampments. *None.* He found the path that cut through the bluff at an angle leading down to the water. He remembered it from when he was a boy. He would need to haul up water to prime the pump in the dwelling. With luck, that's all he would need to do to get it working. He grabbed a length of rope and stretched it tightly between two trees, before returning inside.

Only one of the blankets stripped off the beds in

the two bedrooms appeared salvageable. He would burn the others, which had been riddled with rodent droppings and shredded for nests. But, first things first. He tied another length of rope to a tree by the narrow chasm leading down to the water. He remembered the rocky slope being slippery when wet, and he wanted to make sure he could haul himself back up. He dumped the blanket in the lake and beat it against a rock to clean it. After a while, he slung the wet blanket over his shoulder and used the rope to pull himself back up the path.

He suspended the wet blanket across the line he had tied between the trees and hoped it would dry quickly.

He found an old broom and swept out the interior of the dwelling. The dust made him cough, and his fit of coughing—coupled with hard work—tired him out. He sat down to rest and stared at the tranquil lake. Like a mirror, its surface appeared smooth and calm. He looked past it to Bukno, the community on the opposite side. He could make out the outline of the buildings but couldn't see individual features. *That's good. If I can't see them, they can't see me.*

RYDEN SIMMDRY SPENT most of the day in the Library of Origination gazing upon the oracle, hoping for illumination. Several truths emerged from the haze within his thoughts. *I love Pru Tellerence and could not bear to lose her.* Unfortunately, that's why he had created the clause in the Ultimium Codi barring deans from sentimental or intimate liaisons. Nothing good could come of Terrorians learning he had fathered a child with Pru Tellerence. *Bel would be the perfect hostage.* The child of two overseers would have superior power due to both her parents' Longevicus Blessings. *Nero 51 will only be stopped when we recover the time machine.*

Three truths. He needed to act on them immediately. He had to find the time machine. But first, he needed to find Pru Tellerence.

SEVERAL SOLDIERS CHECKED their gear in the basement of the not-so-abandoned building where Nero 51 had unknowingly carried Pru Tellerence and Horatio Blastoe. The curator threw his cloak on a pile of weapons, and the miniaturized overseers climbed off and hid discreetly in a dimly-lit corner.

★*I do believe we have found the time machine.*

✠*And considering we're hiding within a cache of weapons, we can confirm that the Terrorians did not steal the vehicle to benefit society.*

"Troopers," Nero 51 said loud enough to get everyone's attention, "you are being deployed to Romantica. Our first wave of soldiers on that realm has already managed to imprison a number of citizens including the curator of their library. This mission will deposit two dozen of our best troopers on that realm. Your assignment is to go door-to-door and capture the inhabitants, bringing them here. Once a property has been vacated, burn it to the ground. We can't have anyone sneaking back into territory we've already conquered and using vacant buildings to hide in and strike back from. We will mark our front line as we take it.

The curator pointed to the nearest troopers. "You will be the first of this wave to arrive. Defend yourselves if you must, but do not strike out on your own until all the forces are in place."

The Terrorians boarded the time machine with Nero 51, who transported them to Romantica. Pru Tellerence grabbed Horatio Blastoe's arm. ★ *We must return.*

✣*I think we should wait. There is a lot more to be learned here.*

★*I must go. It's important.*

✣*As you wish, Pru Tellerence. I will hold out here as long as I can, so I can relay information about Terrorian troop movement to the college.*

★*Be illuminated.*

Horatio Blastoe smiled. ✣*As illuminated as I can be while hiding in the shadows.*

PRU TELLERENCE ARRIVED inside the home of Ingur Aguri, behind a coal scuttle. She had chosen to remain miniaturized just in case there was trouble.

The witch slept in a chair by the fire with Bel cuddled in her arms.

The overseer relaxed, but immediately stiffened again, when the front door to Ingur's cottage flew open.

The sound of the door slamming against the wall woke the witch, as well as the child who started crying.

"I'm glad to see you're not busy," Dame Erato said, using every ounce of her strength in an attempt to sound strong.

"How dare you?" Ingur shouted. "I should have left you to die in the meadow."

Selestra's whimpering turned into wails.

★*Enough.* Pru Tellerence grew to normal size,

grabbed the child and tried to comfort her.

"Pru Tellerence," Dame Erato said, slumping into the nearest chair. "It's good to see you escaped the Terrorians."

★ *What is going on here?*

Ingur Aguri stood up, placed her hands on her hips and glared at Dame Erato. "My sister does not know how to say thank you."

Dame Erato barely had enough energy to whisper, even though she was trying to complain at the top of her lungs. "I don't know how to say thank you? I gave you the locket. That was enough."

"I visited you yesterday to mend fences. I brought my granddaughter so you could meet her, in the hope that once again we could be a family. But you spurned me. Now, get out of my home."

Dame Erato managed to shriek, her voice the tiniest bit louder. "You don't have a granddaughter!" The effort left her breathing heavily.

★ *She is my daughter.* Pru Tellerence looked from one face to the other. ★ *I brought her here for safekeeping, not to live in this atmosphere of hate.*

Dame Erato stopped panting. "What are you talking about? Overseers can't have children."

★ *It's not that they can't have children. It's that they don't. There is an ancient mandate that forbids love, marriage, and children, so deans can remain free to make decisions without being encumbered by a threat to their loved ones.* She stroked Selestra's hair.

Dame Erato straightened her shoulders and lifted her chin, trying to make herself look as formidable as possible. "You mated with a man? From what realm?"

★ *That is not your concern.*

Ingur Aguri took a step closer. "The last time you were here, you asked me if Selestra showed any special powers?" The witch's eyes widened. "You mated with another overseer."

Dame Erato's eyes widened as well. "Who?"

GOLD-ARMED SCIENTISTS agreed they needed to introduce a substance to the Adventuran sun that would cool its temperature, reducing its current rate of solar flares.

Prophet DAVID l. put down his stylus and looked over his notes. "We have some of the knowledge we need, but the picture isn't complete."

"What do we lack?" Prophet DANIEL p. asked.

"Our experiments with low-energy nuclear reactions have gone well, but alone, they are too small to make a discernible difference," DAVID l. said. "We need a catalyst—something that will exponentially increase the effect of our cold fusion detonations."

DANIEL p. nodded. "We need a detailed blueprint, as well, of where to place those devices to most effectively cool down the sun."

"We don't need a massive number of them," DAVID l. theorized. "Just enough to rein in the solar flares. Just enough," he repeated, "so we can take back control of our power grid and return our realm to the status quo."

"That's a good beginning," Prophet PATRICK c. said. "Unfortunately, we don't have any idea what that catalyst might be, or even if we can create one in time."

DAVID l. shook his head vehemently. "I have

to find the catalyst. I'm going to find the catalyst." He slammed his hand against the counter. "I must find the catalyst."

CHAPTER FOURTEEN

Marbol searched for Peer Meap while the other Juveniles worked on the fort. He found the curator in his residence in the library.

"Marbol, what are you doing here? The library is off-limits."

"We've been in here plenty of times while you were gone. We're the ones who found you."

"That's true, but now, the library is restricted. I'm just gathering a few of my things to take to Sweetie Pies. Waxmo and Pokkie said I could stay at the apartment above the bakery. The library isn't safe with the Terrorians running around abducting people."

"That's why I'm here. We think they're going to return, and we want you to tell the old guys to come back and wait for them here. We're building a fort, so they'll be well-protected. Tell them to bring chocolate."

Peer Meap coughed to cover a laugh. "I can't do that. It's impolite."

"It's okay. They gave us chocolate when I let them copy my scrambler. Just tell them they can copy more of them. Then they'll pay us with chocolate."

Peer Meap scratched his head. "What is your scrambler, exactly?"

"I've got two of them, and they're different. I guess I should name them." He twisted his wrist, which held one of the scrambles. "I'll call this one Glassy, because it dissolves glass, but you can't tell it's missing." He pulled the other scrambler from his waistband. "I'm going to call this one Foggy, because it clouds people's brains. Yeah. The old guys copied Glassy, but they didn't copy Foggy. I bet if you tell them they can copy Foggy, they'll come back and get me and then give me chocolate. It would be good if you tell them to take a whole bunch of us back with them, 'cause then they'll give each of us candy. If enough of us go, we'd have enough chocolate to fill a rub-a-dub tub."

"Do you have any of that chocolate left?" Peer Meap asked.

"I just got this big chunk that's three different colors. It's my favorite."

"How do you know, if you didn't eat it yet?"

"Because Duddu had one," Marbol said turning red as he lowered his voice, "and I may have snitched it."

Peer Meap snatched the piece of chocolate away. "So, this isn't yours at all. It belongs to Duddu."

"No," Marbol replied. "I ate that one. This one is mine."

"That's not how it works. Promise me you'll give

this to Duddu to make up for the one you took."

Marbol sighed. "Yeah. I guess."

"Once you do that, I'll contact one of the overseers and ask if they are planning to return."

Marbol raised his eyebrows, "And bring chocolate?" His shoulders slumped when Peer Meap silently shook his head.

PROTEUS BLIGH, MAL, and Hue the Elder did not find Dron in the first cave they visited. Instead, they found several scared—and a few irate—citizens who wanted to return to their homes.

"You may not be safe there," Mal said.

"My wife and child are waiting." The speaker, Drefol blanched. "I hope they're all right. Tensia is a formidable priestess, but Garon is a baby. Tensia can take care herself, but I don't know if she can safeguard him, too. I need to protect my son."

"There may be a way to do this," Mal said. "Tell me where you live."

The man drew a rough map.

Ψ *You have an idea, Malcolm?*

Malcolm led the overseer away from the others and lowered his voice to a whisper. "I could transport to his residence and assess the danger. If there is none, I could return here and transport him home. The only thing giving me pause is that we didn't want the Mysterians to know I have the same powers as an overseer."

Ψ *Yes. I could see how that could be a problem.* Proteus Bligh disappeared.

"Why did the overseer leave?" Drefol asked.

Before anyone could answer, Proteus Bligh returned. He walked over to Drefol and took his arm. A moment later, they both disappeared.

For the rest of the day, Mal and Hue the Elder mapped out where everyone lived, and Proteus Bligh escorted each of them home.

The trio traveled from cave to cave helping as many people as possible get home without being seen. They warned each person that if they ventured out, it would be at their own risk.

"Am I to be stuck inside my dwelling forever?" a priest asked. "How will I get food?"

Ψ *If you must go out, do so with great caution.*

"Forever?"

Ψ *When the risk has passed, the library bell will ring. That will be the signal that all is safe. Until that happens, you must assume danger prevails.*

Pru Tellerence took a deep breath as she looked from Dame Erato to Ingur Aguri and proceeded to tell her story.

★ *I met Ryden Simmdry when I first traveled to Lumina to undergo the Longevicus Blessing for new curators. It was a frightening experience for me. It was the first time I ever traveled away from Romantica. I felt proud to be considered for the curator position on Mysteriose, but it also scared me because I knew nothing more than I had learned at the hands of the then-curator of the Romantican library—Essa Essenza. Romantica, as you know, is a type V library, but for some reason, I was unable to vacation in any of the books about the other realms. So, leaving home to visit a world that I knew little about was as frightening as it was exciting.*

★*It must have been obvious, because Ryden Simmdry seemed to go out of his way to be kind to me. And I developed a huge crush on him. I looked forward to his frequent visits to my library, not knowing at the time how unusual those visits were. Then, one day, when we were walking in the library garden, he plucked a flower off a vine and tucked it over my ear. I remember holding my breath. All my nerves tingled and I wondered if that's what love felt like.*

★*I looked forward to his visits—each one felt more special than the one before it—and I wanted him to come by more frequently. But I wouldn't dare tell him, after all, he was Master of the Overseers, and I was a lowly curator. I didn't know that overseers were banned from having romantic attachments. I yearned for his touch—a touch he withheld for a very long time.*

★*Our relationship blossomed in the most unusual way. An outbreak of tuberC was wiping out the population, especially children, and was so deadly that few people volunteered to take care of them. It was heartbreaking to think no one would help ease their pain in their final hours, so I said I would do what I could. I covered the youngsters shivering with chills and fanned those burning up with fever. One priestess took it upon herself to nurse the children, and I tried to help her in every way I could until I, too, felt unwell. My symptoms mimicked theirs. I had a fever and cough and worked until fatigue prevented me from doing any more. I collapsed on my way home from the cave where the children had been taken to die.*

★*Ryden Simmdry found me. He had come to visit, and when he didn't find me in the library, someone told him where I was. He carried me back to the library and took care of me. He made a potion—a vapor—for me to inhale, and he kept a cauldron of water boiling on the hearth, to add steam to the room to ease my breathing. He made an amulet and placed it around my neck to protect me. He fed me soup he'd made himself, and slowly, I began to grow stronger. My recovery amazed everyone who knew me because tuberC is usually deadly. I owe him my life.*

★After that, our relationship changed. He became very protective of me—gentle and caring—and intimacy resulted. That's when he told me about the provision in the Ultimium Codi banning overseers from relationships. We tried to resume a simple friendship, but it was impossible. Our passion had grown.

★The College of Overseers eventually selected me as a candidate. By that time, I knew a lot about the libraries that made up the Illumini Constellation and the overseers' relation to them. I took the challenge. They selected me, and I became dean of Mysteriose. It was a great honor, and it meant I could see Ryden Simmdry much more often. It never occurred to me I might conceive a child. I assumed he would do whatever was necessary to prevent that from happening. I was mistaken.

★I couldn't tell anyone, after all, we were both overseers—subject to the ban by the Ultimium Codi. I was too afraid of the Majorious Longevicus Blessing being reversed. I didn't want to turn to dust and die. Instead, I confided in an old witch, Josefina Charo, who had been a dear friend of my mother. She helped me conceal my pregnancy as long as was practical. After that, the stress of living a lie overtook me, and I was granted time off for nervous exhaustion. No one expected that Josefina had me sequestered on Romantica until I gave birth. She agreed to take care of my baby and keep her

existence a secret.

★I visited infrequently, too afraid that my secret would be found out. And then, one day, I visited Josefina and found someone new had taken over her home. Everyone I asked said Josefina had been in ill health and had gone somewhere to die. I was distraught. My child had vanished and I had no idea what happened.

★Whenever I could, I would travel back here to look for her, but my search seemed futile, until someone mentioned that Josefina may have gone to Fantasia.

★Being from Romantica, traveling here seemed natural, but going to Fantasia would be unheard of. Overseers seldom travel to realms outside their home worlds, Lumina, and the realms they're assigned to. I had no opportunity to visit Fantasia until I met Johanna Charette, who became the Fantasian curator. It gave me the perfect opportunity to escort her back home and search for my missing child. It was an exhaustive search, but I persevered and found Bel, or as you now call her, Selestra.

"What will happen to you, now?" Dame Erato asked.

★That depends completely on Ryden Simmdry and the College of Overseers.

ALL NIGHT LONG, Jackson obsessed about Johanna wanting to explore her relationship with Cameron and, consequently, got very little sleep.

The next morning, he watched Chris chug a cup of hot cappuccino like it was nothing. *That's what I need.* Jackson slid into the chair next to his brother for breakfast.

"What happened to you?" Chris asked.

"What are you talking about?"

"You've got bags under your eyes. Or maybe it just looks that way because they're kinda purplish."

"I couldn't sleep."

"That's too bad," Chris said, "cause you're not going to be able to eat, either."

"And why is that?"

"Because your phone pinged this morning and Emily texted you saying she would see you in front of her house at 8:00 sharp. That was two minutes ago."

"Damn." Jackson leapt from the chair.

"You have to eat something," Mrs. Roth said.

He picked up a slice of his mother's toast, kissed her on the forehead and ran out the door.

Emily frowned when she saw him. "You're late. I've been waiting here for 15 minutes."

Jackson checked his watch. "But I'm only five minutes late."

"I got here ten minutes early because I was excited to see you," she said, handing him her backpack and linking her arm in his.

He yawned loudly.

Emily pulled away from him. "Am I boring you?"

"No. I didn't sleep well."

"Why?"

What am I supposed to do, tell you how much I miss Johanna? "I'm worried about my final project in English."

"We still have two weeks before it's due."

"Yeah, but I haven't started it yet," Jackson said, and realized it wasn't a lie. *I wonder if Johanna's new boyfriend could help me? Or maybe I'll just open a book by Edgar Allen Poe and ask him if he actually had a raven that could talk.*

*

PETER DAKION MADE his presence known in Lumi. He visited cultural sights, studied Luminan history, and dined out for every meal, so people would get used to seeing him around. What he really needed, however, was a home. Living in a hotel did not give him permanency. He wanted to call Lumi "home" for the foreseeable future, and that meant investing in a dwelling. Price was no object. He would be paying with someone else's money.

He walked into domicile dealer Milver Dunstable's office to ask about vacancies.

"How much are you willing to spend?" the dealer asked.

"Whatever is necessary to make me comfortable. Why don't you show me the best you have to offer, and we'll take it from there?"

Milver's eyes widened to match his smile. "I have just the place for you."

THE NEXT DAY, Logan felt trapped in school. He had a presentation due just before lunch and a test in his last class. It didn't pay to zig zag between GRUNT and school. He would have to tough it out at Exeter High for the day, with Cassie hanging on his arm.

Jackson studied him when they got together for lunch. Emily and Cassie gossiped about all the other students, while Logan pouted. Jackson waited until the girls got up together to visit the restroom. "What's going on? You look worse than I do, and I feel like roadkill."

Logan stared at Jackson for a moment before speaking. "Who do you love: Johanna or Emily?"

"Johanna. You know that."

"Yeah. Well ever since prom night, I've found myself drawn to Emily."

Jackson stiffened. "What are you talking about?"

"I don't know why everyone is trying to cover up prom night, but I sure as hell know what happened because I was there. I was with Emily, and we were into each other. That's enough to sway me. I'm so over Cassie, I'm ready to give her the heave-ho."

"Look. You want to work at the library. If anyone finds out what happened at the library, all hell will break loose. Everyone in my family has been sworn to secrecy and you will be, too. The thing is, if you dump Cassie to date Emily, it will throw Johanna and Emily together when we all go out. Not to mention, me and Emily. Both of those are giant *fails*. So, get over it."

"And stay with someone who turns my stomach?"

"Cassie turns your stomach? You were in love with her a week ago."

"No, I wasn't. She was already starting to annoy me. I saw her true colors when she fixed up you and Emily and then organized our prom plans. All that crap with flowers and tuxes and paying for catering and the cabin. Although, the cabin turned out to be a pretty good idea, after all was said and done."

Jackson picked up his books and stood. "You're going to have to make a decision. It's a job at the library or Emily. It's your choice."

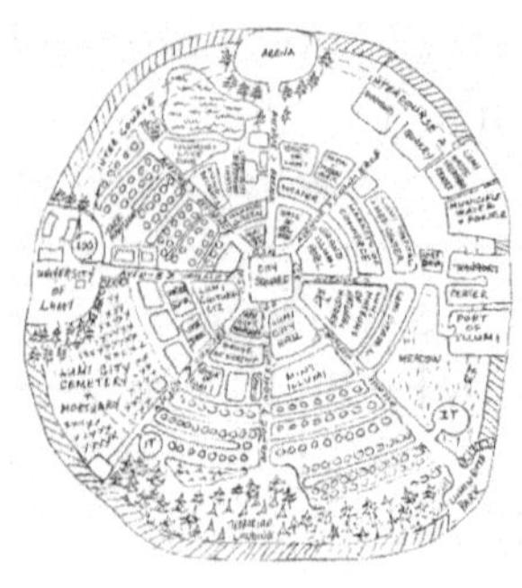

CHAPTER FIFTEEN

A DISTURBING DREAM AWAKENED Dungen, who thrashed about his grandparent's bed entangled in the still slightly damp blanket he had washed the previous afternoon. He relaxed when he realized where he was, but then his stomach growled, signaling that he had not eaten in a while. He slowly got out of bed. The cabin was cold, and he didn't have anything warm to wear other than the clothes on his back and his cloak.

He started a fire and grabbed some *brot* and dried meat from the food box he'd left on the table. The pump worked, although the water coming out looked a little muddy. He could smell the minerals and clay that caused the discoloration. Little matter; he waited for the sediment to settle and drank it anyway because he was thirsty. It didn't stop him from feeling disgruntled. *This is no way to live. It's Pondor's fault for turning his back on me.* Dungen's ringlets tightened. *My father is probably the only person who might be able to figure out where I am.* He clutched the cup in his hand so hard, he crushed it.

After he ate, he sat quietly as a plan took shape. He knew his father liked to tend his garden when he had time off from work. The garden of the house where Dungen grew up had a high wall and a peaceful ambience. Pondor always seemed to lose track of time when he was there. *He loves that garden more than he loves me. So be it. It's time to grant Pondor's greatest wish. I'll visit my father at home and plant him in his garden, so he can spend eternity with his precious flowers and vegetables.*

HORATIO BLASTOE HAD followed Terrorian troop movement throughout the night and conveyed all he learned, telepathically, to the other overseers. Not only did Nero 51 increase his invasion forces on Romantica, Juvenilia, and Dramatica, he also sent a small contingent of troopers to Comedia. From what he had learned of those people, they seemed simple and would be easy to conquer.

NELI FLO RODE a fat pig across the town square as she headed toward home. Music filled the air. The streets of Comi—Comedia's capital city—overflowed with revelers celebrating the city's second millennial anniversary. Balloons floated from every surface, even the spire atop the astronomical clock on the town hall.

Everyone in the city had looked forward to the celebration for a very long time, but as much as Neli wanted to take part in the festivities, she knew if she didn't lock up her favorite pig at home, she might find him roasted on a spit for dinner.

"Get in there, Tropo," she said, poking the pig in his ham with a gnarly branch. She never had any trouble getting him to enter his hut when he was tired or hungry, but it was a nice day, and Tropo wanted to party as much as she did. "You can't come with me," she reasoned. "I'm not in the mood for pig-on-a-stick, especially if it's made out of you. Be a good boy and go in your hut, and tonight, I'll let you sleep on my bed as a special treat. It's warm and soft." Her voice took on a sing-song quality. "You'll like it."

"Rhnt, rhnt," Tropo replied, trying to gain his freedom.

"Be a good pig, just this once. It's for your own good." She lowered the stick.

Tropo saw his chance and bolted. "Nooo," Neli screamed, and gave chase. But Tropo could sprint with the best of them and managed to evade Neli and her stick.

RYDEN SIMMDRY HATED the idea of transporting to Terroria, but knew he had to find Pru Tellerence. He channeled his nemesis Odyon and transported in as a breeze of fresh air. He spotted Horatio Blastoe and appeared in miniature, right next to him.

✠*Ryden Simmdry, to what do I owe this honor?*

The master of the College of Overseers looked around. ⌘*Isn't Pru Tellerence with you?*

✠*No. She said she had to go back.*

⌘*Back to…*

✠*I thought she meant Lumina. Isn't she there?*

⌘*No. Are you sure she didn't say anything else?*

✠*I'm positive. I remember it distinctly. Nero 51 had*

gathered more troops to ship to Romantica, and she said she had to go. That it was important.

Ryden Simmdry clasped Horatio Blastoe's arm. ⌘ *Thank you, my friend.*

PROPHET DANIEL P. FORCED Prophet DAVID l. to hook up to a nourishment and recharge station. The latter had been working all night on a catalyst to use with Adventura's low energy nuclear reactors, and he had just started showing progress when DANIEL p. dragged him away from his work.

DANIEL p. hooked up DAVID l. but was called away on a minor emergency before he could switch off DAVID l.'s power. As a result, DAVID l. refreshed more slowly because his brain floated in a twilight state, instead of in complete darkness. Permutations continued to bounce around DAVID l.'s brain making synaptic connections without being fettered by forced logic.

DAVID l. felt like he had been chosen to witness celestial fireworks in ultrafast motion. The birth and death of stars and battles within the cosmos forced systems to change dynamically. As he witnessed the massive metamorphosis, the synapses in his brain fired in unusual sequences, delineating the catalyst he sought to find.

THE JUVENILES' FORT was a sight to behold. A wall of rocks formed the front and side barriers, which were held in place by boards lashed to upright supports that were planted in the ground. Tiny peepholes and openings—just large enough to fit the muzzles of the scramblers, scorchers, and the decimators the Juveniles found in the library—dotted the rock wall. Peer Meap summoned Zenith Fullova and asked him to explain to the youngsters how fatal the decimators could be, lest they start picking each other off for fun.

The overseer appeared in front of the fort and nodded. §*You have all been very busy, I see.*

Marbol stared at the newly-built edifice like a proud papa. "She's a *trubie*," he said, puffing out his chest.

Peer Meap came rushing out of the library with two boxes of belongings and put them down under a tree, then hurried over to make sure the Juveniles didn't bombard Zenith Fullova with requests for chocolate. "Thank you for coming so soon," the curator told the overseer. "Marbol, did you ask Zenith Fullova your question?"

Marbol stared at the overseer for a moment before speaking. "You copied Glassy," he said, holding up his second scrambler. "But you didn't copy Foggy."

§*What does Foggy do?*

Marbol tapped the side of his head with one finger. "It makes you foggy, up here."

§*How unusual. Can you show me how it works?*

"Are you sure you want to see it in action?" Marbol asked.

§*Of course. I wouldn't want to copy it without knowing what it can do.*

"Okay then," Marbol said, before turning around and shooting Peer Meap.

Zenith Fullova pulled the scrambler out of Marbol's hand. §*I didn't mean for you to use it on Peer Meap.* His words came too late. Peer Meap received a full scrambler charge.

§*Peer Meap, are you all right?*

The curator stared at the overseer and blinked.

§*You can hear me, can't you?*

Peer Meap squinted at the overseer and started backing away. Zenith Fullova put his hand on Peer Meap's shoulder in an attempt to stop him. Peer Meap broke away and began running away from the gathering of people at the fort.

§*What have you done?* Zenith Fullova asked Marbol.

"He'll be okay," Marbol answered. "It only lasts for a little while, then it wears off. I made it to protect my sister from a bunch of bullies. They went wandering around like no-brainers when I used it on them, but they were fine when I saw them later. It's just temporary. It confuses people and makes them scared of their own shadows."

§*And you say it's okay if I make copies of this?*

"It's okay," Marbol looked down at his shoes as he tried to steel his courage, "if you give us a basket of chocolate. All of us," he added.

§*I see. Come with me.* He took Marbol's arm.

"We all need to go," Marbol said, but before he could finish the sentence, he was in the duplicloner room on Lumi, and Zenith Fullova was cloning Foggy. As soon as Marbol realized what had happened, they were back on Juvenilia, a basket of chocolate at his feet.

"If you only give me chocolate," Marbol said, "I could probably use it to swap for favors, but that will make a lot of people mad." He took a deep breath. "But if you gave us each a bunch of chocolate, we'd all be even."

Zenith Fullova nodded and after a moment, he snapped his fingers. A basket of chocolate appeared at the feet of every Juvenile at the fort.

"Wow!" Waxmo shouted.

Pokkie fell to his knees and hugged his basket of candy.

The air wavered and the time machine appeared.

§*Oh, dear.*

Dame Erato could hardly believe Pru Tellerence had given birth to a baby girl. "Does Ryden Simmdry know the child is his?

⌘*I do.*

Dame Erato nearly jumped out of her chair, while the other women gasped collectively—startled by Ryden Simmdry's sudden entrance.

⌘*Pru Tellerence. You are needed at once. The Terrorians are escalating their plans.*

★*I wanted to make sure Bel…Selestra is all right.*

"You say Selestra is your spawn—the child of two overseers. What makes you believe this is your child?" Dame Erato asked.

★*She is the right age, and she has the birthmark.*

⌘*The birthmark?*

Pru Tellerence turned to Ryden Simmdry. ★*A star, behind her ear.*

Ingur Aguri checked behind the child's ears. "There is a mark behind her ear, but it appears to be a scar, not a birthmark."

★*I believe it was done in the institution on Fantasia where I found her. I believe they burned her skin to hide the mark.*

"As the child of two overseers, she will grow into a very powerful young woman."

⌘ *Too powerful, perhaps.*
★ *Only time will tell.*

THE POUNDING ON the door of a home near the Town Center startled the Mysterian politician and priestess who lived inside. "Someone must have stupidly gone out and is now running for his life and thinks we'll be fool enough to open the door."

"You must open the door," his wife said. "If you were outside for some reason, you would want our neighbors to open the door to you, wouldn't you?"

"This is against my better judgement," her husband said as he opened the door a crack.

A tentacle snaked inside and grabbed the politician around his neck as a Terrorian pushed in the door. The priestess screamed and turned to run but soon found herself immobilized. A second Terrorian turned the decimator on the priest as well, placing him in a force field.

The Terrorians removed the captives and searched the house.

"There's no one else here."

One soldier carried the prisoners to the field behind the library, while the other threw an incendiary device inside the dwelling. He pulled the door closed and walked away. Moments later, an explosion inside the house reduced the contents to charred timbers, similar to all the other homes located near the Town Center.

JACKSON, LOGAN, CASSIE, and Emily slid into a booth at Piccolo Italia after school.

"I thought this day would never end," Emily said. "For some reason, everyone seems to have changed overnight, and I don't know why."

"I'll tell you why—" Logan began to say before Jackson's sneaker connected with his ankle.

Before Logan could say anything, Jackson leaned forward and called out to his brother. "Chris. What are you doing here? You're supposed to be working."

"Wrong. I called Johanna, and she said don't worry about it. She has everything well in hand."

"She can't do everything by herself," Logan said to Jackson. "That's why I should be working there."

Emily pulled the wrapper off a straw before sticking it in her soft drink. "It's just a library. It's not like anything earth-shattering would ever happen there. Even if someone folds the edge of a page to mark their spot, it's no big deal."

"Besides," Chris said, "I think that guy from Cranford University is visiting her. She was all happy when I returned home today to grab my wallet. You know how she gets, humming and dusting and dancing around like Prince Charming is coming to visit."

Jackson felt his fists clench. *She should act that way over me, not him.*

Cassie made a face. "She has to dust the library? That must take forever. Why doesn't the library get a cleaning service?"

"Really," Emily agreed.

A waitress delivered their pizza, and Logan let Emily and Cassie each take a slice before he took two. "Eat up, Jack-o, because if you don't, I'll eat your share before you know it."

"Ew." Emily made a face. "Don't call him Jack-o. That sounds horrible."

"Come on, Jackson, take this," Cassie said handing him a slice. "I don't want *Lo-go* getting fat, because he ate your share."

Milver Dunstable used a grand sweeping gesture to open the door to a dwelling right outside the gates of the University of Lumi. "This is one of our premier homes. It used to belong to Eldrith Tare before he moved to the Governor's Palace. Everything here is designed to meet the most exacting standards of Lumi elegance."

Odyon walked through the home and thought about what he could do to make it his own. It looked elegant, by Lumi standards, but he had gotten used to the comforts of Fantasia. Still, if he wanted to call Lumi home, this would have to do. *It's certainly better than those other two hovels he showed me.* "How much?"

Milver grimaced. "It's not inexpensive, after all, it is one of the most sought-after homes in the city."

"If it's so sought after," Odyon said, "why is it still available?"

"Not everyone can afford such exacting refinement."

"How much?" Odyon asked again.

"Twenty billion credits."

Odyon tapped on his *Digi-Tab*, which served as a personal electronic device, identity card, and wallet. "Where shall I send the payment?"

Milver crept closer and looked over Odyon's—a.k.a. Peter Dakion's—shoulder and spied the number of credits in his balance.

Milver quickly opened his own Digi-Tab and replied, "Account 4B-5094K10-R." He made a sweeping gesture with his arm. "Welcome to Tare Manor, your new home."

Odyon stiffened. "Not Tare Manor. The governor no longer owns it, and the sooner that is known, the better. From now on, this home is only to be referred to as Illumini Palace."

"Whatever you wish," Milver agreed. "Is there anything else I can do for you?" he asked as he pulled up a document on a portable tablet.

"Yes," Odyon said, waving his hand toward the entrance. "You can leave."

"Here's the *digicode* to get in," Milver said, handing Odyon a keycard. "If you'll just give me your thumbprint on this screen, I'll embed a copy of the particulars for you."

"Fine." Odyon pressed his thumb on the screen. Milver tapped his tablet against Odyon's Digi-Tab and a verification of the sale along with a deed to the property appeared in Odyon's file.

Odyon placed the flat of his hand against Milver's back and literally propelled him toward the door. "It was my pleasure to serve you," Milver said as he was pushed out.

"Goodbye," Odyon replied, before ordering the door to close and lock.

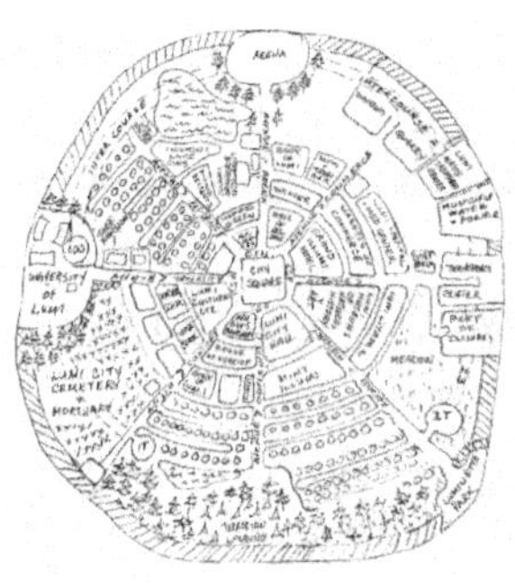

CHAPTER SIXTEEN

Cameron Thorne loved spending time at the Library of Illumination despite knowing all hell could break loose at any moment. That afternoon, Johanna had introduced him to the Bard, as well as Myrddin. She asked Cameron who else he would like to meet.

"Who have *you* met?" he asked.

"Too many people to count," she replied.

"Just tell me some of the ones you remember off the top of your head."

"Einstein, Jeeves, Adam and Eve, Frankenstein's monster—"

"You met Frankenstein's monster? What was that like?"

Her mind recreated the image of the monster trouncing *the three little pigs*. "He wasn't very pleasant, and he nearly wrecked the library. As it was, he injured

Casanova."

"Casanova? *The* Casanova?"

"One and the same. But I'd rather not talk about it."

"You know who I'd like to meet?" Cameron asked.

"Thor?" Johanna replied. "If so, he's upstairs guarding the portals. I had a hard time convincing him he had to use the decimator instead of his hammer. I had to use the decimator to place his hammer in a force field, so now he can't pick it up."

"What comic book did you get him out of?"

She shook her head, smiling. "*The Encyclopedia Britannica*. Thor is a Norse god. He predates comic books and movie scripts."

"Does he speak English?"

"I used a translation spell on him so we could understand each other. Come on up. Maybe he'll tell you all about his father, Odin. Among his many other talents, Odin was apparently a sorcerer who, I think, could have given Myrddin a run for his money."

"I've never met a god before, and I'm sure meeting him would be educational. Maybe, we could even develop a mythology lecture series based on what we learn from different gods firsthand."

"Okay. Let's go up."

Before they reached the cupola staircase, Jackson burst in the front door. "Hey."

Johanna turned. "I'm surprised you're already here. Rumor had it you were stopping at Piccolo Italia for an afternoon snack."

Jackson placed his backpack behind the circulation

desk. "How much pizza can a guy eat?"

"You're just in time. We're going up to meet Thor," Cameron said. "Johanna has separated the god from his hammer, and I think he might be peeved. There could be fireworks. But if you go, maybe the saying 'strength in numbers' will prove to be true and protect us."

Jackson pushed away from the desk. "Thor? Really? I'm in." He followed Johanna and Cameron up to the cupola hoping to be entertained. And maybe his presence would throw a damper on any intended flirting.

PRU TELLERENCE GAVE a lot of thought to Ingur Aguri's theory that Selestra could exhibit special talents over and above what her overseer parents might have.

⌘*Considering there has never been a child born to two overseers before, we have no way of knowing what effect the Majorious Longevicus Blessing would have on our offspring. She could end up being the greatest sorceress who ever lived.*

⌘*Or, considering the babe is never exposed to the pure protective light of the enchantment, it stands to reason she might develop normally, with no powers whatsoever.*

All the color drained from Pru Tellerence's face. ★*No.* She approached Ryden Simmdry until she was so close he could feel the warmth of her breath on his face. ★*That can't be.*

⌘*It may or may not be.*

★*That would mean without the Majorious Longevicus Blessing, Bel would not have the advantage of aging slowly.* A tear spilled down her cheek. ★*If that were true, our child would be long dead. Dust. And Bel—no relation to us whatsoever. I cannot accept that.*

She walked over to the child, bent down and embraced her. ★*You are my child,* she whispered, and kissed her.

⌘*It is time for us to go.*

Dame Erato sighed heavily. Annabeth took the woman by the arm. "And it is time for you to return home and rest."

"No," Ingur Aguri said. "My sister will stay with me and Selestra for a few days. I will take care of her. My potions will bring back her strength, long before any soups or brichi you may concoct would help her." She grabbed Annabeth by the arm. "I'm sure your help is deeply appreciated. Now go back," she waved her arm, "and do whatever it is that you do."

"The militia," Annabeth said as an afterthought.

"Yes. Whatever," Ingur Aguri said as she pushed her out the door.

Back on Lumina, Ryden Simmdry did his best to console Pru Tellerence.

⌘*There is no definitive proof that our child is dead and that Bel...Selestra...is not our child. You said it yourself—you believe she has the star-shaped birthmark you remembered behind her ear. Now, lift your head, relax your shoulders, and breathe.*

Pru Tellerence followed Ryden Simmdry's advice and took several deep breaths. *He is right, of course,* she thought. *It is all just talk. It doesn't mean Bel is not our daughter.* Then she had a more urgent thought. She looked him in the eye.

★*What about the Ultimium Codi? Are we to be*

turned to dust? Would it matter if our child is dead, if we will be joining her soon?

He sighed. ⌘*I believe it is time to convene a full meeting of the College of Overseers.*

ONCE HORATIO BLASTOE had a chance to study Nero 51's chain of command and the rhythm by which the Terrorian launched his attacks, he felt he could almost predict the curator's next moves. At first, the overseer had been surprised to see the curator personally escorting troops to the different realms, but then he realized Nero 51 had a flaw that could be exploited. *The Terrorian is obsessed with control. If we derail his train of logic, he will stumble.*

The overseer studied the Terrorian machinations and was ready to propose a scheme when he received the telepathic message from Ryden Simmdry recalling all overseers to Lumina. He would discuss his discoveries with his brethren and they could formulate a plan together.

NELI FLO CHASED Tropo through the backyards and gardens of all the houses in her neighborhood. She was quickly running out of homes, and if her pig ran as far as the meadow, there would be nothing to slow him down. Finally, at the last house in the row, Tropo entered a yard that was fenced on all sides.

"Got you now," Neli said, as she slowly approached the pig with a noose attached to the end of a rope. "Come on, Tropo," she coaxed, "let's go for a ride."

Tropo grunted a few times as he approached the rope.

"That's a good boy," she cooed. Neli loosened the

noose and prepared to throw it around the pig's neck. "And when we get home, I have some nice, juicy carrots for you."

"Rhnnt."

"Sweet boy," she said in a gentle voice as she tossed the noose at Tropo's neck, but he was too fast for her. He escaped the noose and knocked her down as he bolted past.

Neli Flo had not underestimated Tropo. He ran full tilt into the meadow and picked up speed with every step, until a glass bubble suddenly materialized and Tropo crashed into the first Terrorian to emerge. The stunned pig squealed at the top of his lungs. Tropo was dazed, but not as much as the Terrorians who thought they were being attacked.

The pig backed away, snorting and squealing.

"Get out," Nero 51 ordered the troopers, "and capture that…thing."

"What if there are more?" a soldier asked.

"Ensnare them."

But the trooper whom the pig had collided with remained too stunned to move. The Terrorian next to him pushed the first soldier aside and took aim with his weapon. He wasn't quick enough. Tropo was on the move once again and ran straight for Neli Flo. When he was in striking distance, she threw the noose at him again, causing him to change direction. A second shot by the Terrorians failed to reach its mark.

Neli suddenly realized the odd, ugly thing shooting at her pig shouldn't be there, and she ran screaming from the meadow. Before long, a number of neighbors were running behind her, like a long tail, trying to find out what she was babbling about.

*

As soon as the Terrorians appeared on Juvenilia, Marbol ran at the time machine, alternately blasting them with Glassy and Foggy. A moment later, the machine disappeared. Marbol stopped and stared. Peer Meap and Zenith Fullova rushed to the boy's side.

"Do you think I killed them?" Marbol whispered.

§*I don't think so. I think you just scrambled their brains enough that they feared for their lives and went home.*

Marbol slipped Glassy into his belt. "Okay. I think now we have to go into the woods and search for Selly and Cici."

§*I don't think you'll find them here. The Terrorians have been taking their captives back to Terroria. As far as I can tell, Selly and Cici are no longer on this realm.*

"We have to make sure," Marbol said. He walked over to Duddu and told him what the old guy had said about Selly and Cici being gone, but then he stressed that they had to make sure and search the woods. "You take the scorchers and the decimators. Just leave Bungie here with a decimator to man the fort. I'll stay, too, and use my scramblers to scare the monsters away if they return. That way, if they don't respond to me, Bungie can blast them away.

Like all the hu*bots on Adventura, Prophet DAVID l. did not show excitement through facial expression because his face was robotic; however, his vocal volume increased and his speech pattern sped up as it responded to the excitement in his brain.

"Hold on," Prophet CARL a. said as he studied the

monitor next to DAVID l. "Apparently I failed to switch off your power when I hooked you up. It prevented you from fully charging."

"I don't care," DAVID l. said. "I must not forget what I need to do to formulate a catalyst. I must go to my lab now to work on the solution for the solar flares. I believe I know what to do."

CARL a. knew allowing DAVID l. to work in his diminished capacity could turn out to be a terrible judgement call, yet a part of him did not want to impede the progress of a possible fix. "I will give you three hours. But then, I must hook you up for a full charge in a completely dormant state."

"Agreed."

"Don't shoot, Thor," Johanna called out as she, Cameron, and Jackson neared the top of the cupola steps. "I'm bringing some people to meet you."

Thor narrowed his eyes as he studied the two men. "Why have you brought them here?"

"When they heard a god was guarding the portals, they wanted to honor you."

"Where is their tribute? What do they sacrifice?"

Johanna's eyes widened. "Could you be more specific?"

"I do not ask for much," Thor said. "Small animals are enough."

Jackson leaned in close and spoke quietly in Johanna's ear. "Where's the open book?"

"Downstairs on the circulation desk," she whispered.

Jackson nodded at Thor. "I forgot my tribute downstairs. I'll go get it." He backed up toward the staircase and hurried down when he felt the handrail.

"What if I have no tribute?" Cameron asked brazenly.

Thor's face hardened. "Perhaps you are here to challenge me?" He lifted the decimator onto his shoulder.

"No," Cameron said, taking a step back. "I have no wish to challenge you."

"I am Thor. Many people have challenged me in the past. I know a usurper when I see one." Thor aimed the decimator at Cameron. An instant later, it clattered to the floor.

Cameron jumped.

"Are you all right?" Johanna asked.

"What just happened?" Beads of perspiration appeared on Cameron's upper lip and brow. "Did he aim it in the wrong direction?"

"Jackson probably closed the encyclopedia." As Johanna spoke, the thumping of Jackson rushing up the cupola steps punctuated her words.

"Is everyone okay?" Jackson asked as he reached the top.

Johanna turned to him and smiled. "You were just in the nick of time. Thor decided Cameron was a usurper and was about to decimate him."

Jackson nodded but stopped when his eyes alit on Thor's hammer. "Look what got left behind!" He tried to pick it up but was repelled by a force field. "I can't touch it."

Johanna picked up the decimator. "Step back."

When Jackson was far enough away, she shot the hammer, releasing it from the force field.

"Now we're talking," Jackson said as he reached for the hammer and pulled it. "Is it fused to the floor? It's not budging."

"It's Thor's hammer. Only someone as worthy as Thor can lift it," Cameron said. "I'm afraid the hammer doesn't think you're worthy."

Jackson's face reddened, partially from what Cameron said, and partially from his exertion trying to lift the hammer. "Maybe you should try it," Jackson said to Cameron. "Maybe you're worthy."

Cameron walked over to the hammer and tried to lift it. "That's really amazing. It won't budge."

Jackson gave it another tug. "I wonder if one of the overseers could move it?"

"Probably," Johanna answered. "They seem pretty worthy."

"If they can't, it's here forever," Jackson said.

ON THE OPPOSITE end of town, Cassie checked the instructions again. They hadn't changed. She was still pregnant, and she needed to do something about it. She had dated Logan for the past four years, ever since they met on the first day of ninth grade. She hoped he would be happy, after all, it was his baby. She allowed herself to daydream. Surely his parents would give them money as a wedding gift that they could use to set up a home of their own. They couldn't afford a house, but a nice little apartment in town somewhere would be nice. *Two bedrooms, of course. The baby will need her own nursery.* She felt sure her friends would help by giving her a bridal shower. *I'll set up a bridal registry so they only get me things I want. And a baby shower.* Although, she might keep the baby a secret from them until after she and Logan got married. *It will be perfec*t.

So why was she having such a hard time getting up the nerve to tell Logan?

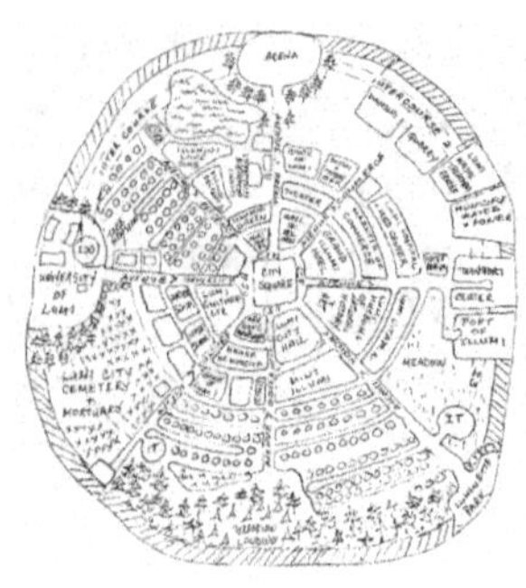

CHAPTER SEVENTEEN

THE GOVERNOR OF Lumi had furnished his previous home in a style that could best be described as minimalist. At least he had left a comfortable bed to rest on, but as far as Odyon was concerned, it was the only usable piece of furniture in the dwelling.

However, other things were more important, like resetting his locks and digicode. He didn't need any unexpected visitors dropping in on him. Afterward, he wanted to relax and think about the changes he should make, but his barren surroundings left him cold. He had found no food, linens, or decorative items in the former Tare mansion, and the shelves in his library were bare. The longer he thought about his surroundings, the more compelled he felt to change them.

He tried to think about something else. *I wonder how Nero 51 is faring on his own? What a fool. He probably doesn't even realize I'm gone.* Odyon finally fell asleep after planning how *he* would have invaded the other realms if *he* were Nero 51. *I could easily kill Nero 51 and take on his appearance. Maybe when he gets closer to his goal. I'll let him handle the mess, for now. I can always swoop in at the last minute when he's nearing the finish line.* Odyon smiled. *The spirit of Garpa would absolutely explode.* Sleep finally overtook him, and he rested soundly.

The following morning, he felt recharged. He was now a resident of Lumi with a new identity and his own palace. He wanted to learn more about the people and customs of the area before pulling the rug out from under them. He still wanted to rule Lumina, but he didn't want to engage in a messy battle to take it. He preferred to win his battles with cunning.

If I bide my time, I should definitely be able to have it all.

Logan showed up at his GRUNT internship bright and early. Too early, in fact. The door was locked.

A few minutes later, Jennifer entered the building holding a large coffee while she rummaged through the oversized bag suspended from her shoulder with her other hand. She smiled as she pulled out her office keys and said, "Voila!"

He waited while Jennifer settled into her desk to start her workday. She ignored him as she read the newswires and scanned the police reports looking for stories she wanted reporters to cover. Finally, she stopped to drink some of her coffee, but only got the cup halfway to her mouth when the police scanner announced a possible bomb at the Gainesford Mall.

"Do you want me to sign out a camera?"

"No. It's your first week and you're still learning the ropes. If you want to go with Channing on this and observe, that's okay. Or, I could send you out on your own story. But this will probably be our top story tonight, and I need a seasoned reporter on it."

Logan looked away from her. "Right."

A few minutes later, Luke Harris, the program manager, arrived.

"Hey, Luke, could you put together a setup for Channing? They're talking about a bomb at the mall, and I need to push him out the door as soon as he gets here."

"No problem. Send him back when he arrives."

Logan felt torn. He understood why GRUNT might want someone with more experience on a big story, but that didn't stop him from wanting it.

"Hey Logan," Jennifer called out, "the circus is supposed to arrive by train this morning. If you want your own story, ask Luke to help you sign out a camera. There's not a working reporter around who hasn't done a circus story at least once. But if you want to go with Channing, I'll understand. I can always give this to someone else."

"I'll wait for Channing. Even if I'm not covering the story myself, I can probably learn something just by experiencing the situation and watching how he covers it."

"Fine."

He walked into the equipment room where Luke had packed up Channing's camera. He took out his phone and used it to snap photos of the camera model number and tripod manufacturer and took close-ups of everything else that went into the setup. *The sooner I get my own camera, the sooner I can prove that I know what I'm doing. Maybe I'll even pick up a police scanner.* He wanted to cover top stories, and with his own equipment he wouldn't need GRUNT to do it. But he also wanted his own stuff so he could do an exposé on the Library of Illumination.

The sooner I get a camera of my own, the better.

PONDOR WHISTLED WHILE he weeded the border plants in his flower bed. The weather was perfect, the sky storm-free. His home was a visually pleasant, stacked stone structure surrounded by a high wall made of the same stone. It was located near the town hall but far enough to make someone think twice, before disturbing him.

The Dramatican judge embraced his day off by working on flowering beds and vegetable plants with his hands. Between his wife and son, he had spent too many years perpetually worried that one of them might hurt someone, and he did his best to keep track of them—not easy for a justice who spent long days listening to mostly petty grievances and accusations. He wished to appease those who complained, while trying to guide citizens on the losing side to an outcome that would help them avoid finding themselves in similar situations in the future. He had a demanding job.

Now, with the sun on his face and his hands in the soil, he felt his shoulders relax and his mind clear.

A HALF-DAY'S RIDE away, Dungen armed himself. He slid a dagger into a sheath on his belt and secured the decimator under an old cloak of his grandfather's that he had found in a trunk. Fortunately, the metal trunk was vermin-free and the cloak in good condition. His own cloak, which he had made sure was highly embellished with jewels to set him apart from "lesser individuals" in Dramoni, would be too recognizable for the task he had in mind. His grandfather's cloak was voluminous, and had a hood with a chin strap that would help hide his identity. Its nondescript color belied the quality of the finely-woven fabric. It would be easy to blend among people when he needed to, and it would easily hide the decimator.

He set out for the city, keeping his head down to avoid being recognized. He maintained a brisk step but tried not to appear overly hurried, which in itself might be remarkable. He very nearly reached his destination before his stomach grumbled. *Proke*, he cursed to himself. He had not thought to take any food with him, and surely, he could not stop anywhere because it would increase the risk of being identified. *There are obi trees in the glen south of the meadow.* A few of the succulent fruit would surely fill the void. *And I won't have to go out of my way.*

Before long, he saw trees with branches heavy with fruit, not too far in the distance. His stomach grumbled again but he ignored it, knowing he could soon eat as much fruit as he wanted. *Perhaps on my way back home, I will stop and fill a sack with fresh fruit to take back to Ulster. Pondor must have some sacks in his storage shed.* He smiled. *He won't have any need for them after today.*

CASSIE LOOKED FOR Logan at Exeter High School the next morning, and when she couldn't find him, she texted him.

WHERE R U
GRUNTING
NEED 2 TALK

She kept checking her phone for a response but didn't receive one. It made her nervous. She tried to calm herself. *He's my boyfriend. Everything will be all right. He's just busy at his internship.*

She sat with Emily and Jackson at lunch but didn't feel much like talking. She noticed that Jackson was quiet as well. She asked a couple of questions about Logan, but Jackson didn't have any answers and seemed distant. Emily, on the other hand, had a one-woman monologue going about an outfit and shoes she had seen the night before at the mall and how it would be "perfect" for so many occasions. Cassie marveled at how Emily could keep on speaking to no one in particular, oblivious to whether anyone listened to her or not. *Did Jackson just say something about Logan?*

"What did you say?" Cassie asked Jackson.

"I said, Logan is spending a lot of time at Graydon Ransom University, even though his internship doesn't officially begin for another month."

"He wants to be their 'star reporter,' but it seems someone named Channing already holds the title. I think Logan is trying to dazzle them with his dedication."

"That's so ridiculous," Jackson said.

Cassie dumped the uneaten half of her sandwich on her lunch tray. "Why?"

"Because he told me he'd like to work part-time at the library, but he doesn't really seem to have any time to do it."

"It's not like he needs to work," Cassie shrugged. "His parents are loaded."

Jackson didn't want to talk about Logan out of turn, even if Cassie was supposed to be his girlfriend. Jackson remembered how easily Logan dumped her for Emily at the senior prom. That appeared to have been reversed by Ryden Simmdry's memory flash, but Jackson felt sure the flash hadn't worked on Logan. And there was more. *Something about Logan now seemed almost sinister. Like the Terrorians in the cupola cast a spell on him on prom night.*

Prophet DAVID l. put down his tablet. *My calculations are correct. I know they are. We just need to bombard the sun with a generous number of carefully formulated ultrafast light pulses bonded to negatively charged catalytic ions. The result will stall hydrogen conversion and...*

Prophet CARL a. hooked DAVID l. up to the recharge station and switched off his circuitry.

And—DAVID l.'s thoughts trailed off as he stilled completely. He would not be attending the meeting the ruler*bots had scheduled. CARL a. hurried out the door. He did not want to be late.

"As you all know," Prophet ANDREW r. began, "everything that has meaning to us is at stake in our struggle to survive the devastating effect of solar flares. If our future looked dire before, it is even worse now, for our window of opportunity has a definite endpoint. Six days."

"Six days!" DANIEL p. exclaimed loudly. "I thought we had six weeks."

"That was a miscalculation," Prophet PATRICK c.

said. "We have only so much organic fuel that we can use for generators. We mistakenly thought there was more in storage tanks but they hadn't been checked during the past century because we no longer had need for it. According to the contingent of hu*bots responsible for amassing our fuel, the old storage tanks have disintegrated in place, allowing the fuel to leak into the ground. Most of the tanks are empty."

DANIEL p. groaned. "It will take more than six days to bombard the sun with anything that might help. And now, it sounds like we don't even have enough fuel to project a missile that can escape velocity."

CARL a.'s brow furrowed as he shook his head. "DAVID l. has a formula he says he knows will work."

"Where is DAVID l?" one of the hu*bots asked.

"Hooked up to a recharge unit. His energy level is dangerously low."

DANIEL p. knocked on the counter surface with his fist. "Don't let him end up like prophet IAN c."

"Don't worry about Prophet IAN c." CARL a. said. "He is going to be fine. Basically, I looked in on him earlier, and I found his test results promising. I took him off charge just long enough to examine him, and while some of his synapses are sporadically misfiring, it appears to be a temporary reaction to becoming so rundown. By this afternoon, he should be nearly back to normal."

"And DAVID l? When will we have him back?" PATRICK c. asked.

"About the same time," CARL a. answered. "Working together, they are our greatest hope. I will work beside them to make sure the job gets done."

"You'll have to," ANDREW r. responded, "or our civilization may be doomed."

THE TERRORIANS WORKED methodically to remove all the residents they could find in the capital city of Myst, then they branched out into the other cities on Mysteriose, trying to capture as many people as possible. The internment camps on Terroria were soon filled beyond capacity and troopers were forced to create detention camps on the individual worlds.

Nero 51 had believed the Mysterians would side with him rather than become his prisoners. Their refusal surprised him, and his surprise grew when his soldiers easily captured the residents of Myst. *For a culture known for their fiery dispositions, my invasion of this realm has occurred much too easily.* Yet, he refused to stop and consider why.

LOGAN AND HIS father pulled into their driveway at the same time.

"You're home early," Logan said.

"You said you wanted to shop for camera equipment."

"Yes. I do," Logan said, barely containing his excitement. "Do you want to go now?"

"Just let me touch base with your mother before we head out."

A few minutes later, Logan climbed into his father's car and gave him directions to the camera store. As they drove, Logan pulled out his cell phone and found the information about the camera and the equipment that went with it. It didn't take them very long at the store for

Logan to find everything he needed.

"Shall I ring this up?" the salesman asked.

"Just one more thing. Do you sell scanners?" Logan asked.

"For a printer?" the salesman asked.

"No," Logan replied. "The kind you hear police and fire calls on. I need one for my car."

"Right over here." The salesman led them to a nearby aisle.

"How much are these?" Michael Elliott asked.

The salesman picked one up. "This one mounts inside the car for less than a hundred dollars."

Michael Elliott relaxed. "That's not too bad."

"We'll take it," Logan said before his father changed his mind.

THE OVERSEERS WORE a mask of solemnity. Master Ryden Simmdry had just opened up a full meeting of the deans and had allowed them instant access to the memory of his secret love affair with Pru Tellerence and the child they begat. Thought-strings telepathically floated between the deans regarding not only the Ultimium Codi and the sudden revelation of a child of two overseers but also of the escalating war and impending peril for Adventura.

Their minds literally hummed as they perused their own thoughts and feelings on the various subjects and played them against the thoughts and feelings of the others.

During the process, both Ryden Simmdry and Pru Tellerence considered everyone's input, while keeping their own feelings under wraps. It was not their place to sway the vote one way or another, and they had agreed to accept the decision of the college.

Finally, the abbreviated group of deans reached a consensus. Plato Indelicat, having been an overseer longer than anyone else—save Ryden Simmdry—assembled their thoughts into words.

Ω*We have each considered the Ultimium Codi in great detail, and fully embrace the Code of Honor that says, 'Sentimentality can cloud the mind. Love can color our decision-making. Fear for the safety of our loved ones can immobilize us.' And that 'we must be free to act in the best interests of the many,' and should not be allowed to fall 'victim to the interests of the one.'*

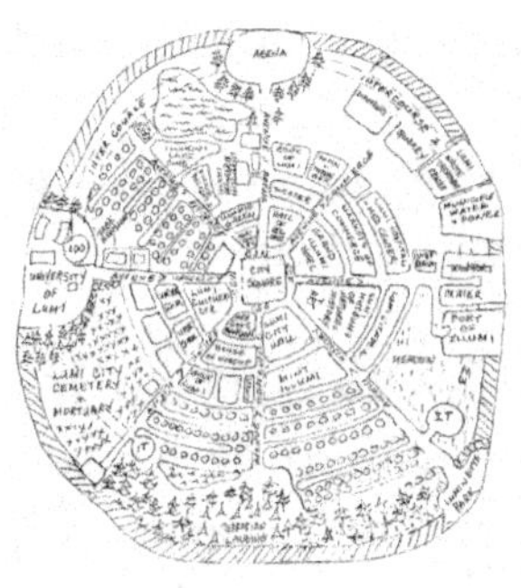

CHAPTER EIGHTEEN

THE TERRORIANS WAITED all night for the Comedians to return, but Neli Flo and her pig were snugly ensconced at home. She had planned to inform everyone that something in the meadow shouldn't be there, but when everyone started following her like a tail, it turned into fun, and in light of all the festivities in the town square, she stopped to eat a *danglidot* and play some games.

When Neli Flo had arrived home, Tropo was fast asleep right in front of her door, awaiting her return.

The Terrorians did not know what actually happened and lay in wait for a counter attack, thinking the Comedians had all been forewarned of their arrival. They had patrolled the area carefully and found cover at the edge of the adjoining woods.

"Do you think they will attack soon?" Plasto 9 asked Ryke 42, the team leader.

"Attacks are more efficient when they are a surprise. We have lost the element of surprise. That now belongs to the Comedians, but we cannot allow ourselves to be lured into a trap. We will await their move."

Pru Tellerence and Ryden Simmdry visibly stiffened when Plato Indelicat reinforced the wisdom of the *Illumini Codi* Code of Honor. Pru Tellerence gripped the edge of the table until her fingers turned white. The deans were right, of course. She and Ryden Simmdry had broken a promise and deserved whatever punishment the college saw fit to hand down.

Ω*The wisdom of the Ultimium Codi is for our own protection and the protection of the realms. It does not consider the union of two overseers. However, are we not already in a dependent relationship, one upon the other? Would we not do what is possible to save each other? And so, it appears that while you would have violated the Ultimium Codi by forming an attachment with an outsider, a union between two overseers only reinforces our strength. And said child, when it reaches adulthood, will increase our rank from twelve to thirteen deans. At that time, the dean holding the least seniority can adopt an at-large position to fill in for any one of us who may be unavailable for some reason to see to our normal responsibilities. As the child in question is said to be very young, it may be some time before this can come into play.*

✠*Let the Ultimium Codi be rewritten to reflect our findings today.*

℥*Done.* And eleven right forefingers rotated in an upward spiral to note their approval.

Pru Tellerence's shoulders relaxed while tears of

relief spilled onto her cheeks. Ryden Simmdry grabbed her hand and squeezed it. He looked at her and whispered aloud, "Our union is blessed."

RYDEN SIMMDRY HELD Pru Tellerence back when the other overseers left the conference room. He shielded his thoughts, so only she could share them.

⌘ *That went amazingly well.*

★ *Better than I could have ever dreamed.*

⌘ *I think many of our number were surprised to hear we have a child.*

★ *Some of them outright wondered where the child might be. I wonder if we should bring Bel here and introduce her to the other deans.*

⌘ *It could be dangerous for her. Right now, no one other than our fellow overseers and Mal know about her.*

★ *And Johanna and Jackson.* Pru Tellerence hesitated, ★ *And Dame Erato, Ingur Aguri, and Annabeth, the young Romantican woman who has been aiding Dame Erato since she nearly died.*

⌘ *The list grows dangerously long.*

★ *I've sworn the Romanticans to secrecy. I believe Ingur Aguri loves our child and will do everything in her power to protect her.* She hesitated. ★ *We have not asked Johanna and Jackson to keep our secret.*

⌘ *I would trust them with our lives.*

★ *As would I, which is why I would like to invite them, as well, when we introduce Bel as our child. It would be a celebration of her special place within our family, by which I mean the entire college of deans, Mal, Johanna and Jackson.*

⌘ *No bigger than that. And no pomp. We don't want*

to attract too much unwanted attention.

★We will introduce her as Bel. She is known as Selestra on Romantica and will remain as such. As long as we prevent any outsiders from knowing about our plans, everything should proceed smoothly.

⌘We can only hope.

GUARDING THE PORTALS could get boring at times, and Johanna started to daydream.

> *Jackson slammed a pile of books down on top of the circulation desk. "Aren't you done packing those books yet, Cameron? If you want to continue to work in the library, you're going to have to pull your weight around here. And right now, you're not."*
>
> *"I don't know what you're talking about. Johanna just told me I'm doing a 'great job.' But all you seem to do is find fault with me. And, may I point out, I do not 'work' here. Johanna's really busy, and I'm just here as a friend, helping her out."*
>
> *Johanna swept down the curator's steps like a fashion model. "Enough you two. Can't we all get along like one, big, happy family?"*
>
> *"Jackson seems to find fault with everything I do," Cameron complained.*
>
> *Jackson appealed to Johanna's good sense. "What good is having Cameron help out if everything he does has to be redone correctly?"*
>
> *Johanna sat down on the chair behind the circulation desk and hid her face behind both hands as she sighed.*

"It's either going to be him or me," Jackson declared. "And considering I'm your co-curator, I guess we know who's out."

Johanna lifted her head and stared at Jackson. "You don't get to make hardline decisions like that. I'm the 'prime' curator, and don't ever forget it."

Cameron threw up both hands as if he were surrendering. "Look, Johanna. I don't want to cause any trouble. Maybe it's best if I go."

"No!" she replied. "This is my call. I'll decide who stays and who goes."

She jumped when a body appeared in front of her.

"Don't shoot. It's just me," Mal said, throwing up his hands just the way Cameron did in her daydream.

She walked over to the former curator and gave him a hug. "I was a million miles away. Sorry if I scared you."

"It's not that you scared me." Mal paused for a second. "That's a lie. Actually, you did scare me because I could have placed you in a force field, or worse, decimated you before you knew what hit you."

Johanna shuddered. "There has to be a better way to guard the portals. It can get boring, especially during the middle of the day when nothing else is going on and no one else is around."

Mal rubbed his beard. "I wonder if the overseers could put a similar enchantment in place like they had when you were serving your first sentence on Terroria."

"My first sentence, as opposed to my second sentence, which occurred after a time rift shifted us back three weeks, or my subsequent incarceration as a prisoner of war?"

Mal gave her a one-armed hug. "When I brought you in to replace me, I had no idea I would put you through so much turmoil. Forgive me?"

She smiled. "It's not your fault. Nero 51 is hell-bent on invading the realms, and we could be experiencing worse problems if I hadn't been sentenced to work on Terroria."

"All because Jackson couldn't contain his curiosity."

She thought about how Jackson acted in her daydream, but then put it out of her mind. She refused to let her imagination get in the way of their relationship.

Mal remarked about how quiet she'd become. "Is there a problem?"

"Yes, but it's all in my head."

"Anyway, I'm here to invite you to a secret celebration."

"If it's a celebration, why is it secret?"

"Because it could endanger Bel."

"Oh. What's the celebration?"

"You *could* call it Bel's coming-out party."

Johanna smiled, but knitted her brows together at the same time. "She's only three."

"I guess you and Jackson will just have to travel to Lumina to learn more."

AFTER ONE DAY in her sister's care, Dame Erato felt more like herself.

Ingur Aguri had treated her sister's wounds with a special poultice, and she chanted over the compress each time she refreshed it with a potion of her own design.

As Dame Erato's strength returned, she played with Selestra, weaving ribbons into the child's hair and teaching her to sing nursery rhymes.

"You're spoiling my granddaughter," Ingur complained.

"I'm entertaining my grandniece," Dame Erato replied.

Ingur tried to hide her emotions. "How long do you think the overseers will allow us to keep the child?"

"That is a question I cannot answer," her sister replied. "We must keep their secret at all costs."

"If it is still a secret."

"I'm sure we'll find out what they plan to do—sooner than we want."

Across town, Annabeth knocked on Milencia's door. The militairre let her inside, quickly searching the surrounding area to make sure she didn't see any lurking Terrorians.

"I am ready to return to duty. What are your plans to reinvigorate the militia?"

Milencia busied herself boiling water. "I don't know what I can do on my own. The Terrorians have Natalia and my sisters, as well as all the other enlisted militairres."

"Perhaps, but weren't you going door to door to recruit new members—like me?"

"Yes, and we have about twenty new, but unfortunately untrained, members. We can hardly use the field to train them. It would be foolish to practice out in the open like that, and we lack the weapons we had before the invasion."

"That may be so, but I know I don't want to stand

around and do nothing while I wait for invaders to upend my life. Even if we are stuck inside, arrows can be made, and you, at least, still have a decimator. We may not have as much to work with as we had before, but we have enough resources to try to prepare ourselves for our enemies' return."

THE DETENTION CAMPS on Mysteriose were shoddy at best. The Terrorians put up several quickly-built long huts with dirt floors; rudimentary sanitary facilities, which were nothing more than giant holes dug in the ground; and the Terrorians' most involved engineering achievement: water pumps.

The caves would have actually been better places to house the prisoners of war, but the Terrorians couldn't figure out how to open the gates. They tried, but soon learned the effects could be devastating after they lost seven troopers who attempted to blast the gates and surrounding walls with their decimators.

The time machine traveled back and forth continuously with supplies for reinforced fences and a poisonous emulsion they could paint over it to keep prisoners from attempting to escape. That, too, led to Terrorian deaths, until the invaders forced the Mysterians to take over the deadly job. The two Mysterians tasked with painting quickly discovered that the poison, while deadly to Terrorians, had no effect on them. But they pretended to weaken and suffer, to prevent the Terrorians from learning their poison wouldn't have the desired effect.

By far, the biggest problem the Terrorians faced was keeping the prisoners from starving. Nero 51 had been using the replicator in his library to supply simple foods, but the sheer number of prisoners his soldiers had captured proved to be daunting. *If I could use the duplicloners in the libraries on each realm, it would allow local forces to take over maintaining the food supplies and would free up the time machine, so I could move more troops to other worlds.* But he knew it was impossible. Most of the libraries were sealed, and he could not gain access to the duplicloners without the curator of each library.

My next step must be to imprison the curators. All the curators. All at once. This will require some thought.

COMEDIAN CURATOR ABBELLO Abbato couldn't believe his ears. "Are you sure, Neli Flo? You are describing Terrorians. If they're in the meadow, we face a very, very dangerous situation.

"Of course, I'm sure. If Tropo could speak, he'd tell you he's sure, too."

"You'd better show me where you found them." They walked outside and the curator climbed into his SOTA—his single occupant transport apparatus. It was like a stubby kayak attached to a balloon that never lost its shape. As soon as he lit the flame, it began to rise. "I'll follow you, Neli."

Neli Flo climbed upon Tropo's back and nudged the pig toward the meadow.

Abbello Abbato pushed a lever forward and little wings lifted up from the sides of the balloon as a propeller on the front began to spin and a thruster at the back of the SOTA croaked out a puff of smoke. Tropo was a fast mover, but Reichel Bean—the dean for Comedia—had made some alterations to the curator's vehicle. It may have looked dodgy, but it could move as quickly as the pig it now followed.

As the unlikely duo sped across the open field, they were, indeed, observed by Terrorian troopers, who did not hesitate to shoot at them.

Neli Flo fell off her pig and screamed, "Run, Tropo, run!"

Abbello Abbato wasn't affected by the blast, but his vehicle was, and it stopped abruptly. The curator didn't, however, and was propelled out of the SOTA.

He screamed as he sailed through the open air but stopped abruptly—the wind knocked out of him—when one of Nero 51's soldiers used his tentacles to grab him.

"I demand to know the meaning of this," the curator said in his most forceful voice. "Who is in charge here? Do you know who I am? I'm Abbello Abbato, the curator of this realm."

Moments later, the time machine appeared with fresh troops to replace the ones who had been there for a full cycle. The Terrorian who had caught the curator and the one who caught Neli Flo commandeered the time machine and took their prisoners back to Terroria.

Horatio Blastoe returned to Terroria as soon as his meeting in Lumi ended. The machinations of war moved swiftly, and he knew if he missed too much, he would lose any capacity to help quash the rebellion.

No sooner did he return than Nero 51 came stomping into the hangar.

"Nero 51," one of the troopers said approaching

the curator, "there is a call for more food on Romantica."

"No more food anywhere," the curator bellowed. "Our main concern is capturing all the curators. It must be done at once, and simultaneously. Tell Barzic 922 and Kelsis 384 to report to me immediately."

The trooper rushed off to find the general and the strategist.

Nero 51 racked his brain to figure out how they might capture all the curators at once. *I already have Natalia Dalura and Abbello Abbato. I don't require curators for Lumina or Terroria, so that leaves nine curators to go.* He thought back to his failed attempt to incarcerate the Fantasian curator. *I'll save Johanna Charette for last.* "I want troopers ready to deploy at my command," he ordered a military officer standing nearby.

"I'll assemble the troops right away," Barzic 922 said, saluting Nero 51 with his tentacle.

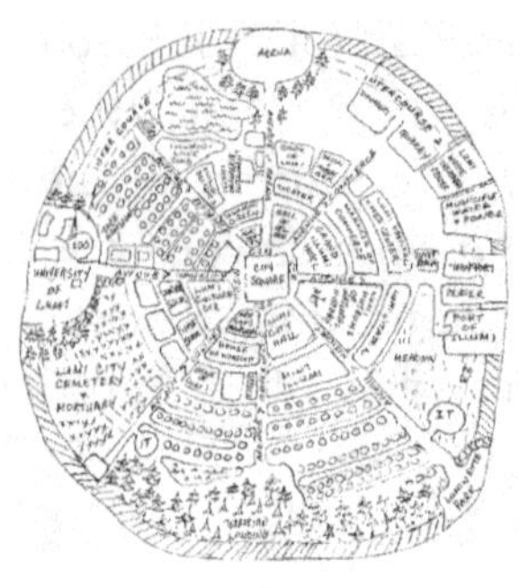

CHAPTER NINETEEN

Selly and Cici were definitely missing, although the Juveniles determined no Terrorians remained in Juvini. They alternated between celebrating the absence of monsters and moaning over the loss of their friends. They refused to leave the fort unattended in case the monsters came back. Zenith Fullova agreed, once again, to make copies of both scramblers, so that any Juvenile guarding the fort had both scramblers and a decimator in his possession.

Waxmo had been standing guard without sleep for more than a cycle, and he found his eyes closing even though he desperately wanted to hear what the old guy had to say.

§*You have to promise me you'll be very careful with the decimators and keep them set on the force field setting rather than the decimate setting.*

Duddu kicked the dirt with his toe. "How can

you expect us to promise that? What if we need to turn something into dust?"

§ *While the possibility exists, I doubt you will need to use such deadly force. If we find you have used the decimator for more than the call of duty, we may be forced to ban all chocolate from Juvenilia in perpetuity.*

Waxmo jerked awake. "What does that mean?"

"No chocolate ever again," Peer Meap explained.

Waxmo's eyes went wide. "Why would you do that?"

§*As punishment for not obeying orders.*

"What orders?" Waxmo continued. "Did I miss something?"

§*Maybe I wasn't clear. I order you to only use the force field setting. I order you to not use the decimate setting.*

Waxmo let out the deep breath he was holding. "Okay. So as long as we do that, we still get chocolate, right?"

Zenith Fullova forced himself not to smile. § *Yes. You are all in control of your fate. If you follow orders, you will still be allowed to eat chocolate.*

Waxmo looked over at the empty basket of chocolate he had eaten to stay awake all night. "Do you think you might let us have a shipment of the stuff in good faith?"

DUNGEN APPROACHED HIS father's home as quietly as possible. His father was smart. Dungen didn't want to give him a chance to defend himself. He circled around to the garden side of the property using a dense hedge to hide behind.

Pondor's whistling annoyed him. *It's time for payback.* Dungen drew in a breath but hesitated. Wanting to kill his father and actually facing the man and pulling the trigger were two separate matters. *Coward. Do it,* he ordered himself. He heard movement. *Now, or Pondor might disappear inside and it won't be as easy while surrounded by all the things that remind me of my mother.*

He slid the decimator on his shoulder and jumped to his feet, taking aim. A Terrorian loomed across from him and he felt a breeze tickle the side of his head. Dungen pulled the trigger, decimating the Terrorian.

Pondor, clearly shaken, stood up and stared at his son. "Dungen, you saved my life." Tears tracked along the justice's cheeks. "Son, you've come home."

ODYON LOOKED OVER his domain. It looked much more appealing than it had when he woke up that morning.

He had visited an inter-realm market at the edge of Lumi and purchased books and rugs and statuary. He had also visited private purveyors in the heart of the city and bought linens and other household goods. He found it difficult to find pillows as Luminans slept without them, but he finally struck gold in a small shop that catered to off-realm dwellers. *It is odd that people so enamored with luxury do not like the comfort of sleeping on pillows.* Lastly, he visited a nursery and purchased several large indoor plants. *I wonder if the Luminans are familiar with the art of feng shui?* The only piece of furniture he added to his new home was an overstuffed *phantiskin* club chair for his library.

He'd paid handsomely to have his purchases delivered immediately and spent the remainder of the day placing his new possessions in his home. The one thing he had not found that day was a place that imported distilled spirits from other realms, but he believed one had to exist. He just needed to find it.

PROPHETS IAN c. AND DAVID l. met in the lab that afternoon. "I feel I have missed so much," IAN c. said, "yet we still suffer from the threat of solar flares."

"I believe I've discovered the solution," DAVID l. claimed. "I know I knew it, but now I can't recall."

"You have to remember," Prophet CARL a. said. "You assured me you knew what to do when I hooked you up to recharge."

DAVID l. drummed his fingers on the metal counter. "What did I say? If you can recollect my exact words, it might trigger my memory."

CARL a. went over his previous notes to see if they would help. "Something about 'ultrafast light pulses' and 'negatively charged catalytic ions.'"

"Oh. YES." DAVID l. picked up a tablet and started computing formulas. He soon covered several tablets and smart boards with numbers and symbols as he worked out the proportions for the catalyst and computed trajectories and probabilities. The process to formulate a solution was not as quick as IAN c. and CARL a. would have liked, but they wanted DAVID l. to be confident in his calculations. There was no allowance for error.

Several hours later, DAVID l. looked up from his tablet and made an announcement. "We need every Phaedra Z07 laser in this hemisphere aimed at the most active solar flares. Awaken DANIEL p. and tell him to ascertain those coordinates." He handed Prophet ANDREW r. a tablet. "He'll need this information as well.

"While that is being organized," he waved a second tablet, "have ChemCharge prepare this catalyst."

"How will they be able to do that without any power?" IAN c. asked.

"Divert half of the available generators to them. They must act quickly."

"Only half?" ANDREW r. questioned.

"The rest need to go to Engyro. Its job is to marry the catalyst to the lasers. This will require a massive effort, of that I am sure, but it's the only way we can save our world."

CARL a. nodded. "I will awaken DANIEL p. and have him map out the most effective strategy. We will do our best. We must all believe it will be enough."

LOGAN COULDN'T WAIT to arrive at GRUNT. He woke a half-hour early so he would be the first one there. He packed all his camera equipment in a padded bag, which looked like a gym bag, and grabbed his tripod.

When he pulled into the parking lot, he saw the program director walking into the building. He wanted a few minutes with him, to make sure he had the right stuff.

"This is nice," Luke Harris said as he inspected Logan's purchases. "Know how to use it?"

"I shot some video last night after I got it, but I'm sure there are things I don't know yet."

"That's why you're here."

"Right."

"Hey, Luke," Jennifer called from the hallway as

she approached the equipment room. When she saw he was with someone, she stopped at the door jamb. "How many camera setups do I have for today?"

"That depends. We're down to two good cameras and one older model. It will be a couple of weeks before we get back the camera Tyson Fried broke."

Jennifer looked at Logan. "If you were hoping to sign out an early camera for a story today, you're out of luck. The cameras have to go to students who are officially registered for the spring semester. I know you're trying hard, but equipment is tight."

"Not for him it's not," Luke said. "Logan bought his own equipment. This is his setup. If you give him a story and he wants to use it today, you have a fourth camera."

Jennifer raised an eyebrow and looked at Logan. "Understood," she said as she turned and walked away.

As the morning progressed, Logan watched Channing leave to cover the governor's press conference. Then, Amy Kobol dashed off to cover a fire. Merrick Henley headed out with the last camera to cover a puppy fashion show for charity. If any other story came up, it would be his.

Jennifer answered the phone on the first ring. She listened intently. "Is it a private plane?" … "Commercial?" … Her eyes opened wide. "Airbus! Where did you say that happened again?" She scribbled down instructions and looked at Logan. "Luke," she called out loud.

He came rushing from the back room. "What's up?"

"A commercial passenger airbus crashed about 10 miles from here. The woman said she saw survivors."

"What do you want me to do?"

"The only camera left is Logan's. But I'm not convinced he's experienced enough to get everything he needs. Besides, if police cordon off the area, he won't be able to get in without a press pass."

Logan turned bright red. "You're giving Luke my camera!"

"Relax. I'm sending him with you. I expect you to shoot all the footage and do the interviews. You can write it up when you return. I'm sending Luke with you so you can get in and to be there just in case you have a technical difficulty or miss a shot he knows you'll need."

Logan's face lit up. "Where is it?"

Jennifer handed the paper with the address on it to Luke. "You'd better drive."

She turned to Logan. "If police start asking questions about credentials, let Luke handle it.

"Now go," she said, pushing them out the door.

"I can't say I'll mind going to Bel's party." Jackson tightened the knot on his favorite black leather tie.

"Yeah, and with Captain Louis Renault upstairs guarding the portals and your mother manning the front desk, we should be fine."

"Who is that guy, anyway?"

"He's from the movie *Casablanca*. I have the screenplay right here." Johanna opened a drawer and showed the open script to Jackson.

"Awesome. So, now, what are we waiting for?"

"Mal. He's the only way we can get to Lumina."

"I remember the last time we waited for Mal to take

us to Lumina," Jackson said. "Nero 51 challenged him for the position of overseer. Then, he stole our time machine."

"I don't think we can rightfully call it 'our' time machine."

Jackson picked up a small booklet on storm chasers. "Yeah. Well, you know what I mean," he said, before he paused to read the back cover.

His mother walked over to the circulation desk, followed by an attendant from the George V Hotel carrying a bar stool from Le Bar. He placed it behind the circulation desk as directed by Niamh Roth. "Merci," she told the man as she tried to hand him a five euro note.

He waved one hand at her as if to say *stop*. "Christophe would never forgive me," he said as he hurried away.

Mrs. Roth blushed.

"Admit it, Mom, "Christophe *loves* you. All the guys in the hotel love you."

She swatted her son's arm. "Stop it. They're just helping out. I want to be comfortable behind the desk. Standing on my feet all day is not the way to do it."

"Do I see new furniture?" Mal had entered so quietly, no one had noticed him.

"My mother stole it from the hotel bar."

Mal smiled but shook his head. "I find that hard to believe."

"I asked if I could borrow a barstool," Mrs. Roth replied, "and the hotel graciously acquiesced."

Johanna handed Mrs. Roth a card. "If you have any problems at all, here's Cameron's phone number. He says he's happy to help out if you need him."

"That's very nice of him." She looked at her son just

in time to see him roll his eyes. "Of course, Chris and Ava will also be here to help as soon as they get out of school."

"True." Jackson said. "You shouldn't need to bother Dr. Thorne at all."

This time, Johanna looked at Mal and rolled *her* eyes.

"Did you pack a small bag? It's not that I think we'll be there more than a day, but we're going to Lumina, and we're in the middle of a series of Terrorian invasions. Anything is possible."

"I've got my stuff right here," Jackson said, pointing to his backpack. He shoved the pamphlet in his pocket for a little light reading in case the party turned out to be boring.

"Me, too," Johanna said, picking up a large leather tote from behind the information desk.

"I wish you hadn't used the word 'invasion,'" Niamh Roth said. "Now, I'll be worried."

"Don't worry, Mom," Jackson said, giving her a kiss on the cheek, "Johanna and I are indestructible. We're a team."

"Be careful," his mother added.

"Shall we go, then?" Mal asked.

Jackson nodded. "Yep."

Mal placed his hands on Johanna's and Jackson's shoulders, and the three of them disappeared in an instant.

MILENCIA AND ANNABETH—armed with a decimator — visited the headmistress of the Roma School.

"You are very brave to have exposed yourself to come here," the woman said.

"We need a place to continue our work," Milencia responded, "and we are hoping we can use the school's lower level. I remember a huge room that you turned into a ballroom of sorts to teach students to dance and move."

"I've been informed by Dame Erato that on some realms, it is called a gymnasium," the headmistress said.

"It has high ceilings and enough open space for us to continue drilling the women remaining in our militia, and it will be hidden from prying eyes intent on stopping us," Milencia added.

"Are children using it now?" Annabeth asked.

"Everyone is too scared to allow their children out of their homes. I'm sure you'll find it quite vacant." The headmistress took two keys off a keyring. "The larger key opens the main door. The smaller one opens the room you're interested in. Be careful. You don't want to mistakenly allow anyone dangerous to follow you into the school."

Milencia pocketed the keys. "Thank you."

COMEDIANS ALWAYS BELIEVED they would be safe in their homes, especially residents whose homes floated. They had nothing against the ground, but the air seemed cleaner when they floated above it. To safeguard themselves from drifting away while they slept, the balloon dwellers used tie lines to fasten their homes together at night—like the tail of a giant kite. The homes at either end of the tail tethered themselves to the ground.

The ground dwellers, on the other hand, built their homes on top of underground stables where they kept their livestock. The air wasn't as pleasant for those residents, but they were rewarded with a steady supply of milk and meat, and they used animals for their transportation.

There were also the rafters. They built their homes

on large rafts, and like the balloon dwellers, they tied their rafts together at night to avoid drifting out to sea.

The most affluent Comedians were cliff dwellers. They had spacious homes built into the sides of cliffs, with personal balloon vehicles hooked outside their doors for transport. There was no front yard to speak of—just miles and miles of open air. They believed their domiciles were the best because they were carved into the rock and could not drift away. They also liked being located above the ground where the air was constantly cleansed by ocean breezes. They had the view of the sea that the rafters prided themselves on, without all the nauseating rocking.

Their sense of security changed, however, when Comedians got word that Neli Flo and Abbello Abbato had been kidnapped by grotesque beings. Everyone—except for the cliff dwellers—no longer felt certain about their future safety. The ground dwellers felt most vulnerable of all, but there was nothing for them to do other than go home and wait.

The only Comedian who ventured out in public was Comi City Mayor Milbo Fatufo. He had seen Neli Flo get captured, and he subsequently managed to capture Tropo without too much trouble. He brought the pig to the town hall and fed him, and then he piled a bunch of rugs, one on top of the other, in the corner of a detention cell for the animal to sleep on. Tropo was the offspring of one of Milbo's own prizewinning pigs, and Milbo didn't want anything bad to happen to the animal.

Little did the mayor realize he was the only Comedian who had not taken refuge within the supposed safety of his home. Everyone else had barricaded themselves inside, hoping for the best.

It didn't take long for them to learn their best wasn't good enough.

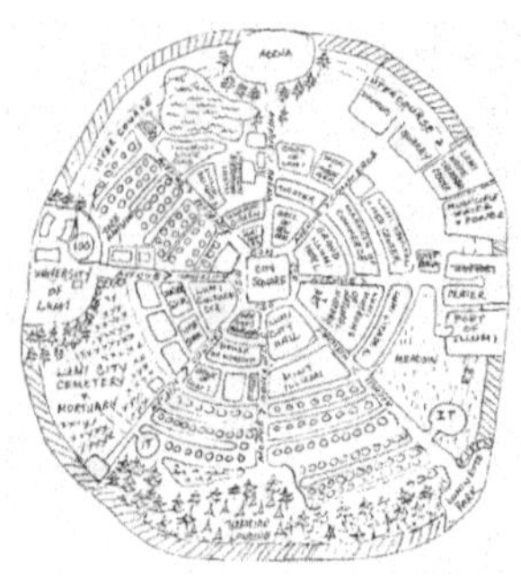

CHAPTER TWENTY

NERO 51 HAD removed himself from the military staging area the previous night "for rest and meditation," although he succeeded at neither. His mind remained too engaged, which prevented him from sleeping. He finally gave up and headed to the facility where the time machine was kept.

His powerful ultimatum the previous evening to Barzic 922 and Kelsis 384 had not gone unheeded. "Imprison curators or pay with your lives."

Overnight, his soldiers managed to capture Numericon curator, Pi; Inspiracon curator, Issiopia; Scientico curator, Galon Senter; and Educon curator, Dr. Infinitis.

It's not a full-sweep, but it's a start, he thought when he arrived at the hangar and was informed of their capture.

"The curators are locked in a containment cell in Building Eight," Barzic 922 said.

"And what are we doing, General, to capture the others?" Nero 51 asked.

"Apprehending curators on realms we have already invaded is more difficult than seizing them from cities that have not yet seen our troops. Realms like Adventura, Dramatica, and Mysteriose are well aware of our intentions, and they are doing their best to thwart us."

Nero 51's demeanor didn't change but his voice carried a menacing stillness. "Are you saying their best efforts are better than our own?"

"N-no," the general stuttered. "We are working on a strategy now that will deliver them into our tentacles."

"When, General?"

"Soon," the general said. "We're working non-stop and will have them in custody very soon."

"You have one day, General. If you and Kelsis 384 do not deliver them by this time tomorrow, you will not live to see the sun rise the following morning."

A platoon of soldiers marched toward the general. The platoon leader saluted Barzic 922 with two tentacles. "We are prepped and ready to go."

"Where are you sending them?" Nero 51 asked.

"Comedia," the general answered. "We've already taken their curator. We are ready to build encampments and start rounding up the rest of them."

"Carry on," Nero 51 said, "but don't forget your primary mission. As I already said, you have one day."

Pru Tellerence may not have planned to have a lot of pomp, but she certainly did not want to introduce her daughter in an atmosphere of gloom. Most Luminans knew nothing of what transpired in the other realms, but they took their cues from the overseers. Ever since the Terrorian invasions began, the overseers had refrained from leaving the College of Deans, and their mood had been grim. The citizens of Lumi, without being consciously aware of it, had dialed down their behavior and acted more soberly than usual if that were possible.

Pru Tellerence wanted to eradicate the somber atmosphere for her child's sake and arranged for music, dancers, balloons, and a menagerie of cuddly animals for the youngster's party.

⌘ *What are you doing?*

★ *Planning Bel's celebration.*

⌘ *We had agreed to keep it low-key.*

Pru Tellerence looked up from her list. ★ *I am keeping it low-key. There is no parade. The public isn't invited. There will be no commemorative souvenirs handed out. I did commission someone to make a doll in Bel's likeness, but only the one doll for Bel herself, and I swore the doll maker to secrecy.*

⌘ *You informed a private citizen that there is a youngster you wish to commemorate with a likeness of herself?* His voice increased a notch. ⌘ *Pruelle, how is that low-key?*

★ *No one here will know. Ingur Aguri is taking care of it.*

⌘ *So, now we're including Romanticans within our trusted spiral of doom?*

★ *As far as anyone there will know, Ingur Aguri is giving her "grandchild" a wonderful gift.*

⌘ *Just…keep it restrained. I do not want anyone outside these walls to know we're celebrating.*

She chewed on her lip. ★ *They might hear the music. Or see the balloons peeping over the top of the walled garden.*

⌘ *Pruelle!*

★ *Is that so bad?*

⌘ *Yes. What do you think people with think— after several realms have been invaded and some libraries destroyed—if we host a celebration?*

⚲ *Excuse me. I'm sorry to interrupt.*

Neither Ryden Simmdry nor Pru Tellerence had seen Reichel Bean, the dean of Comedia, approach. The dean's eyes appeared to be bloodshot.

⌘ *Is something wrong?*

⚲ *Quite. It seems my curator has been captured by the Terrorians. He had his diary in his pocket and managed to inform me. He is not alone. He said he's incarcerated with five other curators, and they surmise the Terrorians are on a spree to capture them all.*

⌘ *Has he overheard any of their plans?*

⚲ *Even if he has, he wouldn't be able to translate what they said.*

⌘ *Of course. I've gotten used to Johanna Charette being able to cast her own translation spell.*

⚲ *She can do that?*

⌘ *Yes. Assemble the others at midiodi. There is something we may be able to do.*

FURST STOPPED AT Pondor's office before going to the library. Pondor's staff told the curator the judge had not come to work that morning, and that he was not at home, or at least he wasn't answering his door.

"Not sick, I hope he is," Furst said.

"Not know, we do," Pondor's clerk answered.

"Go to his home, I will. Find him, I must." With that, the curator spun on his heel and exited the courthouse.

He heard two men speaking loudly, although they did not appear to be fighting. He walked a little closer to hear what they were saying. "Like they were wrapped in glass, our people they picked up, and with them, disappeared. Try to get free, our people did not. Strange, it was."

"Talking about, what are you?" Furst hurried to ask.

"Back, the invaders are," one of the men answered. "Taking prisoners, they are."

"Where," Furst practically shouted.

"The far side of town, I saw them in," he said.

"By Pondor's house, you saw them?"

"Nearby, yes."

Furst took off running, but every few feet, he would leap in order to get there faster. He pounded on Pondor's door. When he got no answer, he opened the door and went inside. There was no sign of the judge. He went out back and saw Pondor's tools scattered about and pulled weeds, wilting from exposure. He picked up a small spade. The handle remained wet from the previous evening's dew. *Treat his tools this way, Pondor would never*, Furst thought. He looked around but found no other signs that Pondor was there. *Terrorians!*

THE ADVENTURANS WORKED through the night, modifying laser guns to shoot ultrafast light pulses. They heard from ChemCharge that the company had already started producing the catalyst. And dozens of Engyro workers were due to arrive that afternoon to start putting everything together.

While they waited. Prophet DANIEL p. coordinated the placement of the laser guns, checking and rechecking Prophet DAVID l.'s calculations every step of the way.

Time quickly evaporated. The actual procedure would not take long, once it was put into place, but they needed recovery time as well. They needed time to re-energize their infrastructure and hook everything up before they ran out of juice.

A MASSIVE NUMBER of people in close quarters with inferior sanitary conditions and food supplies spelled trouble. Mysteriose was the first realm to succumb.

It started with a rumbling cough and crusty eyes. Regardless of who initiated the infection, within hours, almost a quarter of the people in the detention camp were infected. Three hours later, nearly a third were sick, and by the end of the day, eighty percent of the Mysterians in captivity suffered from the illness. By that time, the symptoms had worsened to bloody sputum and diarrhea.

ODYON'S NEW HOME would be deceiving to anyone looking at it from the front. The grand, three-level palace had a sweeping double-door on the main level that took visitors into a large entry hall with staircases on either side leading up to the second level. While it appeared to be just one room on an extensive first floor of a lavish home, it was actually the only room on that floor of the residence, which was built into the side of a hill. The remaining interior spanned the two upper floors. The second-floor drawing room connected to an expansive terrace, surrounded by an intricate stone balustrade. That morning, Odyon had chosen to enjoy his morning cup of coffee—a brew Luminans abhorred, but many off-landers cherished—on the terrace.

The Illumini Palace, as he chose to call his home, was set back from the main byway, next to the University of Lumi campus. The home's location placed it close to the domed enclosure for the Library of Origination and its walled garden.

Odyon could easily observe the dome from where he sat, although he could not see beyond the high wall that surrounded the library. Everything appeared to be peaceful beneath a clear lilac sky, and until Odyon devised a more structured picture of what he wanted his future on Lumina to be, he craved this atmosphere.

If only this chair were more comfortable. He had made some minor purchases for his new home but after sitting on the cold, diamond bench, he suddenly dreamed of a plusher seating option. Unfortunately, the furniture he preferred was not indigenous to Lumina, which had a limited and state-protected supply of trees. He wondered how he could import what he wanted from Fantasia. *Nero 51 and his time machine would certainly come in handy now.*

Zenith Fullova presented Peer Meap with several pairs of scramblers and an equal number of decimators to help the Juveniles protect themselves. He also replenished their rapidly dwindling stores of chocolate.

He carried an especially large basket of chocolate

with him.

§ *Where is young Master Waxmo?*

"I had to send him home," Peer Meap said. "He was asleep on his feet and kept falling over."

§*Do me a favor. Please tell him this basket is especially for him.*

Peer Meap laughed. "I'll do that."

Zenith Fullova handed him the basket before saying goodbye. §*I have business on Lumina and must go. Stay safe, Peer Meap.* A moment later, the overseer disappeared.

Peer Meap called the Juveniles together and handed out weapons, instructing them to be very careful and mindful of each other.

"What about that basket of chocolate?" Pokkie asked staring at the basket.

"Off limits," Peer Meap said. "It's for Waxmo. And to keep you from getting ideas about testing it for him, I'll take it home." He picked up the basket and headed toward his dwelling.

He was only a few feet away when something caught his eye—a large hulking mass. He looked around rapidly, wishing he had kept one of the weapons for himself. Too late. He soon realized he could no longer move.

The Terrorians had captured another curator.

JENNIFER O'LOUGHLIN kept her eye on the newswire feed and listened to reports on the radio all day, writing as much of the plane crash story as possible. Her phone calls to the FAA only told her there would be a late-afternoon press conference. *There's no way I can send a crew out for that. They'd never get back in time.* She would have to work with what she had.

Every crew that returned to the newsroom asked if she had heard about the plane crash. She told them not to worry about any story other than their own. Luke and Logan were the last to walk in.

"What took you so long?" Jennifer asked.

"There's a press conference this afternoon, and I wanted to see what time they would hold it, but Luke made me come back."

"Thank goodness," she muttered. "Luke, could you log a couple of soundbites and check the footage while Logan tells me what he saw?"

"I need to check the soundbites," Logan said. "How can I put together a package without knowing what people said?"

Jennifer sighed. "First, we don't have time for that. Second, you're not even officially on the roster and new reporters have to earn the right to do packages. Third, I've already written most of the story for the anchor to track."

"It's my footage. Shot on my equipment. By me. I own it, and if you don't let me package it my way, I'm walking."

As if on cue, a courier walked through the door. "Hey Jen. Here's the spec footage we shot of the plane crash. Myles says if you use it, you'll have to pay."

"Thanks," Jennifer said taking the package. She turned to Logan. "What were you saying?"

Logan stared at the package in her hand.

Luke rounded the corner. "Hey, Logan, can I have your stuff? I need to get those sound bites."

Jennifer cleared her throat. "Logan's not sure he

wants us to use his video."

Luke's eyebrows shot up. "What?"

Jennifer looked at Logan, "Do you want to tell him, or should I?"

"Forget it." Logan's shoulders slumped. "You can use my video. What do you want me to do?"

MAL, JOHANNA, AND JACKSON materialized in a private corner of the Grand Illumi Hotel.

"Is this the hotel we stayed at last time?" Jackson asked.

"It is. And now, as seasoned curators, you'll probably be considered honored guests."

They arrived at their rooms and unpacked, before heading out with Mal.

"It's still early," Mal said. "The celebration won't be starting for a couple of hours. I need to talk with Ryden Simmdry and get caught up on what's happening. Is there someplace special I could direct the two of you to?"

"There's gonna be food at this shindig, right?" Jackson asked.

"I believe so," Mal answered.

"So, that lets out lunch," Jackson finished.

"Is there a library or a museum we could see?" Johanna asked.

Mal scratched his head. "Well, the library would be the Library of Origination. You were both there for Plato Indelicat's memorial."

"Some memorial," Jackson said, "considering he's still alive."

Mal stopped walking. "Actually, that makes me

wonder."

"About what?" Johanna asked.

"Here I am, thinking you're returning as famous curators who helped keep Nero 51 from infiltrating the College of Overseers. But the Luminans probably think you're here to undergo the testing and initiation for new curators. They won't remember that you've been here before because of the temporal rift. As far as they're concerned, you're new hires."

"Fresh faces in the *land of no*." Jackson made finger quotes.

"There is a museum you could visit," Mal said. "The Luminan Museum of Natural History has an extensive collection of artifacts and exhibits on the formation of the realm and the Illumini Constellation."

Jackson moaned. "I don't want a history lesson. I get enough of that in school."

"I think we should probably go with you, Mal," Johanna said. "Maybe we can help out."

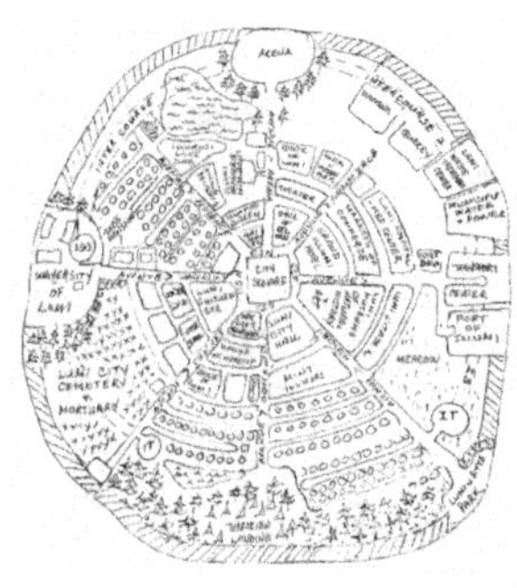

CHAPTER TWENTY-ONE

✠HOW CAN WE *be sure they are specifically trying to capture curators?*

⌘According to Abbello Abbato, they already have six of them.

♱He told me they are being kept together, and he said the room they are being held in appears quite secure.

§What about the other prisoners? I know the Terrorians have transported several Juveniles out of their realm. Where are they keeping prisoners who are not curators?

♱We have no way of knowing.

❊Our question would be answered if a curator and a citizen would volunteer to be captured and both had diaries. Then they could each tell us their final location.

⌘That is a lot to ask. We cannot assure their safety.

❊Of course we can. If we know where they are, we can swoop in using the transporter in our miters and bring them

back with us.

⨎*In that case, why couldn't a few of us transport to Abbello Abbato's location and remove all our curators?*

⌘*An excellent suggestion.*

PONDOR HAD AN excruciating headache. *What happened?* He tried to rub his head but found he couldn't move his arm. *My wrists are bound!* He thought about the Terrorians. He'd almost been killed, but then Dungen had surprised him—saving him from the Terrorian. *So, what happened?*

He could only think of two possibilities. *Either the Terrorians prevailed and I am a prisoner, or Dungen prevailed and has taken me prisoner.* Either way, the outlook wasn't good. As it was, his head was killing him, and trying to move his arms only made the bindings on his wrists tighter.

He was inside a dark place—a blessing in disguise considering how much his head hurt—but it didn't help that his mind struggled to make sense of what had happened.

He took a deep breath and let it out slowly. He didn't like the odors surrounding him, but that was the least of his problems.

He heard a noise nearby. There was a scraping sound as a narrow shaft of light entered the room. In a moment, his questions would all be answered.

MILENCIA AND ANNABETH trod quietly through the shadows provided by the cover of trees. They returned to the area where the militairres had built their encampment before being captured by Terrorians.

Annabeth stepped on a branch, and the resounding

crack sent shivers up Milencia's spine. "Please watch where you're walking," she whispered.

Annabeth simply nodded.

Inside the camp, the remains of a burnt *pallid* hung from a charred spit. Insects crawled all over the food left behind by militairres. Other than that, everything seemed unchanged. Milencia found an assortment of fighting sticks, bows, quivers, knives and decimators in the lean-tos, and together she and Annabeth collected as many as they could hold.

"Isn't that your sister's cape? And there's Patrice's tote," Annabeth said. "We should grab those."

"No," Milencia answered. "Leave them for another day. Right now, our priority is weapons. We must be able to defend ourselves. What good is a cape or a tote, if we're dead?"

Annabeth shuddered but continued to make her point. "If we take the cape, we can bundle all the decimators together inside of it and use the tote to carry the knives. Then we can slip the bows and quivers over our arms."

Together, they carried many of the weapons back to the school, although they had to leave most of the fighting sticks behind because they were unwieldy. The pair returned to the school at a much slower pace than they had used earlier in the day. "I hate leaving uniforms and backpacks behind," Milencia said, "but we can always return for them. And then we can retrieve the fighting sticks, too."

They neared the edge of the woods and hesitated. The open area appeared to be empty, but they could not see through buildings or behind shrubbery.

"Do you want to take a moment to rest?"

Annabeth answered Milencia's question with one of her own. "Why should we rest now, when we're so close?"

"An invader could easily be lurking out of sight, just like we are right now. Once we start crossing the open area, we don't want to be easy targets, so I suggest we run at full speed. But we've lugged a lot of weapons quite a way, so I'd like to know if you want to rest before we need to sprint?"

Annabeth took a deep breath. "Don't worry about me. I can channel my fear straight to my legs for extra energy."

"In that case—"

A twig snapped not too far away, suddenly ending the conversation.

THE TIME MACHINE took shape in an open field on Comedia, and two troopers disembarked. An odd shadow from above caught their attention, and the soldiers looked up to see a large number of structures floating above them—each tied to the next one.

One of the Terrorians raised his weapon to shoot at the vessels, but the platoon leader used the end of his own decimator to push down the barrel of the offending weapon. "Not yet. Nero 51 and General Barzic 922 gave specific instructions not to proceed until our full contingent of soldiers are in place."

The time machine reappeared with more Terrorians.

"It won't be long," the platoon leader said. "We'll be able to strike within one or two measures."

Two more groups of soldiers arrived before the first egg launched. It hit the soldier who originally wanted to shoot down the Comedians without waiting for the others, directly on top of his head. As he wiped it away, he glared at the platoon leader. "Perhaps there are enough of us here, now, for me to take aim?" A soft, squishy vegetable hit him in the eye. He raised his decimator. "No," the platoon leader shouted. "We do this by the book."

Within moments, fruits, vegetables, and other items rained down on the Terrorians from the domiciles above.

"Enough," the platoon leader barked. "Take aim." Immediately, nearly two dozen decimators locked onto the Comedians above.

"Fire," the platoon leader commanded.

JENNIFER O'LOUGHLIN simply wanted Logan to describe what he saw at the site of the plane crash. She wanted his insight into the mood of the responders and the survivors. Then she told him to monitor the live press conference on a local station for anything new. It was almost as if he wasn't there. The anchor, Derrick Martin, delivered the story, and in Logan's eyes, Derrick got all the glory. *He didn't even write the story. Jennifer did.*

Logan went home early and crashed in front of the TV to see how the *real* news stations covered *his* story. He had a lot of the same elements they had, but they had video from the press conference. And because their reporters stayed on the scene, they had live shots and stand-ups. *Why can't we go live?* Logan wondered. *We could live stream from the field onto the Internet.* He grabbed his tablet and started researching live stream hosts. *I bet I could do this myself.* He had a computer. He had video equipment. He would tell his father the monthly hosting fee was for his internship. He also needed his own website. *I'll call it* The Elliott Report. *GRUNT might be okay for picking up a few reporting techniques and making connections, not to mention appeasing my father, but* The Elliott Report *will be more than my claim to fame. It will be the start of my own news empire.*

CREATING PROPHET DAVID L.'s catalyst proved to be a challenge. ChemCharge relied on a combination of energy from fueled generators and a wind bank off the coast of Cada to fulfill its obligation to the realm. They worked non-stop, but some bugs in the system slowed them down. Finally, by the end of the day, they started making progress.

They diverted some power to the vehicles they would use to transport the catalyst and started loading conveyances so the first shipments would arrive in Venit by morning.

Not too far away in the city of Silic, Engyro received word that their workers would soon be required. Skilled hu*bots entered caravans that would carry them to the capital city. The turn of a crank generated a spark that ignited solid fuel within the vehicle, and the spin of its wheels generated additional power to not only get it where it needed to go but also to recharge the workers. Hu*bots hooked up to special outlets inside large trailers that would keep them energized during the trip, so they would arrive ready-to-go.

THE MYSTERIANS' ILLNESS took on a new symptom. As the disease progressed, blisters formed on their skin and slowly grew until their skin could no longer contain the pressure inside. The exploding pustules were reviled by the neighbors of the victims, and exposure insured that all touched by the expelled mucus quickly became similarly infected, until every incarcerated Mysterian had them. Their skin hurt when touched, but the explosions relieved pressure and reduced pain, at least for the Mysterians. Their Terrorian guards soon learned they were not immune to the infection, and their resulting blisters were larger and more painful than those of their prisoners.

HUE THE ELDER kept the overseers informed of the conditions in the detention camps. He had evaded capture and did his best to use his freedom to spy on the Terrorians and the prisoners. Everything he learned was transmitted, via diary, to Proteus Bligh.

THAT EVENING, RYDEN Simmdry and Proteus Bligh surprised Hue when they showed up at the cave where he hid.

⌘ *What can we do to alleviate the discomfort of the afflicted?*

"I assume you mean our own people and not the Terrorians, who are also being felled by the infection.

Ψ *Really? I would think the Terrorians with their thick skin were made of hardier stuff.*

"No. It seems the Mysterians' exploding pustules affect Terrorian skin like acid. They scream out in pain when they are sprayed, and within the hour, they are incapacitated."

⌘ *Unusual, but not unheard of. Many civilizations in the past have been ravaged by the diseases of a conquering nation. Although in this case, the tables have been turned.*

Ψ *Perhaps we could create our own bio-weapon.*

⌘*I think we would serve a greater purpose by supplying a salve for the prisoners.*

"How will we make sure it falls into the right hands?"

⌘*I know it seems like we are asking a lot, Hue, but we would like to transport you into the encampments to disburse it.*

"I could be caught."

⌘*That would also serve our purpose.*

The curator was taken aback. "You wish me to get caught?"

⌘*A number of curators have already been captured and are being held together in an undisclosed location. If you were to be captured, you could be our link to that location, and we could go in and transport the curators back to Lumina. Do you have your diary with you?*

"Always."

⌘*Make sure you hold onto it. It will be the beacon that allows us to liberate you.*

Ψ*But first, you must make sure the Mysterians are medicated. I will transport you into the camps. Once that is done, you can allow yourself to be caught.*

"Do you have this salve with you?"

⌘*No. I must first visit the prisoners to determine what they need, and then return to Lumina to create it.* Ryden Simmdry removed a small pouch and took out a pinch of powder and chanted a spell as he sprinkled it on himself, and then on his fellow overseer, and on Hue the Elder. ⌘*That should protect us from contracting the ailment. Let us go now. The sooner I know what we need, the sooner we can administer it.*

*

GENERAL BARZIC 922 FELT his tentacles droop. "We have only captured one other curator?"

"Yes, General. The one from the realm with all the kiddlets."

The general toughened up. "Nero 51 will not be content with that. He wants all of them captured. Now!"

"They are very well-defended," another soldier said.

"Kelsis 384," the general barked, "which curators remain to be captured?"

Kelsis 384 looked over his chart. "Prophet IAN c. from Adventura, Furst of Dramatica, Hue the Elder from Mysteriose, and Johanna Charette of Fantasia."

The first soldier rubbed his tentacles together. "Mysteriose and Adventura were previously our allies. They will not respond well to our aggression. And Nero 51 has said repeatedly he wants to save Johanna Charette for last and capture her himself."

"Why haven't you taken Furst?" the general asked.

"I will, General. I will return to Dramatica now and do my best to capture him."

The general thought about the ultimatum Nero 51 had given him and Kelsis 384. He decided to share their fate. "Your life depends on it."

FURST RETURNED TO his library. He didn't care if there were Terrorians arriving in droves in Dramoni. *Scared, I am not. Write to Pru Tellerence, I will. Together, to stop them, something we can do, there must be.*

Instead of entering the library through the front door, he leapt from the front path to the bell tower opening.

Through the secret passage I will go.

Furst took the hidden tunnel from the bell tower to the library stairwell. Quietly, he poked his head out looking for Terrorians. *Here, no one is.*

Breathing a sigh of relief, he entered the library and used his diary to contact Pru Tellerence.

Furst, I cannot visit you right now. I have personal business to attend to on Lumina.

Furst sighed, still staring at the diary. A lot of Dramaticans were being captured, and he felt hopeless. The pages riffled. *Better yet, why don't you come to Lumina. I cannot leave right now, but I will come in a little while to escort you here.*

He closed the diary and placed it in his pocket. He made sure everything looked secure before walking to the front door to leave. It was newly built and well-fortified and looked more like a work of art than a simple entry door.

He pulled it open, and his eyes grew wide. Before he could utter a word, he found himself captured in a force field. He tried to wiggle his diary out of his pocket but found it impossible. *Pru Tellerence,* he thought. *If write to her I can't, and more Terrorians have arrived tell her, surely captured herself she will be.*

NOT SO FAR away, Pondor struggled with the knowledge of his own abduction, except in his case, he was taken prisoner by his son. "Why, Dungen?" he asked when he first realized who had bound him and tied him to a chair. His son snarled at him. "You took me prisoner, first. You sent me to jail. I thought I'd share the experience with you."

"They will find you, you know," Pondor reasoned with him. "I'm a judge, and as soon as I don't appear in court, they will start searching for me."

"Terrorians have invaded our world. No one is going to look for you. They will think you were taken prisoner. Your life is in my hands. And your death will be, too."

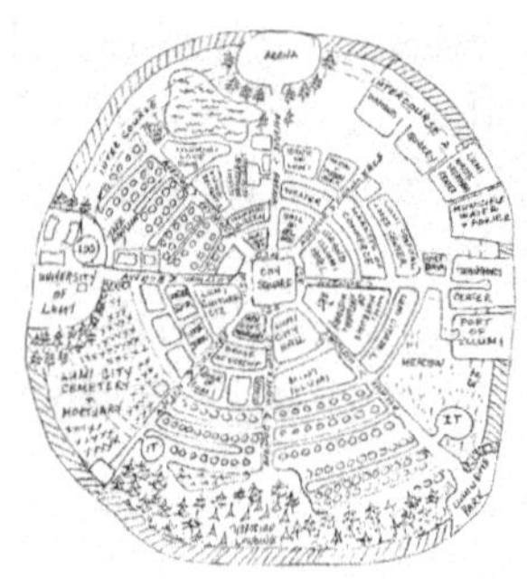

CHAPTER TWENTY-TWO

The Library of Origination was buzzing with activity. One overseer festooned the walls with balloons and banners, while another created an enclosure for small animals.

"Wow," Jackson said. "It looks like they're giving Bel the royal treatment."

"She is royalty," Mal stated. "She's the child of two overseers. You can't find a greater pedigree than that."

"Does she even know what that means?" Johanna asked. "Or is she like most three-year-olds, just trying to navigate her way through life?"

The bleat of a small animal interrupted their conversation. "This is definitely a little kid's party," Jackson said. "A classmate once invited me to a party celebrating his and his baby sister's birthday. They were four years apart in age but were born on the same day. So, his friends ate pizza and burgers and played Xbox, while she and her friends petted baby animals, and wore hats made out of balloons by a clown."

"I can understand that happening at home, "Johanna said. "I guess I thought a party here would be different."

Mal laughed. "I imagine three-year-olds throughout the universe are all attracted to furry little creatures and big, bright, shiny things that float."

"But isn't Bel supposed to be thousands of years old? This is pretty childish for a three-thousand-and-three-year-old." Jackson waved his arm to encompass the entire space and smacked an armful of balloons carried by a Luminan girl walking behind him. One of them escaped her grip and floated away. "Sorry," he said, as he helped her corral the remaining balloons. "I didn't realize you were there."

"It's okay," the girl answered. "There are so many balloons here, I don't think anyone will miss that one."

Johanna and Jackson helped with the decorations until every last ribbon was curled and every flat surface held at least a dozen balloons.

Pru Tellerence stopped Ryden Simmdry. ★ *There is an odd enchantment on the library that is preventing some of the animals from entering. Would you please remove it?*

⌘*If there is a spell in place, it is there for a reason.*

★*Please. Just for this gathering. Then you can put it back in place.*

He closed his eyes for a moment before murmuring a few words, then looked at her. ⌘*It is done.*

Pru Tellerence surveyed the garden. ★*Everything looks perfect.* She chanted something before raising both arms outward. At first, it looked like a mist formed above the garden, but as Pru Tellerence lowered her arms, what appeared to be a film settled down on everything, slightly dulling its shine.

"What is that?" Johanna asked.

Jackson squinted. "Is it dust?"

★*It's a protective layer. It will keep the decorations in place and protect the food. It will be impossible to tell this was set up early. Everything will be bright and fresh, and after a period of rest, so will we.*

"If I wanted to heist one of those little cakes from the edge of the table, would I be able to?"

★*Go ahead. Try it.*

Jackson nonchalantly walked over to the edge of the table and surreptitiously slid his hand toward the cake stand. When he got within an inch of his target, it repelled his hand. He tried again, more blatantly. He still could not grab the confection. "It's protected by a force field."

★*If that's what you want to call it. I think of it as more of a sealant. It keeps out air and seals in freshness. It stops the balloons from bobbing every time someone walks past and keeps them from getting loose and possibly flying off. It allows us to freeze everything in place for a short time, until we need it—and allows everything to return to use at full advantage.*

"How did you do it?" Johanna asked.

★*It's a chant Ryden Simmdry taught me that he said he picked up on Fantasia, so you may be familiar with it.* She lowered her voice and whispered it to Johanna. ★*You also need a summoning spell, which I perform with my arms. Together they give me the desired result.*

Johanna took the blade she had used to curl ribbons

and placed it in front of her. She recited the chant Pru Tellerence had taught her and moved her arms in the same way. A tiny veil of mist formed and settled over the blade. She turned to Jackson. "See if you can pick it up."

Jackson reached for the blade, but his hand was repelled. He tried again. He looked at Johanna. "I want to learn how to do that."

"When we get home."

"Why not here? Now?"

"Would you feel embarrassed if you tried and it didn't work and everyone here saw you fail?"

One side of Jackson's face pulled into a lopsided grimace. "Yeah."

"At home, you can practice."

"I guess."

"I'll work with you until you can do it."

His face relaxed. "Okay."

"Okay," Johanna repeated.

ODYON RETURNED HOME content that his order would be carried out. It would take a little time, but apparently, they made something similar to what he requested on the outcrop of Myco.

He had also stopped to buy books on the history and culture of Lumina and decided to enjoy an afternoon of reading on his terrace.

He draped one of the smaller rugs he had purchased across a hard, diamond chair and tried to find a comfortable position. As he read, he found the voices coming from behind the university walls annoying. *What happened to the peace and quiet of this morning?* He glared at the open space above the walls, as if commanding the very air to muffle the sound of the occupants. Instead, he saw a single balloon rise into the air. *A balloon?* It piqued his curiosity.

Why would the College of Overseers have any need for a child's plaything? The absurdity of it played on his mind. He could devise no answer to what the balloon might mean, other than the possible future deafening screeches of small children disturbing his peace.

He considered changing into a beam of light to inspect the overseers' premises but knew it would be a waste of time. He looked for the balloon that had escaped and saw it floating off in the distance, appearing to be no larger than a pea. Finally, it disappeared.

He switched his gaze back to the garden wall and waited to see if another balloon would follow its predecessor to freedom.

Dee-Dee watched in horror as the Terrorians captured Peer Meap, and she screamed when the monsters carried him away. Her fellow Juveniles stopped what they were doing, to focus their energies on their beloved curator's abduction. Instead, they should have paid attention to everything else going on around them, which is why they soon found themselves trapped in similar force fields.

Capturing Peer Meap turned out to be the Terrorians' only easy accomplishment on Juvenilia. Building detention cells that would hold Juveniles was something else, entirely. It wasn't that the troopers couldn't build the facilities. They knew exactly what they needed to do. However, they wanted Juvenile prisoners to do some of the work, and that proved to be too much to ask.

When asked to dig, the Juveniles threw shovels full of dirt back at the Terrorians. When placed in holding cells, which had dirt floors, the Juveniles tunneled out. And whenever they found a large rock, they set it aside to use as ammunition.

To make matters worse, the older kids who had managed to hide their scramblers from their captors, would silently aim Foggy at the nearest trooper, and pull the trigger. Those soldiers would wander aimlessly, while the Juveniles hooted with laughter.

"This is more fun than Bullaroot," Waxmo said.

"Yeah," Guffle and Flugle agreed.

Whenever they "fogged" one of the troopers guarding the camp, Duddu and Marbol would work on the locks holding the pens closed. "It's not much of a lock," Marbol said. "It's more like a long pin slipped through a bunch of holes with a knot tied at the bottom to stop it from sliding up."

Duddu got to work untying the knot, and they were soon able to come and go as they pleased. However, many of them preferred to return to the pens and wreak havoc on the Terrorians' sanity.

Milencia hoisted one of the decimators to her shoulder. "Run. I'll cover you."

Annabeth took off across the field. Milencia heard another twig snap and shot with the decimator in that general direction.

"Oh—"

That doesn't sound like an invader, Milencia thought to herself. She silently made her way through the trees until she found Stasia frozen in a force field. "Sorry, Stass," Milencia whispered as she reversed the force field. She turned quickly to check on Annabeth and watched her enter the school. "We have to make a run for it across the field."

"I'm ready when you are," Stasia answered moving her arms to make sure she was all right.

The two of them took off across the field and were nearly at the door when they were immobilized. Milencia tried to crane her head to see where the shots came from and saw two Terrorians come out of the woods. "Like I said, sorry, Stass."

The Terrorians took their time and were about halfway to their victims when one of them stopped moving, and then, the other. A moment later, Milencia and Stasia felt their force fields evaporate and hurried toward the school. Annabeth let them inside.

"We can't stay here," Milencia said. "They saw us enter and will immediately barge in here when their friends find them."

"Maybe they won't say anything," Stasia reasoned.

"There's only one way to keep them from talking," Annabeth answered. She looked at Milencia and Milencia nodded. Annabeth returned to the window she had just used to shoot the Terrorians and eliminated them completely.

"We still can't stay here," Milencia said.

"Why?" Annabeth asked.

"Because if any of their friends saw what we just did, we're as good as dead."

THE FORCE FIELDS that formed around the balloon homes affected the exterior shells but not the people inside of them. The Comedians were able to climb between vessels and go about their usual business. Many of them had had a peaceful night of sleep because their homes didn't knock into one another like they usually did when the wind caught them. So, they slept soundly and woke up fully rested.

Unfortunately, the Terrorians pulled their victims down shortly after first light, and the Comedians found themselves in their enemies' clutches. Once again, they threw everything they had at the invaders, but it wasn't enough. Soon, the balloon dwellers, the ground dwellers, and the rafters, all found themselves being herded into a makeshift detention camp.

Mayor Milbo Fatufo prided himself on being a trusted user of the Library of Illumination and a close friend of Abbello Abbato. When the curator first told Milbo about a possible invasion by Terroria, the two had studied up on the threatening realm, learning everything they could about its residents. Milbo had laughed when an anxious Terrorian shot out of the open pages of *Laevus Terroria* running for his life while being pursued by a small white cat.

As Milbo watched the chaos unfold below his cliff dwelling, he thought of the scene from the book and hatched an idea. It required a bit of work, but Milbo wouldn't be able to venture out anyway, because of the invaders, so he may as well put his time to, what he considered, good use.

He found a trunk of animal hides in the back of the cave and looked for one he knew he owned—the pelt of a giant albino bornivor, a huge rabbit-like animal about as big as a wild hog—just the right size to repurpose into a feline costume for Neli Flo's pig, Tropo.

Milbo worked all morning, using odd bits to

fashion a cat's ears and the quills of a *pattootu* plant to create the whiskers. *Tropo is going to hate wearing a mask, but we must hide his snout.*

When he finished his work, Milbo sat back and chuckled. It would be worth it to see how the Terrorians reacted to a rampaging Tropo disguised as a big, fat, white cat.

AFTER SPENDING THE night preparing a salve for the Mysterians, Ryden Simmdry and Proteus Bligh traveled to Hue the Elder's location on Mysteriose, and all three of them transported to the detention cells.

Their sudden appearance startled some of the occupants. "Hue has been caught, and so have two overseers," one person gasped. Others soon gathered around to see if he spoke the truth.

"We have not been captured," Hue explained. "We are here with salve and potions for your ailments."

"We are dying," a witch said. "Save yourselves, if you can."

Ryden Simmdry mumbled something unintelligible and waved his hands. He and Proteus Bligh shrunk until their size and their clothing soon resembled the other Mysterians. They still wore hats, but their headgear now resembled close-fitting turbans.

"My goodness," Hue the Elder exclaimed, "that was interesting."

Ryden Simmdry smiled. ⌘*Pass out the salves and potions.*

Hue handed a vial to the witch who had spoken. "Drink this."

She eyed it warily and then gulped it down. Nothing happened. Several minutes passed. "What is it supposed to—" She closed her eyes, dropped the vial on the ground, then took a deep breath before reopening them. "My lungs. I can breathe." She nudged Ryden Simmdry. "You have salve?"

He pointed to a small container and she quickly opened it and spread it on her arms. Once she did, everyone else became eager to follow her example. After everyone in that cell responded to treatment, the trio traveled to the next one, and when they had completed their rounds at that detention camp, they traveled to others.

Their work was too extensive to go unnoticed, and soon they heard Terrorian guards entering the enclosure where they worked. ⌘*Do what you must*, Ryden Simmdry informed Hue the Elder, and the overseers disappeared before the Terrorians ever saw them.

ON ADVENTURA, THE earliest deliveries of the catalyst coincided with the arrival of the first convoys of workers, and soon, Venit buzzed with specialists readying laser guns for their eleventh-hour effort to save their world.

A group of leader*bots decided their curator needed to be on the scene as they readied to put their plan in motion. Prophet IAN c. had steadily recovered while attached to a charging unit, and Prophet DANIEL p. retrieved him for the final thrust.

At first, IAN c. appeared disoriented, having been in a semi-comatose state for a while. But once prophets DANIEL p., DAVID l., and PATRICK c. explained what had transpired since his collapse, his thought processes gelled, and he began to regain the efficiency of mind and the unique abilities that made him a superior leader.

The four hu*bots strode into the main laboratory, now being used as a control center. Several large lasers were strategically placed in this facility alone, with the progress of other laser locations being shown on dozens of large screens.

IAN c. nodded. Hu*bots couldn't smile, but if they could, the curator would be grinning like a clown. When he was last awake, their condition had seemed hopeless. Now a spark of optimism warmed his heart, if not the other parts of his body.

He climbed up a short flight of stairs to take his position at the front of the mezzanine that overlooked the work floor, then realized he had forgotten his tablet.

"I'll get it for you," PATRICK c. said.

"No. You are all too busy, here. I will return in a moment."

He left the lab and crossed the hall to the staircase. A door opened and before the curator knew what hit him, he was unable to move.

A Terrorian scanned IAN c. with a small device and gasped when it informed him they had caught another curator. "We must return to Terroria, now."

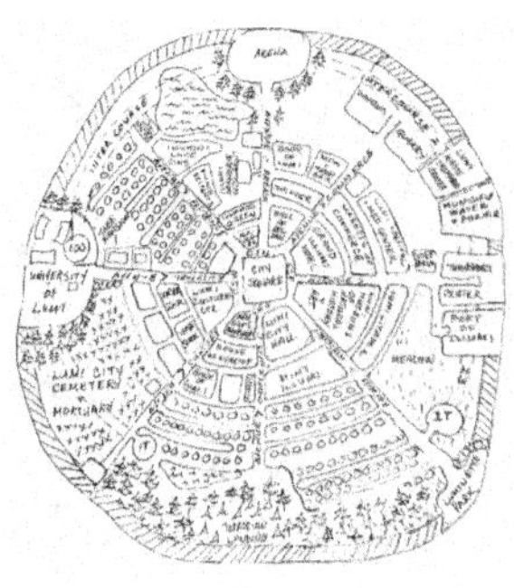

CHAPTER TWENTY-THREE

Milencia, Annabeth, and Stasia argued all night about where to train the new recruits. Realizing they would have already been attacked if seen by the Terrorians, the trio decided to stay put. They assessed the new militairres' skills and divided them into platoons. Whenever a disagreement occurred, Milencia pulled rank and outvoted the other two, citing her former and continuing status as a commander. She ruled with an iron fist. Her demeanor remained cool and calm, but inside she was divided. Part of her was scared, and she feared she would not know what to do when suddenly faced with danger. But, another part of her brain had entered its own little happy zone, and she thrived on being in charge.

"We didn't have much of a dinner," a woman named Lei called out, "and we didn't get any breakfast. So, please tell me we're getting lunch."

Milencia blinked. She had been so overwhelmed by her sudden power, she had completely forgotten about food.

"This is a school. It must have a place to eat. Take two others with you and take stock of what food is available. I'd also like suggestions of how to prepare it to our best advantage. We don't know when or if we can replenish it. So, if there is some, it may have to last."

Lei grabbed two women, and they left in search of a kitchen.

"Wait," Milencia called out.

Lei made a face. "What is it?"

Milencia thrust a decimator in her hands. "Stay alert. And don't be afraid to use this. You never know what you may encounter."

As the three women searched the halls, every unexpected sound caused them to gasp in fright. "Maybe you want to walk with that thing over your shoulder and ready to shoot," one of the women said to Lei, "because the way you're holding it now, we'll be dead if we find one of those beasts out here."

Lei handed her the decimator. "If you're so ready to shoot on sight, you take it."

Nicoletta took the weapon and shouldered it. She aimed it at a chair in the middle of the hallway and pulled the trigger. The chair disappeared. "This will work nicely."

Lei listened at a double door, and when she didn't hear anything, she slowly pushed it open, and finally poked her head inside. "Tables and chairs," she said. "Come on."

The three of them walked inside and then approached another door in the back of the room. Lei put her ear to the door. Her eyes widened. "I hear something," she said so quietly, the others barely heard her. Nicoletta square up in front of the door and nodded. Lei took a deep breath and slowly pushed open the door.

LOGAN'S CELL PHONE rang, yet again. *This is the fifth call from Cassie. Doesn't she realize I'm in the middle of something? If I wasn't busy, I'd have answered her by now. Or not.*

He had awakened early and gone out for a *boffo* coffee—the largest size the Java Joint sold. That and a giant slab of crumb cake sustained him. During the past few hours, he had used the Java Joint's Wi-Fi to purchase a domain name and web host and created *TheElliottReport. com.*

He uploaded the first story he ever did for GRUNT and had just started editing his footage from the plane crash into a package. *I should drive down to the site later and shoot a standup and get additional footage.* Investigators would probably be there for weeks. He planned to follow the entire aftermath on *The Elliott Report.*

He also needed to shoot more footage of the school, and his friends, and the Library of Illumination. That was another story he planned to delve into but right now, the crash was the big story on everybody's mind. And if he could establish his credibility with the plane crash, people would have to believe him about the odd events at the library.

IT DIDN'T TAKE long for Odyon to develop a habit of enjoying breakfast out on his terrace. The weather on Lumina was usually mild under lilac skies, and sitting outside watching a light breeze sway the tops of the trees behind the walled gardens of the Library of Origination was hypnotically pleasing. However, on this particular morning, the annoying hum of voices—loud enough to hear but too quiet to understand—made him scowl with irritation.

The shapeshifter changed himself into a breeze and gently wafted high above the wall to the library garden. He couldn't believe his eyes. *They're defiling the Library of Origination for a child's party?* Everywhere he looked he saw decorations, small animals, and games. *That explains the balloon I saw floating away.*

Pru Tellerence appeared to be all aflutter as she organized everything. *This would be a woman's doing,* Odyon thought.

He quickly lost interest and returned to his terrace, picking up the remains of his breakfast and carrying it inside. At least, there, he wouldn't have to listen to the buzz of droning voices.

Nero 51 stormed into the hangar. "General Barzic 922," he yelled. "Report. Kelsis 384, report."

The two Terrorians stopped what they were doing and rushed over to Nero 51. "Are all the curators residing in my cell?"

"Yes," General Barzic 922 stated, "with the exception of Johanna Charette, for whom, you said, you have very specific plans."

"I have plans for her demise," Nero 51 said flatly. "Not for her capture. You are certain every other curator is in custody?"

"Yes, Nero 51," they said simultaneously. "Except you," General Barzic 922 added.

Nero 51's tentacles stiffened as he stared at the general. "Take me to them," the curator ordered.

They led the curator back to library and descended to subfloor one hundred and one. They followed the maze-like halls to a room at the center and opened the door. Inside, Natalia Dalura, Prophet IAN c., Dr. Infinitis, Galon Senter, Peer Meap, Furst, Abbello Abbato, Issiopia, Hue the Elder, and Pi sat on the floor with their backs to the wall, talking quietly amongst themselves.

Nero 51 stared at each one of them, making sure the General and Kelsis 384 had not made a mistake.

The ten curators all looked up at the Terrorian. "Why have you brought us here?" Dr. Infinitis asked.

Nero 51 didn't answer. Instead, he slammed the door and walked away. *They'll learn why they are here in due time. In the meantime, they can imagine the worst, and then they'll find their idea of the worst is not half as bad as it really will be.*

NEWS OF FURST'S capture by the Terrorians traveled quickly and by morning, everyone knew the curator was no longer there to protect them. Dramaticans tried to fight the invaders but did not do as well without Furst's leadership.

Dungen heard about Furst's capture when he ventured out for supplies. The shopkeeper did not stop boarding up his windows as he told Dungen he would be closed for the foreseeable future. Dungen bought as much as he could carry back to the cabin, and then returned for fuel and tools and whatever else he thought might help if the Terrorians came to Cirra Lake.

He returned to the cabin and built brackets inside the door that could hold a log, in case an invader tried to force the door. Also, he made sure he had a large supply of wood stacked inside along the length of one wall for the fireplace. He had cleaned the shop out of candles and fuel for the oil lamps. He bought as much food as he could find on the shelves and asked the shopkeeper if he had more in the back. When the shopkeeper said no, Dungen suspected he was lying but didn't want to call attention to himself by challenging him.

Pondor watched his son put away his supplies. "If you're thinking of locking me in," Pondor said dryly, "you should consider putting the security bar on the other side of the door."

"You can try to escape if you want. You probably won't get very far. Not even your *wonder boy*, Furst, could escape the Terrorians. They took him prisoner last night, and I say good riddance."

Pondor's curls tightened. "They've captured Furst?"

"Yes. So, he will not be coming to your rescue. No one will."

THE DOOR TO the cell containing the captured curators had barely closed behind Nero 51 when Master Ryden Simmdry and deans Selium Sorium, Plato Indelicat, Zenith Fullova, and Horatio Blastoe appeared within the makeshift prison. The curators all rose to their feet.

"Master Ryden Simmdry," Prophet IAN c. said, "have you come to liberate us? It's important that I get back to Adventura at once."

⌘*In due time. Our first task it to remove you all en masse. Then we can sort out where you need to be.* Each overseer touched two curators and within seconds, they all stood within the Library of Origination.

★*How wonderful that you're here,* Pru Tellerence said. ★*You're just in time for a party.*

⌘*I think some of them feel a greater need to return to their own worlds.*

★*I understand. But if any of you would like to stay, you're more than welcome.*

Artemus Rexana hurried into the room. Σ *Prophet IAN c.'s world is in great danger,* he explained. He turned to the curator. Σ*I will escort you home, immediately.*

"Thank you."

✠*We understand it appears unseemly if some of you stay for a celebration while the residents of your world suffer. I'm sure Pru Tellerence will understand.*

"I'm always up for a party," Abbello Abbato of Comedia said. "What are we celebrating?"

"The existence of a most extraordinary life—the child of two overseers."

"We love children on Comedia," he replied. "I'd like to stay."

"As would I," Peer Meap added. "I know my world is in dire straits, but I can assure you, the young citizens of Juvenilia are much more innovative and up to the task than I. They will not miss me."

The rest of the curators agreed to stay, including Furst, who reasoned that the child must be the offspring of his own dean, Pru Tellerence. They were shown to quarters where they could clean up and rest before the celebration began.

*

Johanna spent some time trying to teach Jackson how to perform the summoning spell Pru Tellerence had used to create a protective film around objects. But try as he might, the co-curator could not perform magic. He dragged his hands through his hair, mussing it up. "I don't know why this works for you and not for me?"

"Let's try it again," she said.

Before they could, Mal arrived to take them back to the Library of Origination. He noticed the look of defeat on Jackson's face. "Did something bad happen?" he asked.

"Johanna can do that trick that Pru Tellerence did, but I can't. I did everything she told me to do," Jackson said, "but nothing happens."

"Not everyone has magical abilities," Mal pointed out. "But some people can do it naturally. Johanna is just one of those people."

"Or maybe," Jackson said, "when she grabbed Beck's wrist the day Odyon escaped, he passed some of his magic onto her."

"It's a possibility."

"It's just not fair."

Mal raised his brow. "By now, you should have realized that very little in life is fair. It's not fair that the Terrorians are invading other realms. It's not fair that the time machine was stolen. It's not fair that it took three thousand years for Pru Tellerence and Ryden Simmdry to be able to say they have a child."

Jackson jumped on a transport disc. "It's hard to believe that little rug-rat is three thousand years old. It's hard to believe she's even three years old."

Mal took Johanna's arm as she stepped on the disc. "That's the beauty of the Majorious Longevicus Blessing," he said. "If you ever rise to the rank of overseer, you too will age that slowly."

"Tell me about it. I'm stuck being age seventeen for the next ten years."

Mal smiled. "I can think of worse things. Besides, the only thing slowing down is the aging process. As far as Fantasia's legal system is concerned, you're aging normally, just like all your friends, except you'll retain your boyish charm."

INSIDE THE LIBRARY of Origination, the festivities got off to a good start. Bel arrived with Dame Erato and Ingur Aguri and was equally fascinated by the animals and the decorations. The Romantican women tied balloons to her wrists and placed her on an animal that looked like a cross between a pony and a goat.

"What is that?" Jackson asked.

"That's an equid. It's native to Romantica, but there have been equids on Lumina since before the Two Millennia War."

Their attention was diverted by the arrival of several other curators.

"Natalia Dalura," Jackson said in amazement. "I thought she was taken prisoner by the Terrorians."

Horatio Blastoe heard Jackson and joined the Fantasian trio. ✠*She was, indeed, but we liberated them all. The only curators not incarcerated on Terroria were you and Johanna.*

"How did you manage to get them away?"

✠*It was easy once we thought about it. We have the ability to transport ourselves at will, as long as we wear our miters, or in Mal's case, his chaperon. We just transported into their cell and brought them back with us.*

Jackson's laughter sounded like a bark. "Nero 51 is going to be so pissed off."

✠*Perhaps. We will deal with that when it happens.*

Governor Tare rode past his former home on his way to the Library of Origination. He felt an inexplicable pull and ordered his transport disk to stop. He knew an off-lander had purchased the home, and the governor decided he needed to meet the new resident of Tare Manor.

Odyon transformed into Peter Dakion before reluctantly opening the door. "Can I help you?"

Governor Tare pulled back his shoulders and raised his chin so he could look down on this interloper who was living in *his* house. "I'm Governor Tare—the former owner of this home. I want to meet the new owner and answer any questions he might have. Is he in?"

"Do *you* often agree to see people who visit you without an appointment?"

Tare jerked back. "If this is a bad time, I'll leave you to it." He turned to step away.

"You just happened to be passing by?" Odyon's words dripped with ice.

"If you must know, I'm on my way to a celebration at the Library of Origination," Tare answered.

That triggered Odyon's curiosity. "What are they celebrating?" he asked with a touch more warmth.

"The offspring of two overseers," Tare answered.

"The first of her kind."

"That's impossible!" Odyon declared.

"I assure you, it is not," Tare replied, straightening out his hat.

Odyon had to remind himself that he was now Peter Dakion. "I was told," he said carefully, "that overseers were not allowed to have children."

"I don't know if that was ever the case, but even if it were, it certainly isn't anymore. I'm on my way to meet the child."

Odyon decided to go out on a limb and challenge the governor. "I don't believe it."

"You need proof? Come along with me as my guest and meet her. But once you have satisfied your curiosity, I would ask that you leave."

"You're an invited guest?"

"Yes."

"And you will escort me inside as your guest?"

"That's what I said," the governor replied, shining his fingernails on his sleeve.

"I'll take you up on that," Odyon said holding the door open. "Please come in for a moment while I change my jacket." *Perhaps as Peter Dakion, a guest of a guest, I will be able to enter the library.*

Tare stepped inside and while Odyon was gone, he studied the rugs and the art the new homeowner had placed around his house. *Heathen*, Tare thought.

Odyon quickly returned. "Let us go then and see this amazing child who is supposedly the offspring of two overseers." He literally pushed Tare out the door and led him to the Library of Origination.

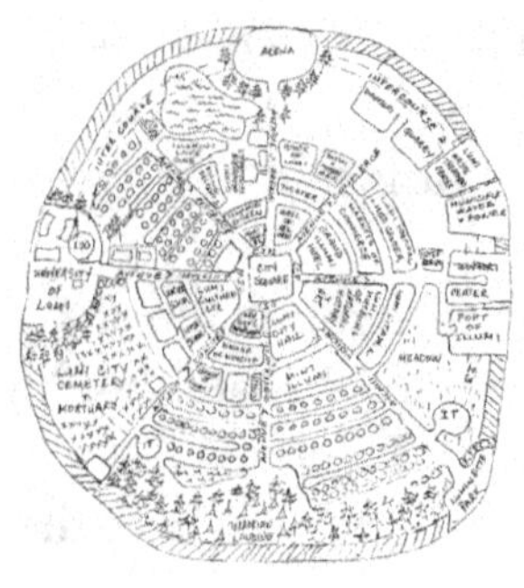

CHAPTER TWENTY-FOUR

JUVENILE BODIES WERE sprawled across the dirt floor of the detention cells. They were deep asleep—using each other as pillows—following an exhausting night of mischief. They missed seeing a new group of troopers arrive and depart.

That group of soldiers, shocked by the mental deterioration of the troopers they'd come to relieve, reported to their superiors that something on Juvenilia had driven their predecessors insane, and they demanded to be returned to their home realm.

General Barzic 922 told them he could not leave Juvenilia unattended, but the replacement troopers argued that the soldiers who were already there could continue to monitor the kiddlets. When the general asked the previous group of troopers if they minded staying, they had no idea who he was or where they were.

Marbol's brain scrambler had been quite effective.

*

Nicoletta saw movement as soon as Lei opened the door at the back of the school dining room. She hesitated before shooting and thought, *What if it's a Romantican child?* It wasn't. Instead, they found a kitchen with an open exterior door and a wild pallid routing through a box of apples.

"Don't shoot," Lei hissed. She took a step toward Nicoletta and flipped the switch from decimate to force field. "Okay, now."

Nicoletta took aim and captured the pallid in a force field. They warily entered the kitchen. "Secure that door," Lei told the third woman, Marin.

Nicoletta covered Marin's progress with the decimator, just in case. "The lock is broken," Marin said." Maybe the pallid threw itself at the door and broke it open. Do we have a blow torch?"

"Like I would know," Lei answered, her lip curling.

Marin looked at Nicoletta. "Help me move this." Together, they pushed a prep table against the door.

Lei sneered. "That's hardly enough to ward off an intruder."

"We're not done," Marin said. She motioned for Nicoletta to follow her into the dining room. "Let's move this table inside." They butted it up against the prep table and then pushed a third table against them. A small gap remained between the tables and the wall. Marin looked around and found a bunch of folding chairs stacked against each other. She grabbed a few and lodged them between the last table and the wall. "Let's look for rope or chain or anything we can wrap around the legs of the adjoining tables to keep them from separating if someone tries to force the door open.

"I saw some in the room we're practicing in," Nicoletta said.

"Okay, we'll go back for it later." Marin grabbed an unused bin and piled whatever apples they could salvage into it. Lei reached for an apple, and Marin slapped her hand. "No. We all eat together or not at all."

Nicoletta pulled open a heavy, metal door and found an ample supply of food. "We've got a bonanza of bread in here," she looked in the corner bins, "and vegetables." On the shelves, right next to the door, which she couldn't see until she was fully inside the storage area, were more supplies. "Plus, nut butter, oils, and preserves. Lots of them."

"Fine," Lei said. "Let's pack it all up and take it with us."

Nicoletta looked at her and just shook her head. "And where are we supposed to cook anything? We need this kitchen."

"Can I make a suggestion?" Marin asked. The other two turned toward her. "I suggest we take the apples, nut butter, and bread back to the practice room with us, so everyone can have something to eat. Now. Then I suggest we take a few more militairres and search the school for any more open doors, so we can secure our place inside."

"Fine," Lei answered. "Go ahead."

"I need your help. Nicoletta is protecting us, so I don't think she should put down the weapon. Grab some of those plates and knives while I fill this bin with bread."

Lei bristled. *I was leading this mission. How did she get to be in control?* But she did what she was asked, and they found a cart with wheels in an adjoining storage room, which they used to wheel their bounty back to the gymnasium.

Milbo looked outside and noticed most of the invaders had moved down the beach to an area adjacent to a meadow. If he leaned out of the opening to his cave, he could see them building pens. It was depressing to see so many of his friends and neighbors lined up in rows like frozen audience members. *They should sing*, he thought. *They're all together and their voices on a beautiful day like this would sound incredible.* He thought about sending a message bird. He didn't own one, himself, but he knew his next-door neighbor, Grouse Allecci, had one. If they could teach the bird to fly down and say, "Sing the anthem, sing the anthem," maybe the prisoners would catch on and raise their voices in song. They would probably never be all lined up like that again. *It's such a unique opportunity!*

He used his balloon vehicle to travel to the next cliff dwelling.

"Greetings, Grouse. I have a favor to ask."

His neighbor agreed to teach his bird the message but said it would take a while.

"That's fine," Milbo answered. "I have to go dress Neli Flo's pig in a new outfit."

"I hope it's not another one of those flowery capes she always makes the pig wear."

"No. This one is a surprise. It's a shame Abbello Abbato isn't here. He would really appreciate it."

"What is it?"

"You'll see," the mayor said with a smile. "You'll see."

*

RYDEN SIMMDRY STOOD next to Pru Tellerence, who smiled proudly at the little girl, sitting on a miniature, tufted wing chair that suited her perfectly. The overseer wore her miter, but she had removed the white hair that had been attached to it to make her appear more like the other overseers; her still-auburn locks, subtly enhanced by threads of gray, cascaded around her shoulders.

Music played in the background, and local Luminan children played with the animals, while Bel opened packages wrapped in colorful paper and ribbons. It looked a lot like a child's birthday party, although it was something else entirely.

Odyon held his breath as Governor Tare pulled him into the library. *Either they've turned off whatever blocked my DNA*, Odyon thought, *or the guise of Peter Dakion is masking it. Either way, I win.* They inched their way into the circle of onlookers surrounding the child. "How unimpressive," Odyon muttered.

Tare made a face—as if he smelled something foul—and edged away from Odyon. Odyon didn't care. In his new guise as Peter Dakion, he felt sure no one would recognize him or care that he was there.

Bel stared at the box she had just rescued from too many layers of wrapping tissue, and Dame Erato moved over to help the child open the lid. Inside lay a tiny gold bracelet that Dame Erato had chosen to give the child.

Next, Ingur Aguri handed Bel a bundle wrapped in silvery cloth. As Bel pulled off the ribbons that held it together, the cloth turned out to be the present—a silky, silver coat with a lattice overlay at the bodice that had ribbons and feathers woven into it.

Horatio Blastoe presented the youngster with a carved chest made out of a cloudy material that looked like a cross between diamond and mica and appeared to be incandescent. ✠ *This is a box you can store your treasures in. Touch it.* He took her hands and placed them on the chest. Then he waved his hand over the box and said a short chant. ✠*And now, no one but you can open it.*

Zenith Fullova presented the child with a small doll that looked like a fairy princess. §*I have it on good authority that every little girl on Juvenilia loves dolls like this one. How could I go wrong? Even if it's not as luxurious as this handsome chair that Marsh Kierand brought you from Inspiracon.*

Bel hugged the doll and said the first thing any of the visitors heard her say all day long. "More."

⌘*I guess she's not so different from children everywhere.*

Ingur Aguri removed an apple from her bag and handed it to the little girl. "Here's a nice treat," she said, and hoped the youngster would be satisfied.

Jackson and Johanna stood nearby and heard Bel's comment. Jackson leaned in to whisper, "I don't know if I ever said 'more' as a kid. We were pretty poor, and I think I always knew there would never be much more."

"I know what you mean," Johanna said. "I grew up in an orphanage. 'More' didn't exist for us."

"Actually, Bel grew up in an orphanage, too," Mal said quietly. "But I guess with overseers as parents and Ingur Aguri and Dame Erato as her unofficial grandmother and great aunt, she learned 'more' pretty quickly."

Reichel Bean and Abbello Abbato disappeared for a

moment, and when they returned, they presented the child with a box with holes in it. Bel began to rip the cover off when an impolite sound emerged from within.

Terrorian guards on Mysteriose were surprised to see so many prisoners moving about the pens. Earlier in the day, most of their captives had appeared half-dead, but now, they seemed revived.

One trooper, who felt especially bad after having been sprayed by one-too-many exploding pustules, said, "Maybe there is a chance I will soon feel better, as well." But the troopers had neither the potion nor the salve, and their condition continued to eat away at them, sapping their strength and comfort.

I need more memory cards. Logan stopped at a store to pick some up for his camera, as well as a storage case and notebook. He planned to keep a running log of all his video and interviews. He also stopped at a printer to have business cards made for *The Elliott Report. I have to start thinking like a businessman.*

In his bedroom, he logged the footage he'd previously shot and slipped the cards into the storage case. *Today was a good day.*

His phone rang. *Cassie.* He sighed as he reluctantly answered it. "Hey, Cass."

"Where have you been? I've been trying to reach you all day."

"I was busy with my new internship. They're all experienced and I'm the new guy, so I need to get up-to-speed."

"Well, my parents went to visit my older sister for the weekend, and I thought I'd make you a steak dinner."

He made a face. "You're going to cook?"

"Yes, I'm going to cook," she said. "I've made you spaghetti before, and pizza."

"Yeah, but steak is pretty tricky."

"What makes you such an expert on steak?"

"I help my old man barbecue all the time."

"Great. You can grill the steak, while I make the salad and the baked potatoes."

"You got dessert?"

"Pistachio ice cream rolled in chocolate cake."

He looked at the clock. It was late and he knew his parents were having dinner with friends. "Okay. I'm done here. I'll be there in twenty."

"See you then."

CASSIE DISCONNECTED THE call with a smile. She'd been worried when she couldn't reach Logan, but now he was on his way. She wanted this dinner to be perfect. She had used the pregnancy test one last time, and she was definitely preggers. *Tonight's the night.*

She put on Logan's favorite music and walked around lighting candles. *The way to a man's heart may be through his stomach, but it never hurts to seduce him, as well.*

She had already made a salad, so all she had to do was throw the potatoes on the grill with their steaks. She put a bottle of sparkling wine on ice but had a six-pack of Logan's favorite beer in the fridge in case he didn't want wine. *He'll need to drink something to dull the surprise.*

On the coffee table, a small box was tied up with

ribbon. She smiled. *This will mark the first step on the path to our future together.*

"WHAT DO YOU mean, 'they're unconscious'?" Nero 51 barked. Now that he was escalating his invasion, he needed the troops who were already placed on other realms to pull double shifts. He had advised them he would pick them up after one full cycle, but now, he needed them to stay for two. He sent a trooper in the time machine to inform the soldiers on Mysteriose that their pick-up would be delayed, only to learn from Senet 83 that they were too sick to guard the prisoners.

"As of right now, you are assigned to Mysteriose until further notice. Take two soldiers with you and send the other three back."

"They may be too sick to operate the time machine," Senet 83 said.

"If that is the case, use your decimator to put them out of their misery permanently, and bring the time machine back here. I'll have the next set of troops drop you off."

The trooper nodded. He didn't want to serve on a world that made Terrorians sick, but he didn't have much of a choice. With Nero 51, it was do or die.

General Barzic 922 approached the curator. "Our troops are getting sick on one of the realms."

"I've already heard, General. How nice of you to inform me of something I already know. You should have told me about Mysteriose as soon as you knew."

"Mysteriose? Are our soldiers getting sick on Mysteriose, as well? I came to tell you about the troops on

Juvenilia. They're not well enough to function."

Nero 51 felt all his tentacles stiffen. "So, they're becoming infected on two realms. The overseers probably have a hand in this. Cancel all inter-realm military deployment and amass all our troops in the town square. If the overseers want to engage in battle, we'll battle them. Round up the curators we've captured and bring them to the square, as well."

We can both play this game.

DUNGEN COULDN'T STAND being cooped up in the cabin with his father, who endlessly questioned him and tried to reason with him. Instead, he patrolled the woods outside, looking for signs of Terrorians.

The woods remained quiet, but not the lake. What looked like hundreds of boats were heading to the furthest shore—away from Dramoni. They were already pretty far from the capital, but apparently the Dramaticans didn't want to take chances after hearing their curator was captured.

Dungen's stomach growled. There was food in the cabin, but it made more sense to capture live meat while he still could. Before the sun set, he'd caught, skinned and roasted his dinner. Only after cooking the meat, did he realize the smoke from an open fire may not have been a smart idea. He grabbed a bucket of water, doused the flames, carried the meat inside, and bolted the door.

Pondor stared at his son as the chair he pulled from the table scraped across the floor. He watched Dungen eat with gusto. Dungen could feel his father's eyes boring into him and cut off a small portion of the animal, which he tossed to him. It landed on Pondor's lap. Pondor looked down at his hands, which were bound.

Dungen sighed. After eating for a few more moments, he threw down his food and reluctantly got up to untie his father's hands. Instead of going back to his dinner, he sat across from his father with the decimator trained on him, just to make him uncomfortable.

Most Dramaticans considered the north side of Cirra Lake relatively quiet, but sudden bird shrieks accompanied by the flapping of wings and baying of animals signaled something unwelcomed outside.

Dungen walked to a boarded-up window and peered through an opening between the pieces of wood. It was dark out. Too dark to see.

Too dark to see Terrorians standing right beside the cabin.

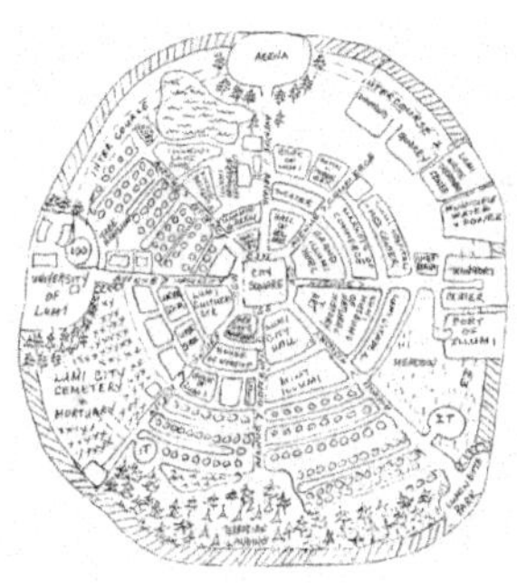

CHAPTER TWENTY-FIVE

Prophet IAN c. went out of his way to pick up his tablet before returning to the lab. He felt incomplete without the constant data stream from all the hu*bots working on combatting the solar flares.

Prophet DANIEL p. immediately stopped working when the curator walked in. "IAN c. are you all right? When you didn't return right away, I was afraid we had taken you off the recharge system too quickly. And then, I couldn't find you anywhere. What happened?"

"The Terrorians happened," IAN c. answered.

Prophet DAVID l.'s head snapped up in a way more human than hu*bot. "What did they want?"

"They abducted me and transported me off-world, where they imprisoned me with several curators from other realms. Apparently, they are trying to take over the entire Illumini system."

"How did you get away?" Prophet PATRICK c. asked.

"The overseers. They came and transported us to their home world. Then Artemus Rexana brought me here. What is our status?"

"Three-quarters of our lasers have been reconfigured and are ready-to-go," prophet CARL a. said. "This morning, we uncovered a dozen more generators. And basically, just two hours ago, we discovered several more lasers. DAVID l. has been calculating additional trajectories that will do the most good, while DANIEL p. is overseeing the movement of completed laser systems to the farthest regions for more expedient coverage, that way the ones that are not yet complete won't have as far to travel and can be brought on line more quickly."

"Do we have an estimated time of detonation?" IAN c. asked.

CARL a. looked at his tablet. "Not yet. I'll inform you as soon as I know."

Jackson took Johanna's hand. "Can we get out of here? This party is to introduce Bel to all the mucky-mucks here in Lumi. I don't feel like our constant presence is required. At least, not until the desserts arrive."

"Where do you want to go?" she asked.

"I heard someone say there's an observatory with a telescope in the library cupola. I'd like to see what overseers gaze at when they're not busy keeping the Illumini Constellation safe."

They easily found the cupola stairs and slowly made their ascent, Jackson pulling Johanna by the hand.

Jackson looked up. "There's a cloud in here. We're going to have to climb through it. Is this library taller than the Libraries of Illumination?"

"I have no idea," she answered.

They climbed through the cloud and when they could finally see again, the staircase split in two, each side spiraling upward and outward to connect with the outer edges of the cupola floor. "I can't see the Curator's Key from here. It's blocked by that flat thing over our heads. What is it?"

"I'm sure we'll be able to figure it out once we reach the cupola. There are catwalks connected to it."

The divided staircase felt less sturdy, like it was made out of rope rather than metal. It took all their concentration to keep their balance as they climbed to the top. Finally, they felt the firmness of the cupola floor beneath their feet. "I'd like to know how the overseers get up these steps without breaking a leg," Jackson said. "They're all pretty old, and these stairs are treacherous."

"Overseers don't need to climb the stairs. They only need to think about standing in the cupola, and they're there."

"That's true," he answered. "I wasn't thinking." He turned to look at the platform they had spotted from below. On it sat a giant mechanism with several telescopic arms that extended outside the library's glass dome. Each arm appeared to have elbows that allowed it to bend in different directions. "Wow. I've never seen anything like this, before. They're sticking right out of the roof and curving all about, but from outside, you can't even see them."

"Kind of like the portals' windows," she murmured.

"Come on." He grabbed her hand and led her across the catwalk. Each telescope had two chairs that looked like old-fashioned dentists' chairs. "Let's go try them out."

They climbed a small flight of steps built into the base of the mechanism, and Jackson lifted Johanna into one of the seats. As she sat back, a padded leg rest slid down from the seat and a headrest folded up. Jackson walked around to the adjoining seat and slid into it. "Wow."

"It's a lot more comfortable than it looks," Johanna said, laughing.

"We could hunker down here all night, looking at the stars," he noted. "Who needs a hotel?"

"Do you know how to make this work?" Johanna asked, nodding toward the telescope.

"Give me a moment. I'm sure, between us, we can figure it out."

CONFUSING MONSTERS WAS fun, but it quickly became boring when there were no new monsters to torment. Slowly, the Juveniles began walking away from the detention camps. There was a lot more to entertain them in their homes, and they had already finished all the candy they had with them.

"We can't leave the monsters wandering around like they are," Marbol argued. "If we don't continue bombarding them with Foggy, they'll eventually get their wits back and start hunting us again."

"Not if we lock them up," Boxer said. "Let's tie them up and stick them in the cages and padlock them closed."

"What if they pick the locks?" Waxmo asked.

"We'll pour glue in the locks!" Boxer said.

They used the scrambler on the Terrorians again, and led them to the holding cells, where they tied them up and braided the ropes through the metal fencing. They poured glue on the Terrorians tentacles and the ropes binding them, then locked each enclosure with multiple padlocks, and poured glue on them, as well. "This should hold them," Boxer said.

THE NEW MILITAIRRE recruits cheered when they saw Nicoletta, Marin, and Lei return with food.

"There's more where this came from," Lei said.

"A little more," Nicoletta said. Then she smiled widely, "And a wild pallid waiting to be roasted."

"Right now, I think I'd gnaw on a wooden box," Annabeth said, "although, this apple is much more preferable." She took a bite, relishing the crunch and not caring about the juice running down her chin.

"I don't suppose you saw any water or wine?" Milencia asked.

"No," Nicoletta answered, "but that doesn't mean there isn't any. There could be some in storage. Although I doubt there's any wine. This is a school."

"None of that matters, really," Marin said, "because there's running water in the kitchen. You can all rehydrate until you're ready to explode."

"Unless the Terrorians find us," Milencia pointed out.

Marin nodded. "I told Nicoletta and Lei that we should form groups and patrol the school to make sure all the doors and window are locked."

"There are a lot of windows. I think they'd be easy enough to break if the invaders want to get inside," Lei said.

"Maybe so, but we'd hear the glass breaking," Annabeth said. "If we don't check that everything is locked and a window is open, we may not hear them come in. I'd rather be warned than surprised."

"We're safest in here," Milencia pointed out, "and it will be getting dark soon. So why don't we split up right now and check the perimeter, and then meet back here."

The others agreed, and they split up into six groups.

MILBO TOOK THE long route to Neli Flo's home. All the invaders were on the other side of the city, so he felt safe enough. He opened the gate to the stable and walked inside. He was able to corner Tropo by feeding him hard boiled eggs. Tropo loved eggs and eagerly ate while Milbo draped the costume over the pig and secured it under his chin and belly. Tropo pulled away when Milbo pulled the mask over his snout and snorted loudly. Milbo tried to soothe the animal, but Tropo darted away, shooting out the open gate.

Milbo gave chase, but the pig proved too fast for him and disappeared down a path leading to the beach. Milbo waved his arms to get the pig's attention, but that only made Tropo run harder, and when he reached the packed sand on the beach, he made a sharp turn and ran in the direction of the detention camp.

Milbo stopped running, leaned over and put both hands on his knees while he tried to catch his breath. He had hoped to be somewhere safe with a spyglass so he could watch the Terrorians' reactions when they spotted what appeared to be a giant white cat. But he was so out of breath, he didn't know if he'd be able to get back to his vehicle in time, and then home.

It was a such a fun gag, he couldn't help but laugh out loud. But then, the thought of missing the outcome made him sad.

Too bad, because he had his camera all set up right inside the door to his dwelling.

Milbo raced home. Maybe, if he hurried, he could still see the "show."

At the top of the hill, he noticed one of the ground dweller's vehicles. He was pretty sure the owner had been taken into custody, and Milbo promised the universe he would return it as soon as he could.

He stepped into the vessel and threw off the tie lines that held it in place. A moment later he was airborne and puttering back home. A brisk breeze hindered him from going in the direction of the cliff dwellings but helped him travel along the waterfront. *If I'm high enough, the Terrorians shouldn't be able to reach me, and I'll be able to watch their reaction to Tropo.*

Indeed, Milbo was making better speed than Tropo, who stopped occasionally to poke at a shell sticking out of the sand. Soon, the mayor flew directly over the pig, and slowed his vehicle enough to watch Tropo storm the detention camp.

He could hear the captured Comedians singing the national anthem, but they stopped and laughed when they saw Tropo running around in his costume. Milbo had expected that. He didn't expect the horror expressed by the Terrorians, who instead of trying to catch the pig, screamed as they ran into the water. Moments later they had all disappeared under the surface.

Milbo wasted no time. He swooped down in the borrowed vehicle, grabbed a tie line and jump out when he neared the ground, securing the vehicle. He quickly went to work releasing the prisoners.

Meanwhile, Tropo ran around, frolicking at the water's edge, oblivious to everyone's sudden joy.

BENEATH THE WAVES, the Terrorian soldiers all had the same idea, activating their biometric bands. One soldier after another committed suicide rather than face the wrath of a giant, demonic white cat—an obvious emissary of the devil.

ON A DISTANT REALM, a similar but much smaller teacup piglet jumped out of the box and darted around the Library of Origination, amid the comments, shrieks, and laughter of the people standing around. It was fast for a little pig and nearly impossible to seize.

The squealing little fuzz ball pin-balled around the room as guests tried to either avoid it or catch it. Finally, with a wave of his hand, Ryden Simmdry calmed the creature, picked it up and handed it to Bel. The youngster planted a huge kiss on its snout and hugged her new pet.

⦿ *We have never had pets at the College of Overseers.*

Ψ *That's because aside from exhibits of small animals, like the one here today, pets are not allowed in Lumi.*

Ω *Oh, dear. That may prove to be a problem.*

Governor Tare had been staring at the piglet since

it first popped out of the box. He looked at the three overseers, whose exchange he had heard, and then at Master Ryden Simmdry. He might be the governor, but he knew the Master of the Overseers outranked him and everyone else on Lumina. "I do not believe it will be a problem," Governor Tare said. "She's a very special child." *With very powerful parents.*

THE SOLDIERS SENET 83 encountered on Mysteriose appeared close to death. He had bridled when Nero 51 told him to put sick troopers out of their misery permanently, but he could see how it would be more of a mercy than anything else.

"Do not kill me," one of the troopers pleaded with Senet 83.

"You are dying. You look like you're in pain. It will end your distress."

"The prisoners were sick," the dying trooper gasped, "but they are recovering. Maybe I will recover, too."

"If any of the enemy find you in your weakened state, they will not hesitate to kill you, and it could be much more torturous than you imagine."

"Please, Senet 83—."

And if Nero 51 finds out I spared you, against his direct orders, I would be signing my own death warrant.

MYSTERIAN PRISONERS WATCHED as a lone, new arrival decimated the Terrorians who had captured them. No one knew what was going on, but they couldn't ask because they couldn't translate the Terrorian language. They prayed he would not start obliterating them next.

Instead, he stopped for a conversation with the only remaining soldier. Eventually, he returned to the time machine and left.

"Why do you think he left him alive?" one of the prisoners asked.

"Maybe as a sign to others that this is a place of death," another prisoner answered.

THE DYING TROOPER took Senet 83's admonition to heart. The prisoners might turn on him and try to torture him. That didn't hurt as much as knowing Nero 51 had ordered Senet 83 to kill the sick Terrorian soldiers. *That* made his blood boil.

It took a lot of effort, but he stretched his tentacles toward the closest cell. He grasped the door and pulled himself closer so he could see what he was doing. In a dying effort, the Terrorian opened the enclosure. As soon as the prisoners were released, he pressed on his biometric armband and ended his life.

LOGAN WAS SURPRISED to find Cassie in such a playful, compliant mood. They had been going out together for years, and she had started taking advantage of their relationship and acting bossy during their second year together. He hadn't minded. Cassie was pretty and their relationship was intimate. Besides, he had someone to take to parties and go to the movies with, although lately, she had turned into a little Hitler.

He fired up the barbecue, and while they waited for the grill to heat up, they drank together. He started with wine, but when he opened the refrigerator to get the steaks and saw his favorite beer, he switched. He felt mellow. He had been thinking about Emily a lot, ever since the senior prom. *Am I the only one who remembers what really happened?* But tonight, Cassie was easy-going and seemed a lot lower-maintenance than Emily. He had watched Emily with Jackson. She had acted a lot like Cassie was acting toward him right now, all sweet and kittenish, but then he'd listened to Cassie and Emily making plans together, and he realized he had witnessed Emily's evil twin. She had grabbed him as her prom king without any regard for Cassie's hurt feelings, and he knew if they got together again, she would try to manipulate him. *Maybe Cassie's not so bad.* With her, he knew what he was getting.

Cassie tossed the salad and placed it on the table. She refilled her wine glass and went outside. Logan took his steak off the grill and called her over. "Is this done enough for you?" He sliced it so she could see the center.

"It's perfect," she said, rising on her toes to kiss his cheek, "just like you."

He smirked, removed her steak, and carried their dinner inside. While they ate the main course, they talked about classes, tests and graduation. Over dessert, they segued into discussions about college and the future.

"So, how's your internship going?" she asked.

"Once I show them I'm better than this Channing guy they all idolize, things will be great. And I have a plan for that." He told her all about *The Elliott Report* and what he had done so far. Then he handed her one of his new business cards.

"You're really serious about this."

"Damn straight. I even saw something online today about monetizing a website. That would be perfect."

"I don't know what that means, exactly."

"It means using the site to make money. It's selling ad space and affiliate marketing. I even read something about adding a button to accept donations. How cool would that be? I might be a publishing mogul by the time I turn twenty."

"So, you're not looking for a job?"

"I am, but it may not be as necessary as it was before. My old man is paying for my education, and I'll automatically get room and board staying in the dorms, so I should be fine. He'll support me as long as I stay in school. I get a decent allowance, so I'm covered. Income from the website would be icing on the cake."

"What about off-campus housing? Would he pay for that, too?"

"First-year students aren't allowed to live off campus."

"What about married students?"

"What about them?"

"Are they allowed to have their wives with them?"

"Don't know. Don't care. Not married."

Cassie started chewing one of her fingernails. "It's something you should think about."

Logan had drunk several bottles of beer and a glass of wine, but he was sober enough to understand where the conversation was heading. "We're not getting married. We're too young. We have our whole lives ahead of us."

She grabbed the gift box off the table and handed it to him.

"What's this?"

"A present."

He ripped off the ribbon and opened the box. "You got me a coffee mug?" He looked at her as he pulled it out of the box. "For my dorm room?"

She held out her palm as if inviting him to read what it said.

His face turned white as he read the only word on the front of the mug. *Daddy.*

When Pru Tellerence found Bel and her new piglet cuddled together fast asleep under a table, the celebration started to wind down. Lumi officials and their children headed home. Workers arrived to wrangle the animals, remove their enclosure, and clean up. As far as Pru Tellerence was concerned, everyone appeared to accept that two overseers had a child and were introducing her to the community. She considered the day a success.

Ryden Simmdry was a little more concerned. He didn't know there would be local officials and children at the celebration. Aside from the overseers and curators, he had only expected Dame Erato and Ingur Aguri. *Too many people know about Bel, and it will be difficult to protect her location, especially if anyone saw the distinctive tattoo on her throat or heard Dame Erato and Ingur Aguri talking about her being a Maroqi priestess.* He hadn't recognized a handful of people, and he wished he had never allowed himself to be talked into the celebration.

Pru Tellerence had taken the two sisters and Bel to their guest quarters and tucked the toddler into bed, where she slept soundly, even without the comfort of her piglet, who was snuggled into Dame Erato's shawl in a box in the corner of the room. Ingur Aguri sat down to rest for a moment and passed out. Dame Erato looked like she was about to do the same when Pru Tellerence finally left the trio.

Governor Tare was the last outsider to leave the Library of Origination. Ryden Simmdry's eyes narrowed. He was sure Tare had arrived with another man—a stranger—whom he hadn't seen leave. The master looked around but everyone he laid eyes on belonged there. He sighed. *Perhaps I'm overthinking this.* He had always relied on his gut, however, and his gut told him something was amiss.

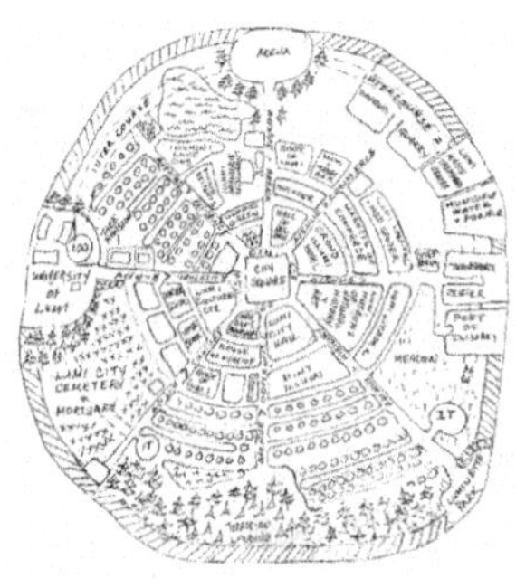

CHAPTER TWENTY-SIX

HIGH ON A WALL inside the Library of Origination, where the rays of the sun glanced off the surface, a separate glint of light mingled with the sun's reflection. Odyon watched and waited for the people within to say something useful. He had once been a curator, a fact he kept hidden beneath a flesh-colored glove. But he had never been an overseer, and zeroing in on their internal conversations was difficult at best. He could eavesdrop on the curators' conversations, and he could hear what the overseers wanted the curators to hear, but he was sure there were thoughts the overseers kept hidden.

It didn't matter. He had lived a long life, and spending a few hours on a wall in the library was a drop in the bucket of time. If he could sense a weakness or a course of action that would suit his plans for the future, it would be worth every second of the tedium leading up to it.

*

THE DOOR TO the cabin rattled. *Someone is trying to get in.* Dungen, who had been waving the decimator in his father's direction, switched position and trained it on the door. He could hear grunting on the other side, not words, but sounds and clicks.

Come on in, he thought. *I'm ready for you.*

The grunting decreased in volume.

Dungen waited. And waited. Pondor fell asleep, his untied hands hidden within the folds of his tunic. Dungen refused to remove his full attention from the door to the cabin. The cracks between the boards blocking the windows grew visible, changing from dark gray to the steamy color of light fog. Dungen got up and looked outside. He walked to every window and looked through whatever opening he could find. No one appeared in view.

Pondor awakened at the sound of Dungen's shuffling. He watched his son move around the room but immediately closed his eyes again whenever Dungen turned toward him. He needn't have bothered. He was the last thing on his son's mind.

Light flooded the cabin when Dungen opened the door. Pondor opened his eyes in time to see his son leave.

Outside, Dungen moved stealthily and tried to stay in the shadow of the cabin. He didn't see any movement, and as he continued to explore—undiscovered—he made his circle of investigation increasingly wider. When he reached a high point near the roadway, he allowed the decimator to slide around to his back and climbed a tree. The view was exceptional. He could see over the descending treetops to the lake, down the roadway on either side, and past the fields and farmland to his north. *Nothing.* Not a Terrorian in sight. Nor a Dramatican. *Where is everyone?* The sound of a wild bird's mating call broke the silence. It was the only sound of life he could discern.

INSIDE THE CABIN, Pondor took advantage of Dungen's absence. He reached over and untied the rope on one foot and then the other. The sound of leaves rustling alerted him to someone approaching. He quickly wrapped the rope around his ankles, so it would look like he was still bound and closed his eyes to the point where he could just make out what was going on from beneath his lashes. A dark shadow blocked the light that had illuminated the open door.

JOHANNA AND JACKSON controlled a very powerful telescope. They quickly discovered the one they had chosen to sit at was focused on a burnt-out Library of Illumination.

Jackson rubbed the stubble on his chin. He used to be able to go without shaving for two or three days, but that had recently changed. His fair coloring was the only thing that camouflaged his emerging beard. *So much for only aging one year for every ten that pass.* "That library is a mess," he told Johanna. "Where do you suppose it's located?"

"It has to be Romantica. Didn't Ryden Simmdry mention their library went up in flames when trapped Terrorians burned books and furnishings for heat?"

"They died, didn't they?"

"Yes. And that's probably the library where it happened."

Jackson readjusted his position in the seat. "So, let's look at the other realms. Maybe we can spy on my brother from here. Or Logan."

"Why do you want to spy on Logan?"

"He's been acting strange since the senior prom. Mean. Angry. The whole thing changed him. Like maybe he inhaled too much Terrorian vapor."

"Have I become meaner and angrier?"

"No."

"Then it isn't the vapor."

"I don't know if we'd be able to see him from here, anyway."

"I think the reason why there are so many telescopes is because the realms are scattered widely across the heavens."

Jackson leaned over and counted the telescopic arms. "You're right. There are six arms and twelve of these nifty chairs. That means every overseer can check out their realm from here. There's a chair for each of them, although, they probably have to play *odds and evens* to decide whose world they're going to look at first."

"I think Romantica is realm two," Johanna said, "and we're realm eleven. So, let's slide over there," she looked at the next telescopic arm to her left, "and maybe we'll be able to see Fantasia."

"Or Terroria," Jackson added. "Sounds good to me." They quickly changed seats and focused the telescopic arm. "It's just some abandoned building somewhere with a bunch of weeds growing out of it."

"Can you magnify it? Bring it in closer?" she asked.

Jackson played with the controls. A moment later,

the building filled their eyepiece. "Look. Something is moving."

Johanna looked on as the ground opened up, revealing a staircase. Moments later, Nero 51 climbed out. "Terroria," they said in unison.

Johanna and Jackson lost track of time as they telescope-hopped and zoomed in on all the different realms, studying the areas surrounding the Libraries of Illumination. They talked about what they observed and compared it to what they knew about each realm. Their rapidly growing wealth of knowledge became so mind numbing, they eventually lapsed into sleep.

NERO 51 BARELY CONTAINED his rage. "What do you mean the curators are gone?"

Bener 411 could feel the curator's hot breath on his face. "The room was locked when I got there. I had the guard open it up, and it was empty. I asked what happened to the prisoners, and he said he did not know, but he confirmed that no one had been admitted since your last visit."

Nero 51's first impulse was to lash out at the underlings who had lost his prisoners. But for some reason, the vision of Odyon—shapeshifting—entered his mind, followed by his knowledge of the overseers' ability to appear and disappear at will and transport others with them. He could feel his gelatinous substance—which flowed through Terrorian's veins instead of blood—boil.

He approached the town square, which overflowed with recently deployed soldiers, speculating about why they had been summoned back to Terroria so suddenly. Nero

51 stood before them, and he took a deep breath while considering his options. When he felt in control of the situation, his voice rang out. "Our plans have changed."

The buzz died leaving only the echo of Nero 51's words hanging in the air. He made eye contact with as many people as possible during a short pause. "As long as the overseers are allowed to roam among worlds, we will never achieve our goal. They must be prevented from interfering. The only way to stop them is to focus all our attention on them alone and attack their home base."

"Is that wise?" a strategist said out loud before realizing his question would be most unwelcomed.

"It is what must be done," Nero 51 stated emphatically. He turned to Kelsis 384. "Make sure these soldiers know everything there is to know about Lumina within the next few hours." He raised all four of his right tentacles straight into the air. "WE ATTACK AT DAWN!"

The soldiers followed suit raising their tentacles into the air. "Victory," one of them shouted out, and soon they were all chanting, "Victory…victory…victory."

Nero 51 turned to General Barzic 922. "Do not wander away, General. You and I will be engaging in a little night reconnaissance. Meet me in the underground hangar at the darkest hour."

BY THE TIME the Adventurans were ready to launch their lasers at the sun, very few of the leader*bots still functioned. Those crucial to the actual launch operation had plugged themselves into recharge units, while others worked through the night making sure everything was ready. At dawn, Prophet PATRICK c., who had worked through the night, roused prophets IAN c., DAVID l., DANIEL p., and CARL a., as well as a half-dozen others, and asked CARL a. to hook him up for recharge. PATRICK c. would not be witnessing his civilization's last-ditch effort to save their world. "May technology endeavor—positively," he said, wondering if he would ever awaken.

THE RECHARGED LEADER*BOTS took their places, while hu*bots who had worked through the night left for recharge stations, hoping there was enough power left in them for another day of existence.

DAVID l. checked with each of the laser operators before approaching IAN c. "We are ready to detonate."

"On my signal," IAN c. said.

Everyone stood ready, waiting for the word.

Adventurans did not believe in prayer. They were a technology-based civilization. Yet, the moment before uttering the command to fire the lasers, IAN c. came as close to silently praying as any commander ever would.

"We've got to get this done," DANIEL p. muttered.

"I couldn't agree more," DAVID l. whispered back.

A long moment of silence followed.

"Has the sun cleared the horizon?" IAN c. asked.

"Fifteen measures ago," DANIEL p. answered.

"Fire lasers, now."

LOGAN COULD NOT find the motivation to get out of bed. He felt safe within the cocoon of his blankets, and something in the back of his mind told him he would remain so if he just stayed in bed. He rubbed his arm and winced. He moved it by his face and saw a jagged red scar caked with blood. *Arrgghh. Cassie.* He hadn't reacted well to the *Daddy* mug, throwing it against the wall. Cassie hadn't handled his response very maturely. She'd picked up one of the jagged halves—tears spilling down her red face—and lunged for him, cutting his arm. He managed to wrestle the broken cup away from her and quiet her down with the false promise that he needed more time to think about "what would be best for them."

Is there such a thing as a pre-marital divorce? There was no way he would let her cramp his style. *A baby?* He didn't want some *mistake* ruining his future. He quickly learned that communicating a lot of those thoughts with Cassie was not a good idea. He needed a plan. *Too bad it's the weekend.* He would have to wait until Monday to call Graydon Ransom University to see if he could get a dorm room for the summer. *If I could just stay at school through the summer, fall, and next spring, I'll be okay. Out of sight, out of mind.* That and a new phone number would make it difficult for Cassie to bother him, but it wouldn't resolve the *kid* issue.

How much does an abortion cost? Maybe she would agree to get rid of the baby, that way, she could continue her education, as well. He would have to appeal to her intellect. That would settle any future *kid* issues. They had both taken a course called *Advanced Adulting* about the realities of life beyond high school. He distinctly remembered Mrs. Merkle lecturing, "It costs more than a quarter million dollars to raise a child until its eighteenth birthday." He thought he was worth way more than that. In retrospect, he didn't want to be the one paying it, at least not yet. *No.* Cassie had to agree to get rid of the baby. *It's the only way.*

And then he'd dump her.

*

Zenith Fullova escorted Peer Meap back to Juvenilia. They materialized in a private nook behind the town hall and quietly made their way toward the detention cells. Both were surprised to find grumbling Terrorians incapacitated within the cells.

"Where are the children?" Peer Meap wondered aloud.

§*Probably at home, all snug in their beds.*

They turned at the sound of scraping feet. "Marbol," Peer Meap asked, "is this your doing?"

"I just scrambled their brains," the boy answered. "The others gathered them up and led them into the cages." He winced. "Do we have to feed them?"

Zenith Fullova could not hide his smile. §*Yes, you do.*

"I thought we might. What do you think they eat?"

A moment passed while the overseer engaged in communal telepathy. A moment later, Ryden Simmdry appeared.

§*Master Ryden Simmdry will handle their nutritional needs.*

The master chanted to himself and raised his joined hands, palms up, and as he separated them, small discs appeared floating in the air. The overseer straightened his arms and the discs flew into the pens, easily fitting between structural openings, each one attaching itself to the neck of a Terrorian.

"What is that?" Marbol asked.

⌘*Sustenance. It will provide their minimal nutritional needs until it is not needed anymore.*

"We don't have to give them stuff to eat?"

⌘*Not anymore.*

Marbol's shoulders relaxed. "I'm sure glad they don't have to eat candy. I didn't want to have to give mine up to feed monsters."

⌘*Would you have if I weren't here?*

"I guess," Marbol said, kicking a rock.

⌘*You managed to pull off an impossible feat here. I would like to talk to you and your friends. Where are the others?*

"We're having grain-plops for breakfast. Duddu chose it. They're all at the town hall making batter and stuff. Some of them will have jam-whammies in them. Those are my favorite. Want some?"

⌘*I would very much like to talk to your friends, but I wouldn't think of depriving anyone of…jam-whammies. I will leave those for all of you.* Ryden Simmdry swept his arm in the direction of the town hall. ⌘*Lead on.*

Milencia awoke feeling refreshed, except for the crick in her neck from sleeping on a hard floor. She checked with the women who had patrolled overnight, and then grabbed a piece of fruit for breakfast. "Annabeth, I'm taking you with me. We're going to patrol the perimeter of the building."

"You want to go outside in plain sight?"

"Nope. I want to check on the inside to make sure everything is okay, and then I want to go up on the roof and survey the surrounding area from there."

"We'll be visible on the roof."

"Then we'll stay low and wiggle across the surface on our bellies if we have to."

"Why can't we just look out the windows on the

top floor?" Annabeth asked.

"Because I want to be able to engage the enemy without their return fire breaking a window. The glass is our early warning signal, remember?"

"But if these weapons can obliterate something without a trace, the invaders can shoot at the windows and the glass will disappear without a sound. So, our early warning system is not really as wonderful as you would like."

"Why do you have to give me new issues to worry about?" Milencia whined. "I was just starting to feel in control of something."

Annabeth grabbed a weapon. "It's the least I could do. Come on. Let's go patrol your perimeter."

They quickly checked all the outer rooms, starting with the lowest level. The building remained locked and the view of the surrounding area appeared clear. The two women made their way to the roof and crawled to the edge. Everything looked peaceful under a bright sky.

"You'd never know we were under attack," Annabeth stated.

"I know. I can hear birds tweeting and crickets chirping—the regular sounds of morning, just like before the Terrorians arrived."

"Now that you mention it, do you remember hearing those sounds since the Terrorians arrived?"

"I was too preoccupied with staying alive to listen for birdsong."

Annabeth sighed. "It's just that it seems so normal and I don't see a sign of them anywhere. I would love to go home."

"If your home still exists," Milencia answered with a sigh.

✠*Now that we are quite sure the Terrorians have the time machine, we must devise a plan to return it to its rightful owner. Malcolm, your thoughts?*

"I agree with you. It's the one thing allowing them to continue their invasion. Of course, we have to hope they did not use the device as a template to make more."

⌘*I do not believe they would be able to replicate it. The vehicle, itself, is too large, and the technology is too advanced for the Terrorians to grasp at the current time.*

"We would need to obtain the crystals that power it, along with the conveyance. That may not be easy. I'm sure Nero 51 keeps those with him at all times."

⌘*The vehicle is Fantasian. Can't you procure a duplicate set of crystals from the creator?*

"Without a time machine, I can't travel into the future to get them."

⌘*I could help you with that.*

"You can?"

⌘*Explaining myself would take too much time. Instead, we should go and—in your words—shoot from the hip.*

Mal grinned. "Let's do it."

⌘*Horatio Blastoe and Plato Indelicat, I ask that you do one service for us while we're gone.*

Ω*How can we help you?*

⌘*Travel together—incognito—to Terroria. Horatio Blastoe knows where the time machine is being kept. Plato Indelicat, as dean of Terroria, you know the lay of the land*

and the disposition of the residents. Verify that the machine is the only one of its kind and that it is still based there. The Terrorians have already hidden its location once. There is nothing to stop them from doing so again. You must not be detected.

A SHIMMER OF LIGHT sitting high upon the wall morphed into a breeze and floated among the dust motes down to the cloak of Plato Indelicat. Odyon had no way of traveling between realms on his own, but he could hitch a ride with the overseers and warn Nero 51 about their plans. Not that he liked Nero 51, but the Terrorian curator would need to invade Lumina for Odyon to fulfill his dream of ruling the thirteenth realm.

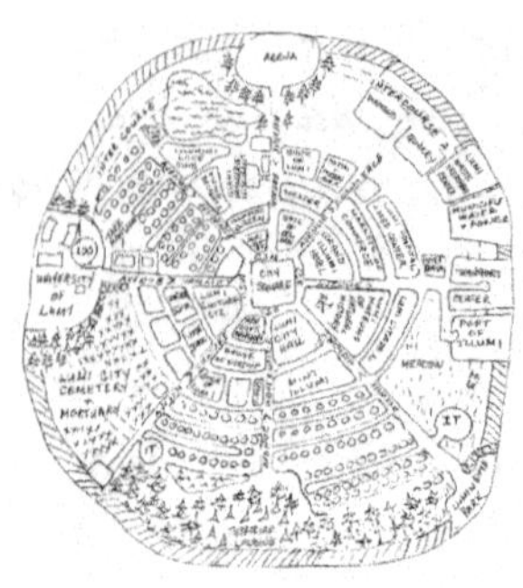

CHAPTER TWENTY-SEVEN

THE MYSTERIAN PRISONERS were appropriately mystified. *Have the Terrorians given up? Is this a ruse to get more people out of their houses, so the invaders can scoop them up? Where are the invaders?* The former prisoners, thankful they had been released, were surprised to find the Terrorian dead. His last act had been compassionate, but he was only one among the many before him who had made their lives miserable.

They didn't waste time standing by the detention cells to chat about it. They felt more inclined to rush home to see how their families, friends, and neighbors fared.

SOME OF THE newly-freed Comedians picked up weapons left behind by the Terrorians. Benzi Camma hoisted a weapon over his shoulder and aimed it at a crab crawling up the shoreline. Behind him, Milbo began screaming.

His fellow citizens pulled the weapon out of Benzi's hands, explaining he had been holding the weapon backwards and had shot the mayor.

"Help me, help me, help me…" Milbo cried as he struggled unsuccessfully to break free.

"How do we release him?" one of the detainees asked.

"When the invaders wanted to release one of us, they shot us a second time," a former prisoner answered.

"So, do it!" Milbo shouted.

"But sometimes, they'd shoot at something—like a rock that got in their way—and it disappeared," the former prisoner continued.

Milbo went silent as he froze in place.

The speaker grabbed the weapon, turned it around, and shot at the crab. The crab stopped moving. He shot it again. The crab once again crawled up the beach. He turned the gun on Milbo.

"Ohhh!" It sounded more like a moan from Milbo than a statement.

He pulled the trigger.

Milbo felt his arm go free and relaxed. "Good job," he mumbled, although he had a hard time believing his own words.

"Do you think they'll come back?" a young man asked.

"They might, so I think we should all find a safe place to spend the night," Milbo answered.

"That's easy for you to say. You're a cliff dweller. We were pulled right out of the sky by our anchor line and our homes were turned to dust by the invaders."

"You must all know some cliff dwellers or ground dwellers. It's best to stay with them for a while, until we ascertain our safety."

"We're ground dwellers, and we were taken hostage," the head of a family stated.

"How did the invaders get inside?" Milbo asked.

"They knocked on the door," the family man answered.

"And you opened it?" Milbo asked.

"That's what we always do when someone knocks."

"Well, don't," Milbo stated.

The former prisoners started drifting away from the beach. Some requested accommodations from their neighbors or offered the same if their homes still existed. A few wanted to stand around and talk about their ordeal, but most Comedians didn't want to be on hand if the invaders made their way back from the sea or appeared out of nowhere again.

HORATIO BLASTOE AND Plato Indelicat materialized in miniaturized form inside the Terrorian hangar where Nero 51 kept the time machine. Odyon floated away as a dust mote, in search of the curator. The two overseers began their methodical search for duplicate apparatus. A time machine stood in plain sight, but it appeared inactive at the moment. They needed to verify that it still remained one of a kind.

Odyon found the curator on sub-level 333, beneath the Library of Illumination. He watched while Nero 51 practiced humming the way Odyon had taught him. "You may yet learn to shapeshift, Nero 51, but today, something more important is afoot."

The curator glared at him. "Do not interrupt me!"

"You're going to want to hear what I came here to say."

"I've been planning the next stage of my invasion all night, and I would like some time to meditate before putting the plan into action.

"There are curators on your realm, right now, preparing to relieve you of your, or should I say 'their,' time machine."

The curator jumped to his feet. "You are sure of this?"

"I arrived with them. And I must depart with them if I don't want to be stuck on this infernal world with you or your kind. So, I'll leave you to do whatever you must do to protect the vehicle. I must go find my return ride to Lumina."

Nero 51 slammed the elevator door shut as he and Odyon began their ascent to ground level. "Where are they?"

"In your underground hangar. I guess it's not as secret as you thought."

"*Fegt.*"

Once they left the library, Odyon turned into a whisper and floated back to the hangar to find the overseers.

RYDEN SIMMDRY AND Mal arrived on Fantasia in the middle of the twenty-third century. They materialized in the office where Mal had originally borrowed the time machine. Their clothing dated them, yet they did not appear odd, as many of the people who had gone to that location to request transport were from different eras, and their clothing varied wildly.

Mal pointed out one man in particular. "That is Sir Arthur Breckenridge. He is the man I dealt with the last time I was here." They approached the balustrade that divided the room but were told they would have to wait their turn.

Ryden Simmdry hummed.

⌘*He will want to see us immediately.*

The man who had stopped them cocked his head, then said, "Wait here." A moment later, Sir Arthur approached them. He recognized Mal and smiled. "Returning our vehicle?"

"I would like to," Mal answered. "But I seem to have misplaced the crystals. If it wouldn't be too much bother, we would like to acquire a duplicate set, so we can return the time machine."

"Let me pull up your records." Sir Arthur handed Mal a small ball. Mal already knew holding it would identify his DNA and recall his records. A moment later, Sir Arthur swiped the virtual documents that appeared in mid-air and nodded. "I see we have done much satisfactory business with you over the past six hundred years or so. If you will wait here, I will see about a duplicate set of crystals." Sir Arthur disappeared behind a door of substantial size.

⌘*Do you enjoy traveling through time, Malcolm?*

"It has its benefits, especially for curators of the library."

⌘*So you do not do it for pleasure.*

Mal laughed aloud. "I'm sure it could be fun, but I've only changed time zones, so to speak, in the service of righting wrongs."

⌘*I could teach you to time travel if you like. Not all the overseers can do it, nor do they want to. But you are already familiar with the peculiarities of the space-time continuum, and I could teach you to travel on your own.*

Mal snapped his fingers. "Just like that?"

⌘*You would have to wear your chaperon, since it is necessary for tele-transportation, but I could easily show you the rest.*

Mal smiled. "I may take you up on that." He stopped speaking when Sir Arthur reappeared holding two crystals. "These should work with the vehicle in your possession." He slipped them into a small kidskin bag and handed it to Mal. "Enjoy your travels."

No sooner were they out the door than they were back on Lumina, where they waited to hear from Horatio Blastoe and Plato Indelicat.

THE TWO OVERSEERS popped into and out of potential Terrorian hiding places in quick succession, looking for duplicate time machines. After a thorough search of the library and surrounding buildings, as well as the hangar, the town hall and town square, they decided their task had been completed.

✠*There are no other time machines here, but it appears the Terrorians are amassing for something major. We need to return to Lumina and hope that Malcolm has taken possession of a duplicate set of crystals.*

Ω*I agree. Let's take one last look inside the hangar, and then depart.*

ODYON FLOATED OVER to Plato Indelicat's robe and rested upon it as a speck of dust. Moments later, the two overseers and the stowaway were back on Lumina.

*

A GOLDEN-ORANGE GRID crawled through space, en route from Adventura to its sun. Through a telescope, it appeared to be a gossamer web. It looked ethereal, yet too uniform to be anything spontaneous. Prophet DAVID l. estimated it would take approximately 7.6 minutes to reach the Adventuran sun.

Prophet IAN c. and the others waited in complete silence. The curator knew DAVID l. would inform him at the estimated time of impact. While he waited, he remembered select bits and pieces of his many lives. Because Adventurans were cloned replicas of their previous selves, their past lives stayed with them. They were all historians, so to speak, although their scope of deciphering past events focused on each Adventuran's immediate environ. IAN c. thought of his years as curator of the Library of Illumination. He knew how the libraries operated on other realms, having been to both the Luminan and Scientic facilities. His library was a mere shell compared to the others, if only because of the Adventurans' post-nuclear proclivity to download information directly onto hard drives implanted near their brains. The libraries in other realms seemed ancient and fusty, yet they held a charm all their own that inspired wonder and enchantment. His facility was more of a museum than a working library. *It is how we know what books, manuscripts, and scrolls looked like. That's when we had endless trees and plants with which to make paper to print everything on. Or when we had skins to use in lieu of paper, or parchment to serve that purpose.*

"Five minutes to engagement," DAVID l. announced.

Prophet CARL a. sighed uncharacteristically. "These will probably be the longest five minutes of our lives. It brings to mind the words of a Fantasian philosopher, one Friedrich Nietzsche, whose work I studied years ago. He said, 'That which does not kill us makes us stronger.'"

"That about sums it up," DANIEL p. whispered to DAVID l.

"I didn't know you studied off-world philosophy," IAN c. said. "We do not maintain many downloads under that category."

"I did not come upon his work through a download. Basically, I plumbed the depths of your library looking for noted philosophers from other worlds, and I read those words on the brittle pages of a dusty book deep within the bowels of the library's many sub-levels."

DAVID l. studied his console. "Four minutes to impact."

"I wonder if others would have benefited from using the library?" IAN c. mused. "I always believed it to be too badly damaged after the nuclear devastation following the Two Millennia War. However, in retrospect, most of the damage affected the above-ground levels. A wealth of information has always remained available in the libraries sub-levels." He appeared to sigh—an altogether unusual mannerism for hu*bots, because they have no lungs. "Perhaps, I am not the best choice for curator. Perhaps another could have done more for the Library of Illumination."

"'Perhaps' we'll never know," DANIEL p. muttered.

DAVID l. stared at DANIEL p. for a moment before returning his gaze to his console. "Three minutes to impact."

"This civilization came back to life after one period of almost total destruction," IAN c. continued. "While we may not all survive the next few days, there are some who may. Some whom the overseers might discover in stasis and re-invigorate after the current crisis ends. Every so often, the old ways must be abandoned to allow for the growth of new ideas. Lives must be sacrificed to allow a rebirth to take place. Civilizations come and go, but the thread of existence often finds other ways to carry on."

"Sometimes, forgetting what has come before increases the chance of making mistakes anew," CARL a. said. "We can always learn from our mistakes."

"If this mission fails," IAN c. said, "if our civilization ceases to exist, what will prevent those who come after us from plunging this world into another nuclear nightmare?"

CARL a. smiled. "Your very own Library of Illumination. As long as the sub-levels continue to house the archives of all that came before, anyone who comes after us has the potential to learn from our mistakes."

"Two minutes to impact," DAVID l. said.

"Could we talk about something other than philosophy and dying?" DANIEL p. asked. "This entire conversation will be meaningless if what we are doing works. It's a whole lot of useless introspective blubbering. Let's just try being upbeat for a moment and imagine what we'll do if we succeed in reducing the solar flares. It should not take long for us to see if all our work is effective. What then? Are we prepared to repair the power grids? Have we identified the best way to set a recovery plan in motion?

What is our recovery plan?"

IAN c. cocked his head—another unusual movement for a hu*bot. "I've been concentrating so much on how to fix the problem, I haven't considered what we should do in the eventuality that all the measures we've worked so industriously on, come to fruition."

"Wouldn't this be a good time to start thinking about that?" DANIEL p. asked.

"Indeed, it would," the curator answered.

"One minute to impact."

IAN c. began to pace. "Our first action must be to re-energize the power grids."

DAVID l. shook his head. "How do we do that without an initial, substantial power source? We can only turn the grid on one section at a time. As soon as we do, the endless draw from all the online recharging stations will trip the circuit breaker, shutting it back down. The first grid will need to be backed up by a substantial amount of power in order to sustain the load."

IAN c. stood a little taller. "The Library of Illumination."

"How is a mostly-defunct library going to save us?" DANIEL p. asked.

"I may be wrong, but I believe the first sub-level of the library is intact. CARL a., when you last used the library to research philosophy, do you remember how far down the damage went?"

"There is no damage below ground level. If there were, I would never have ventured further."

"Impact."

All eyes went to the viewing screens. Instead of

several large eruptions on the sun's surface, a hundred smaller, barely noticeable flares broke out uniformly across the surface. A minute passed.

"Did it work?" DANIEL p asked.

"It will take a little while before we can tell for sure. Right now, surface eruptions appear to be uniform, dividing the strength of the massive flares that plagued us into smaller ones we can handle," DAVID l. answered. "That must continue, in order for our plan to work."

"Let me put it another way," DANIEL p. said. "Have we failed?"

"It is too soon to tell," DAVID l. said.

"No." DANIEL p. spun around. "If there were continued, huge, out-of-control eruptions like there were before, you could say we failed. But there aren't. As of this moment, we have not failed." He turned to IAN c. "What's in the first sub-level of the Library of Illumination that's going to help us re-fire our grid?"

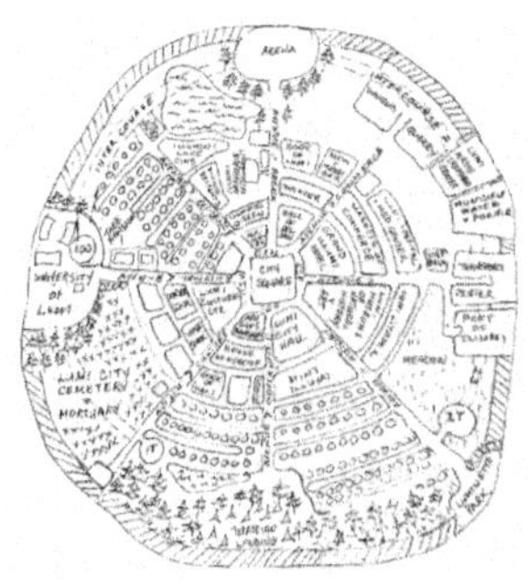

CHAPTER TWENTY-EIGHT

RYDEN SIMMDRY AND Mal arrived back on Lumina at the same time as Horatio Blastoe and Plato Indelicat. Mere moments later, all the overseers convened in their meeting room.

✠*The time machine is hidden in an underground hangar on Terroria and was there when we left.*

⌘*Malcolm and I have procured a set of crystals to operate it.*

Mal opened his hand to reveal the crystals. "I should go immediately, if we want to retake the machine before it is used again."

⌘*I couldn't agree more.*

Ω*I'll return with you,* Plato Indelicat said, Ω*and show you where it is located.*

"Excellent."

*

ODYON DRIFTED HOME, squeezing himself under the door as a wind gust. He regained his human appearance and embarked on his usual morning routine as if nothing had happened. He carried his news tablet and his breakfast outside and settled down in his favorite seat.

No one even missed me. How sad. And how very, very fortunate.

JACKSON'S SNORE WOKE Johanna. Her wrist slammed into the telescopic arm as she stretched, and she nearly bumped her head when she tried to sit up too quickly. The adaptive chairs they sat on had sensed their lowered respiration and stretched into a more reclined position. But as Johanna suddenly awakened, the chair rose back into position causing her to lose her equilibrium. When the room stopped spinning, she slid out of the chair and descended the stairs. "Jackson," she shouted.

"Just five more minutes," he mumbled as he tried to turn over. Comfortable as it might be, the chair wasn't a bed, and Jackson slowly opened his eyes when he realized something was amiss. He looked at the chair next to his, which was empty. "Johanna?"

"I'm over here," she said from a few feet away. "I'm surprised you didn't want to sit in *those* chairs," she said, pointing well above his head.

Jackson leaned out of the chair and craned his neck but couldn't see what she pointed at. He took a deep breath and stretched as he slid out of the chair and walked over to her. He turned to look up, and his eyes settled on a much higher telescope that was directed downward at a sharp angle. "That's not pointing at another realm."

"No. It looks like someone's keeping tabs on something here in Lumi."

He stretched. "We've seen everything else. But I feel like our reconnaissance wouldn't be complete without investigating that last telescope."

"I agree," she said. "How do we get up there?"

There was no simple staircase leading up to the higher telescope, just ladder-like bars that looked like handles extending out of the central stem of the mechanism.

"I think a little climbing is in order."

"I'm game if you are."

"Okay." He rubbed his stubble. "Do you want to go first? That way I can stand down here in case you fall."

"And catch me?"

"That's the idea."

"Who's going to catch you, if you slip and fall?"

Jackson leaned over the edge of the platform. "Furst," he called out, too low for anyone to hear him.

"Stop joking around," she said. "I'm going." She climbed up the extensions and when she reached the top step, one of the seats swung over and nudged the back of her knees. She grabbed one of the armrests and sat down. It retracted to its original position. She looked down at Jackson. "Your turn."

He climbed to the top and the remaining seat moved over to collect him. A moment later, he was at her side. "Actually, that was pretty easy."

"It was. Let's turn this thing on and see what's so exciting to look at on Lumina."

Jackson adjusted the focus, and they found themselves staring down into a flower bed. "This is an awfully sophisticated piece of equipment to use just to take a look at your neighbor's garden."

Johanna played with the controls and the shot widened out. "Look. One side is the garden behind the Library of Origination. I recognize the statues on that section of wall from Plato Indelicat's memorial."

Jackson looked through the eyepiece. "The flowers are on the other side of that wall. One of the overseer's must have garden envy."

"That would be the house on the right as you enter the grounds," Johanna said. "I think that's where Governor Tare used to live. But Mal said he sold it—" she paused to think for a moment, "—to someone from Fantasia."

"Really? I wonder if we can redirect this thing to look in a window?" He played with the controls but could not maneuver the telescopic arm into the correct position. "I can't seem to—wait! Someone is coming out the back door. Look."

Johanna and Jackson shared the eyepiece and watched the new owner of the house emerge.

Old personas are like a worn-in pair of jeans or a really comfortable T-shirt; you never want to take them off because they're easy to wear. Peter Dakion's persona was new, making it more difficult to maintain, which is why Johanna and Jackson nearly jumped out of their seats when they spied Robert Birk, a.k.a. Odyon, sitting down to breakfast on his balcony.

Dungen pulled Pondor forward to cut the cords binding him. They fell off before he unsheathed his knife. "I see you've been busy, old man."

He kicked Pondor's feet apart. The loosened rope fell away. "Why did you stay?"

Pondor used the voice he reserved for his most egregious lawbreakers. "Why did you bring me here?"

"You obviously don't show any public appreciation of me as your son. I wanted to see if you could attach any value to our relationship when outsiders weren't present."

Pondor tried to get up but stumbled; the circulation in his legs had not yet been restored. He finally dragged himself into an upright position with the help of a chair. "You are my son, Dungen, and I will always love you. You're a part of me. But you also share blood with your mother, and she had her share of problems. They were not her fault. She was born with a congenital chemical imbalance. You show the same symptoms."

"You said it was not her fault. If that's true, any symptoms you see are not my fault, either."

"I agree. That is why you have remained free for so long. However, murder is not a symptom. It is an act of cowardice and cruelty, and I am quite sure you murdered the young soldier, Lenc."

"He threatened me!"

"He was a boy. An orphan. He forfeited his childhood to help us fight the Terrorians. I do not see you volunteering to take his place or to assist your friends and neighbors."

"I will not answer to Furst! He is not my leader. I should have been chosen as curator."

"It's odd, my son, but I have never seen you take joy from books. Those I presented to you as a child quickly found their place in the bottom of the hearth. You have no love of the written word."

"Reading is for people who do not wish to lead. I'm a man of action. Wasting my time with printed words is an insult to my intelligence."

"You're wrong," Pondor bellowed. Dungen took a step back in reaction to his father's vehemence. "Reading engages the mind and stimulates the soul. It teaches us about our past and prepares us to enter the future. It expands our knowledge and helps us live our lives more fully. Books are one of our greatest legacies, yet you would cast them aside for action. And what action did you take? Murdering one of our neighbors. You don't deserve to be a curator of a Library of Illumination. You do not begin to possess the skills required for that position, nor could you imagine what to do with those skills if you had them. Your mind is small, Dungen. It is not your fault. But murdering Lenc is, and you must pay for that."

Mal and Plato Indelicat were gone a short measure before reappearing on Lumina.

Ω*Our report is not as expected.*

"As the saying goes, we have good news and we have bad news. Which would you like first?"

Ryden Simmdry already sensed the answer. ⌘*What's the good news?*

"It looks like the invasion troops previously sent to other realms have all been recalled to Terroria. It's evident in the number of soldiers we saw amassing in their town square."

⌘*That is good news. Unfortunately, we already knew*

the bad news as soon as Plato Indelicat re-entered the room. Where do you think they moved the time machine?

Mal hesitated. "It's not that they moved the time machine. It's that they're using it."

At that moment, it was closer than any of them imagined.

NERO 51'S WAR machine moved like the wind, transporting troopers to a wooded area on the southern tip of the outcrop that hosted the capital city of Lumi and the Library of Origination. Few people in the city had reason to visit the forest, and the dark foliage easily hid the vast number of invaders being transported to the planet. At most, only three troopers could be moved in a single visit, but the time machine moved so quickly that by nightfall, hundreds of Terrorians would lay in wait on the outskirts of Lumi. Nero 51 refused to accept defeat. His soldiers were commanded to not engage until he arrived to lead them into war.

It won't be long now, he thought. *This is for you, Garpa.*

"I DON'T CARE about Lenc," Dungen said as he turned his back on his father. Before he could continue, Pondor—fueled by growing anxiety—jumped him from behind.

Dungen tried to wrestle free, but Pondor used one hand to loop the rope that previously bound his feet around Dungen's neck. The younger man tried to tug the rope loose and was too preoccupied to notice Pondor grabbing a lantern. One blow to the head caused Dungen to crumple to the floor. His father used fishing line hanging from a rod on the wall of the cabin to secure Dungen's hands and feet, and he used the rope to tie his son to the bed.

Dungen's eyes fluttered open.

"I will send someone to get you," Pondor said.

"You will never make it out of here. The Terrorians will kill you, and then I'll starve to death in this cabin, alone. That will be your legacy, old man."

"In that case, you had better hope I make it back to the city and send someone to get you."

"Then what?"

"You'll be tried for Lenc's murder. Our society depends on a set of rules to keep us safe. When a rule is broken, someone must be made to pay, or else we'd be living in a state of chaos, and no one would be safe."

PONDOR TOOK THE decimator Dungen had stolen and carried it with him as he carefully made his way to the main roadway. He followed it back to the nearest town. A number of people were gathered on the doorstep of a local store, speaking excitedly.

"Is something amiss?" Pondor asked as he walked up to them.

"The invaders appear to have gone. No one has seen them for most of the night. We are trying to decide if we should return to our homes or continue to migrate west, where they're less likely to find us. From what we've pieced together from other people, they tend to stay close to cities and only send small patrols this far out. I think they've given up out here and returned to one of the cities."

"I need to get to Dramoni. Is anyone going in that direction?" Pondor asked.

"Didn't you hear a word I said?" the speaker asked.

"The invaders have probably returned to the cities. You'd do best to stay away from there."

"Unfortunately, I can't. Perhaps you could lend me transportation."

The man narrowed his eyes as he looked at Pondor. "It will cost you."

Pondor loosened some jewels from his caftan and handed them to the speaker.

The man nodded before he turned and walked to a bush next to the store, where he had hidden a Dramatican version of a bicycle. It worked on the same principle, but instead of a solitary wheel in the front and back, it used double wheels that were attached to each other with spacers in-between them. The seat looked like a bucket seat, and instead of handlebars, it had more of a half-steering wheel.

Dramoni wasn't close, but Pondor knew this could be his only way back to the city. And if everyone gathered here was right, he'd be safe for most of the trip.

"It's Odyon. C'mon. We have to capture him," Jackson said as he tried to figure out how to make his chair move back to the ladder rungs.

"He's not going to just open the door. We need Ryden Simmdry's help. He can transport us there with me holding the little black cube in my hand."

"Okay." He paused. "How do we get down?"

Johanna tried to move the seat forward by jerking her hips. "Hmmm…that's not working."

"Getting up here seemed so easy," Jackson whined as he pushed the eyepiece away with a decided thrust. His chair moved toward the wall. He grabbed onto the rungs and climbed down. He looked up. "C'mon. What are you waiting for?"

"What did you do?" she asked.

"I pushed the eyepiece away."

"But it's not even near me." Johanna leaned forward and grabbed the eyepiece, pulling it toward her and then pushing it away. Her chair moved to the central stem. "Did it," she called down.

Together, the teens negotiated the unsteady, split staircase and then dashed down the cupola stairs as quickly as possible. They looked for Ryden Simmdry in the main part of the Library of Origination, and when they couldn't find him, they went in search of the library's executive board room.

The teens burst through the door, and the overseers turned in unison. Johanna and Jackson stopped as abruptly as if a line had been drawn on the floor.

"I hope we're not interrupting," she said, "but we just saw Odyon having breakfast on the terrace of Governor Tare's mansion next door, and we thought, if you could transport me there, I could capture his essence in the little black cube."

⌘ *You have the cube with you?*

"I carry it everywhere, hoping to run into Odyon."

⌘ *Then we shouldn't delay. Take out the cube.*

Johanna fished inside her pocket and produced it.

Ryden Simmdry placed his hand on her shoulder. A moment later they were gone.

"Hey, what about me?" Jackson complained, after they left without him.

"I wouldn't worry, Jackson," Mal answered. "They

were probably in so much of a hurry, they didn't realize they left you behind."

"That's what I'm afraid of," Jackson said, his chin dropping to his chest. *She probably feels like she doesn't need me anymore.*

A ROMANTICAN WOMAN emerged from the woods at the edge of the field. She broke into a sprint as she ran for the school. "Open the door," she screamed, afraid invaders might be on her tail.

"Quickly, get inside and call out for someone to open the main door," Milencia ordered Annabeth. Annabeth scampered across the roof to the nearest window and re-entered the building. "Open the main door," she yelled. She ran down the stairs as fast as she could and arrived on the first floor to find the woman already inside the building and the door barred. "What happened out there?"

"I've been hiding in the woods. I was away for a while, and when I returned, I saw many homes destroyed and ugly brutes with tentacles patrolling the town square."

"Just now?" Annabeth clarified.

"No. Yesterday. I've been hiding in the woods. I didn't know where to go, but I saw someone climb out of the window onto the roof of the school, and I decided to make a run for it, hoping to find shelter here."

"Did anyone pursue you?"

"No. Why?"

"We're trying to determine what happened to the invaders," Milencia said from the staircase. "I stayed on the roof and watched in case they were following you, but

I didn't see, or hear, anything unusual. I wonder where they've all gone?"

"Try the town square," the visitor answered.

Milencia looked around. "Anyone care to join me for an excursion to the town square?"

No one answered. Annabeth grimaced. "I'll go with you."

"No. You'd better stay here. As far as this group is concerned, you're next in line in seniority as a militairre."

"You can't go alone."

"I'll go with you," Marin said. "Can I take one of those with me?" she asked, nodding at the decimator.

"Here," Stasia said, handing Marin a weapon.

"You have to follow my lead," Milencia said as she led Marin toward an unobtrusive back entrance. "If I say run, don't question me, just run. Your life could depend on it."

"What are you hoping to find?" Marin asked.

"Nothing. I'm afraid we'll find something, but if I had my choice, I don't want to find a single solitary thing that wasn't here months before the library burned down."

They sprinted for the tree line and followed the woods to a row of burnt-out houses that led to the village. They hid behind the charred remains of what was once their friends' and neighbors' homes. Everything seemed eerily silent, except for the wildlife.

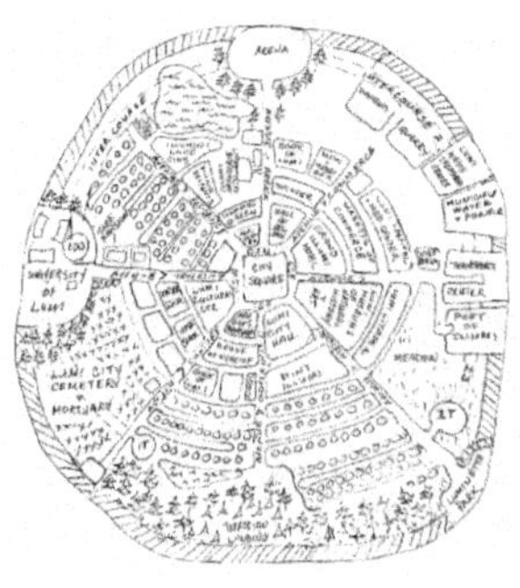

CHAPTER TWENTY-NINE

THE COMI SHORELINE had always been pristine, but that afternoon, the reverse came true. At first, it was just one Terrorian carcass. By sunset, two dozen dead Terrorians littered the beach. The carnage could be described as horrific, but also eerily comforting. The invaders were dead, and any new invaders would be greeted with an obvious sign that their kind weren't welcome on Comedia.

CURATOR IAN c. AND prophet CARL a. slashed through the webs that shrouded the staircase leading to the lower levels of the Adventuran Library of Illumination. IAN c. led the way to the Chamber of Doors and used the insignia on his left palm to obtain access.

"A locked door leading to more locked doors, Prophet IAN c? I am intrigued."

IAN c. approached the door to the nuclear reactor.

"For many millennia, the library has maintained its own source of power. If we are lucky, it will allow us to use it for another purpose."

"Adventurans as a population do not believe in luck. We work toward a goal until it is realized."

"Well then, let us work toward our goal." The curator opened the door and nodded at a glowing blue orb that sat in the center of the darkened room. The orb drifted toward the door.

"Come, CARL a. It will follow."

The two hu*bots climbed the steps to the main level, and the blue orb followed. They crossed the town square, and still, the blue orb followed. They continued on until they reached the lab where the others waited.

"Please tell me we are maintaining a measure of success on the sun's surface."

"The eruptions remain a manageable size," DAVID l. stated. "What's our next step?"

"Your next step, DAVID l., is to stay here and monitor the surface. Contact us immediately if there is any change.

"DANIEL p. Please unhook a cohort of charged hu*bots and send a few of them here to assist DAVID l. Dispatch the others to the city's power stations. They will need to switch on the individual power annexes in precise order to ensure we don't overload the grid. Have each group contact me in the central power plant when they are in place.

"CARL a., you and I will take our blue friend to the main plant and put it to work as backup."

*

ODYON BARELY HEARD the whisper of sound behind him, yet he felt the hairs on the back of his neck prickle. *What—?* he thought, but he was too late. He felt himself pixilate and twisted to see Johanna Charette holding a black cube in her hand. In the time it took him to comprehend what had happened, he was sucked into it.

PRU TELLERENCE AND Furst arrived on Dramatica together after learning Terrorian troopers had abandoned the other realms. The detention cells were empty. "Freed, everyone has been."

★ *That is a positive sign, but where is everyone?*

"In the barracks, they will be," Furst said. "Meal time, it is."

As they walked, they looked at damaged buildings. The Terrorians had destroyed buildings and homes but not as many as on some of the other realms—a testament to Dramatican bravery and fighting ability.

Inside the barracks, Furst proved right. A large contingent of men and women shared a meal under a sign that read: *Kinship—United on All Fronts.*

★*I didn't realize you had women soldiers.*

"Not soldiers. Lost their homes, they have, perhaps."

★ *Yes. Of course.*

The crowd cheered when they saw Furst.

"Won the war, we have," Ozzro said, jumping up from his seat and slapping Furst on the back.

★*I'm afraid not.*

"What?" someone asked, before the others at the table lapsed into silence.

"Moved the fighting front, the Terrorians have. To ask for volunteers, we have come. On Lumina, we need to fight."

"That, where is?" one of the women asked. She looked at her mate. "Gone long, will he be?"

"Far, it is," Furst answered. "Important we fight, it is. Or, lose all the knowledge in the library, we could. When that happens, erased, all our books and papers will be."

★*Including the saying on the sign above your heads.*

"Impossible, that is," one of the women said.

★*It is very possible unless we stop the Terrorians where they fight. Those who volunteer would be transported to Lumina. It's on another world, far beyond your sun."*

"Furst," the woman asked, "true, is what she says?"

"Yes," he answered. "Going, I will be. Stand with me, will any of you?"

Every man in a military tunic stood. Then others stood to join them.

"Volunteer, only those past the age of majority may. Should not volunteer, anyone who has already lost someone in this fight. Benger and Lylle, for volunteering, thank you, but a son," Furst nodded at Benger, "and a brother," he nodded at Lylle, "you have lost. To maintain the peace, stay here. Running, keep Dramoni. Rebuild. Sacrifice enough, your families have.

"Everyone else, thank you," Furst continued. "Leaving shortly, we will be. To your families, say goodbye. And meet me here, gather your gear. In a quarter-cycle, we leave."

When the volunteers returned, Pru Tellerence

instructed them to grasp the next man's arm and form a circle. After the circle formed, the volunteers disappeared from sight.

"So, it's agreed," Hue the Elder said. "The unused caves on the Eastern shore will be used as temporary housing while we rebuild."

"It shouldn't take long to rebuild," one of the politicians pointed out. "The side walls to all the earth shelters remain intact. Only the frames that held the thatched and sod roofs were burned by the Terrorians. We could have a third of the available workers clear out the debris, while another third construct frames for the roofs, and the last group goes out into the meadow and gathers sod and thatch. This will allow some people to start refitting their homes more quickly, rather than waiting while everyone does the same job at the same time."

"Who will choose whose home is fixed first?" High Priestess Usterice, asked.

"We shall start in the west and work our way eastward. That way, those who must live in the caves the longest will have less to travel in the end."

"No!" shouted a priest named Sirge. "My home will be one of the last ones fixed. I do not agree with your plan."

"I see," Hue the Elder said. "Then I suggest you start fixing your house right now, by yourself." He conferred with the other elders for a moment and then raised his voice. "Anyone who does not subscribe to the plan the elders just laid out can fix his own home, but by withdrawing from our plan and doing it yourself, you are agreeing to do the work without anyone's help, nor with the donated materials we are acquiring for the project. If you choose to put yourself first, you must rely on your own resources. If you choose to work for the good of the community in a way that will allow us to do the most work in the quickest manner, you will benefit from the pooled resources and talents of all."

"That's not fair," Sirge argued. "I will need someone to help me build the frame and to cut and transport the sod."

The murmuring of voices inside the now roofless pit increased. Hue held up both his arms. "Who would like to drop out of the plan to help Sirge rebuild his home first and lose out on community resources?"

"When you say it like that," Sirge bellowed, "no one will want to do it."

"Precisely," Hue said.

Ψ*Excuse me.*

No one had noticed Proteus Bligh's arrival in the back of the discussion pit, and they all turned when his greeting interrupted them.

Ψ*It would seem that you have your recovery well in hand, but we need something from you.*

"What could you possibly need from us?" Usterice asked.

Ψ*The Terrorian invasion has not ended. It has just changed location. We believe troops will be amassing in one location, and we are asking each realm to supply us with warriors to help quell the Terrorians for good.*

"Wave your arms and perform your own sorcery," Sirge shouted. "We don't owe you anything. How dare you make such demands?"

ΨIt is not a demand. Only a request.

"We have lost too much already," Usterice called out.

Ψ The Illumini Constellation has been guided and protected by the College of Overseers for many millennia. It has always been a give-and-take system, although in the past, we have never needed to take anything in return. But now, Lumina is threatened. We do not ask all your able-bodied citizens to help us. But any you could spare would be helpful in keeping the Illumini Constellation protected. Without Lumina, you would lose your library and the written source of your knowledge. Your future generations will struggle to remain literate, and they might lose that battle. If anyone can be spared, please see Hue the Elder. I will be in contact with him. It is, after all, only a request, but it is one of the most important requests that will ever be put before you.

A young priest named Davo responded. "If I agree to help you, I will miss the opportunity to have my home rebuilt because I will not be here to take part in the plan."

ΨA moment. Proteus Bligh stood quietly, as if lost in thought. In reality, he engaged in telepathic communication with the other overseers. He regained focus. *Ψ If you choose to fight with us, we will make sure you home is rebuilt by the time you return.*

The sound level increased, as everyone reacted to the offer Proteus Bligh had just made to Davo.

"Would that be true for me also?" a politician asked. "I have a family. Would they have to wait for my return? What if I don't survive the battle?"

ΨAnyone who fights will have a home to return to. Those with families will have their homes rebuilt once they engage in battle. Hue the Elder will see to it. He nodded at Hue, who nodded back.

"Then I will fight," the politician announced.

"And I," Davo called out.

ACROSS MANY OF the realms in the Illumini System, individual overseers sought the same recruitment. Some were more successful than others, but they all managed to transport warriors—male and female, old and young—to Lumina, where they gathered inside the same arena where the Curator Orientations and Overseer Challenges were held.

HORATIO BLASTOE POINTED at each of the doors to the detention cells holding Romantican prisoners. The women cheered as they were released. They told him how the Terrorians all seemed to disappear after the time machine arrived that afternoon.

✠*About that,* Horatio Blastoe said. ✠*There appears to be a change in plans. I am looking for militairres who would volunteer to fight on Lumina. Most of you have basic training and know what's at stake if you lose. We know Lumina is a long way off, and many of you may not wish to leave your homes, but we are in desperate need of your fighting strength to protect the Illumini Constellation.*

"Of course, you know I'll go," Natalia said.

"Me, too," the Jolen sisters said in unison.

The new co-captains all agreed to go. In fact, only two of the younger girls, who did not want to leave their families, agreed to carry the fight to Lumina.

✠*You have made me proud.*

Someone in the distance shouted. Everyone turned to see Marin and Stasia running toward them. "You freed them," Stasia called out happily.

"Most of us," Natalia admitted, "but not all. We believe some militairres were taken off-world."

✠ *They have been taken to Terroria. Plato Indelicat, the overseer for that realm, is at work, right now, endeavoring to free them. He will take everyone to Lumina. Those who wish to return to their home worlds will be allowed to return. But we are hoping many, like yourselves, will heed the call and fight.*

LOGAN THOUGHT GETTING information about abortions—without explaining why he wanted it—might be tricky, so he told the people he spoke with that he needed the information for a story he was doing for GRUNT. Unfortunately, he found himself referred to other offices, which were apparently closed on Sundays. He groaned. The sooner he took care of this, the better. He only hoped Cassie would be patient until he found a solution to their problem.

CASSIE COULD NOT stop crying. *Why is Logan being so mean about the baby?* It didn't take a rocket scientist to know he didn't want anything to do with the child he fathered.

Her parents wouldn't help. They were divorced, and each had remarried and had other children. Her father, whom she lived with, often complained about money because clothing and feeding his younger offspring seemed to drain every cent he had. She wouldn't be getting any financial assistance from her father, and she knew her step-mother would never agree to take care of her baby while she worked. They would probably kick her out. Cassie's mother would be even less helpful. They had never gotten along. Her mother always belittled Cassie for not being attractive enough or smart enough, even though Cassie was pretty and did well in school. No matter how hard she tried, she would never be able to live up to her mother's impossible expectations.

Her cell phone buzzed. *Logan.* "Hi."

"I've been looking into options for us and I think I found a way to get past our problem and preserve our future."

"How?"

"I don't have all the info yet, but I've heard about a clinic in Caldwell that performs discreet… terminations."

"Terminations. You mean an abortion? You want me to abort our baby?"

"Cass, I'm still looking into possible solutions, but so far, this seems like the best one."

"Do you even love me?"

He hesitated a little too long. "We've got our whole lives ahead of us—"

She disconnected the call. *Bastard.* She thought about what it would be like to be a single mom with a minimum-wage job and a baby to take care of. *I can't do it,* she thought. *Not by myself.* Her shoulders shook and her face crumpled as her emotions overwhelmed her.

While her father and step-mother busied themselves with their younger children, Cassie quietly snuck into their bedroom and ransacked their medicine chest for sleeping pills. Between her father's Ambien and her step-mother's

Xanax and Zoloft, she had more than three-dozen pills to end her anguish.

She hid them under her pillow. Then she went downstairs and raided the liquor cabinet. She took a nearly-full bottle of vodka back to her room. She drank half of it as she mourned the fate of her unborn child. She used the rest to wash down the pills she pilfered. As she lay down on her bed to wait for everything to take effect, a single tear escaped the corner of her eye.

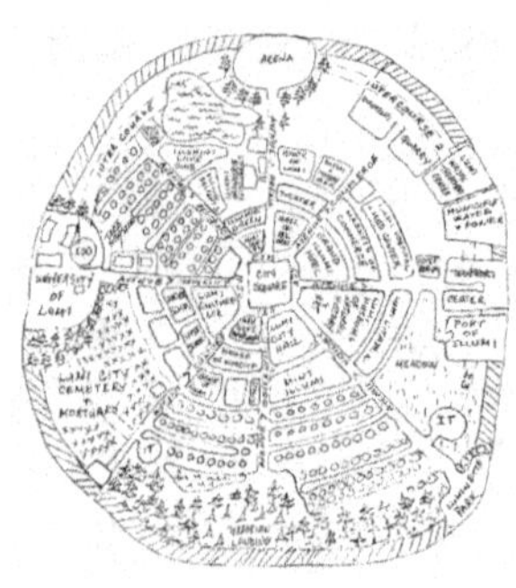

CHAPTER THIRTY

Hu*bots stationed in the various power plants awaited their orders from Prophet IAN c.

Meanwhile, the curator stood in the middle of the central power plant preparing to telepathically communicate with the blue orb. He took a deep breath and raised his arms, then he lowered them until they pointed to the main generator. Afterward, he used a Com-Link communications device and asked each deployed hu*bot for his exact location. He gave each one a number instructing him what to do when the number was announced.

A dry run proved everything was ready.

"Prophet CARL a. stand by. You are first in line. When I say 'one,' pull the handle to switch on the grid.

"Stand by," he told everyone over the Com-Link.

Once again, he looked at the orb. Then he re-focused on CARL a. "One."

CARL a. pulled the handle and the main generator roared to life.

"Two. Three. Four. Five." IAN c. counted aloud until he accounted for every annex.

A speaker sputtered to life. Prophet DAVID l. announced, "The power is on. Prophet DANIEL p. is up in the observatory and says the whole city is coming back to life."

A flurry of voices on the Com-Link made the same claim.

CASSIE'S STOMACH SEIZED and she rolled over in bed, violently vomiting a mixture of semi-dissolved pills and alcohol. She tried to gasp for breath but inhaled her own vomit, causing sudden spasms of choking.

One floor below, her step-mother complained to Cassie's father, "What on earth is going on with your daughter upstairs?"

"If it bothers you," he said, "go up and take a look."

"She's *your* daughter."

"When you asked me to place that wedding ring on your finger, you chose to become her surrogate mother."

Something above them crashed to the floor.

Cassie's step-mother finally stood up. "Since you don't care about your own daughter, I'd better go—before she wrecks the place."

Cassie's father reluctantly followed his wife up the stairs. He watched his wife try to turn the doorknob. It was locked, and when Cassie wouldn't open the door after their many requests, he threw himself against it. CRACK. The wood gave way, and he fell into the room. He managed to stay on his feet. His wife wasn't as lucky. She passed out right after she screamed.

He looked at his daughter. Cassie's face had turned blue and her eyes were bugged out as her body twitched a few last times. A bedside lamp lay shattered on the floor beside a pool of vomit, a victim of the teenager's flailing.

Cassie's father called for an ambulance and answered a few questions. "Actually, she's quieting down now."

Probably because she had stopped breathing.

MORE THAN A THOUSAND troopers in the forest on the outskirts of Lumi received their orders.

"What if the overseers' army is much larger than ours? A thousand troops are not a very large number of soldiers to take over an entire world," General Barzic 922 said.

"Lumina is an unusual world," Nero 51 noted. "It is not made up of large landmasses. It comprises a series of outcrops that stand high above a planet covered almost entirely by water."

"They can attack by air or sea?"

"No, General. They have no airships. No missiles. The outcrops are too high for naval involvement. Even the largest outcrops are not very large. Lumi is only 500 sectors, and it is the capital city. The only larger outcrops are Agrili and Meccan, which are agricultural outcrops. Once we have taken Lumi, the others will be easy. Since Lumi's population is limited by its land mass, we should be able to achieve what we need with the thousand troopers we have here, not to mention, the ten-thousand troopers who remain on Ter 0 awaiting deployment."

"The sky is brightening," one of the troopers said aloud.

"Indeed, it is," Nero 51 concurred. "Line up in formation. We march when the sun breaks the horizon."

JOHANNA AND JACKSON stood in the center of the arena, observing all the volunteers from the other realms who had chosen to continue the fight against the Terrorians on Lumina.

"I can't believe they recruited an entire section of kids to fight," Jackson remarked, after seeing a number of volunteers from Juvenilia. "What good could they possibly be?"

§*Don't let their apparent age fool you. They may appear young and act childish at times, but those kids, as you call them, were the most successful realm in defeating Terrorian invaders. We freed many people trapped in detention cells on some of the other worlds. But when we arrived on Juvenilia, the cells were filled with Terrorians. The Juveniles were free. They are quite inventive and have contributed two new weapons to our arsenal.*

Jackson looked surprised. "Really?"

Johanna pointed to another area of the arena, populated by attractive women in flowing uniforms. "Romantica?"

§ *Yes. Those are the militairres, led by Natalia Dalura.*

Jackson perked up. "Natalia is here?"

§*She is in the stands with her commanders, discussing strategy.*

"I can't help but think," Johanna mused, "that the Terrorians will know better than to make themselves easy targets."

§*Not if the Juveniles are successful. Their weapons, "scramblers" if you will, interrupt the targeted victims' brainwaves and confuse them. They're quite effective.*

"Are some of those people in the far corner sitting on pigs?" Jackson asked.

⌘*They are Comedians. That is their way.*

Johanna pointed into the stands. "Something's on fire."

⌘*The Mysterians are conjuring victory spells.*

"They're all part of the Illumini System? I didn't realize we were part of such a diverse group," Johanna said. "I guess I should have known after meeting Nero 51 and Furst that residents from the other realms would be different from us. Seeing them all here in the same place really drives the point home."

"Who are all the people with the really big heads?" Jackson asked.

⌘*The Numericons.*

"And the short guys with hairy ears?" Jackson continued.

⌘*Scienticons.*

"In the far corner on the left," Johanna pointed. "Is that one group or two?"

⌘*The beings all dressed in silver with swords at their sides are Inspiracons. Those dressed more conservatively are Educons. When you get closer, you'll notice the Educons also bear the distinction of having two irides in each eye.*

Jackson held up a finger. "What are irides?"

"Irises—the colored part of your eye." Johanna answered.

"Cool. So, there are soldiers here from every realm," Jackson frowned, "except Fantasia."

⌘*And Adventura. They are battling a major life-threatening problem, not related to the Terrorian uprising.* Ryden Simmdry placed his hand on Jackson's shoulder. ⌘*You, Johanna, and Mal are here to represent Fantasia.*

"I'm sure my mother and my brother would have volunteered," Jackson said.

◉*Perhaps. However, I don't believe Ava would have appreciated being left behind.*

"Cameron would have probably fought, as well," Johanna added.

⌘*Do you wish to return to amass your troops?*

They didn't have time to answer. The bell in the front of the Library of Origination tolled the arrival of the Terrorians.

THE TERRORIANS MARCHED in formation up the Avenue > Governance, with Nero 51 centrally located in the third row. Troopers kept a sharp eye out for any resistors hiding in the trees that surrounded them on both sides. They saw no beings of any kind, anywhere.

After several minutes, General Barzic 922 quickened his pace to catch up with Nero 51. "I thought Lumina had an advanced civilization and was a place of light with bright buildings made of gemstones. I never expected to see all these trees. Are you sure we're in the right place?"

Nero 51 felt his nerves contract. "Of course, we are. All the realms have forests."

"You said this outcrop is only 500 sectors. Is it mostly trees?"

"It is not." The curator's words were clipped.

Barzic 922 slowed his pace to build space between himself and the prickly curator and asked one last question. "Do they practice sorcery here?"

Nero 51 stopped walking. The soldiers walking behind him crashed into him and nearly knocked him down.

"Hold up," General Barzic 922 commanded. The others stopped walking.

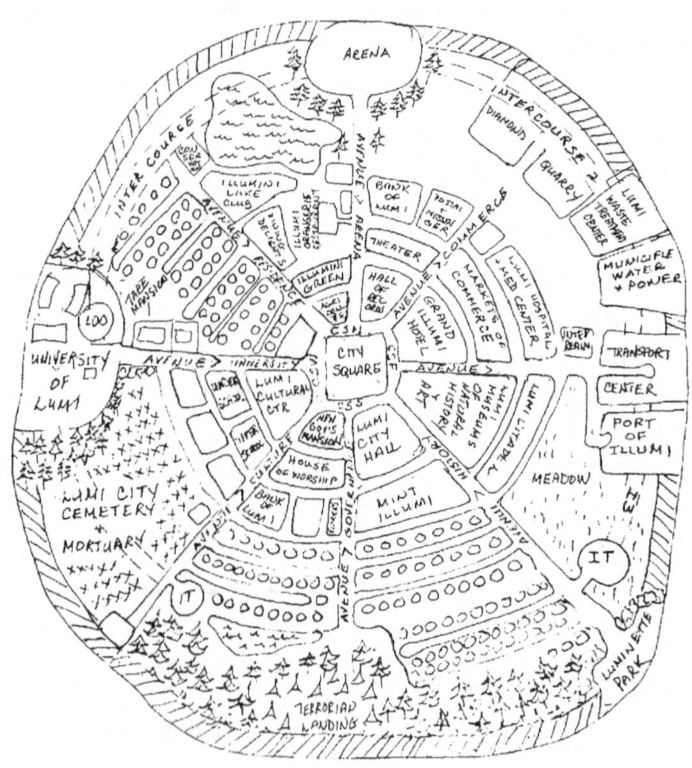

Nero 51 strode to the left. He saw only trees. He returned to the others and then passed them pushing several sectors to the right. Again, trees. *Fegt. I will make the overseers pay for their little game.* "Continue on."

"Onward," the general called out, and the Terrorians marched on.

"Who's ringing the library bell?" Jackson asked. "I thought everyone was here?"

⌘*Plato Indelicat. He doesn't have anyone in the arena to represent because he is Terroria's overseer. He is in the observatory monitoring the invaders. Apparently, they are on the move up the Avenue > Governance.*

Johanna pulled a crude map of the Lumi outcrop from her pocket. "Where is that, exactly?"

◉*If you go out the main entrance of the arena and head straight south, cutting across City Square, the name of the roadway changes to Avenue > Governance and leads straight into the forested park where the Terrorians have been amassing.*

★*It cuts right through the middle of a residential area. Have we taken any precautions to safeguard the residents of Lumi?*

⌘*I have placed an enchantment on the residential areas. As far as the Terrorians are concerned, all they will see is more trees. We have also informed everyone to stay within their homes or workplaces today.*

★*Do you honestly think they'll listen? The residents of Lumi have never had any reason to be afraid to venture outdoors.*

⌘*It was a very persuasive message, whether they realize it or not.*

Mal nodded. "That limits civilian involvement. May I suggest, rather than waiting to defend ourselves, that we take some offensive action."

★*Are you suggesting we attack first?*

"I'm suggesting we use the intercourse," Mal answered, "to covertly move some troops out as far as the lines go, so we can flank the enemy."

⌘*An excellent idea, Malcolm.* Ryden Simmdry looked for Furst in the crowd and waved him over. ⌘*I would like you to take your men to the end of the line on the west intercourse, which will allow you to exit between the cemetery and the forested park. The Terrorians will be on the move northeast of you.* He waved at Natalia Dalura. ⌘*I would like you to take your militairres on the eastern intercourse to its terminus. You will be where the meadow borders a residential area and the forest. Horatio Blastoe will accompany you. I will give you further instructions when necessary.*

⌘*Before either of you go, I need Galio Abbingdon.*

The dean of Scientico appeared almost immediately and handed Ryden Simmdry wristbands.

⌘*Thank you.* He handed one to each of the curators. ⌘*This will allow us to communicate telepathically. It can be confusing to have so many overseers' thoughts in your heads, so I have asked Galio Abbingdon to limit it to my thought waves alone, to keep the chatter down. I will give you updates automatically and will monitor your thoughts so we can keep in constant contact.*

"That is so cool," Jackson said, eyeing the wristbands.

⌘*I'm glad you think so,* Ryden Simmdry said, handing him one.

Jackson put it on and then looked at Johanna. "Aren't you going to give Johanna one?"

⌘*I'm pretty sure Johanna doesn't need one. Ever since her encounter with the Eahta Frean fram Drycræft, her abilities have increased.* He turned to Johanna. ⌘*Am I wrong? Do you require a wristband?*

Johanna shook her head. "No. I'm good."

Jackson's mouth opened and his eyes grew as large as half-dollars. "You can hear them telepathically?"

"I always could."

⌘*Not necessarily. Only when we wanted you to hear us. But I believe you have surpassed that phase.*

She shrugged. "I guess."

Jackson grabbed her arm and led her away. "When were you going to tell me you could do that?"

"I didn't know you couldn't. I thought we were both privy to the overseers' thoughts."

"Yeah, well I guess this marks the big difference between you being the prime curator and me being a plain old curator."

"You've got a wristband." She rubbed his arm. "It's just as good."

"For now," he said, looking dejected.

The library bell pealed once. ⌘*The Terrorians have reached the city square. Johanna and Proteus Bligh, take the Mysterians and Scienticons on the intercourse to the Library of Origination. Jackson, you and Pru Tellerence take the Educons and Inspiracons to the Transport Center and approach City Square by way of the Avenue > Art.*

⌘*The Juveniles, Comedians, and Numericons are with Malcolm and me on the Avenue > Arena.* He looked at Marbol and Duddu. ⌘*Are your scramblers charged and ready to go?*

"Yep." "Yes, sir!" they answered.

Ryden Simmdry's thought rang out as clear as if he said it over a loud speaker. ⌘*We are on the move.*

As the Juveniles walked, they were mesmerized by the glistening diamonds that sat along the edge of the walkway. Marbol scooped a few up and placed them in his pocket.

⌘*You do not want to do that, young man. They will explode if you try to remove them from Lumina.*

Marbol removed most of them and threw them back on the ground. He kept a couple in his pocket, just so he could get a closer look at them before he left for home.

Mal placed a hand on Ryden Simmdry's arm. "Is Plato Indelicat alone?"

⌘*Dame Erato, Ingur Aguri and Bel are also inside the library.*

"Do any of them have weapons?"

⌘*Ingur Aguri is not without her bag of tricks.*

"Plato Indelicat?"

⌘*No weapon that I know of. However, there are enchantments in place to protect the people within the library.*

"I would feel better if I took a decimator and joined them. The Terrorians may swarm the outcrop, but the essential fight is to control the libraries and the Illumini System. I'm sure that is where the fighting will culminate."

⌘*Perhaps you are right. Go, Malcolm. I will miss your counsel at my side, but you will only be a thought away.*

BEFORE LONG, THE Terrorians reached the city square. The enchantment didn't work as well with the large buildings of the inner city. Nero 51 felt more sure of himself. He recognized the Lumi City Hall on his right and the city square in front of him. Across the square, off in the distance, a crowd headed his way. "Take the square. Hold position but stand ready to engage, General."

"Colonel Endrie 1101," Nero 51 continued, "take a small battalion of troopers and split to the right following the Avenue > Transportation." He pointed it out on a map. "There is a Transport Field and direct access to the Port of Illumi at the edge of the city. Secure those areas. We don't want anyone arriving to help the Luminans."

"Captain Zenner 3, you and your men are with me."

General Barzic 922's head snapped. "Where are you going, Nero 51?"

"You are to continue forward, General. I will take the captain and his men west to the Library of Origination. It is the overseers' seat of power, and I particularly want to insure its downfall."

The Terrorians split, spreading across the outcrop.

JACKSON WISHED HE had Johanna at his side. He felt a little bereft without her. They had always worked so well together, he was stunned by their separation.

★*Cheer up, Jackson*, Pru Tellerence said, having read his thoughts. ★*I'm sure Ryden Simmdry split you up because he believes you are equally capable.*

Jackson's shoulders lifted a little and he raised his head. "You really think so?"

★*Of course. You have proven, time and again, that you have a quick mind and respond well in the face of adversity.*

So does Johanna. Having the two of you flanking the enemy is the wise way to proceed.

Jackson nodded. "Thank you." He turned to her and smile. "I needed that."

LUMI CHILDREN WERE among the most well-behaved youngsters in the Illumini Constellation; however, the overseer's enchantment had a strange affect upon them. It may have shielded them from the invaders, but it also increased activity in their brains, triggering aggressive behavior in normally docile children. One young man dwelled on the information that a war was about to be waged right outside his door and that he wasn't doing anything to help. The more he thought about it, the more his anxiety escalated, until he grabbed a walking stick and ran out the door in the direction of the Avenue > University.

At first, the trees confused him, but having lived there his entire life, he charged on toward the main road.

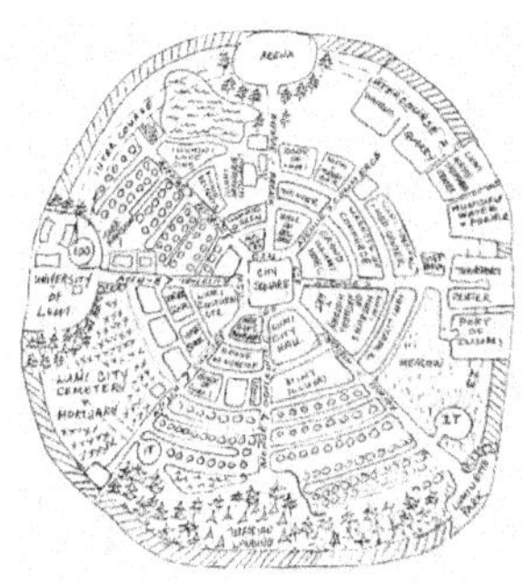

CHAPTER THIRTY-ONE

"Hey, Mom," Ava said dropping her backpack on the floor next to the circulation desk. "Any word yet from Jackson and Johanna?"

"Not yet. Why are you home from school so early?"

"We only had a half day; they're holding teacher conferences this afternoon."

"I guess you can take the place of the young corporal upstairs who's guarding the portals. I tried to get General Ulysses S. Grant to do it, but he let me know in no uncertain terms that his rank was too high to be placed on guard duty. He ordered a nice young soldier to take his place, except I don't know how much good he'll do. He insists on protecting the portals with a musket rather than the decimator, which he waved away."

"Fat lot of good that'll do him against Terrorians," Ava said. "I'd better go relieve him."

"Call me when you get up there, and I'll close the book," her mother said.

Niamh Roth's nerves were put to ease knowing Ava was taking care of library business, but her daughter had reminded her that Johanna and Jackson still hadn't returned from what should have been a one-day trip.

Johanna and Proteus Bligh disembarked at the intercourse station beneath the University of Lumi. The campus appeared tranquil. No one ventured outdoors, although Johanna knew Dame Erato, Ingur Aguri, and Bel were sequestered within the oracle chamber under the Library of Origination, which was protected by various protective charms. The main gate to the university was closed, and while Johanna didn't see a lock, she knew it would be difficult for the enemy to enter. But she couldn't relax. *The Terrorians are so big, they'll probably pull themselves up and over the walls with their tentacles. It would be like child's play for them.*

Proteus Bligh surveyed the campus. Ψ*All is secure.*

Johanna looked out the gate and watched the approaching crowd. "Not for long."

"What is our strategy?" one of the Mysterians asked.

"Protect the library. Use whatever talents you have to immobilize the Terrorians. I don't know how we can stop them from getting inside the walls of the university, but we must stop them from gaining control of the library."

She turned when she heard Terrorians right outside the gate speak in their distinct syntax; she used a translation charm so she could understand them.

"Ready…aim…" The line of four Terrorian troopers stood with their decimators trained on the gates.

"They're going to shoot out the gates," she told the Mysterian and Scientic volunteers. "Move out of the line of fire."

"That should be their undoing," one of the Mysterians said. An explosive percussion caused the air around them to gain brilliant clarity and color, then it appeared to melt and quickly fog over.

Johanna stood stock still for a moment, determining she was unharmed. "Is everyone okay?" she asked.

Ψ *Yes. These gates have the same protection as the gates in the caves of Mysteriose. A decimator is a poor choice of instrument to use on them.*

When the air cleared, four decimators lay scattered in the street, the only remnants of the initial line of Terrorians who had tried to gain entrance.

Ψ *That should keep them at bay, until they learn it's easier to scale the wall than to shoot out the gates.*

"And when they do realize that?" Johanna asked.

Ψ *We will be forced to fight back.*

Jackson stationed the Educons and the Inspiracons along the perimeter of the Transport Center and asked if they had any questions about the way their weapons worked.

"This looks like a toy gun," Elan Coates, a Educon said. "Grappho Pluck assured me it is a weapon and told me to aim it at the nearest Terrorian and pull the trigger for ten seconds. I tested it on a bush outside the arena, but it didn't do anything."

Jackson nodded. "It's a scrambler. Ryden Simmdry told me about these. They only work on something with a brain."

Coates bristled. "Just because some of your kind do not believe that plants have brains like higher levels of beings, does not mean it is so."

Jackson hung his head for a second before lifting his chin and continuing patiently, "It's a scrambler. It scrambles someone's brain waves and confuses them. It makes them feel scared and vulnerable. I don't know. Can *you* tell when a bush is feeling scared and vulnerable?"

The Educon made a face and his double irides in each eye moved apart. "This, does that?"

"Yes," Jackson said looking away. He found Educons' eyes very disconcerting.

★*I would suggest you use your weapon right now. They are approaching.*

"Okay," Jackson said. "Everyone with a scrambler," he grabbed the device and held it above his head so everyone could see it, "shoot now."

At least a half dozen Educons aimed at the Terrorians and pulled the triggers of their scramblers, but nothing appeared to happen. The Terrorians continued to come closer.

"Again," Jackson called out, "and keep the trigger pulled in for at least thirty seconds." He watched as they shot, and still, the Terrorians approached.

Natalia, Horatio Blastoe and the militairres emerged from the transit terminal to find themselves at the edge of a meadow banked by towering trees.

The militairres split up. Horatio Blastoe accompanied half of them up the Avenue > History toward the square, while Natalia and the others cut through the residential streets and shadowed the Terrorians as they marched up the Avenue > Governance.

Natalia didn't want to make a move until she heard from Ryden Simmdry, but she started to worry when the invaders took possession of the city square and split apart in two other directions.

She knew the wristband would allow her to hear the overseers' thoughts, but she wasn't too sure if it would allow them to hear hers. *I might as well take a chance.* She moved away from the Terrorians before telling the wristband where the invaders were headed. She felt foolish speaking to her wrist, but if it worked, her embarrassment would be well worth it.

CHRIS ENTERED THE library much more quietly than usual.

"Christopher," his mother said, "is anything wrong?"

"Yeah, Mom." He busied himself with his backpack. "It's all over school. Logan's girlfriend Cassie committed suicide." He looked at his mother with disbelief in his eyes. "She's dead."

Niamh Roth gasped. "She was just here with Logan for prom night."

"Right." Chris sighed. "And now she's gone."

"How is Logan taking it?"

"Who knows? Nobody's seen him all day. One of the students said he spends all his time trying to get in good with the people running his summer internship, so he'll start at the top of the pecking order instead of the bottom."

"An admirable idea, except he hasn't graduated high school yet, and I think that takes priority."

Chris shrugged. "Is Ava upstairs? I can take over for her. It will give me some time to think."

"Are you alright? I know you must be feeling sad and confused about Cassie. I'm here if you want to talk about it. Cassie must have felt like she had a hopeless problem with no solution. I want you to know I will always be here to talk to and help you, if you ever think you've reached a dead-end like that."

Chris sniffed. He turned away from his mother because he didn't want her to see the tears in his eyes. "Thanks." *I should be stronger than this. If she sees me cry, she'll baby me.* Still, he appreciated having his mother offer to talk things out with him. *Not that I'll ever need to take her up on it.*

NATALIA HESITATED AFTER Ryden Simmdry gave her a direct order. She wanted to fight the Terrorians, not turn around and march into the forest to secure the time machine. She knew the time machine was important but argued with herself that it was something someone else could do while she used her skills to fight Terrorians.

She asked Milencia Jolen to take Patra and half the militairres to secure the time machine. "Be careful. They may have left a patrol in the forest to protect it."

Patra, the co-captain of archery, was ready to take on the assignment. "What does the time machine look like?"

"A giant glass bubble. It's transparent, so it may be difficult to see in the shadows of the forest. And you'll have to hunt for it because we have no idea where in the forest it might be."

"Don't worry," Milencia said. "We'll find it, and we'll protect it." They headed back down the street.

"Are we to engage the enemy in city square?" one of the remaining militairres asked.

"We do not have any direct orders at this time. I do believe we have been positioned here in case the Terrorians try to retreat. We're here to box them in and prevent them from getting away."

"That doesn't sound very exciting," another recruit said, "although, after being kept in a detention cell, I guess being at liberty, no matter how quiet it is, has its advantages."

WHEN THE TERRORIANS reached the gates of the Transport Center and could go no farther, they looked at each other for a moment, before wandering around in a daze.

"They work!" Jackson kissed the scrambler. "I can't believe those kids created a weapon that actually scrambles brains. I could have really used one of these all during high school."

★ *We have stopped them temporarily, but they will be back, and there are too many of them to confuse. Eventually, someone is going to get through and do some damage.*

"How long does the charge last?" Jackson asked, staring at the scrambler in his hand.

"What do you mean?" asked Dr. Infinitis, the curator of Educon.

"The power source," Jackson answered. "It must have a limit. How long will this weapon continue to work before it runs out of juice?"

"That is a question for the inventor," Dr. Infinitis said.

Jackson asked his wristband and wondered how long it would take for Ryden Simmdry to get back to him.

General Barzic 922 faced his men, about to give the order to shoot on sight, when a tall, lanky Luminan suddenly ran out from behind a building and slammed him in the head with a walking stick. The general went down, stunned. The Luminan swung the stick wildly from side to side until he found himself immobilized in a force field.

"We have our first prisoner of war," the trooper who fired the shot shouted, and a roar of victory erupted from the troops.

§ *Oh dear, that can't be good*, Zenith Fullova said telepathically to Ryden Simmdry.

⌘ *You are right, old friend. Something has changed the status quo.*

§ *Unlike other wars, these weapons are all so silent, it's difficult to tell when there has been fighting.*

⌘ *Yes. However, I have not received distressing messages from anyone, other than Natalia. I can't help but wonder what has made the Terrorians so boisterous?*

"It is only one capture," General Barzic 922 announced. "Let's not get ahead of ourselves. Is everyone in position?"

"Yes, General."

"Kroay 89, take your men forward and shoot on sight."

The small group of Terrorians continued their march north of the city square, with their weapons already aimed at the overseers and Juveniles just a block away.

Johanna edged her way over to the gate and surreptitiously peeked out, trying not to look too obvious. It was difficult to differentiate among the Terrorians. She moved toward the center of the gate to get a better look and stubbed her toe on what she thought was a rock. *Ouch. Note to self: never wear sandals to a war.* She bent down to rub her toe and spotted a loose diamond next to the large uncut one that tripped her. The loose gem didn't look raw like the others she had seen on Lumina. This one looked like it had been polished and worn as a jewel. *This looks like it might have fallen off Furst's uniform.* She slipped it in her pocket to give back to him as she continued to keep watch. A Terrorian strutted to the front of the group and spoke. *Nero 51.* She saw him lift the decimator and flip the Omicron Key and watched as tiny lights illuminated the other troopers' weapons. *Uh-oh.*

She returned to Proteus Bligh's side. "It's looks like they abandoned the idea of taking prisoners. I think they're going to shoot to kill."

Ψ *First, they have to get past the wall.*

Johanna took her decimator and flipped it over her shoulder, firing past the overseer's head. A Terrorian—trapped in a force field—hit the ground and rolled into a corner.

A Scienticon, standing a short distance away,

suddenly disappeared. Johanna swung around and took another shot. Another Terrorian fell inside the walled compound.

Before she could register it happening, a third Terrorian jumped on the wall and shot at the first prisoner, releasing him from his force field. The Terrorian whirled around, and Johanna managed to flip the key on her weapon, but not before the other soldier was freed and two more Terrorians were on top of the wall. "Our people are not fighting," she screamed at Proteus Bligh.

He telepathically commanded them to use their weapons, but many of them were too afraid to shoot because they thought what happened to the first line of Terrorians would happen to them, as well.

Logan was content to trail along with Channing on his story Monday morning. The phone call in the middle of the night telling him Cassie had died, and asking if he knew why she would commit suicide, had been very unsettling. He told her parents he had no idea why she would do such a thing, and he hoped they wouldn't find out she was pregnant. He knew she hadn't told them, yet. She had made that perfectly clear. She told Logan she wanted him with her so they could approach her parents, as a couple, to say they were getting married. *As long as they just plant Cassie in a box and bury her, everything will be fine.*

It wasn't like *he* had killed her. And now that she was dead, he should be in the clear. But he knew his father would be disappointed in him for allowing such a terrible thing to happen, after all, if he had taken care to use protection, or abstain from pre-marital sex entirely, this never would have happened. He tried to put the thought out of his mind. *What my old man doesn't know can't hurt me.*

Logan was sorry Cassie was dead, but he was more relieved. *At least now, I don't have to talk her into an abortion or break up with her.*

THE WRISTBANDS WORN by Jackson, Furst, and Natalia allowed them to see past the enchantment Ryden Simmdry had placed on the residential sections of Lumi.

Furst hurried through the Lumi City Cemetery and leapt up onto the roof of a neighboring building to get a bird's eye view of the invasion. He could clearly see how the Terrorian troops had split and were spreading out across the outcrop. He searched in particular for Nero 51 and spotted him nearby, just outside the gates of the Library of Origination. His ringlets tightened when he saw Terrorians breach the university wall.

Furst chose to use his bow and arrow rather than the decimator strapped to his back to stop them from storming the library. In quick succession, he fired off three arrows at three Terrorians. Their squeals told him he had hit his marks.

He jumped down hoping he hadn't been seen. He searched his quiver for an arrow coated with flammable material. Taking a deep breath, he lit the end, jumped back up on the rooftop, and aimed it at Nero 51.

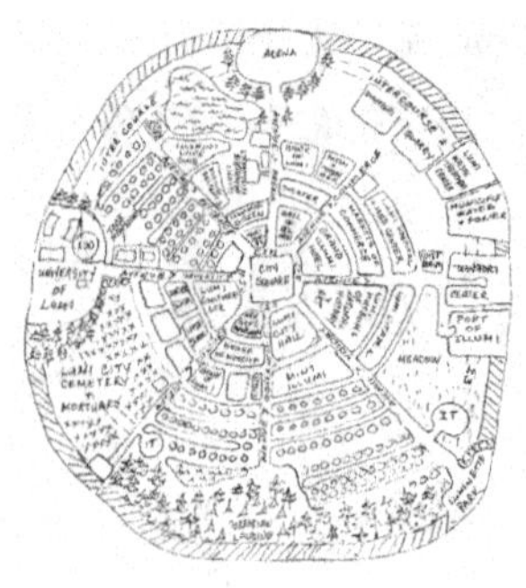

CHAPTER THIRTY-TWO

AN UNEXPECTED FLAME on a rooftop caught Johanna's eye. She watched as Furst took aim with his arrow and followed its projected path into the crowd. She immediately knew Nero 51 was the intended victim.

NERO 51 NOTICED THE same flame and grabbed Captain Zenner 3 by the tentacles, pulling the soldier in front of him. A second later, the captain squealed, and Nero 51 pushed his body away, grabbing a decimator and aiming for the shooter, but Furst was long gone, having jumped back behind the building for protection.

Nero 51 immediately dispatched a group of soldiers to find Furst and eliminate him. He turned back toward the university and stared inside the gate. He could see Johanna Charette standing there, as clear as day. But he knew he couldn't shoot at her without being killed himself.

Fegt! These overseers with their tricks and enchantments. He threw back his head and roared. It was unusual for anyone to see Nero 51 lose his control, but his scream was primal, as was his desire to kill Johanna Charette and take over the Library of Origination. He pulled himself up on top of the wall in a mad rush to kill his rival curator.

During the single moment it took to reach his new position, Johanna Charette had disappeared. The others scattered as well, seeking refuge within buildings and behind greenery.

Run, like the scared mught *you are, Johanna Charette. You can't hide from me.*

The Terrorian curator jumped down inside the walls of the university campus, followed by many of his soldiers. The fighters from the other realms were now well-hidden.

"Kill everyone you find, except the girl. Bring her to me."

At first, Furst hadn't thought much—one way or the other—about the enchantment that turned most of the Lumi landscape into a virtual forest, but now he applauded it. It allowed him to hide from the Terrorians who were confounded by walking head-on into buildings when they actually thought they were ducking between trees. Furst leapt through the cemetery in a wide arc until he jumped across the university wall onto the south side of the campus, which was the area farthest from the Library of Origination. He took care to pick his way around the grounds, avoiding Terrorians and looking for places he could retreat to, if spotted by the enemy.

He crept along the west wall that bordered the edge

of the outcrop. It had a stunning view of the water below, and of the Fridi outcrop in the distance, but Furst scarcely had time to notice. Instead, he stopped to watch Terrorians force their way inside locked buildings, only to emerge again, a short time later.

He stayed low, creeping behind lush foliage until he reached the edge of the walled garden. When he felt certain he wouldn't be seen, he leapt over the wall that separated the College of Overseers and Library of Origination from the rest of the university.

CONSTANT INPUT FROM the various fighting factions put Ryden Simmdry's consciousness to the test, and it very nearly prevented him from directing the volunteers who accompanied him. He was too busy staying in contact with everyone else, monitoring their thoughts.

They were less than a block from the city square when the master of the overseers realized his weakness. Neli Flo seated atop Tropo had forged ahead and was nearly decimated when Terrorians took a shot at her. Luckily, Tropo had spotted an interesting weed on the side of the road and bounded out of harm's way at the last second. A distance marker embedded in the roadway suddenly disappeared.

⌘*Marbol, it is time.*

"Be careful there, Neli Flo," Comi Mayor Milbo Fatufo called out. "Tropo almost lost his bacon. And another thing—"

Marbol pulled Foggy's trigger while nodding at the other Juveniles to begin. Unfortunately, their scramblers had a short-distance range, so only the closest Terrorians were affected. However, decimators could shoot much further. That became evident, when Mayor Milbo Fatufo evaporated mid-sentence.

⌘ *We're being fired on from the city square.*

THE TERRORIANS IN the city square would have continued firing on the Juveniles and Comedians if they hadn't been attacked from behind.

Natalia had heard Ryden Simmdry and instructed her militairres to fire with decimators or bows and arrows. The stick fighters and grapplers would not be of much use in this particular battle, except as backup for those fallen in combat. Sometimes, the victims' weapons clattered to the ground and were picked up by the next wave of militairres; however, more often, the weapon disintegrated with the person bearing it.

Since the militairres' weapons were exact duplicates of the Terrorians' own weapons, their Omicron Keys had been activated at the same time as the enemies, so when the militairres took aim, they shot to kill. The Terrorians quickly signaled Nero 51 they were under attack and needed backup. However, Nero 51 had plans of his own that didn't include backing up the troopers in the city square.

ONCE JACKSON HEARD Ryden Simmdry was under attack, he made up his mind to a take more aggressive action. A quick survey of the Terrorians outside the gate to the transport center told him they were getting closer, even if the troopers at the front of the line appeared to be confused.

Just shooting at them with decimators wouldn't be enough.

One of the Inspiracons screamed when her companion disintegrated. An Educon disappeared a moment later.

An Inspiracon pulled his sword and rushed toward the nearest Terrorian, twisting his sword's hilt. He aimed at the Terrorian, and a bolt of lightning shot from the tip of the sword, electrocuting the Terrorian. The smell of burning flesh permeated the area. Other Inspiracons followed his lead, killing any Terrorian too surprised, or too slow, to use his decimator. It was a good plan, but Terrorian decimators allowed for a longer range of attack, and many of the Inspiracons were vaporized before they were close enough to use their weapons.

Jackson grabbed the booklet he had shoved in his pocket before leaving Fantasia and opened it up. A truck filled with weather-related instruments appeared. He flipped a few pages. Suddenly, a tornado popped up and appeared to be bearing down on them. He turned the booklet to face the other way, and the tornado changed direction, as well. He watched, wide-eyed, as Terrorians were picked off the ground by the swirling vortex and hurled through the air. Weather conditions remained eerily calm inside the Transport Center, but all hell had broken loose outside the gates.

★*Jackson, that's…*

He whirled around to face Pru Tellerence, and in doing so, he changed the direction of the tornado again.

★*Jackson, no!*

He saw Pru Tellerence's face contort as she stared over his shoulder, and he turned in time to see the tornado at their gate. He snapped the booklet shut.

Bodies fell to the ground. Detritus landed more softly. The Avenue > Transportation appeared to be in ruins. Whatever Terrorians Jackson could see, lay immobilized on the ground. Most of the larger buildings, remained standing, but they had broken windows, and items from inside the buildings had been sucked out and now littered the ground. The small Inter-Realm Market, which had been constructed of man-made materials, hadn't fared as well as the buildings constructed out of diamond. It was completely demolished, its wares from distant worlds, scattered about. An antique Mysterian double-sided halberd had become implanted in one of the stanchions holding the Transport Center gates. It looked like Excalibur from the Arthurian legend, embedded in stone.

★ *Thank the Ancients this isn't a residential area.*

"I'm sorry. I wasn't thinking. I just wanted to stop the Terrorians."

★*And you did, very effectively. I am not criticizing your actions. I am merely pointing out an additional benefit.*

"Do you think we should go to the city square and do it again?"

★*I think a tornado in the city square may be too dangerous. By all means, carry the booklet with you but only use it as a last resort.*

Jackson pulled some of the Educons and Inspiracons aside and told them to remain at the Transport Center to keep it from being overrun by Terrorians.

He and Pru Tellerence led the others past the devastation on the main roadway that connected them directly with the city square.

*

WAVES OF ADVENTURANS were quickly recharged, and as backup leader*bots were brought up to speed, those who had worked to save the realm received much-needed sustenance and rest.

"All freezing units have been brought back online, and we have a large contingent of hu*bots taking inventory, cataloging, and verifying the location of living tissue and cloning materials," a worker reported.

Prophet IAN c. walked into the lab, having just come off a six-hour recharge. "Make sure every refrigeration unit is backed up by a generator that is ready to operate."

"I believe we have everything in hand here, IAN c. No need for alarm."

"It's not alarm," the curator said. "It's precautionary. Just because it is in place, doesn't mean we will need it. But if we need it and it isn't in place, our circuits are fried."

"Point taken," the worker replied.

Artemus Rexana walked into the room. *∑ Good day, Prophet IAN c. I have been looking for you. The situation has become dire on Lumina, and assistance is intensely needed. Once conditions here are in hand, the College of Overseers could use your help along with a contingent of hu*bots, especially those fitted with weaponized arms.*

"Of course," the curator replied. "Just give me a short period to ensure everything that needs tending is being taken care of, and I will assemble an army of hu*bots ready for battle."

It didn't take long for Adventura's military to be called into action and assembled in the town square. "How do you propose we get them there, Artemus Rexana?" IAN c. asked.

*∑Have each hu*bot join grasp his neighbor's arm. Be aware, fighting has been going on for some time. The Terrorians have decimated many. Stand ready to fight, immediately. They formed a large circle and the overseer joined it, transporting them instantaneously.*

INGUR AGURI SNUCK out of the Oracle Chamber in search of fruit juice for Selestra. Her nerves were on edge, and she screamed when she saw Furst entering the library through a back door. She had been too wrapped up the day before with Selestra's party and hadn't even noticed that Furst was a guest. As far as she was concerned, he did not belong there, and her reaction was instinctive.

"No." Furst whispered. "To help you, I am here." But the damage was done.

NERO 51 BANGED AT the front doors of the library with all his might. When the doors remained steadfast, he waved over more of his troopers and told them they had to gain entrance. Throwing their bodies forcefully against the doors didn't work, so they pulled a sapling out of the ground and tried using it as a battering ram. It was too weak to withstand the activity and soon bent and splintered. The troopers threw it aside and started hurling themselves against the windows, to no avail.

"There has to be a way inside," Nero 51 shouted. "Find it."

PLATO INDELICAT ALSO responded to Ingur Aguri's scream. He had asked her not to leave the confines of the Oracle Chamber where she had been sequestered with Dame Erato and the child, but she insisted Selestra was thirsty, and she needed to find refreshment.

He quickly nodded at Furst and led Ingur back to the chamber after she grabbed juice, bread, and cheese. As he hurried her away, Ingur grabbed a container of rat poison. She stuck it in her bag. *A little, thrown into the face of the enemy, might come in handy*, she thought.

Ingur screamed again when Mal suddenly appeared in the Oracle Chamber.

Ω*Malcolm, my friend, it is good to see you.*

"The ability to transport makes scouting the area easier, although I had a close call when a Terrorian spotted me outside. I managed to disappear before he could do any damage. I must say, whatever is in our hats that allows instant teleportation is a wonderful thing."

Ω*The key is in the miter, I always say. Without them, we are less than we can be. Are the Terrorians making great advances, Malcolm?*

"I don't know. I was looking around the university campus for weak spots where invaders could gain access, when they started pulling themselves over the walls. That's when I came inside."

The weapon moved on Mal's shoulder, and he looked down to see Bel patting it like it was a toy. "No, no, no," he said pulling it out of her reach. "You can't play with this. We don't want to make any holes in the ceiling of the chamber."

"Play dah!" the child demanded.

"No," Ingur said taking the little girl's hand. Bel pouted and returned to the chair she had received as a gift and plopped herself down with her lips clamped together.

"I see you've been decorating," Mal said, nodding at the chair.

"We wanted to make the room comfortable for Selestra," Dame Erato said. "She's only three years old and will quickly tire of being stuck in this dark, little room."

As soon as she said the words, the oracle grew brighter.

"You said Selestra, but I assume you mean Bel?"

"I renamed her Selestra," Ingur stated, "for her own protection. However, Pru Tellerence has apparently forgotten and introduces her everywhere as Bel."

Mal tried to placate her. "Once this Terrorian incursion settles down, I'm sure our lives will return to normal."

"If there *is* any such thing as normal," Dame Erato added.

Furst remained upstairs in the main entry hall of the library. Just a few feet away, troopers made a racket as they rammed the doors and windows, but Furst stood ready to protect the library and its occupants. He concentrated on their progress and this time, he chose to use a decimator rather than a bow and arrow. It worked more quickly in close quarters and completely eliminated retribution by an injured victim.

Compared to the assault from outside, his breathing was the only noise within. He counted his breaths, waiting for something to happen.

A tiny *snikt* sounded when the back door opened. He whirled around, and while he knew he should fire immediately, he held back a second. His eyes widened.

*

As Pru Tellerence and Jackson walked past battered Terrorians, the overseer recited individual incantations that would keep any of the survivors in a deep and lengthy state of unconsciousness. *No need having them sneaking back up on us,* she thought.

Closer to the city square, arrows crisscrossed the area, and bodies disappeared.

★*Stay alert. There is danger ahead.*

Jackson took his decimator and settled one end on his shoulder. The hair on the back of his neck prickled when an arrow flew past his head, close enough for him to feel the displacement of the air. He looked over at the militairres. "I'm not the enemy here," he called out to no one in particular.

The militairres didn't respond, but a Terrorian saw him clear as day and aimed his decimator at Jackson. One of the Jolen sisters nailed the Terrorian with an arrow, nodded at Jackson, and then shot the same Terrorian in the head, killing him.

Jackson looked past her and caught sight of Natalia Dalura standing atop a small wall. *Is she trying to get somebody to shoot her? She's a perfect target.* He took a quick look around to see if any of the Terrorians had noticed.

One definitely had.

Furst took a deep breath and relaxed his shoulders. "You Johanna Charette, I almost killed."

"Thank you for controlling yourself," she said with the hint of a smile. "I wouldn't be much help here if I were dead."

She closed the back door to the Library of Origination and bowed her head as she recited an enchantment. She waved both arms in an outward arc. The doors and windows on the sides and back of the building became as impenetrable as the ones in the front. The windowpanes took on a milky haze as well to prevent anyone from seeing inside.

"Who else is in here with you?" Johanna asked.

"Plato Indelicat, I saw. The child in the Oracle Chamber, Dame Erato and the Mysterian witch have, he says. No one else, I have seen."

She startled at a particularly large crash against the door, but it continued to hold. "If you wouldn't mind remaining here, I want to go up to the observatory and see if anyone is monitoring Nero 51's troop movements.

"All over, they are, but here, Nero 51 is."

"You almost got him, Furst. It's a shame he saw the flame on your arrow. I think this whole war would fold if he were stopped."

"Another man, is there not? Working for Nero 51, a shapeshifter?"

Johanna's hand unconsciously touched the cube in her pocket. "He's out of the picture for now. It's Nero 51 we have to stop." Another giant *thud* shook the front door. "I will be back, soon, to help you." She scrambled up the cupola steps until she reached the observatory. She had expected to find someone there and was surprised to see it empty.

Ω*I will return to monitor everything, Johanna Charette,* Plato Indelicat said from afar, reading her thoughts. Ω*But right now, Dame Erato and Ingur Aguri are* *keeping me busy.*

Johanna climbed to the top seat and slowly viewed the whole of Lumi through the telescope. Her heart quickened. The area outside the Transport Center looked like a war zone, and she immediately worried about Jackson. "Jackson, tell me you're okay," she said aloud. When he didn't answer, she wished she had taken a wristband. *Maybe that's the only way he can hear me. Unless…* She searched frantically for a glimpse of him, directing the telescope from Transport Center to the city square. She watched the active fighting and saw a Terrorian train his weapon on Natalia. "Natalia, on your right!" she shouted, hoping the Romantican curator would hear her telepathically.

The Terrorian who stood poised to shoot her suddenly disappeared. She looked around and saw Jackson, with his decimator aimed in that direction. She relaxed. He had saved Natalia. Then she felt her stomach tighten. *Jealousy? Jackson and Natalia?* She shook it off. Now was not the time to let their relationship, or lack thereof, intrude upon what needed to be done.

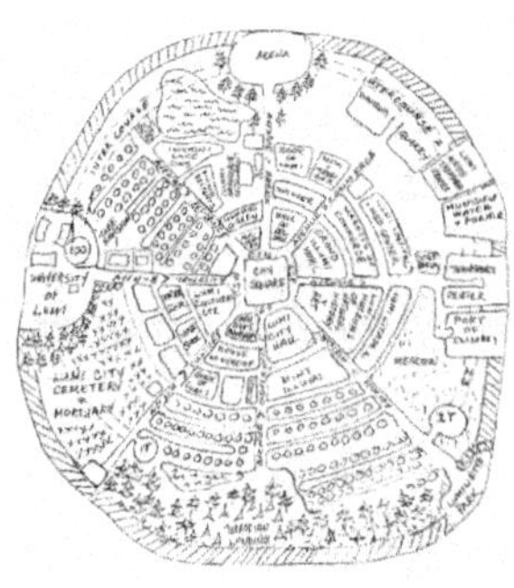

CHAPTER THIRTY-THREE

The city square was an important landmark, and would be considered a coup for invaders to command, but it was clear the Terrorians had not expected so many inter-realm volunteers to fight back.

Ryden Simmdry tensed a bit when he spotted Pru Tellerence right at the edge of the fighting. He saw a Terrorian train his decimator on the female overseer, and the master screamed aloud, "Pruelle, no!" but then took a breath and relaxed when she raised her hand and redirected the shot back at the trooper who fired it.

She carefully circumvented the city square, until she reached Ryden Simmdry's side. ★*What news have you of Bel?*

⌘*As far as I know, she is still safely ensconced within the Oracle Chamber. Although, I do know Terrorians have gained entrance to the campus and are actively trying to break into the library.*

★ With only Plato Indelicat to protect them?

⌘*Malcolm, Johanna and Furst are inside the library with them. If Nero 51 breaks through my protections, he'll still have to deal with two of the finest curators we have and our chancellor of the exchequer.*

A victory cheer erupted from the city square. The Terrorians there had been defeated.

⌘*Do not claim victory so quickly, friends. Many Terrorians remain and have overrun the University of Lumi, where they are trying to take over the library. I had hoped by bringing the battle to the square, we would prevent them from reaching the library. But that has not come to pass.*

⌘*Natalia, I would like you and your militairres to hold the square against any other waves of invaders. Deans Grappho Pluck and Marsh Kierand, please stay to assist her. Everyone else, follow me.*

Ryden Simmdry turned up the Avenue > University followed by his ragtag team of resistors. Pru Tellerence stayed by his side, but Jackson, Marbol, Neli Flo and Tropo surged ahead of them, ready to take on the battle for the Library of Origination.

LOGAN'S DAY IN the newsroom dragged on. He hadn't been assigned a story and without a deadline, there was no adrenaline rush. *It beats being in school. I'll bet Cassie is the big story today. Thank God, I don't have to pretend to be all sad and lost without her. I hope she didn't confide in anyone that she was pregnant.* His head began to throb. He didn't necessarily want to stay in the newsroom, but he sure as hell didn't want to go back home, or hang out anywhere

where people he knew might be.

He thought about going to the mall to look for a job. He had asked Jackson for one, but that was before the huge prom debacle. And something about Jackson turned him off. *He's too self-righteous. And he'd be even worse if I worked at the library because he'd be my boss. That's not going to happen. Ever. I'm my own man. I'm going for a job at the mall.*

THE NOISE LEVEL increased as Ryden Simmdry neared the university. Jackson grabbed the front gate and tried to pull it open, but it held solid.

⌘*Allow me to help with that.* The overseer nodded, and the gate sprang open.

★*Is that wise?*

⌘*The Terrorians are already inside.* He gestured toward the library.

Pru Tellerence and the others turned to see a large faction of invaders trying to ram their way inside.

★*That can't be all of them…*

⌘*There are Terrorians scattered about, but that is the bulk of those who remain. Many have been decimated. You told me yourself, scores were killed or rendered helpless by the tornado.*

★*Wouldn't there be many more of them on Terroria waiting to fight?*

⌘*Perhaps. It depends on whether or not Nero 51 felt secure enough to leave the crystals that operate the time machine in anyone else's possession. I believe he carries them with him, which means the vehicle cannot be used by the troopers he left behind to protect it, or by those who await his return on Terroria.*

   ★*So, it is a finite group.*
   ⌘*For the present.*

JOHANNA CONTINUED USING the telescope to sweep the area. She spotted a few Terrorians in the forest to the south protecting the time machine but nearly missed the stealthy militairres who crept up on them. *Good job!* she thought as she watched the women surround the Terrorians.

The rest of the eastern half of the outcrop appeared quiet. She aimed the telescope straight down and saw Ryden Simmdry and Pru Tellerence advance toward the university behind Jackson, Marbol, and a girl riding a huge pig. The pig appeared to be smiling, which made Johanna laugh out loud. Then she shook her head. *War is nothing to laugh at, especially if the girl and her pig get hurt. Or worse.* The girl didn't appear to be carrying any weapon, which made Johanna wonder why she was leading the volunteers toward the campus.

Jackson suddenly dropped and rolled, then aimed his decimator and fired. Johanna looked for the enemy, but didn't see anyone. *Jackson probably found his mark.*

A sudden sadness washed over her. Jackson was just graduating high school. He should be celebrating the last weeks of school with parties and beach blasts. Instead, he was fighting for his life on a foreign world. *He's lost his innocence.* She gasped, realizing they had both killed people. *So have I.* A single tear made a track down her cheek. She didn't have time to wipe it away when she saw Ryden Simmdry falter.

*

Jackson broke away from the group when he spied the Terrorians trying to gain access to the library. He ducked out of sight. "Johanna, where are you?" he whispered into his wristband.

Inside the observatory in the Library of Origination, he heard her say in his head.

"It's not safe in there. The Terrorians are trying to smash in the door."

They haven't succeeded yet. I just saw you, but now I can't find you. Where did you go? she asked him.

"Behind a small building across from the library on the opposite side of the entrance to the university," he whispered.

I can see the building, I just can't see you.

Jackson stepped out so she would have a clear glimpse of him on the telescope. She no sooner spotted him than a bush right next to where he stood, disappeared.

"Uh-oh." He jumped behind the building.

One of the Terrorians is coming. Get out of there.

Jackson ran a zig-zag pattern away from the building, looking for a place to reposition himself so he could take out his pursuer. He darted behind a building and ran around it as fast as he could, so he could fire on the Terrorian from behind.

"I sure hope none of your buddies are close by," he muttered as he ran out from behind the other side of the building in plain sight. He shot wildly and cursed.

The Terrorian whirled around and lifted his weapon, but Jackson's second shot was better.

"Score," he whispered into the wristband.

*

Ava hardly touched her dinner.

Niamh Roth knew better than to ask her youngest child what bothered her. She knew exactly why Chris hadn't said a word and why Ava hadn't eaten a thing. Being young meant feeling immortal. At their age, they believed only old people died. Knowing someone their own age had died by her own hand, was another story altogether. Both her children seemed to dwell on it.

"Is the school district planning a memorial service for Cassie?"

Chris shrugged. "I don't know," he said in between bites. "Brittanie said they're having grief counselors come to the school to talk with students. Whatever good that will do. It sure won't bring her back to life," he said without looking up.

"But it may help other young people deal with their feelings about death and teach them how to handle similar thoughts of suicide they may have had themselves.

"Have you ever thought about killing yourself, if even just for a moment?" she asked her son.

"What, are you crazy? Why would I want to kill myself?"

"I'm just saying, sometimes we all may feel so depressed that we wonder what it would be like if we were dead. Do you remember the movie, *It's a Wonderful Life?*"

"Every time a bell rings, an angel gets his wings," Ava said in a sing-song voice.

"That's the one," her mother said. The character, George Bailey, is so desolate, he wishes he had never been born and tries to kill himself. Clarence, who is trying to earn his angel wings, shows George what life would be like for the people around him if that had happened. And it was terrible. His existence meant so much to so many people. Yet, he felt like killing himself.

"I'm just saying," she continued, "if either of you ever feel that bad, come talk to me, or someone, anyone, and remember that film."

"I guess," Ava said.

No one spoke for a while. The quiet was deafening.

"And I promise," their mother added, "whenever you tell me you're depressed, not only will I listen to everything you have to say with an open mind, but I'll also treat you to ice cream afterward to lift your spirits, just for confiding in me."

"Mom, I'm really depressed," Chris said. "Rocky Road with hot fudge sauce would really help."

"Me, too," Ava added, "with whipped cream and nuts."

Their mother shook her head. "I feel like I may have diluted my message."

"Nope. Not diluted it. Just sweetened it a bit," Chris said. "As a matter of fact, I'll even call in the ice cream order to room service."

"In that case, I'll have some, too," Mrs. Roth said. "We could all benefit from something sweet, right now."

THE MASTER OF THE College of Overseers stood just behind the mob of Terrorians battering down the library door, and his voice echoed at full volume from the heavens.

⌘*LAY DOWN YOUR WEAPONS.*

A Terrorian at the edge of the mob picked off one of the Numericons standing behind Ryden Simmdry, before the overseer could flick his wrist and send the soldier flying into a tree. The tree cracked and the top half fell on the trooper, killing him.

The dead trooper's brother slowly backed away into the shadows, which had lengthened as the afternoon wore on. He moved slowly along the wall toward the main gate to get behind Ryden Simmdry. The trooper's movements were slow and graceful, and his dark coloring helped him blend in. No one paid much attention. They were much more interested in the confrontation between Ryden Simmdry and Nero 51.

The trooper watched and waited. He couldn't tell the overseers apart from behind, but it didn't matter. He would take a life in payment for the life his brother forfeited. He raised his decimator.

Nero 51 knew his weapon's power would be turned back upon him if he fired it, but he did not intend to give up easily.

"Keep working," he snarled at his soldiers, who continued pummeling the door to the library.

⌘*Nero 51, you have lost.*

"NO!" shouted the curator. "It is you, who have lost. You think you are powerful, but I've watched and waited. Your power wanes with each new moon. You are old, many millennia old by your own calculations, while I am young and strong. In a fight without your powers, I would prevail, but you hide behind a lifetime of magic and sorcery. Your only goal seems to be hoarding knowledge in the Library of Origination, which you will not share with the realms. We are supposed to be a single system yet you do little to unite the libraries."

⌘ *You desire knowledge you are ill prepared to comprehend. Each realm will receive what it needs when the time is right. Not before.*

"Each realm will receive what it needs on my say-so, once I am head of all the Libraries of Illumination."

⌘ *One man alone is not strong enough to oversee the entire Illumini System. It is a large enough job for the entire College of Overseers.*

"I will have the assistance I need from those who are loyal to only me."

★ *You cannot win.*

"I would no sooner listen to you, a woman, than anyone else." The Terrorian spit on the ground. "You do not know your place."

Pru Tellerence felt her muscles tighten. In an instant, she transported to the Terrorian curator's side and slapped him across the face, before disappearing again and reappearing slightly behind Ryden Simmdry.

An errant shot from the aggrieved Terrorian trooper caught her arm as she disappeared. Her limb and the sleeve that swathed it disintegrated, leaving a gaping wound in its wake. Pru Tellerence screamed out in pain.

Ryden Simmdry's defenses faltered when the primal nature of her scream caught him off-guard, weakening the enchantment he actively struggled to maintain on the front entrance. In an instant, the Terrorians' battering ram crashed through the front doors of the Library of Origination. The soldier who shot Pru Tellerence was no longer alive to celebrate their victory. Ryden Simmdry didn't need a decimator to remove him from the scene. He mentally bombarded the soldier with information, images, and minutiae until the Terrorian's brain overheated, split, and fatally hemorrhaged.

The master asked one of the curators to keep watch over the Juveniles as well as Neli Flo and Tropo.

⌘*Lead them back toward the Square if you can. It may be safer. Pruelle needs me and I don't know if I can continue to give some of the others the protection they need.*

Johanna heard Pru Tellerence's scream as clearly as if the overseer were standing right next to her. Then she heard the door smash open. She took a deep breath, and in an instant, she appeared on the floor below, right next to Furst. She was stunned by her own ability to teleport, not having the miter or chaperon the overseers and Mal used. But she had little time to reflect on it. Instead, she grabbed her decimator, jumped out of the way of what would surely be the first line of fire, and started shooting Terrorians.

Furst jumped behind a statue of Mingus Ob, the first Master of the College of Overseers, as he nocked an arrow and quickly let it fly. He worked as fast as he could, trying to stop as many Terrorians as possible from overrunning the library, but he only had a half-dozen arrows.

The statue disappeared and Furst leapt into the air, swinging the decimator on his back over his shoulder and taking three separate shots before he landed—hitting his mark each time.

Mal suddenly appeared just inside the door, and he used a decimator to pick off the Terrorians who made it through the door, from behind.

"We're seriously outnumbered," Mal noted, as a Terrorian shot disintegrated the decimator in his hand.

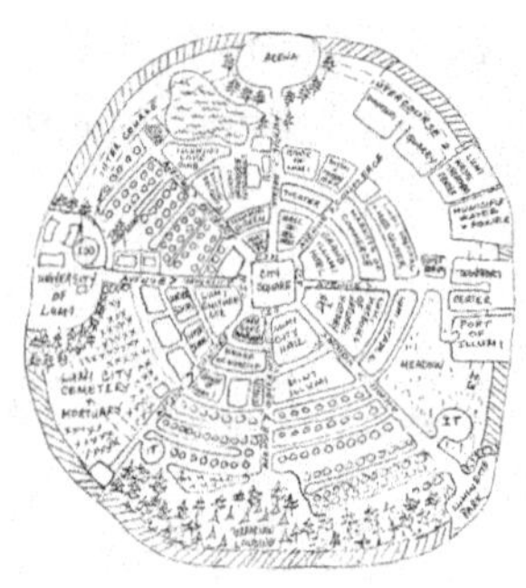

CHAPTER THIRTY-FOUR

Jackson heard Pru Tellerence's scream and was astonished to see the Terrorians gain access to the library. He ran toward Ryden Simmdry and Pru Tellerence and shot at every Terrorian who came into view, but many of the ones on campus had already entered the building. Those who remained outside the gates were held at bay by the Juveniles and Numericons, although the number of remaining volunteers from both realms had plummeted. Jackson did his best to protect the overseers as the master used his powers to cauterize Pru Tellerence's missing limb.

A moment later, Mal appeared and scooped a decimator off the ground.

"That's the ticket," he said, as he and the weapon transported back to the residence level of the Library of Origination, where he picked off swarming Terrorians like a man at a shooting gallery. Every few moments, he used the power of the miter to disappear and change locations, making it difficult for the invaders to aim at him.

IN HER WEAKENED state, Pru Tellerence failed to hide many of her thoughts, and while she bravely did her best to tolerate the pain, she worried at the effect it might have on her hope of eventually being able to raise Bel. *I won't even be able to hug her*, she thought.

⌘*You only need one arm to hug the child, Pruelle. I will supply the other arm to close the circle.*

She was touched by his sentiment but still worried about the toll her loss would take on her ability to be an overseer.

⌘*Do not lament what you have lost. Rejoice that you are alive and can still effect change.*

★*Of course.* She sighed. ★*We survive, but for how much longer?*

She had a point. The fighting inside the library, and in small pockets around the outcrop, proved deadlier than anticipated.

SUDDENLY, JACKSON STOOD alone. Ryden Simmdry and Pru Tellerence simply vanished, and the teen didn't know if they had chosen to relocate or if they had been decimated. Either way, he dove for cover and decided to find a way into the library that didn't involve the front entrance.

DESPITE THEIR BEST efforts, the overseers had failed to protect the library.

Nero 51 led a small contingent of Terrorians down

to the lower level, with orders to capture any beings who still remained. He knew an Oracle Chamber existed, but he didn't know its location, and he desperately wanted to find it.

He and two of his soldiers explored the sub-levels of the library looking for anything odd.

"There," Nero 51 said, pointing to a section of the wall.

"What is it?" one of the soldiers asked. "What do you see?"

"Don't you see the faintest outline of light? It's as if it defines a door."

"I don't see anything," one of the soldiers answered.

Nero 51 placed his hands over the outline. "Of course, you don't. It is very cleverly done and visible to only the most discerning eye, which is mine." He could feel a faint vibration. "I believe it is protected by the overseers' sorcery. It will require some finesse to get past."

Zzzttt. A shot bounced off the wall. The Mysterian who fired it disintegrated.

The two troopers turned in a flash and fought off the defenders who dared shoot at them. Nero 51 stepped out of the line of fire and a beseeched Garpa—from a safe distance away—to send him the knowledge he needed to open the wall.

JOHANNA WATCHED MAL disappear and reappear elsewhere, and the maneuver clicked in her brain. *If Mal and I keep this up, and Furst continues to leap to safety, we should be able to put an end to this.*

*

JACKSON HEARD THE precise stomping of feet. He peeked through a hedge in the direction of the sound. Dozens of Terrorians had apparently climbed the university walls and approached the library as backup.

"I don't know if you can hear me," he whispered into his wristband, "but the bad guys have backup. Lots of it. Coming your way. I'd help, if I could figure out how to get into the library."

A moment later, Johanna appeared at his side, grabbed his arm, and they suddenly reappeared in the cupola. "I've got to get back down there. Could you take a quick look through the telescope and update us on who is where?"

"Sure. Go ahead. But be careful."

She laughed. "Being careful requires thoughtful contemplation. All we have time to do is react instantaneously and hope we survive." A moment later, she was gone.

LOGAN SAUNTERED INTO his favorite store. Paul, the manager, rushed over to help him with his selections.

"Not today," Logan said, when Paul pointed out a pair of hiking boots with a royal blue interior. "I'll probably add them to my closet down the line, but for now, I'm actually looking for a way to share my keen sense of style with your other shoppers, which is what I could do if I worked here. Got any openings?"

Paul's head jerked. Logan was one of his best customers and spent a load of money there. He never thought of Logan as the sales-clerk type. But he had just fired a salesman who stole a shipment of very trendy and expensive jeans right off the truck and sold them online on a website that bore the thief's name. How stupid could the kid be? "You know," he said, nodding, "I could use someone like you."

"You could?" Logan asked. "That's great. When can I start?"

"Come into the office and fill out some forms, and we'll work out a schedule for you."

Thank God, Logan thought. *I'll be earning some coin, while building my reporting skills. All I have to do now is graduate, and considering I have advance credits, and my old man is on the school board, I'm good to go.*

"Do you want to start this weekend?" Paul asked.

Logan thought quickly. "I'm available right away. And I don't have any classes on Wednesday. I'm ready when you are."

"Okay. then," Paul said, modifying Logan's schedule. "I'll put you down for a full day of training on Wednesday. I'll meet you by the back entrance at 9:30. You get an hour for lunch at 1:30 and then work another four hours for a full shift. How's that?"

"It sounds perfect to me," Logan answered.

Walking out of the mall, he ran into Fels Rankin, a guy he and Cassie knew from school.

"Logan," Fels said, looking awkward. "I'm so sorry about Cassie."

"Yeah," Logan replied, trying his best to appear sad. "And now I just found out I have to work Wednesday. They'll fire me if I'm not there. I can't even go to her funeral." He slammed the wall with the flat of his hand to demonstrate his frustration.

"That sucks, dude."

Logan looked down and shook his head. "Sorry, bro. I can't talk about it." He walked away quickly with his head down, and even though his shoulders shook, no one would realize it was with laughter and not tears.

On the way home, he stopped at a florist and ordered flowers on his father's business account to be sent to the funeral home.

"What do you want it to say?" the florist asked.

"Say? It has to say something?"

"Yeah, you know, *Cherished Friend, Beloved Sister,* that kind of thing."

Logan smiled. "One word: *Forever.*"

"You got it."

As in, free of you forever, he thought. *And now they can't call me callous for not being at the funeral. I sent flowers. And Fels will tell them why I'm not there.*

MOVEMENT CAUGHT JOHANNA'S eye. Behind the latest line of Terrorians, Selium Sorium suddenly appeared and fired what appeared to be a decimator but didn't have an Omicron Key. *It must be one of the weapons the overseers created,* she thought. She watched as Terrorians were slowly frozen in their tracks. Because they didn't disintegrate, their fellow troopers didn't know they had been compromised, which allowed the overseer to quietly continue his work.

Frozen Terrorians began toppling when another group of invaders pushed into the library from behind. This startled the others, some of who turned and fired, killing some of their own, but also decimating Selium Sorium.

"Nooo!" Johanna screamed when she saw the

dean, who represented Fantasia, disappear. The Library of Origination was overrun. A trooper raised his weapon but was prevented from firing. "Nero 51 wants her delivered to him alive."

Mal grabbed Jackson's arm and transported inside the Oracle Chamber.

"What are you doing?" Jackson frantically pushed Mal away. "We have to save Johanna?"

"Johanna knows what she's doing," Mal answered. "She'd never forgive me if I didn't save you first. I'll go back outside and see if she needs assistance."

ΩYou don't have to. Plato Indelicat waved his arm at the oracle. Above it, an image of Johanna being marched down a flight of stairs appeared. As the troop leading her progressed, Nero 51 came into view.

"Where are they?" Jackson asked.

ΩRight on the other side of this wall, Plato Indelicat answered, nodding toward the wall in question. A door sat in the middle of it.

Jackson ran for the door and grabbed the handle but was repelled.

ΩIt is enchanted. No one can get through without Ryden Simmdry's approval.

"What if Ryden Simmdry is killed in battle?" Jackson asked. "Would we all die in here?"

Mal patted the young man's back. "Of course not. We can leave the same way we entered."

Plato Indelicat smiled and tapped his miter. *ΩIt is like having a self-driving car.*

"Except we wear it on our heads," Mal added.

*

Galio Abbingdon made himself very small and watched from a shadowy niche as Terrorians crammed inside the Library of Origination. There were no overseers or beings from other realms to stop them, and the invaders congratulated each other on a valiantly won victory.

❋ *They have taken over the fifth level and have breached the lower levels as well,* he reported to his brethren. ❋ *They have Johanna Charette.*

Just outside the library, Pru Tellerence snapped to attention, regardless of her injuries. She looked at Ryden Simmdry.

⌘ *Do not worry, Pruelle. Johanna is quite a capable young woman.*

★ *She may seem so, but she is not an overseer. She is young, without the protections overseers enjoy and without the many years of experience other curators possess.*

A moment later, Reichel Bean and Rubicon Zenicon were at their sides.

⌘ *Deans, please assist Johanna.*

★ *No.* Pru Tellerence caressed Ryden Simmdry's face with her remaining hand. ★ *You must do it. You have far greater experience handling this kind of situation.*

⌘ *I will not leave you.*

★ *You must. Reichel Bean and Rubicon Zenicon can escort me to safety.*

Ryden Simmdry kissed her forehead lightly before relinquishing possession. ⌘ *Please take Pru Tellerence to the Oracle Chamber. Ingur Aguri is there and may be able to abate Pruelle's pain.*

*

"NERO 51, WE HAVE—"

The Terrorian curator raised one tentacle into the air. "DO NOT INTERRUPT MY THOUGHTS."

"But sir—"

"Kill him."

One of the two troopers who accompanied the curator turned and decimated his fellow trooper.

Johanna would have smiled if she wasn't so thoroughly appalled by the wanton act.

Every Terrorian stilled and stared at the curator and two troopers. They all knew how important Johanna's capture was to him, but none was brave enough to say *We have Johanna Charette*. And so, Nero 51 continued to seek enlightenment, while his troopers wondered why they had chosen to follow a leader who now seemed unhinged.

Their attention was so focused, no one notice a miniaturized Ryden Simmdry appear behind a wall sconce. The master had witnessed the brief exchange between the curator and his followers and did his best to telepathically incite unrest among the Terrorians.

A LARGE PLATOON OF hu*bots materialized outside the Library of Origination. Artemus Rexana divided the group and urged half of them forward. It didn't take long for the Terrorians to realize they were being cut off from behind. They responded by decimating encroaching Adventurans and soon learned how quick and deadly retaliating hu*bots could be.

The overseer led the other half of his band of hu*bots out of the gates, and they engaged in battle head-on with Terrorians marching on the Avenue > University toward the library.

For the most part, the nature of the weapons did not result in a bloody battleground. However, casualties could be determined by the sheer reduction in forces.

Artemus Rexana rued the loss of life, but he knew it had to be done to keep the Terrorians from backing up Nero 51.

THE TENTACLES THAT Terrorian troopers used to grasp Johanna's arms cut off her circulation and her hands grew colder by the minute, but she dared not move. She could sense Ryden Simmdry's efforts to instigate unrest among the soldiers, and she could feel the tension grow.

Nero 51 had not yet noticed her, and after what happened, no one volunteered the information.

I can always transport myself away, Johanna thought, *if I need to, but then I'd accomplish nothing. This needs to come to a head. I want to look into Nero 51's beady eyes and watch them change as he realizes there's no way I'll let him win.*

⌘*Those are brave words, Johanna,* Ryden Simmdry said telepathically, shielding his words so only she would hear them. ⌘*But don't become so overly sure of yourself that you become cocky. That's how battles are lost.*

She frowned. She knew the master was right, and her face reddened when he chastised her. She didn't want to earn the overseer's disdain. She wanted him to be proud of her.

I understand, she answered telepathically.

INSIDE THE ORACLE Chamber, Dame Erato and Ingur Aguri gathered around the newly arrived Pru Tellerence, lamenting the terrible loss of her arm and trying to make her comfortable. Reichel Bean updated everyone on the fighting outside the Library of Origination. Rubicon Zenicon proclaimed it a miracle that Pru Tellerence lost only an arm and not her life.

Only one person remained uninterested in the news. Bel's stomach growled, and she wandered around the chamber looking for something to eat. Ingur Aguri's bag lay on the floor in a corner. Bel found it and dug inside, looking for apples. She found one, and even though it had some powdery residue on it, she lifted it to her lips and took a bite. The residue made her start coughing.

Ingur Aguri turned to the child and blanched. "Selestra, no!" She rushed to the little girl's side. By then, Bel had turned red in the face and couldn't stop choking. Ingur Aguri saw the residue on the apple and slapped it from her hand.

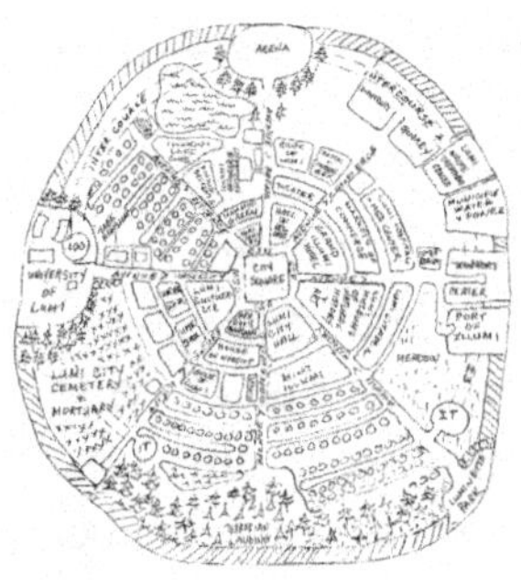

CHAPTER THIRTY-FIVE

MILENCIA AND PATRA were spoiling for a fight. They lay hidden in the forested area of Lumi, keeping an eye on Terrorians who seemed just as restless as they were.

"If the Terrorians come running back, and the time machine is here waiting for them," Milencia surmised, "then our sitting here is useless because we'll be overrun. I think we should take a stand. There are a limited number of Terrorians here, and if we eliminate them one by one, we will have control of the time machine."

"I don't agree," Patra said. "If we take control of the time machine, without having the means to move it, then when retreating Terrorians return, they'll simply kill us and take the machine. Who has the key to this thing?"

"I have no idea, but Natalia might. And even if she doesn't, she has a wristband and can contact the overseers."

"We could send Aerina. She is the fastest runner I

have ever seen. What if we asked her to find Natalia and get the answer?"

"I don't know. This may only be an outcrop, but it has a lot of streets and buildings, homes and trees. Who's to say where Natalia is, right now? What if Aerina can't find her, or worse, what if she's killed running this errand?"

"You're making my head hurt, Milencia. I don't know how you became a commander because your thinking is very limited."

Milencia felt her face heat up. "I am your commanding officer, not the other way around, but I'm going to compromise with you. *You* can go and try to find Natalia. Aerina can stay here with me. Go ahead." She flicked her wrist at Patra as if she were an insect.

"Fine." Without another word, Patra took off through the trees in the direction of the Avenue > Governance.

Milencia sighed. She now had one less militairre with one less weapon to fight the Terrorians. *Maybe Patra is right. Maybe I'm not cut out to be a commander.*

INGUR AGURI RUMMAGED through her bag, looking for whatever she could use as an antidote for the rat poison Selestra ingested. When she had taken the container from the pantry, her intent was to use it against the enemy. It never occurred to her that the tin might open or the child would go into her bag looking for food. The bread and cheese she had brought back from the pantry sat next to the oracle still wrapped in a cloth. She had been so caught up in what was going on, she had failed to protect Selestra. The old witch thought her tears had run dry long ago, but here they were, spilling down her face as she desperately searched for a way to save her "granddaughter," or more importantly, Pru Tellerence's child.

Dame Erato placed a hand on her sister's shoulder. "I may have something that will help."

Jackson chewed on his lower lip while he watched Johanna stand like a statue in what looked like a still life tableau. Except for the slight movement of bored troopers, nothing happened. Even Nero 51 looked like a stone rendering. "Do you think they're still using the time machine to transport troopers here?"

Mal felt in his pocket for the crystals he had picked up on Fantasia. "Not if Nero 51 has the crystals on him."

"At least, that's good news. The Terrorians are all over the place, as it is."

Plato Indelicat smiled and nodded at Mal. Ω*You can go, Malcolm. I will remain here and hold our ground.*

"Where are you going?" Jackson asked.

"I'm going to transport into the time machine and move it."

Jackson shook his head. "What if there are Terrorians inside?"

"I don't think it's a very comfortable place for them to be. They have to duck their heads and squash through the door just to enter the chamber. They're probably waiting outside. If I hold the crystals in my palm, and transport inside the machine ready to fly it to another place, I'll be in and out before they know it. Why? Do you want to come with me?"

"No. I mean, I can't. What if Johanna needs me?"

"I understand." Mal turned to the overseer. "Plato Indelicat, where do you suggest I take the machine?"

The overseer communed with the rest of his brethren and informed Mal of the location.

As time slowly passed, Johanna could feel the tentacles that grasped both her arms loosen. It was as if the Terrorian soldiers reacted in unison. She thought Ryden Simmdry might have a lot to do with that and smiled. Her smile caught Nero 51's attention.

"You have Johanna Charette," Nero 51 said, snarling. "Why didn't anyone inform me?"

"Placid 1486 came to inform you."

The trooper's death flashed in Nero 51's mind. "Regardless. Blindfold her, muzzle her, and bind her hands and her feet. Then take her to the time machine and shackle her to it. If she gives you any trouble, take a knife and cut off a small part of her anatomy. Do not kill her, but torture is acceptable."

One of the soldiers looked like he wanted to argue with Nero 51, but no one dared, lest he be the one whose tentacle was sliced off.

"Nooo," Jackson screamed as he threw himself against the door to the Oracle Chamber, only to be repelled once more. The oracle had displayed Nero 51's orders for Johanna, and Jackson wanted to protect her. He staggered away, rubbing the shoulder he'd smashed into the door.

Ω *There is no need to hurt yourself Jackson.*

"There is every need. I should be by her side. Together, we're invincible. Apart, we're…just apart."

Plato Indelicat smiled. Ω *We are all working to defeat the Terrorians. It will happen, but it may take time.*

"How much time?"

Ω *The last war took two millennia.*

Jackson groaned.

A DISTURBANCE AT THE edge of the forest diverted the Terrorians' attention, and they left the time machine to investigate. While they were gone, Milencia wandered over to the machine and climbed inside. She knew it would be dangerous, but she took the chance to see why it was so important to guard the darn thing. She stood in the middle of an empty bubble. A moment later, she screamed and cowered.

Mal immediately recognized the militairre. "It's okay. It's only me. I've come to hide the time machine from the Terrorians."

"Really? Patra already got through to you?"

"I don't know what you're talking about, so my answer is *no*; I know nothing about Patra."

"We wanted to know who had the keys to this thing so we could move it."

Mal smiled. "I'll take care of that for you. You and your friends can go join the other militairres in the city square."

"Where are you taking this?"

"The less people who know, for now, the better. Why? Are you looking for a quick trip to the square?"

"There are eight of us, seven without Patra, and I don't think we would all fit. Go. We'll rejoin the others using our own two feet."

Mal nodded. "As you wish."

Milencia climbed out of the time machine and a moment later, it disappeared.

The other militairres had gathered close by in case she needed their assistance.

"Follow me," she told them. "There's nothing left to guard. Let's leave before the invaders return." And they quickly fled the forest and headed toward the square.

Not too far away, Patra finally reached Natalia.

"Patra, what's wrong? Why aren't you with Milencia?"

"I came to find you to ask about the key to the time machine. I thought if we got the opportunity, we could steal it from the Terrorians."

"Does Milencia know you're here?"

"Yes."

Natalia spoke into her wristband and waited for an answer.

The exchange took longer than Patra expected.

Several moments passed before Natalia turned to her and said, "It's already done. Milencia and the others are on their way here."

Patra's brows knitted and she frowned. "Who had the key?"

Natalia smiled. "The chancellor of the exchequer. Keep an eye out for the rest of your squad. I want to know when they arrive."

Ava was not expecting any action in the cupola, which made her reaction time slower than normal. That turned out to be a good thing for Mal, who parked the time machine in the middle of the floor.

"How did you get back the time machine?" Ava asked.

"I simply took it when the Terrorians weren't looking," Mal answered with a smile. "I brought it back here because the overseers believe it's safe. But on second thought, this may not be the best choice."

"Why?" Ava asked. "I can protect it."

Mal smiled. "I'm not talking about keeping the machine safe. I'm more concerned with *your* safety."

"Yeah. But if you leave it here, I won't feel so bored." Ava grabbed Mal's hand. "Are you going to stay? We could order room service."

He hugged her. "There's a full-out war being fought as we speak, and I need to return to Lumi. But when I return, it's a date."

"How about Jackson and Johanna? Are they okay? Mom will want to know."

He hesitated. "They were fine when I last saw them, but things are changing rapidly, which is why I can't stay and visit. But I promise we'll be back soon." He hugged Ava again before climbing back into the time machine and heading to a new destination.

MAL LANDED THE time machine inside the cupola of the Library of Origination, but the vehicle blocked the telescopes and sat precariously close to the edge of the platform. He walked a short distance away and stared at the machine before closing his eyes. He recalled an incantation he heard overseers use on several occasions to miniaturize either themselves or other objects. Mal closed his eyes and opened his thoughts to the overseers to ask for assistance, as he held his palms out as if to touch the vessel. He recited the spell, then reluctantly opened his eyes to see if he succeeded. On the floor sat a tiny time machine, no bigger than a softball.

Well, that's a handy little trick. He picked it up and looked around. Niches built into the central column had space for books and globes of the various realms. He placed the time machine among them. *That should work for a little while.*

In the blink of an eye, Mal returned to the Oracle Chamber, where he found the atmosphere leaden. Dame Erato and Ingur Aguri chanted over Bel's limp body, while Jackson's jerky movements and constant pacing signaled nerves at the breaking point.

"What's happened?"

Ω *Young Bel or Selestra, I'm not really sure what her name is, seems to have ingested poison, and the sisters are trying to revive her. Pru Tellerence is already mourning the child. And Nero 51 has taken Johanna Charette prisoner. It has quite upset her young man.*

"Where have they taken Johanna?"

Ω *I believe they want to shackle her to the time machine.*

"If they can find it. They're probably taking her to where they believe it's still located."

Mal placed his hand on Jackson's arm. "Shall we go get Johanna back?"

Jackson's looked at Mal, his face filled with hope. "I thought you'd never ask."

*

THE TERRORIANS TIED Johanna's hands and feet, but contrary to Nero 51's orders, they did not blindfold and gag her. She made a face when one of them picked her up. The smell was awful and his tentacles felt slimy. As he carried her out of the building, she hoped volunteers from the other realms wouldn't fire on the Terrorians without noticing her. She needn't have worried. Nero 51 had explained to the troopers how to exit the university campus from the south gate and cut through the cemetery to the edge of the forested area.

The fighting outside the Library of Origination dwindled, although fighting on the Avenue > University continued amid shouts and screams.

The Terrorians moved quickly and reached the forest in record time, but they were stunned to learn the time machine had vanished. Johanna was unceremoniously dumped on the ground while the troopers talked about what Nero 51 would do to them when he discovered the vehicle missing. They were so consumed by their own conversation, they failed to notice Mal and Jackson suddenly appear behind Johanna.

The two men crouched down, grabbed Johanna, and rematerialized inside the Oracle Chamber where they untied her hands and feet.

"Thank you for saving me, even though I really didn't want to be saved."

Jackson, who had been about to sweep her into a bear hug, dropped his arms. "What do you mean?"

"I want to be able to upset Nero 51's balance of power, and the only way I can do that is if I'm with him and show him up in some way. He'll be ticked off when he finds me missing, even more so when he finds the time machine missing. But I don't think it will weaken him. I think it will make him more determined to win this war."

⌘ *There is a certain amount of truth in what she says*, Ryden Simmdry said, suddenly appearing behind her. ⌘ *The Terrorian's rage will drive his ego.*

THE MILITAIRRES WERE all reunited in the city square and were adjusting to the robotic beings who seemed to have joined the ranks of the volunteers.

"Is the war over?" Milencia asked.

"There's no final verdict on that," Natalia answered. "Some report the Terrorians have been driven from the Library of Origination, but pockets of them remain within the walls of the university campus. Several overseers are holed up in the Oracle Chamber, including Pru Tellerence, who lost a limb in the fighting. Johanna Charette was captured by Nero 51's men, but subsequently freed by Jackson and the chancellor of the exchequer. There's also a story circulating about a civilian death—a young citizen who decided not to stay indoors and was capptured by the Terrorians. Right now, everything seems quiet, but hell may excel, and the Terrorians could return for the kill at any time. We just don't know yet."

Milencia frowned. "What about all the troops who were sent to different Lumi locations? How did they do?"

"Like you, no one is where they were originally sent. We've heard about victories and casualties, and at the moment, we don't really know how many of us are still around to fight."

*

NERO 51 FROZE AS he approached the hall at the Library of Origination's entrance. He expected to see his soldiers patrolling the building, but instead found a dozen Adventurans securing the site. He made a U-turn and rattled doors in the back of the library until he found one that would open. It led to the master's courtyard, a small cubicle protected by high brick walls on all sides. Most people would consider it a dead-end, but the Terrorian ordered one of his soldiers to pull himself up by his tentacles, and when the soldier reported no one awaited them on the other side, they used it as their escape route. Thinking back to the orders he had given the soldiers in charge of Johanna Charette, he, too, followed that path through the cemetery to the forest, all the while fuming about the Adventurans.

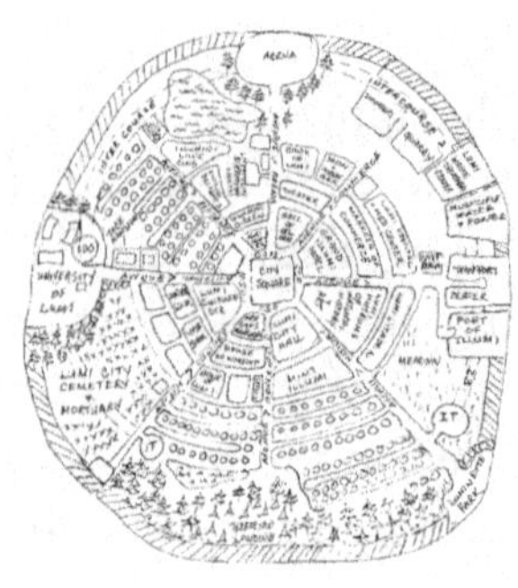

CHAPTER THIRTY-SIX

Johanna led Jackson back to the cupola. "So, now what?" he asked. "Are the Terrorians all gone?"

"Contained, yes. Gone, no," Johanna answered.

"Nero 51 appears to be unaccounted for," Mal said. "He may be hiding out somewhere, or he could have been decimated. We just don't know."

"At least he can't transport anymore troops here unless he stumbled upon the time machine." Jackson gave Mal a sidelong glance. "Where'd you hide it, Mal?"

"I'm surprised you missed it. It's up in the cupola."

"How would it even fit up there?" Johanna asked. "The telescopic arms and chairs take up most of the space.

"I have a little magic of my own. You can't be a curator for four hundred years without learning some sorcery. I was afraid if I rushed it back to 23rd-century Fantasia, and then tried to return here, I might end up stranded here—two hundred years in the future.

"We'll all be dead by then," Jackson said.

Mal laughed. "You're forgetting the Longevicus Blessing. You'd only be in your late 30s."

"I never projected it that far ahead," Jackson said, thumping himself on the head. "That is so cool."

"Except your family will all be gone by then," Johanna said.

Jackson stopped walking and all the color drained from his face.

"Sorry," Johanna said. "I didn't think before I spoke."

Mal began speaking about the time machine again to divert Jackson's attention. "Anyway, I miniaturized the time machine to about the size of a snow globe," he lowered his voice, "and left it on a shelf in plain sight."

"Is that wise?" Johanna asked.

"I live my life by one simple rule: I do the best job I can do, with whatever resources I have on hand, in the time allowed. It hasn't failed me yet.

"Now if you'll forgive me, I want to close my eyes for a while. It's been a pretty tense day."

FOLLOWING HIS RETURN to the Oracle Chamber, Ryden Simmdry rarely left Pru Tellerence's side. Nearby, Dame Erato and Ingur Aguri recited healing chants over their ward. Ryden Simmdry walked away to place an amulet he'd always worn on Bel. ⌘*It will help withdraw any poison from her body and will assist the healing process.*

He was well-aware of the volunteer fighters' progress around the outcrop, and except for the location of the missing Nero 51, he felt secure. After several hours, he left the chamber only long enough to ask the Adventurans to make one final sweep of the Library of Origination. He told them they could leave the premises afterward, although he asked a small contingent to keep watch for the Terrorian curator on the campus grounds.

Back inside, he picked up Pru Tellerence. ⌘*I believe it is time to exit our prison and reclaim our home.* The door swung open on his unspoken command, and he carried Pru Tellerence to his chamber where he rested her on his bed. She looked around in wonder. Even though they had lived in close proximity for several millennia, she had never been inside the master's chamber, even though it was located right next door to her own.

★*Wouldn't it have been better to take me to my own room?*

⌘*We are parents. United in love like husband and wife, we shall live together.*

She smiled. ★*I am not entirely sure my possessions will all fit in here with yours.*

⌘*Then we will break through the wall to your chamber, so that we may share both spaces together.*

★*I wish I came to you whole*, she said, sadly looking down at her missing arm.

⌘*I've had you whole, Pruelle. You are no less vital to me as you are, right now. Your heart and soul were not carried in the arm you lost. They reside within here.* He placed his hand over her heart. ⌘*And here.* He placed her hand on his chest.

★*Together forever?*
⌘*We are one.*

*

INGUR AGURI CRADLED Selestra to her breast, as she dropped heavily onto the bed in the guest chamber.

"Is there any change?" her sister asked.

"She is not white, nor blue, which would indicate impending death, but her pallor remains the palest yellow—not a good color, but something we can work with."

"You have a potion in mind?"

"I do, if you would take Selestra and keep her comfortable."

"Of course." Dame Erato sat on the bed and took the child, wrapping a blanket around her.

AFTERWARD, THE TWO sisters lay sprawled across the giant bed in their chamber, with Selestra snugly tucked between them. In the middle of the night, the child roused, and Dame Erato went in search of a snack. In addition to fruit, she found several bottles of Fantasian *umeshu*.

Ingur Aguri cut the fruit into small pieces for Selestra, while Dame Erato opened the bottles of liquid and sniffed them before tasting.

"Is it potable?" Ingur asked.

Dame Erato licked her lips. "It's some type of fruit juice. It's quite good."

The child drank very little before falling back asleep, but the two women polished off the remaining three bottles of *umeshu*. They, too, fell asleep—very soundly—not knowing each bottle contained an ample amount of alcohol.

THE BRUSH IN the forest was thick, so thick that Nero 51 heard his soldiers talking excitedly among themselves before he actually saw them. Only them. No time machine. No Johanna Charette. His ensuing roar should have awakened the dead.

"Kill them all for dereliction of duty," he instructed the soldiers who had accompanied him. He turned around and stalked off, alone, back toward the Library of Origination. He didn't care whom he had to kill to win this war. He was prepared to show no mercy.

In his wake, a firefight ensued. The soldiers marked for death had no intention of going down without a fight. The skirmish was short-lived, like the lives of the participants. In the end, only one trooper remained. He threw down his weapon and marched alone up the Avenue > Governance with his tentacles held high above his head in surrender. *I have a better chance of survival with our enemies than I do with Nero 51.*

The Terrorian curator re-entered the Library of Origination the same way he had exited. He expected to see Adventurans roaming the halls, but there were none, just one overseer wandering about. *As if nothing has happened.*

He wanted Johanna Charette but would settle for the time machine. Either one would give him leverage.

He carefully inspected most of the open areas. The moon had risen and he suspected most of the overseers had retired to their private chambers. Oddly, their doors had no handles and he did not know how to open them.

He had to wait them out. He looked for a place to rest where he could remain undiscovered until he felt certain all the curators were asleep. His chances of surprising them then, might be better.

The one area he had failed to investigate was the observatory in the cupola. The staircase was too open and daunting, and he was too tired to deal with climbing to the top.

The stone staircase near the front door had a large recess behind the steps. He crouched down and crawled into the space, which was just large enough to accommodate him, and he closed his eyes to rest.

ON THE HIGHEST chairs in the observatory, Johanna and Jackson sat side by side. Johanna had used the telescope to search every street for Nero 51 with no luck. Jackson tried to help, but the adrenaline rush that had fueled him all day had evaporated, and he soon fell asleep. Before long, Johanna, too, gave in to exhaustion.

THE RISING SUN bathed the city square in a wash of gold. Most of the volunteers had taken turns through the night either resting or patrolling the perimeter. Marbol and Pokkie sat in the center of the square with Peer Meap, rehashing their adventure.

"Look what we found," Pokkie said, digging deep into his pocket and brandishing a handful of loose diamonds.

"They're very appealing," Peer Meap said, "and unlike anything we usually see on Juvenilia. But you can't take them with you."

Pokkie scowled. "Why? I found 'em fair and square."

"This is a very unusual place. It's like a world inside a bubble. Nothing that is from here is allowed to leave here. If it does, either the bubble would pop," the curator picked up one of the boy's diamonds and held it between his fingers, "or you would." He handed the diamond back to Pokkie. "You don't want to pop, do you?"

Pokkie stared at the diamonds. "No." He threw them into the bushes.

Nero 51 hadn't meant to fall deeply asleep under the stairs. He had only planned to wait until he was sure everyone had retired for the evening before he searched the Library of Origination. But now, as others in the building awakened, so did he, and he berated himself for an opportunity lost. He was wedged under the staircase in a way that made getting up difficult. He could use his tentacles to seek something to grab onto, but he didn't want to risk being discovered.

Without risk, there is no reward, he told himself, and he was about to reach for the doorway when he heard the creaking of old stairs out in the library, and then the thump of footsteps over his head. The overseers' morning was about to begin. While they didn't need to eat very often, they still needed hydration, and they always started their day with the nectar of the *illio-pell*, a fruit only grown on Lumina.

Nero 51 watched as the shadows of several overseers seemed to dance across the stone floor. When he felt certain the last of them had passed, the curator grasped the doorframe and slowly pulled himself out from under the staircase. He grabbed his weapon and shouldered it. *It's time to demonstrate my invincibility.*

*

Ryden Simmdry and Pru Tellerence did not go down for morning nectar. Pru Tellerence needed to build up her strength, and Ryden Simmdry refused to leave her side. He could conjure almost anything she needed, except for a new arm. He sighed. At least he could create some nectar. The other overseers could handle the aftermath of the invasion without him.

Johanna opened the gate to the pig pen. She emptied the bucket of food she carried into a trough. The pigs snuffled as they scrounged for food. The noise didn't stop—even while they ate. Suddenly, Nero 51 crashed through the gate and obliterated the pigs with his decimator. The snuffling continued...

Johanna sat up suddenly. It took her a moment to get her bearings. The cupola was bright with sunshine and the telescope clued her in pretty quickly to her location.

The snuffling continued. She turned. *Jackson.* She shook him.

"Five more minutes," he mumbled.

"I'm not your alarm clock," she replied. "We'd better take a look and see what's going on." While Jackson thrashed, Johanna grabbed the telescope and surveyed the area. Everything appeared to be quiet.

"What's up?" Jackson asked, as he maneuvered the chair into an upright position.

"It's all pretty quiet. Are you awake?"

"Wait." Jackson got out of the chair and climbed down to the floor. He stretched, and then did a few jumping jacks. "Okay. I think I'm ready."

"For what?"

He scratched his head. "For whatever you woke me up for. What's happening?"

She smiled at him. "Nothing really. You can sleep another five minutes. Or a half-hour if that's what you want."

He groaned. "Now you tell me."

"Sorry. I woke you before I looked through the telescope."

Jackson's stomach rumbled. "Do you think overseers drink coffee and eat donuts?"

"No."

"Wrong answer. I really need a caffeine and sugar-fix right now."

She climbed down from the seat. "They have to have some food here, after all, they just had a party and there was a ton of food."

"Yeah, because the only person eating was Ingur Aguri. Did you notice how she can pack it away?"

"Yours 'not to reason why…'"

"Yeah, yeah, yeah, 'theirs but to do or die.' That's probably on my final this week. If I make it to my final. Do you think we'll be home by Thursday?"

"Definitely."

PROPHET IAN C. HEARD from every hu*bot that he'd sent to scour the Lumi outcrop for Nero 51. All reports were negative.

"The Terrorians suffered heavy casualties," Natalia Dalura told him. "There were so many of them, but now, we have one live prisoner who surrendered overnight. All the others appear to be dead, or to have been decimated."

"I'll report back to the Library of Origination."

"You don't have to." She pointed to her wristband. "I've already told them."

"I do not have a communications device."

Natalia pointed to his deadly arm. "You have something much better."

IAN c. held his arm out in front of him. "I do not have much occasion to use it on Adventura."

She smiled. "Now you know it works."

"It has been a pleasure, as always." IAN c. bowed his head. "I will still check in at the library. I would like to know how long they will need us. Our world is recovering from a series of violent solar flares. I will need to return as quickly as possible in case our perceived solution is merely a false respite."

It didn't take long for the Adventuran to reach the library. When he arrived, he found several hu*bots guarding the door.

"Are there problems?" IAN c. asked.

"None," a hu*bot answered. "We're here in case Nero 51 returns, but he hasn't been seen since last night."

IAN c. nodded again, and entered the library, pausing for a moment to allow his lenses to adjust to the change in light.

Ω *OH DEAR, THIS can't be good.* Plato Indelicat did not think to shield his thoughts, and Nero 51 pivoted when he heard them.

"Overseer," the curator bellowed.

Five stories above, Johanna grabbed Jackson's arm.

"Come on." In a heartbeat, they were on the main level.

Nero 51 had not heard their approach. "You and your kind are responsible for my problems. You must be eliminated." Barely moving, he vaporized Plato Indelicat.

"Nooooooo," Johanna screamed. Nero 51 turned toward her but she flicked her wrist and the slight movement sent Nero 51 crashing backward into the stone staircase.

Jackson gave her a sidelong glance. "You're starting to scare me, again."

EEIIRRKK! The front door scraped open.

Johanna whirled around in the direction of the noise. In a flash, Nero 51 snaked out a tentacle and wrapped it around Jackson. He yanked the teen to his side and with his other tentacles, he placed the decimator against the side of Jackson's head.

Prophet IAN c. entered. "Is everything okay?"

Jackson answered with a groan, "Unh-unh."

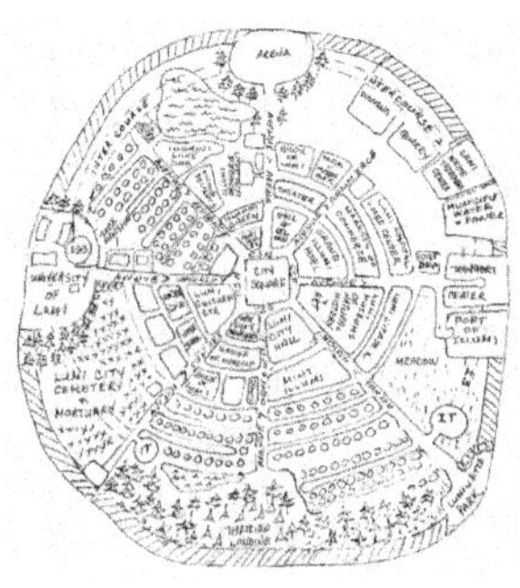

CHAPTER THIRTY-SEVEN

Johanna and Prophet IAN c. stared at Jackson. The teen's face contorted because of Nero 51's ever-tightening grip, and the business end of a decimator jammed against his head.

Johanna tried to rein in her fury. "It's not him you want."

"I have to start somewhere," Nero 51 said. "But I might be willing to negotiate if you vacate the university grounds and lock the gates to the outside. Then, gather every last overseer in this room within one measure."

"Don't try to be a hero, Johanna Charette," Nero 51 continued. "My tentacle is already tensed against the trigger on this weapon, and if you vaporize me, your friend will not survive."

A door opened and the overseers all filed in almost immediately.

Nero 51 shifted position but did not loosen his hold on either his decimator or Jackson. "That's more like it. Where is the time machine?"

Mal rubbed his beard. "In a safe place."

"I want it here, in the courtyard, within the next few moments, or the boy will be the first casualty of your inefficiency."

Mal instantaneously disappeared.

"Where did he go?" Nero 51 shouted.

Ψ *To get the time machine, of course.*

The main door creaked open. Marbol and Pokkie joked with each other as they walked into the library but froze when they saw the Terrorian with a weapon.

Nero 51 reached out two unoccupied tentacles and slapped the scramblers out of the boys' hands. The devices made tiny ticking sounds as they skittered across the floor. "Who else is in this building?" the Terrorian asked.

⌘ *Three elderly women and a tiny child. They can do you no harm.*

"Bring them here immediately. I want to see everyone currently residing within the walls of this library—inside this room, now!"

The door squeaked open again. Everybody tensed.

"The time machine is in the courtyard," Mal said. "I told the Adventurans who were patrolling outside they could leave as soon as they vacate the university grounds. They said as far as they know, this is the only occupied building, but they will check one more time, before leaving."

Time seemed to stand still as they waited for the Adventurans to depart. Johanna nervously fidgeted with the cube in her pocket. The overseers conducted a tense telepathic discussion amongst themselves. Everyone else stared at the Terrorian and Jackson waiting to see what would happen. A disruption occurred when Ryden Simmdry entered carrying Pru Tellerence, with Dame Erato, Ingur Aguri, and Bel holding onto his arms.

Pokkie used the interruption to dive for his scrambler, but Johanna chose that same moment to take a step backward to allow more room for the growing crowd, and the Juvenile banged into her, knocking the black cube from her hand.

SUDDENLY, ODYON APPEARED in the center of the room, and he used only his eyes to take in his surroundings. They stopped at Nero 51. "Am I to believe you have achieved your goal, Nero 51?" he asked.

"Almost. Why don't you take a quick look around and make sure there are no weapons they can use to delay my progress."

A few moments later, Odyon returned carrying very few weapons. "It would seem the curators feel they don't need a lot of firearms to protect themselves."

Nero 51 nodded at the collection of arms. "Destroy them all."

Odyon pulled a decimator out of the pile and vaporized what remained. "And now?"

"Why don't you *breeze* out into the courtyard and make sure the time machine is there and no one else is lurking about."

Odyon changed into a breath of air and the weapon clattered to the ground. He reappeared. "I guess that has to stay here." He placed the decimator in a far corner and departed.

Nero 51 took a chance. He swung the decimator away from Jackson and vaporized the weapon before anyone could move. A moment later, the decimator was again resting against Jackson's head. The move proved successful but left Nero 51 anxious. And his anxiety escalated because he had no way of knowing if Odyon would do as requested and return. The Terrorian began to sweat. Afraid he might lose his grip on Jackson, he held the boy and the decimator even more tightly, which increased his tension level.

Several minutes passed before Odyon came back. "It would appear you and your friends are the only ones left on this campus. I hope you're not planning on cramming them all into the time machine?"

"It's there, then?" Nero 51 asked.

"Yes." The shapeshifter looked in the corner for the weapon. "My deadly toy appears to be missing."

"I got rid of it; better than having someone grab for it and try to be a hero." He held Jackson against him as he took a step forward. "I suggest we all move outside to the time machine."

Marbol's eyes grew wide. His discussion with an overseer did not go unheeded. He dug into his pocket and pulled out the diamonds he'd held onto and casually dropped them to the floor.

Johanna chanted under her breath as she edged closer to Nero 51 and Jackson. She gave a quick, almost imperceptible nod, and Nero 51 tripped over some invisible obstacle, losing his hold on the teen. Johanna grabbed Jackson and disappeared—transporting him to the cupola, away from the Terrorian's reach.

Down below, the Terrorian refused to be distracted. He grabbed the closest person and a moment later, he held the decimator to Marbol's head, much the same way he had trained it on Jackson.

Marbol squirmed and placed his hand on the Terrorian's chest. "Don't hurt me," he begged.

"Move," Nero 51 demanded as he shoved the boy toward the time machine.

"I've got to get back downstairs," Johanna told Jackson.

He grabbed her arm. "You're taking me, too, or you're not going. He's got a new hostage. I'll be okay. Are there any decimators laying around?"

"No," she answered. "Only the one in Nero 51's possession."

He tapped his temple with one finger. "Then we'll just have to use our wits, like we usually do."

She couldn't help but smile. "Okay. You ready?"

They reappeared behind the others, hoping to blend in.

Odyon approached the time machine and stood next to it. "What's your plan?"

Nero 51 pushed the boy toward the time machine. "You. Me. The boy." He paused looking around at the overseers. "And her," he said nodding at Pru Tellerence.

⌘*No.* The thought was telepathic, but its volume unmistakable.

Nero 51 stared at Ryden Simmdry. "You are not in

control here, Overseer. I am." He turned to Odyon. "Get her."

Odyon grabbed for Pru Tellerence's arm, and suddenly realized it no longer existed. He put the flat of his hand against her back and pushed her forward. She winced. He helped her into the time machine, then removed her miter and tossed it to Ryden Simmdry. "She won't be needing this."

★*No*, she cried out. She struggled with Odyon.

Nero 51 lost patience. "What does it matter?"

"If she has it, she can teleport. There's no use in taking her hostage if she can leave at will."

The Terrorian's jaw slackened. He recovered from the revelation almost immediately and pushed Marbol toward the time machine.

"What does this thing do?" Marbol asked.

"Get in," Nero 51 said through clenched jaws.

"How does it work?" Marbol continued asking.

The Terrorian stiffened. "I will kill you now, if you don't get in immediately."

"Someone told me you need these." Marbol opened his hand just long enough for Nero 51 to see the crystals the teen had pick-pocketed. Marbol flung them away.

Nero 51 felt his empty pocket, then pushed the boy to the ground and rushed for the crystals. He grabbed them and ran for the time machine shouting, "Now, Odyon."

Odyon jumped inside.

Nero 51 was barely a second behind him.

It only took that second for Johanna to transport inside the time machine, drop the diamond she believed belonged to Furst and remove Pru Tellerence.

The time machine wavered. BOOM!

The blast knocked Johanna and Pru Tellerence to the ground.

"What happened?" Jackson asked, rushing to their sides.

★*She saved me.*

"I hope I didn't hurt you," Johanna said, helping Pru Tellerence stand.

"The rumble," Jackson said. "Was that the time machine exploding?"

Johanna turned toward Mal. "I'm sorry, Mal. It was the only way I could think of to end the standoff. I hope you don't get into too much trouble for losing their machine."

"How did you do it?" Jackson asked.

"I thought Furst lost one of the gems on his uniform. I found it and was going to give it back to him. But when Nero 51 and Odyon rushed to leave, I may have dropped it." The slightest hint of a smile played on her lips as she winked at her co-curator.

"Why would it explode if it belonged to Furst? I thought only Luminan diamonds exploded."

★*I had Furst's uniform decorated with the finest Luminan diamonds. But we didn't use conventional means to deliver the uniform to Dramatica. We transported it through the eighth dimension to get around any problems.*

"How did you know that?" Jackson whispered to Johanna.

"I didn't," she replied. "I forgot it was only Luminan diamonds that explode. Sometimes, it takes plain, old, dumb luck to save the day."

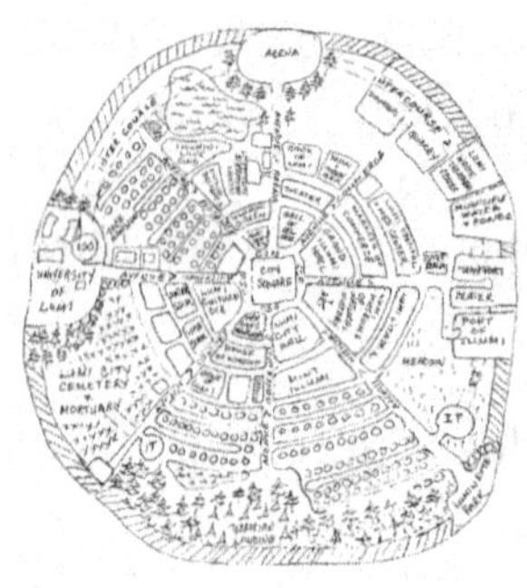

CHAPTER THIRTY-EIGHT

JOHANNA AND JACKSON stayed in Lumi for the memorial services for Selium Sorium and Plato Indelicat, which were held the next day.

"It's like deja vu," Jackson commented in a whisper during the service.

Johanna wiped a tear from her eye. "Losing Plato Indelicat once was sad enough. Losing him twice is heartbreaking."

"What do you want to bet Dame Erato is the next new overseer?"

"Why not Mal?" Johanna asked. "Nero 51 isn't here anymore to mess things up for him."

"True. Do you think they'll invite us to the challenge?"

"In due time."

Pru Tellerence sang *Musi Morti*. Johanna raised her voice in song as well, their two voices complementing one another.

"I still don't get how you know that song," Jackson said.

They released the clamps on the overseers' pallets and watched as they floated away. Several moments passed before the pallets exploded into a cloud of diamond dust, which floated down from the sky.

After the memorial, Johanna, Jackson, and Mal took one last walk around Lumi with Horatio Blastoe.

All around them, small landmarks, trees, and gates were damaged or missing because of the conflict, and a few buildings had clean holes running right through their walls.

"How will you fix those?" Jackson asked the overseer.

✠ *They will be glazed over. We're already referring to them as Terrorian windows, which is ironic, because instead of darkness, they will let in light.*

After their walk, they returned to the Library of Origination.

Ryden Simmdry and Pru Tellerence approached them. ★ *We're leaving to escort Dame Erato, Ingur Aguri, and Bel back to Romantica. We can take you home from there.*

"Bel isn't staying with you?" Johanna asked.

Pru Tellerence sighed. ★ *I can't give her the care she needs with my new disability. For now, it's best that she returns to Romantica with her new "grandmother." She wants to take Neli Flo and Tropo home with her. I had to promise her I would take her to visit them when I'm feeling better. I'm hoping that's soon. Prophet IAN c. has invited me to Adventura to be fitted with a prosthetic arm. It will take some getting used to, but in time, I should be able to do all the things I did before.*

"Maybe you could get one of their blaster arms,"

Jackson said. "There's nothing like carrying a little heat in case of emergencies."

Pru Tellerence could not hide her smile. ★*I'll take that under advisement.*

They heard shouting coming from the edge of the outcrop.

"What's going on?" Johanna asked.

⌘*Apparently, not all the Terrorians were decimated. A few jumped into the water to escape death. Unfortunately, they did not know about Luminan mermen.*

Jackson and Johanna remembered a scene they had witnessed in an open book before they first visited Lumina. "Yikes," Jackson said. "Those guys are really unfriendly."

★*You know about our mermen?*

Johanna nodded.

⌘*A problem for another day. Are you ready to leave?*

"I'll grab our backpacks," Jackson said. "They're right inside."

"I'd like to return to Fantasia with them," Mal told Ryden Simmdry. "Just for a little while. I'll return, soon."

⌘*If I know you, Malcolm, you're going back for some of that excellent bouillabaisse we previously shared.*

Mal's eyes lit up. "I hadn't even thought of that. Thanks for reminding me."

⌘*By all rights, you shouldn't even be hungry with the Majorious Longevicus Blessing.*

Mal smiled. "I guess it takes a while to kick in."

Jackson returned, carrying two backpacks. "Ready when you are."

They followed Pru Tellerence and Ryden Simmdry to where the two sisters and Bel waited. Ryden Simmdry placed a hand on each woman's shoulder. Pru did the same for Jackson. Mal grasped Johanna's hand. A moment later, they arrived in the heart of Romantica: the library garden.

Pru Tellerence looked around and sighed. ★*We have a library to rebuild.*

⌘*We have several that need our attention, but they can wait for now. I know you want to play a large part in that, and you can help put everything right, after your visit to Adventura.*

★*I hate to make everyone wait.*

⌘*The first Terrorian war lasted two millennia. This one played out much more quickly. Restoration will not take longer than a few months. Those who wait will be satisfied.*

Mal studied a statue in the middle of the garden. "I'm sorry for interrupting, but I have to ask, who is this?"

★*A revered Romantican witch. And a friend. She disappeared quite some time ago. No one knows what happened to her. She will always hold a special place in my heart. Someday, I hope to learn her fate.*

"It's so odd," Mal said. "She looks just like a woman I remember seeing on Fantasia, perhaps fifteen years ago."

"Really, Mal?" Jackson said. "You remember some elderly woman from that long ago? What did she do that was so memorable? Give you a winning lottery ticket?"

"I found her in our library clutching a little girl—a three-year-old child. Unfortunately, I never got to speak to her. The woman was dead. Her image is still very clear in my mind."

★*Bel…* Pru Tellerence whispered imperceptibly.

"Authorities searched all over for the little girl's parents but never found them."

Ryden Simmdry's felt his nerves tingle as his senses heightened. ⌘*What became of the child?*

Mal's mouth twisted in a sheepish smile. "She was brought to a foundling home a short distance away. But there was something about her that I just couldn't let go of, so I kept tabs on her. She was exceptionally bright and earned a high school diploma early, but the home wouldn't continue her education. Instead, they put her to work doing menial tasks.

Johanna's head jerked up. "Are you talking about me?"

"Yes. We've spoken about Peakie's before," he said, teasing her. "*Josefina Charo.*"

★*Oh*. It was more than a gasp than an exclamation. Pru Tellerence swept Johanna's hair back from her ear. A tiny star-shaped birthmark clearly alluded to her origins. Pru Tellerence turned to Ryden Simmdry with tears in her eyes. ★*I was wrong. Johanna is our child.*

Johanna's eyes widened. Being the child of Pru Tellerence and Ryden Simmdry explained so many things. Her escalation of magical power. Her innate pull toward and dedication to the library. Her sense of belonging. *I have a family.* Her eyes filled with tears that threatened to break free. "I think I could really use a hug."

Mal and Jackson moved toward Johanna at the same time Ryden Simmdry and Pru Tellerence embraced her. The group hug crackled with power and warmth.

LATER, WHEN THEY were alone, Jackson took a deep breath and dove into a conversation he had been avoiding. "I love you. But now that you're so powerful, I can see why you may feel I'm not at your level. I understand that. You're the daughter of two overseers, and you probably have abilities nobody's even seen yet. I guess you feel like you should marry up, or at least date a guy with more…substance… than me. But it's not my fault that I fell in love with you. And while I know we can work together while we date others, it really hurts every single day. And I don't know if I can live like that."

"Are you talking about resigning? Or are you asking me to marry you? Because I refuse to accept your resignation. And we're too young to get married."

Jackson's face lit up. "Can we get engaged?"

"Still too young."

"Go steady?"

"Maybe. If you give me your varsity letter jacket."

"I don't know," Jackson hedged. "It's a pretty cool jacket."

"I'd let you wear it sometimes."

"You would?"

"But do you really think you'll want to wear it in college?"

"College." His smile faded. "Where Dr. Thorne is the dean."

"Jackson. Get real. Cameron is a wonderful guy and I think he'll become a good friend to both of us. But let's face it, when we are in our 30s in another two hundred years, he'll no longer be alive to watch my back. Besides, he may be a dean, but you're a curator." She grabbed Jackson and kissed him. After a lengthy interlude, they both came up for air.

"You mean I outrank him?"

"I mean I love you."

"Then why did we stop doing this?" He pulled Johanna against him and gave her a passionate kiss. He put every emotion he had ever felt toward her into it, resulting in that particular kiss being remembered for all time in the annals of the College of Overseers, because she could read Jackson's mind, but forgot the overseers could all read hers, as well.

THE END

If you enjoyed reading *Fourth Chronicles of Illumination*, please help others enjoy it as well.

Review it: Most readers rely on reviews to decide what to read next. Help them out by describing what you liked or didn't like about this book.

Recommend it: Tell your friends or book club about it. Ask your local library to carry it.

Lend it: This book is lending enabled. Share it with your friends.

Join my Inner Circle: Receive information about all my forthcoming books and giveaways. Sign up at: www.artiquapress.com/inner-circle/

I love to hear what my readers have to say about my books, good and bad. But especially good. Write to me at: c.a.pack@libraryofillumination.com

Turn the page for a sneak preview of:
FIFTH CHRONICLES OF ILLUMINATION

FRENEMIES

Johanna Charette happily closed the library door behind the delivery driver who had just picked up her outgoing packages. Jackson was away, having decided to take two summer college courses on the same day. The summer semester was shorter than spring or fall, so his courses were three hours each—one day a week, instead of only ninety minutes each—twice a week. Johanna was on her own.

Now that the Terrorian threat had ended, the Roth family had moved back to their house on the other side of town. So, Johanna had spent the day alone, acutely feeling the absence of their camaraderie. She had not had a moment's peace during much of the spring because of one rogue curator's invasion plan against the unusual libraries that, like his own, made up the Illumini System. All the Illumini libraries were enchanted, and each one contained an identical wealth of knowledge, although the books that appeared in the main reading room at one, might be tucked away in the rarely-visited sublevel of a library on another realm.

The books' properties differed as well. Books sprang to life in four of the libraries. In libraries making up the other three classes, books might automatically rearrange themselves in order of importance for *that* particular day; or a genie could pop out of a book to determine a reader's true intention. And in the remaining class of libraries, people could become a character *inside* the book, which proved to be a popular vacation destination on those realms. It could also be a hazard, like it had been on Juvenilia, when the curator of that library entered a literary world, and the book accidently closed, trapping him inside.

In Johanna and Jackson's library, the characters and sometimes entire scenes came to life inside the library, which could be a curse or a blessing. Having Casanova appear and not disappear when the book closed put a lot of stress on her and Jackson, but when they were in need of someone to guard the portals, it was always good to be able to open a book and ask Jeeves, or Buffalo Bill, to lend a hand.

Today, Johanna had chosen to go it alone. She thought Jackson might put in an appearance before the end of the day. He had asked to continue living in the hotel suite inside the library, even though the rest of his family had moved out. *It would be a good compromise,* she thought. Jackson would be nearby, but in separate quarters. *And we could always order from room service for dinner!*

JACKSON FUMBLED THROUGH his wallet for cash, while juggling books in the Cranford University book store. He had just completed his English Literature and Information Technologies classes and had stopped to buy textbooks and supplies.

He had stared at the man who informed him he couldn't download the IT textbook onto his tablet. "You mean I have to buy the actual book?"

"Yes."

"I can understand that for English lit, but my IT book is all about emerging technologies. Shouldn't the university try *embracing* technology by allowing students to download the book?"

"No."

Jackson shook his head, packed up the heavy books, and the five sweatshirts he bought—one for each member of his family and Johanna—and headed toward the car. He wanted to talk to Johanna about living at the library and hoped the sweatshirt might soften her up. *Maybe that and a nice dinner from room service,* he thought, if she hadn't already closed the travel guide that allowed the hotel suite to materialize inside the library.

"Jackson!

He stopped when he heard his name and looked around. Cameron Thorne was walking toward the bookstore. Jackson stood right in his path.

"Dean Thorne." Jackson nodded.

"I think you can call me Cameron. We've both faced Terrorians, although you had a much bigger role to play than I did. I believe we have enough shared history, however fleeting it might be so far, to be on a first name basis."

Jackson shifted his books and bag of sweatshirts and shook the dean's hand. "In case you can't tell, it was my first day."

"How did it go for you?"

"Not bad, but it's a long day. I thought two classes would be a piece of cake. But two *three-hour* classes—not so much."

"You'll thank yourself when the fall semester starts. You'll already have two classes under your belt and can take a lighter load than your classmates."

"I planned to do that anyway. I want to have enough time to do well in college, but still be able to pull my weight at the library."

"I have Johanna in one of my classes on Thursday," the dean said.

"Really?" Jackson voice sounded an octave higher than he wanted it to.

"Yes. Shakespeare 101. She told me she's looking forward to it."

"Oh."

Cameron saw one of his students heading toward them, calling out his name. "I've got to go. It's good to see you," he said, nodding before leaving abruptly.

Jackson's eyes widened, surprised to see Cameron walk in the opposite direction of the young woman calling out for him. He looked at the person who had called the dean's name. She was pretty in a very put-together kind of way; like she tried really hard to look perfect. She wore very precise makeup, and her skirt was short and tight, but not in an overly slutty way. Still, he had no trouble imagining the view a professor would get if she crossed her legs in class. His eyes opened even wider. *Maybe she's a teacher, and it's her students who get the view.*

He felt himself blush. *I have too much imagination*

to be thinking these things. He packed up the car and headed for the library.

BY THE TIME the summer semester officially started at Graydon Ransom University News Tonight—affectionately known as GRUNT—Logan Elliott had already proven himself an able reporter. He had automatically become one of the organization's top choices to cover important stories, because he already had experience, owned his own camera equipment, and he happened to be there during the pathetically understaffed summer semester, when fewer students took courses because financial aid was not available. Logan had volunteered to go in several days a week, rather than the one day required of students and thus, had endeared himself to the people in charge. So much so, he received plum assignments over students who had already taken part in the internship for several semesters.

It didn't hurt that he was rich, good-looking and drove a nice car. The girls flocked to him like moths to a light. But in his opinion, none of them could hold a candle to Emily Brent. She could pass for a model, and he already had *history* with her.

Unfortunately, Emily didn't remember their history. She knew him as her recently-deceased best friend's grieving boyfriend. She did whatever she could to ease his pain, but as far as she was concerned, she was *off men* after breaking up with his best buddy Jackson Roth from the Library of Illumination.

That has to change, he thought. Jackson was a great friend when we were kids. Having him around was like owning a puppy. Jax had a good sense of humor, was always outgoing and friendly, and the guy was a chick-magnet. But

Logan didn't need Jackson anymore. He wanted Emily, and to do that he would have to besmirch Jackson's reputation. He already had a lot of the tools he needed to pull that off, and it would only take a couple more weeks before Jackson, the Library of Illumination, and the library's unusual secrets all became headline news on *The Elliott Report*.

Fifth Chronicles of Illumination coming in 2019

ABOUT THE AUTHOR

C. A. PACK is an award-winning former journalist, who gave up fact for fiction. She was inspired to write her Library of Illumination series after discussing her views on what the perfect library would be like. *Chronicles: The Library of Illumination*, which contains the first five adventures in the series, was named one of the "Best Indie Books of 2014" by Kirkus Reviews.

C. A. is also the author of the *Evangeline's Ghost* series.

She lives on Long Island with her husband, and a picky little parrot who loves to play peek-a-boo.

* 9 7 8 0 9 9 7 9 0 8 4 7 3 *